P9-EKY-537

THE ADVENTURES OF
TINTIN
REPORTER FOR "LE PETIT VINGTIÈME„
IN THE LAND OF
THE SOVIETS

BY HERGÉ

EGMONT

TRANSLATED BY LESLIE LONSDALE-COOPER AND MICHAEL TURNER

EGMONT
We bring stories to life

Tintin in the Land of the Soviets
Artwork copyright © 1999 by Editions Casterman, Paris and Tournai.
Text copyright © 1999 Casterman/Moulinsart

Tintin in America
Artwork copyright © 1945, 1973 by Editions Casterman, Paris and Tournai.
Text copyright © 1978 Egmont UK Limited.

First published in this edition 2015 by Egmont UK Limited
The Yellow Building, 1 Nicholas Road, London W11 4AN

ISBN 978 1 4052 8275 8

64054/1
Printed in China

THE ADVENTURES OF
T I N T I N
REPORTER FOR "LE PETIT VINGTIÈME,,
IN THE LAND OF
THE SOVIETS

BY HERGÉ

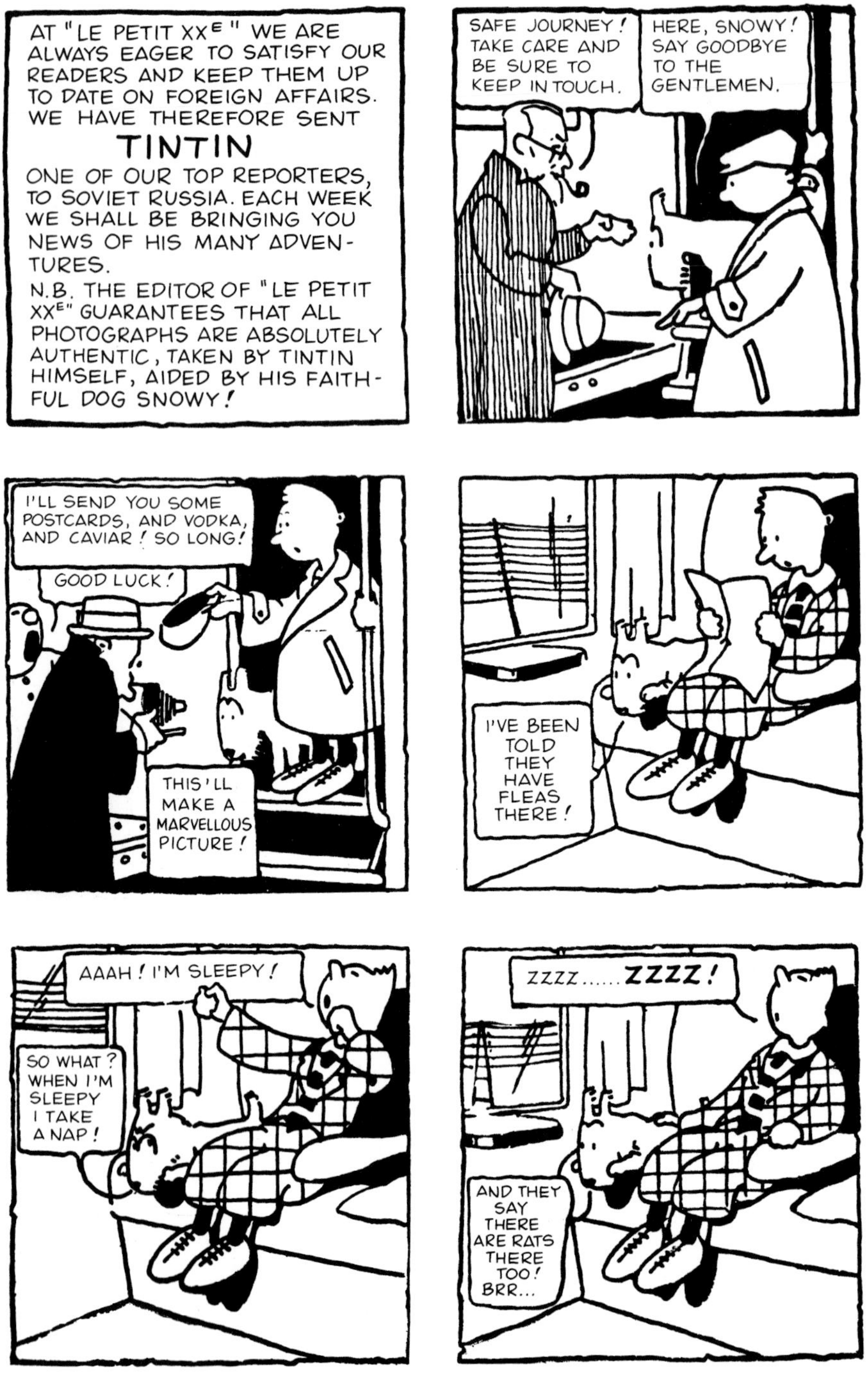

AT "LE PETIT XXE" WE ARE ALWAYS EAGER TO SATISFY OUR READERS AND KEEP THEM UP TO DATE ON FOREIGN AFFAIRS. WE HAVE THEREFORE SENT
TINTIN
ONE OF OUR TOP REPORTERS, TO SOVIET RUSSIA. EACH WEEK WE SHALL BE BRINGING YOU NEWS OF HIS MANY ADVENTURES.
N.B. THE EDITOR OF "LE PETIT XXE" GUARANTEES THAT ALL PHOTOGRAPHS ARE ABSOLUTELY AUTHENTIC, TAKEN BY TINTIN HIMSELF, AIDED BY HIS FAITHFUL DOG SNOWY!
SAFE JOURNEY! TAKE CARE AND BE SURE TO KEEP IN TOUCH.
HERE, SNOWY! SAY GOODBYE TO THE GENTLEMEN.
I'LL SEND YOU SOME POSTCARDS, AND VODKA, AND CAVIAR! SO LONG!
GOOD LUCK!
THIS'LL MAKE A MARVELLOUS PICTURE!
I'VE BEEN TOLD THEY HAVE FLEAS THERE!
AAAH! I'M SLEEPY!
SO WHAT? WHEN I'M SLEEPY I TAKE A NAP!
ZZZZ...... ZZZZ!
AND THEY SAY THERE ARE RATS THERE TOO! BRR...

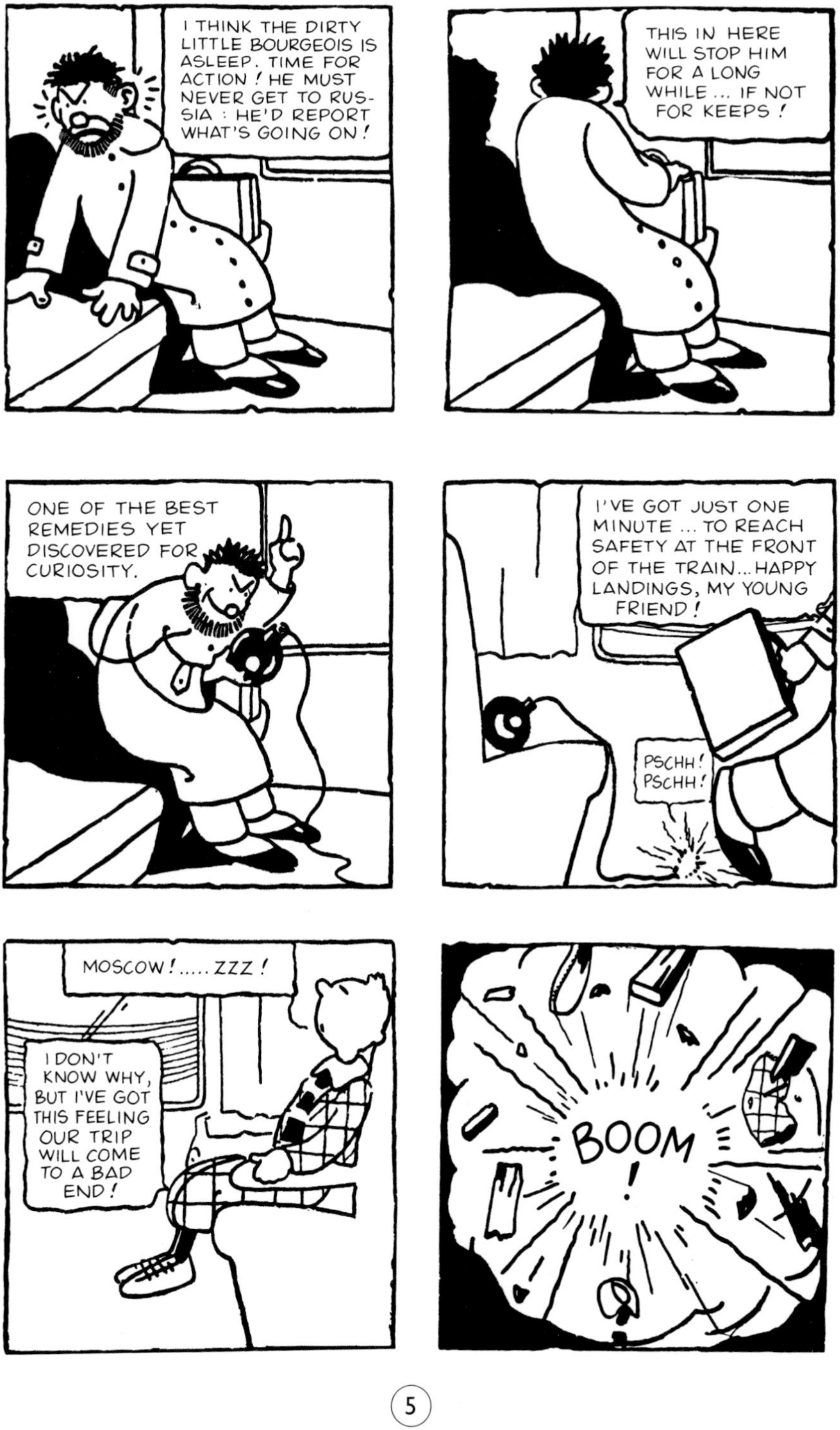
I THINK THE DIRTY LITTLE BOURGEOIS IS ASLEEP. TIME FOR ACTION! HE MUST NEVER GET TO RUSSIA: HE'D REPORT WHAT'S GOING ON!
THIS IN HERE WILL STOP HIM FOR A LONG WHILE ... IF NOT FOR KEEPS!
ONE OF THE BEST REMEDIES YET DISCOVERED FOR CURIOSITY.
I'VE GOT JUST ONE MINUTE ... TO REACH SAFETY AT THE FRONT OF THE TRAIN... HAPPY LANDINGS, MY YOUNG FRIEND!
PSCHH! PSCHH!
MOSCOW!.....ZZZ!
I DON'T KNOW WHY, BUT I'VE GOT THIS FEELING OUR TRIP WILL COME TO A BAD END!
BOOM!

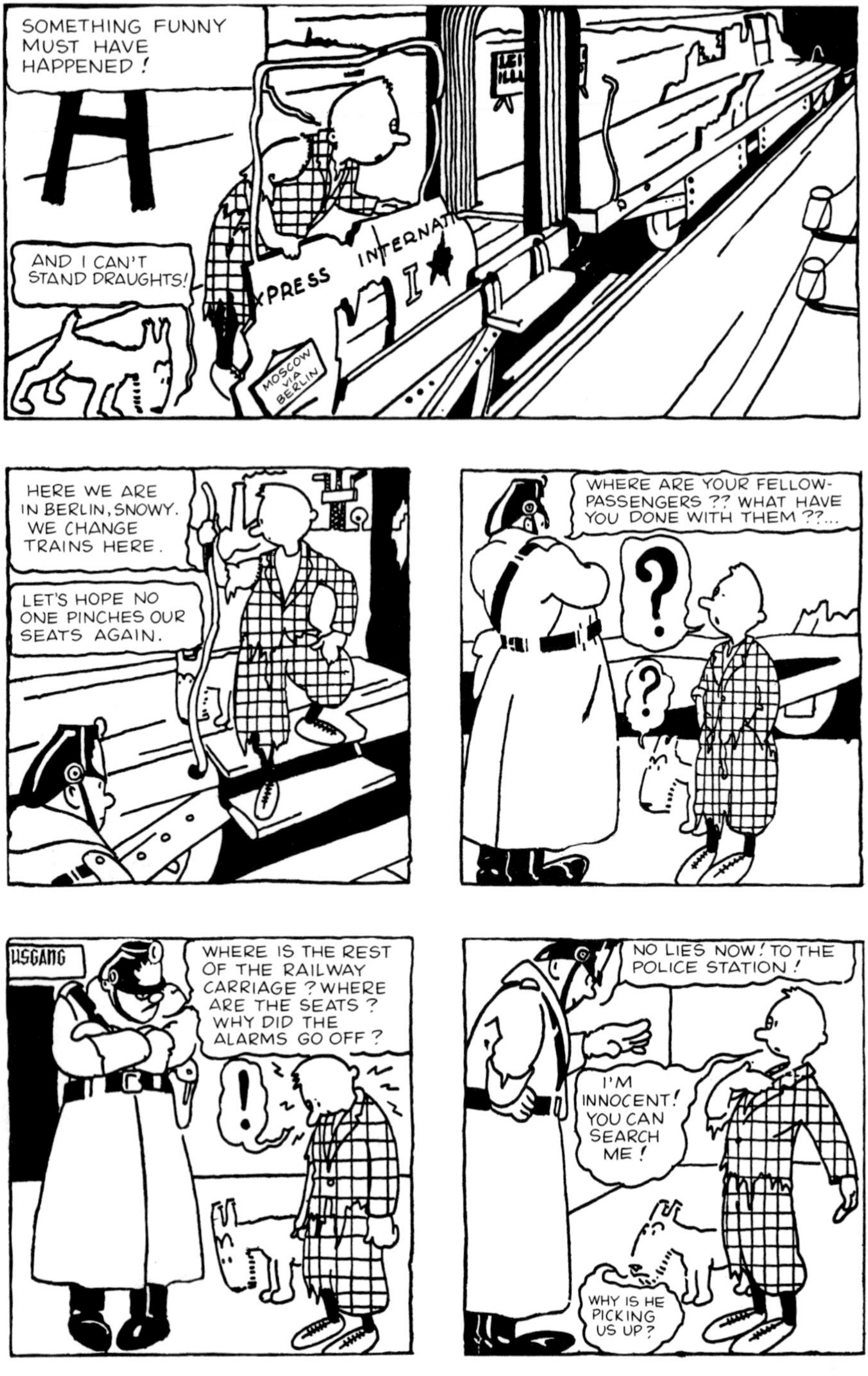
SOMETHING FUNNY MUST HAVE HAPPENED!
AND I CAN'T STAND DRAUGHTS!
XPRESS INTERNAT
MOSCOW VIA BERLIN
HERE WE ARE IN BERLIN, SNOWY. WE CHANGE TRAINS HERE.
LET'S HOPE NO ONE PINCHES OUR SEATS AGAIN.
WHERE ARE YOUR FELLOW-PASSENGERS ?? WHAT HAVE YOU DONE WITH THEM ??...
?
?
USGANG
WHERE IS THE REST OF THE RAILWAY CARRIAGE ? WHERE ARE THE SEATS ? WHY DID THE ALARMS GO OFF ?
!
NO LIES NOW! TO THE POLICE STATION!
I'M INNOCENT! YOU CAN SEARCH ME!
WHY IS HE PICKING US UP?

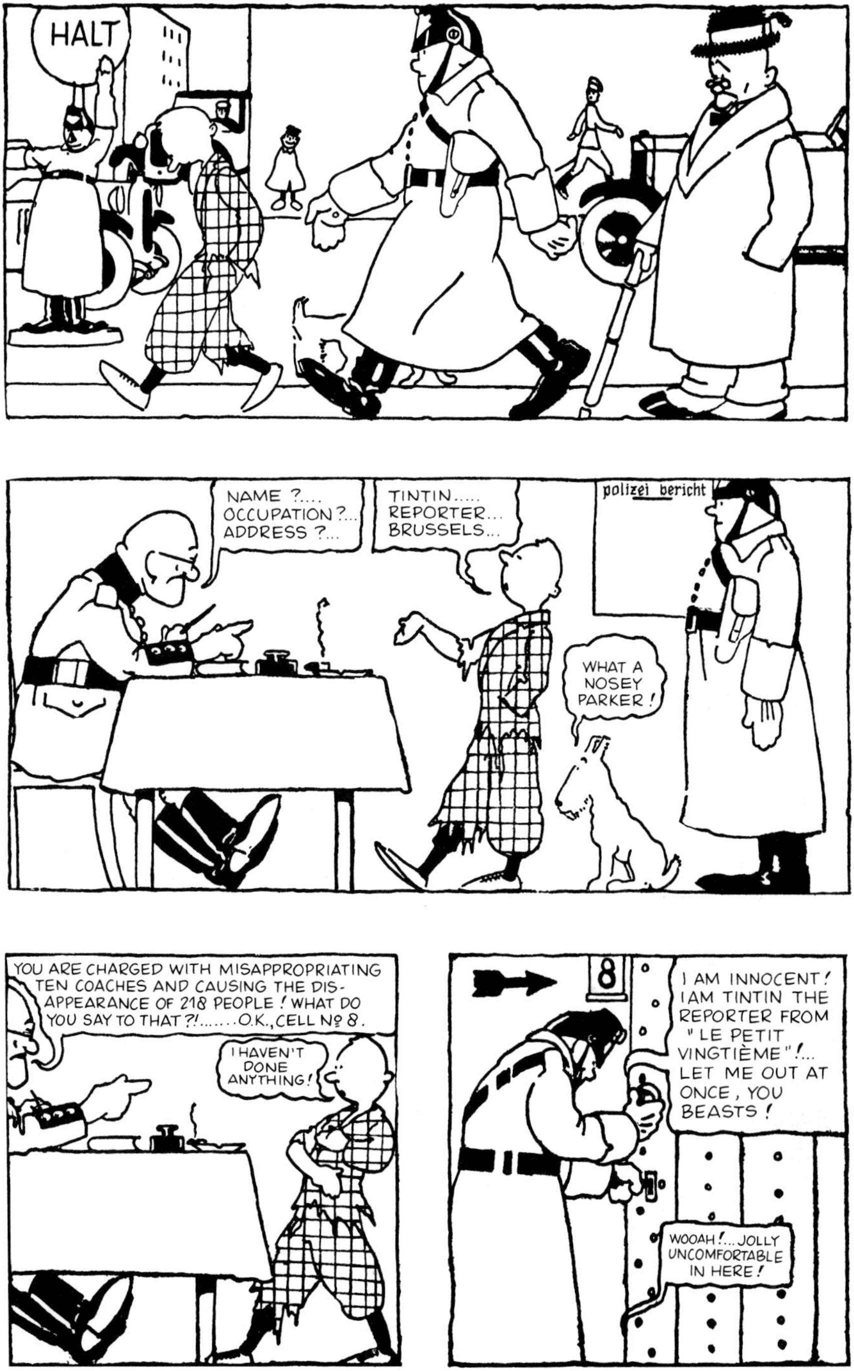
HALT
NAME ?.... OCCUPATION ?... ADDRESS ?...
TINTIN..... REPORTER... BRUSSELS...
polizei bericht
WHAT A NOSEY PARKER !
YOU ARE CHARGED WITH MISAPPROPRIATING TEN COACHES AND CAUSING THE DIS-APPEARANCE OF 218 PEOPLE ! WHAT DO YOU SAY TO THAT ?!....... O.K., CELL Nº 8.
I HAVEN'T DONE ANYTHING !
8
I AM INNOCENT ! I AM TINTIN THE REPORTER FROM " LE PETIT VINGTIÈME " !... LET ME OUT AT ONCE , YOU BEASTS !
WOOAH !... JOLLY UNCOMFORTABLE IN HERE !

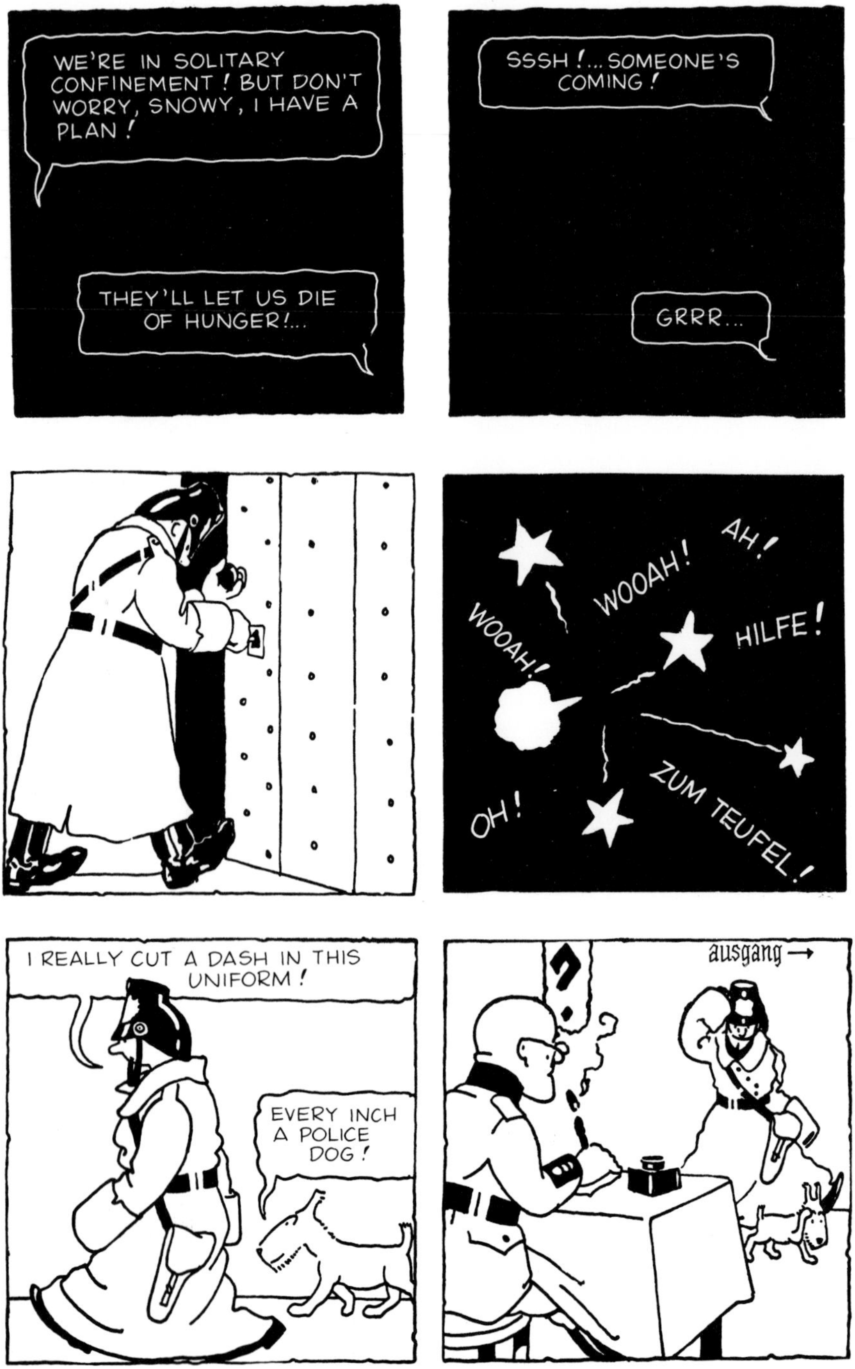
WE'RE IN SOLITARY CONFINEMENT! BUT DON'T WORRY, SNOWY, I HAVE A PLAN!
THEY'LL LET US DIE OF HUNGER!...
SSSH!... SOMEONE'S COMING!
GRRR...
WOOAH!
WOOAH!
AH!
HILFE!
OH!
ZUM TEUFEL!
I REALLY CUT A DASH IN THIS UNIFORM!
EVERY INCH A POLICE DOG!
?
ausgang →

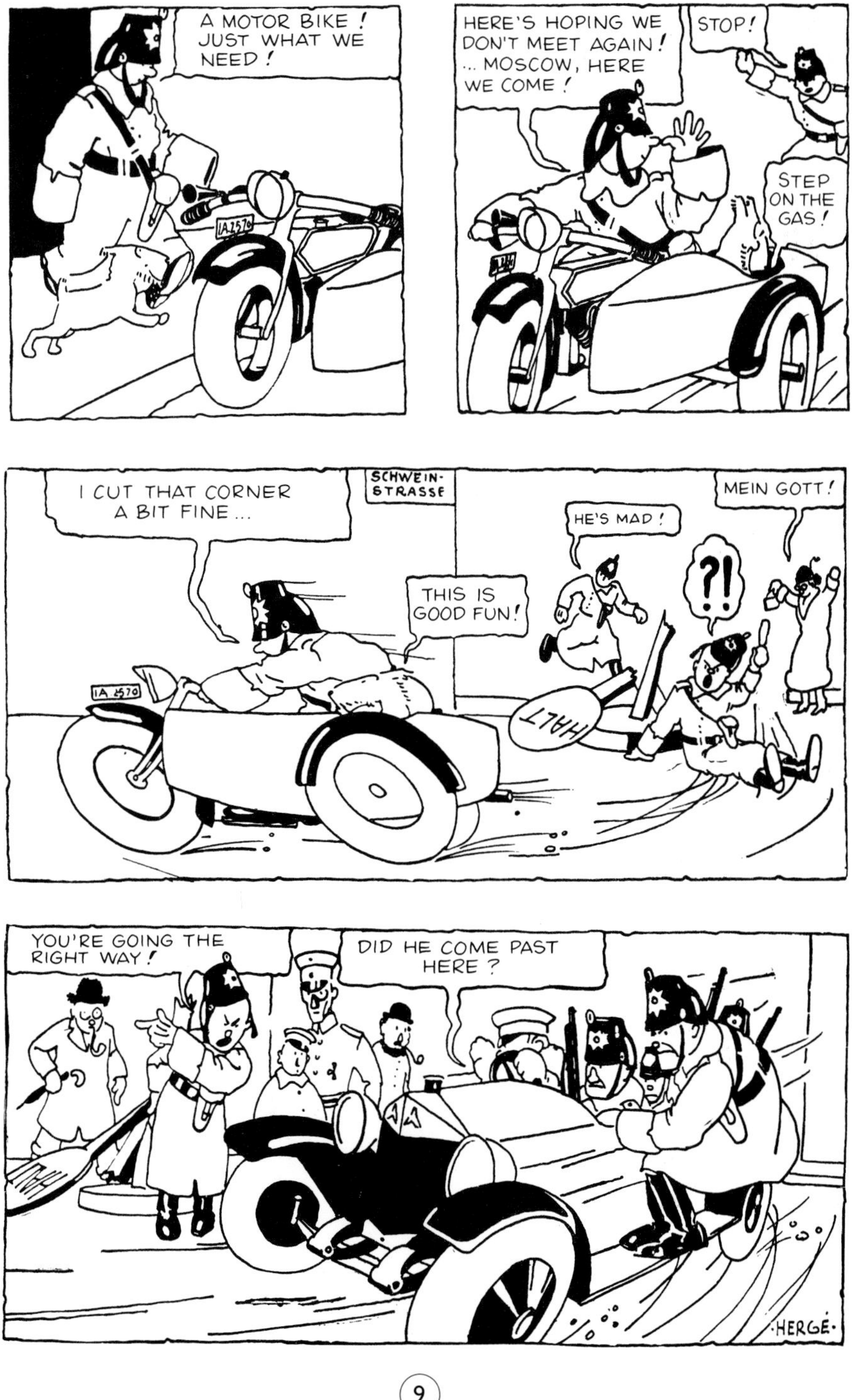

A MOTOR BIKE ! JUST WHAT WE NEED !
IA 2570
HERE'S HOPING WE DON'T MEET AGAIN ! ... MOSCOW, HERE WE COME !
STOP !
STEP ON THE GAS !
I CUT THAT CORNER A BIT FINE ...
SCHWEIN-STRASSE
THIS IS GOOD FUN !
HE'S MAD !
?!
MEIN GOTT !
HALT
YOU'RE GOING THE RIGHT WAY !
DID HE COME PAST HERE ?
·HERGÉ·

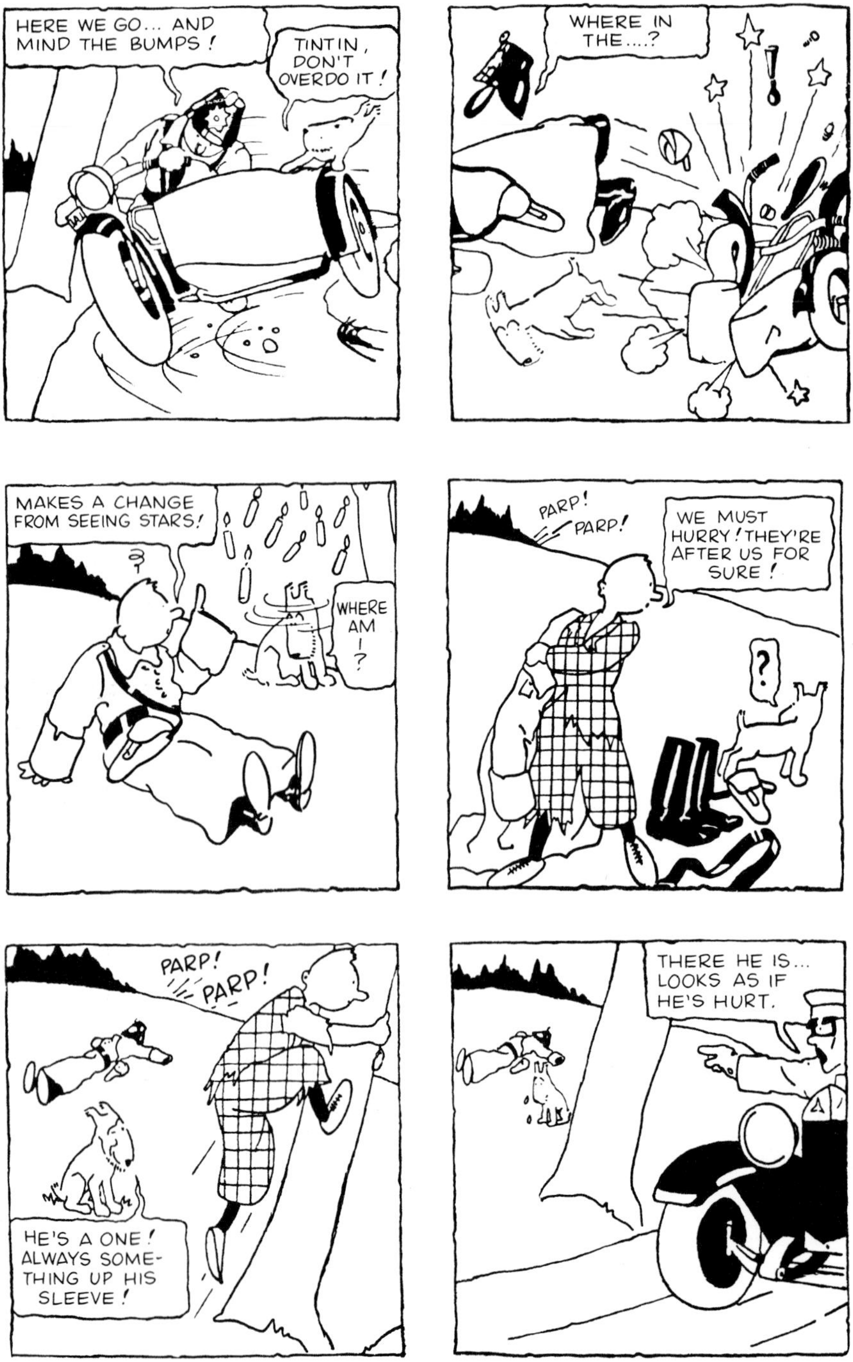

HERE WE GO... AND MIND THE BUMPS!
TINTIN, DON'T OVERDO IT!
WHERE IN THE....?
MAKES A CHANGE FROM SEEING STARS!
WHERE AM I?
PARP! PARP!
WE MUST HURRY! THEY'RE AFTER US FOR SURE!
?
PARP! PARP!
HE'S A ONE! ALWAYS SOME-THING UP HIS SLEEVE!
THERE HE IS... LOOKS AS IF HE'S HURT.

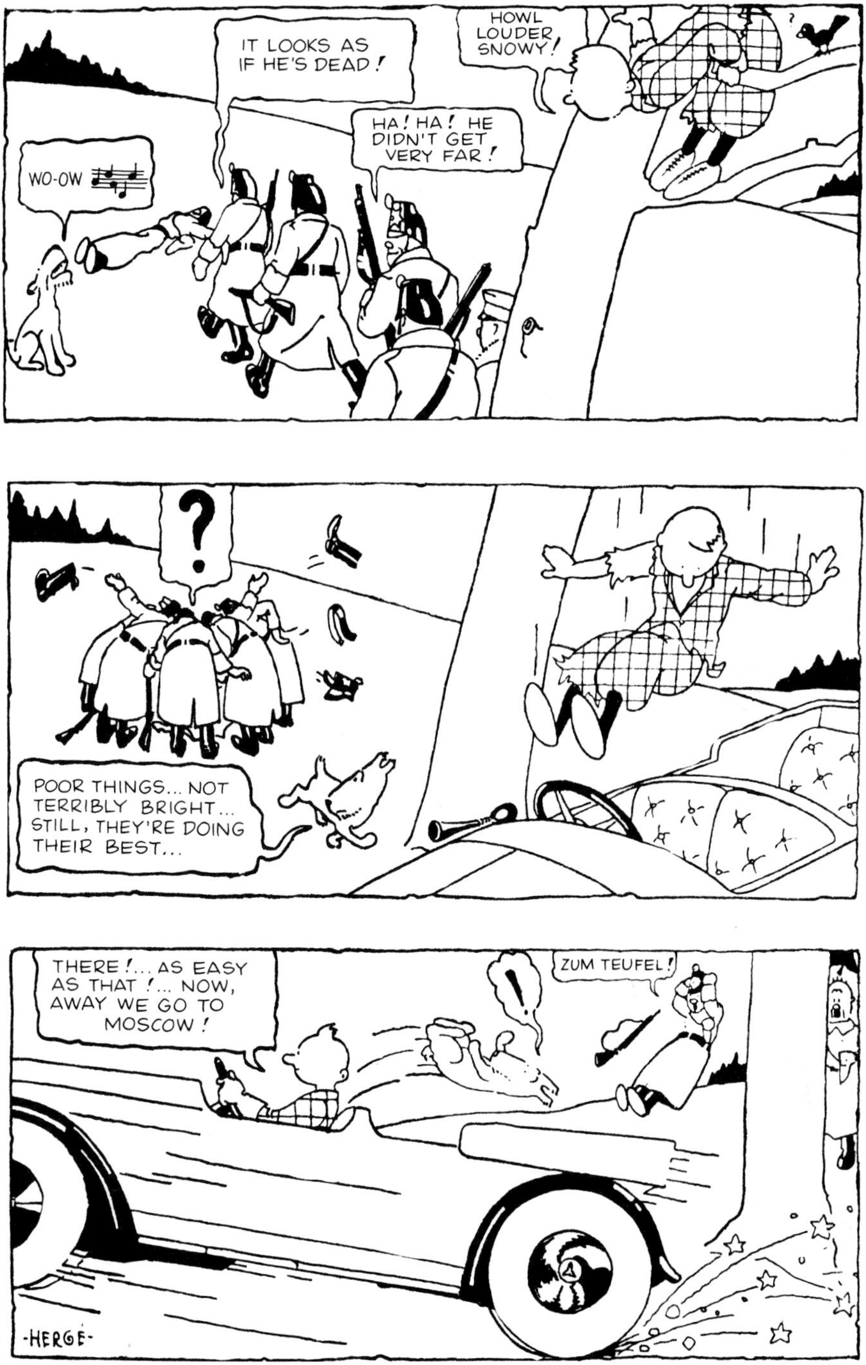
WO-OW
IT LOOKS AS IF HE'S DEAD!
HA! HA! HE DIDN'T GET VERY FAR!
HOWL LOUDER SNOWY!
?
POOR THINGS... NOT TERRIBLY BRIGHT... STILL, THEY'RE DOING THEIR BEST...
THERE!... AS EASY AS THAT!... NOW, AWAY WE GO TO MOSCOW!
!
ZUM TEUFEL!
-HERGÉ-

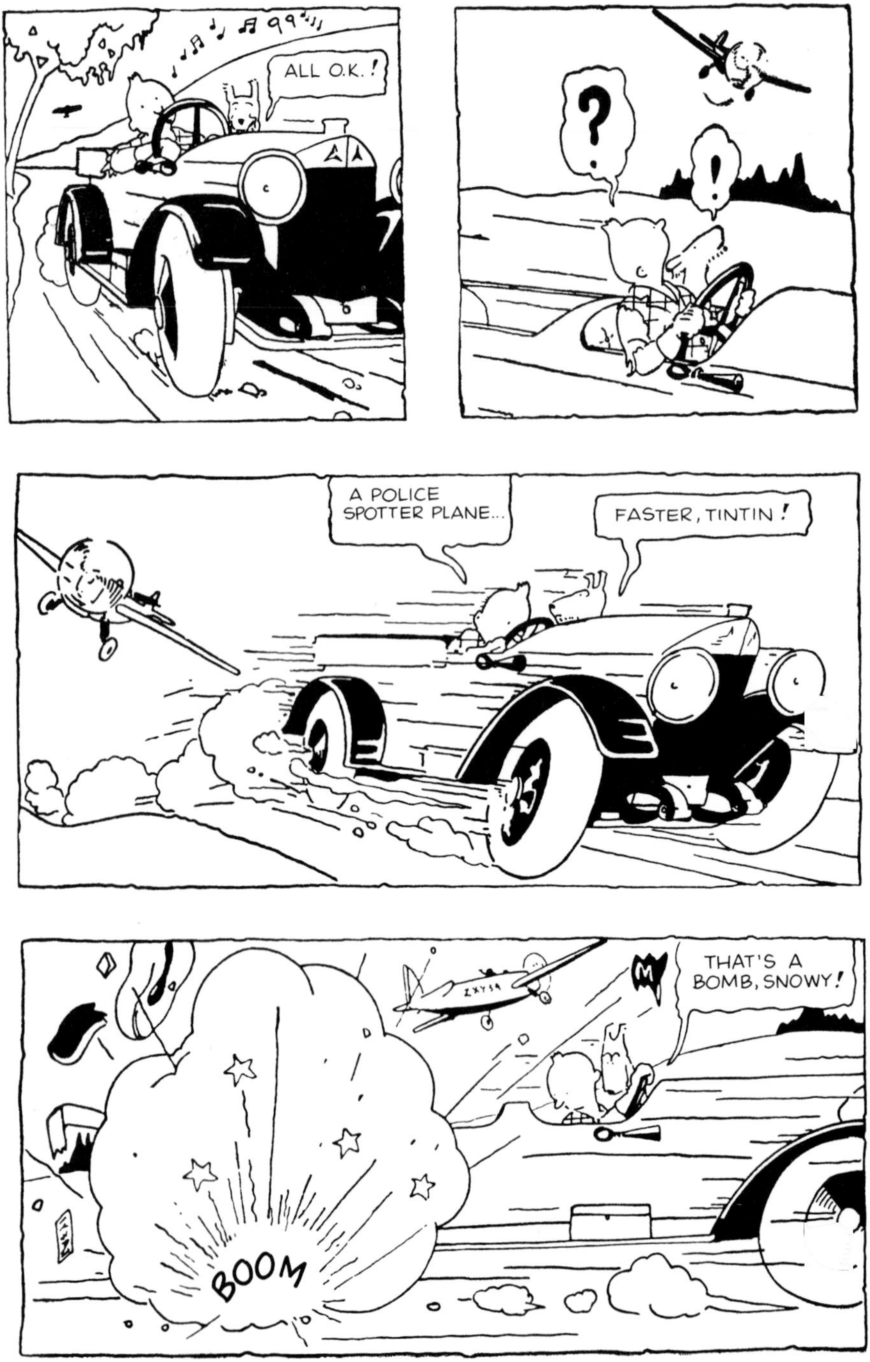
ALL O.K.!
?
!
A POLICE SPOTTER PLANE...
FASTER, TINTIN!
ZXY34
THAT'S A BOMB, SNOWY!
BOOM

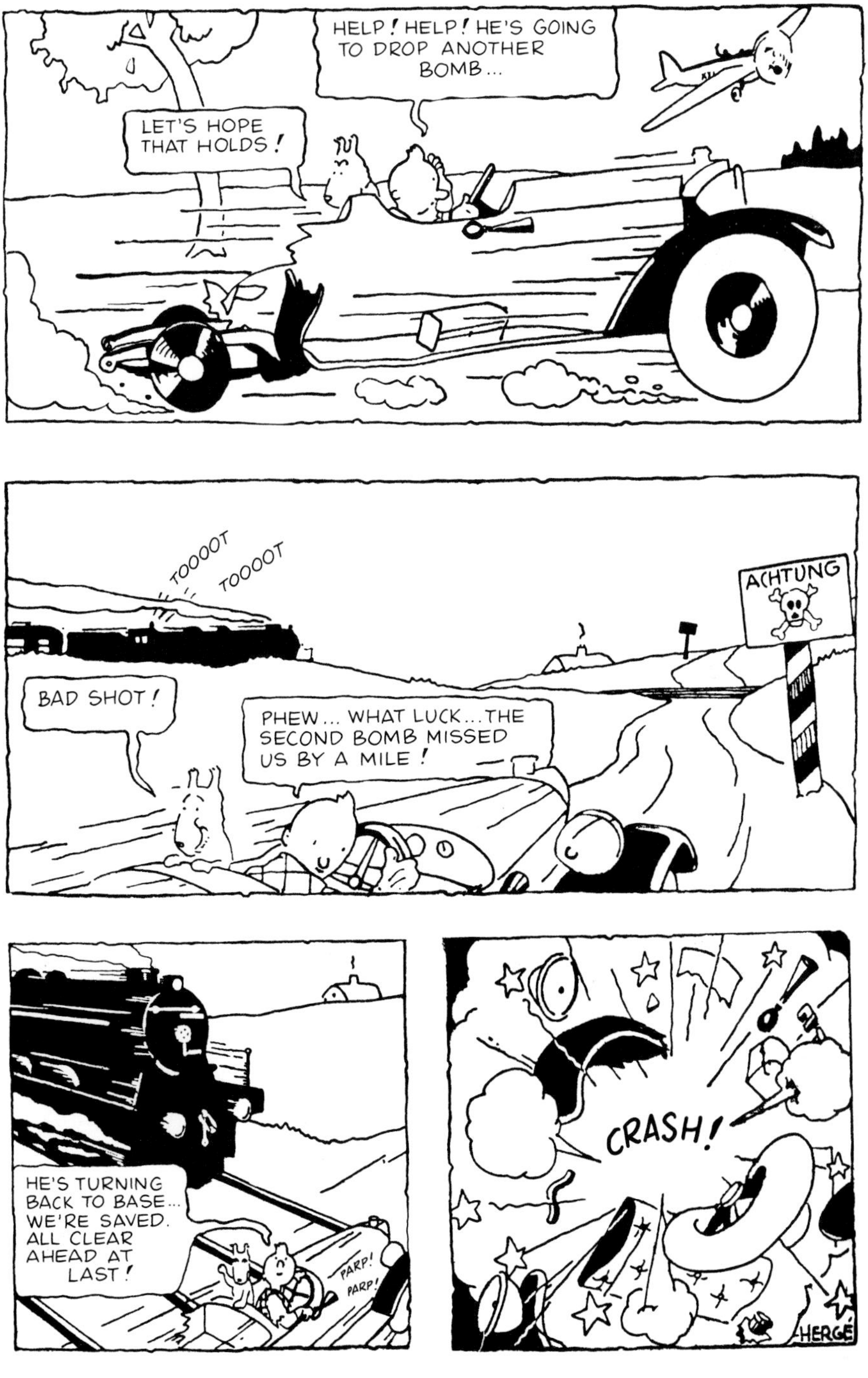
HELP! HELP! HE'S GOING TO DROP ANOTHER BOMB...
LET'S HOPE THAT HOLDS!
TOOOOT
TOOOOT
ACHTUNG
BAD SHOT!
PHEW... WHAT LUCK...THE SECOND BOMB MISSED US BY A MILE!
HE'S TURNING BACK TO BASE... WE'RE SAVED. ALL CLEAR AHEAD AT LAST!
PARP!
PARP!
CRASH!
HERGÉ

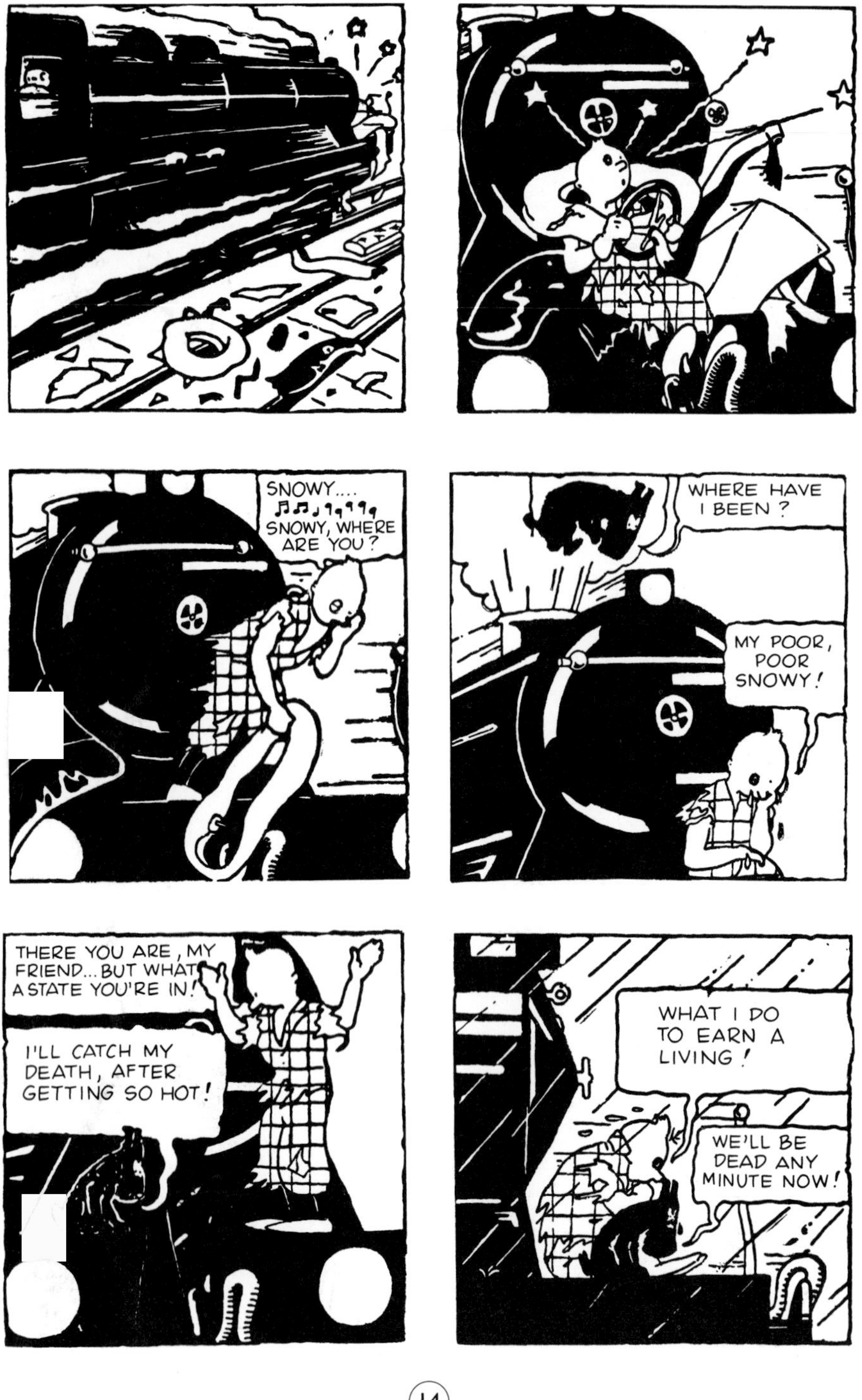
SNOWY.... SNOWY, WHERE ARE YOU?
WHERE HAVE I BEEN?
MY POOR, POOR SNOWY!
THERE YOU ARE, MY FRIEND... BUT WHAT A STATE YOU'RE IN!
I'LL CATCH MY DEATH, AFTER GETTING SO HOT!
WHAT I DO TO EARN A LIVING!
WE'LL BE DEAD ANY MINUTE NOW!

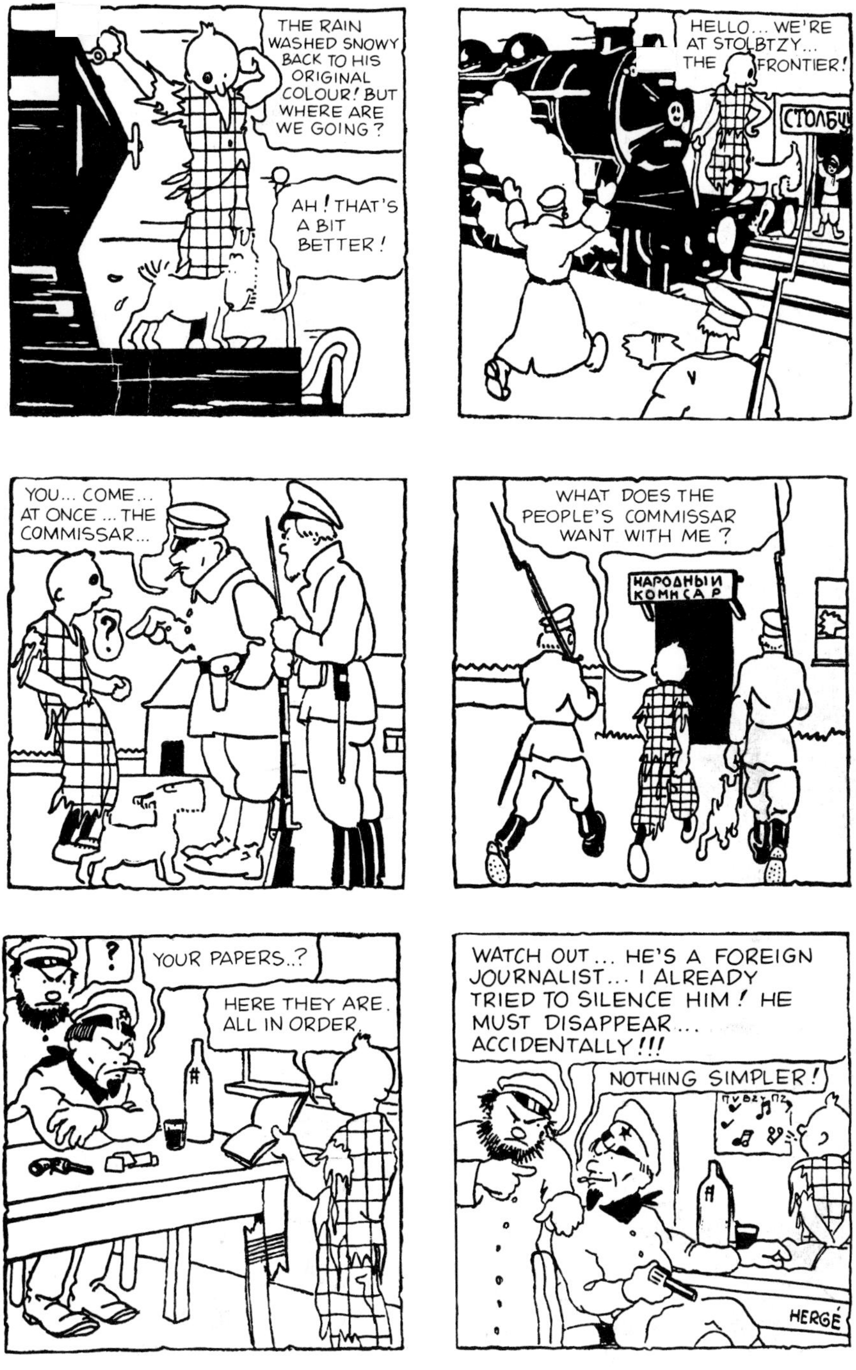
THE RAIN WASHED SNOWY BACK TO HIS ORIGINAL COLOUR! BUT WHERE ARE WE GOING?
AH! THAT'S A BIT BETTER!
HELLO... WE'RE AT STOLBTZY... THE FRONTIER!
YOU... COME... AT ONCE... THE COMMISSAR...
?
WHAT DOES THE PEOPLE'S COMMISSAR WANT WITH ME?
НАРОДНЫИ КОМИСАР
?
YOUR PAPERS..?
HERE THEY ARE. ALL IN ORDER.
WATCH OUT... HE'S A FOREIGN JOURNALIST... I ALREADY TRIED TO SILENCE HIM! HE MUST DISAPPEAR... ACCIDENTALLY!!!
NOTHING SIMPLER!
HERGÉ

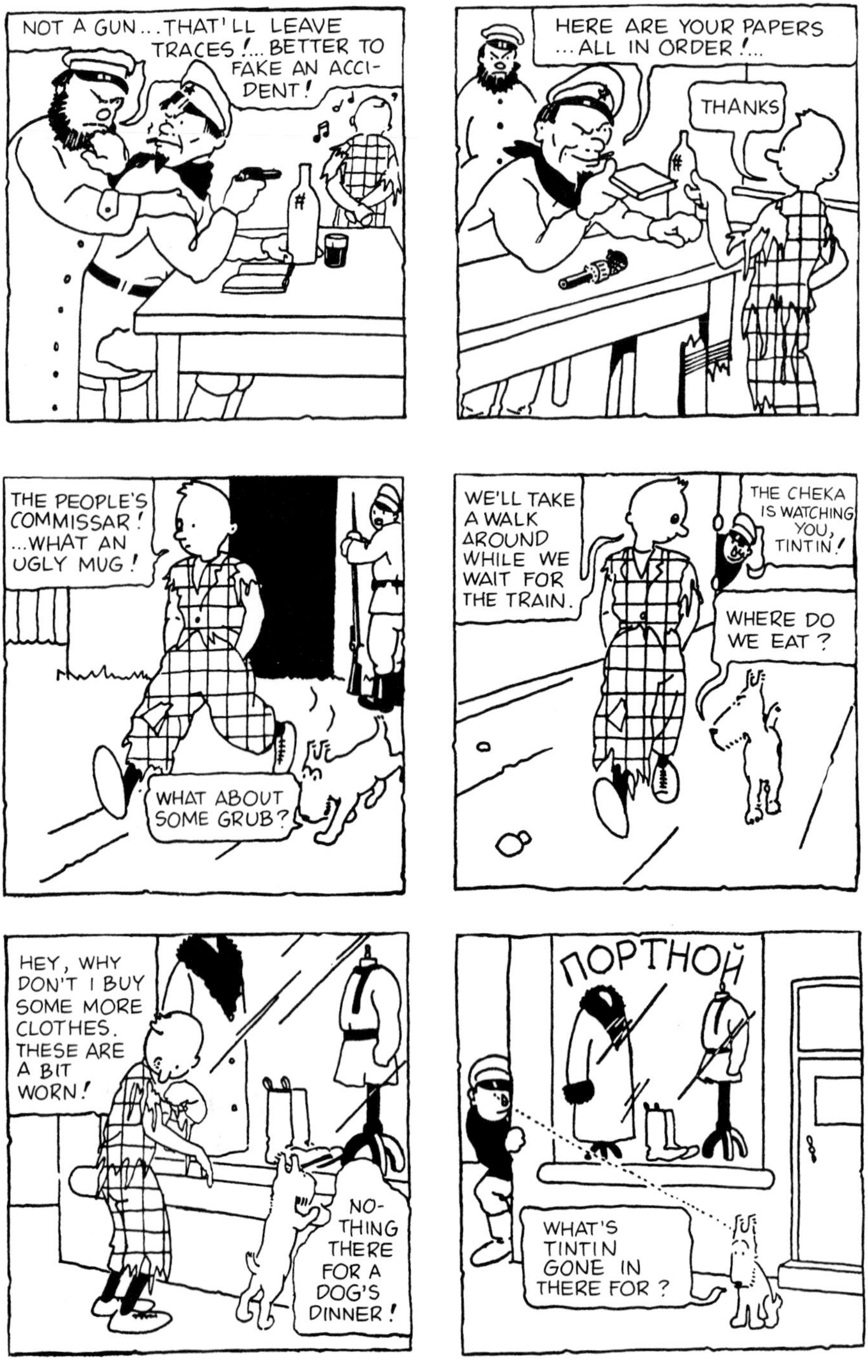
NOT A GUN...THAT'LL LEAVE TRACES!... BETTER TO FAKE AN ACCI-DENT!
HERE ARE YOUR PAPERS ...ALL IN ORDER!...
THANKS
THE PEOPLE'S COMMISSAR! ...WHAT AN UGLY MUG!
WHAT ABOUT SOME GRUB?
WE'LL TAKE A WALK AROUND WHILE WE WAIT FOR THE TRAIN.
THE CHEKA IS WATCHING YOU, TINTIN!
WHERE DO WE EAT?
HEY, WHY DON'T I BUY SOME MORE CLOTHES. THESE ARE A BIT WORN!
NO-THING THERE FOR A DOG'S DINNER!
ПОРТНОЙ
WHAT'S TINTIN GONE IN THERE FOR?

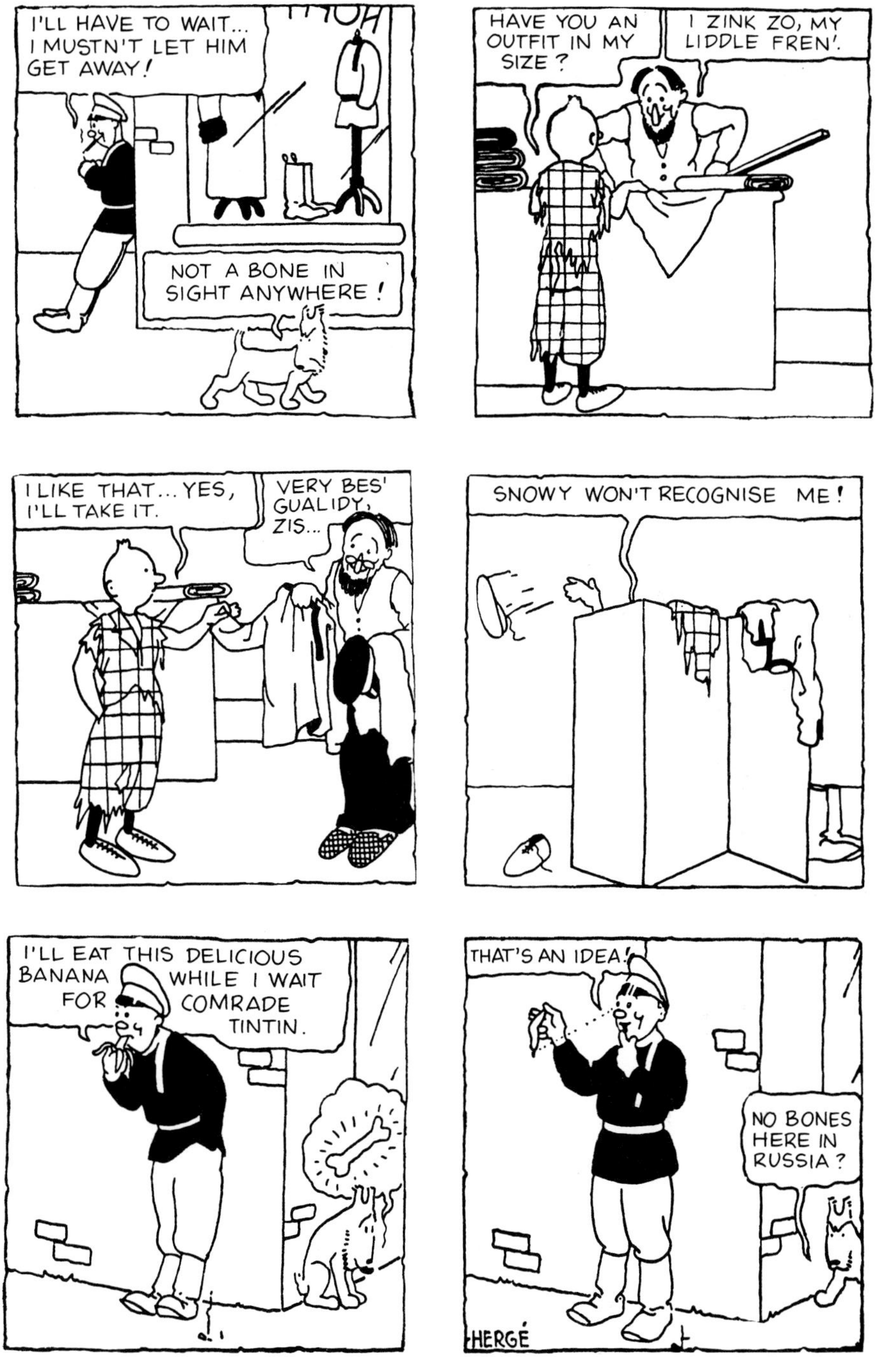
I'LL HAVE TO WAIT... I MUSTN'T LET HIM GET AWAY!
NOT A BONE IN SIGHT ANYWHERE!
HAVE YOU AN OUTFIT IN MY SIZE?
I ZINK ZO, MY LIDDLE FREN'.
I LIKE THAT... YES, I'LL TAKE IT.
VERY BES' GUALIDY, ZIS...
SNOWY WON'T RECOGNISE ME!
I'LL EAT THIS DELICIOUS BANANA WHILE I WAIT FOR COMRADE TINTIN.
THAT'S AN IDEA!
NO BONES HERE IN RUSSIA?
HERGÉ

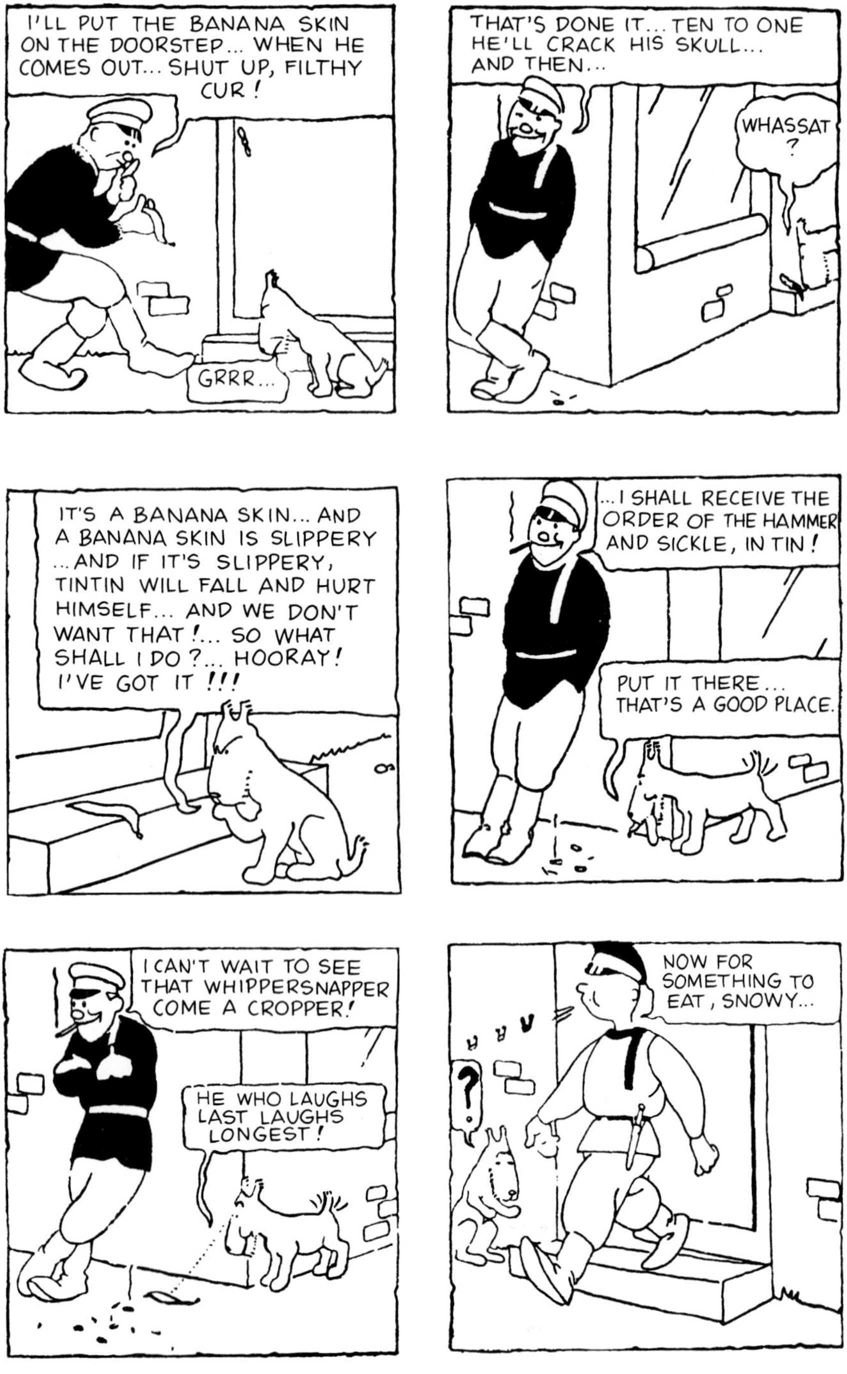
I'LL PUT THE BANANA SKIN ON THE DOORSTEP... WHEN HE COMES OUT... SHUT UP, FILTHY CUR!
GRRR...
THAT'S DONE IT... TEN TO ONE HE'LL CRACK HIS SKULL... AND THEN...
WHASSAT ?
IT'S A BANANA SKIN... AND A BANANA SKIN IS SLIPPERY ...AND IF IT'S SLIPPERY, TINTIN WILL FALL AND HURT HIMSELF... AND WE DON'T WANT THAT!... SO WHAT SHALL I DO?... HOORAY! I'VE GOT IT!!!
...I SHALL RECEIVE THE ORDER OF THE HAMMER AND SICKLE, IN TIN!
PUT IT THERE... THAT'S A GOOD PLACE.
I CAN'T WAIT TO SEE THAT WHIPPERSNAPPER COME A CROPPER!
HE WHO LAUGHS LAST LAUGHS LONGEST!
NOW FOR SOMETHING TO EAT, SNOWY...
?

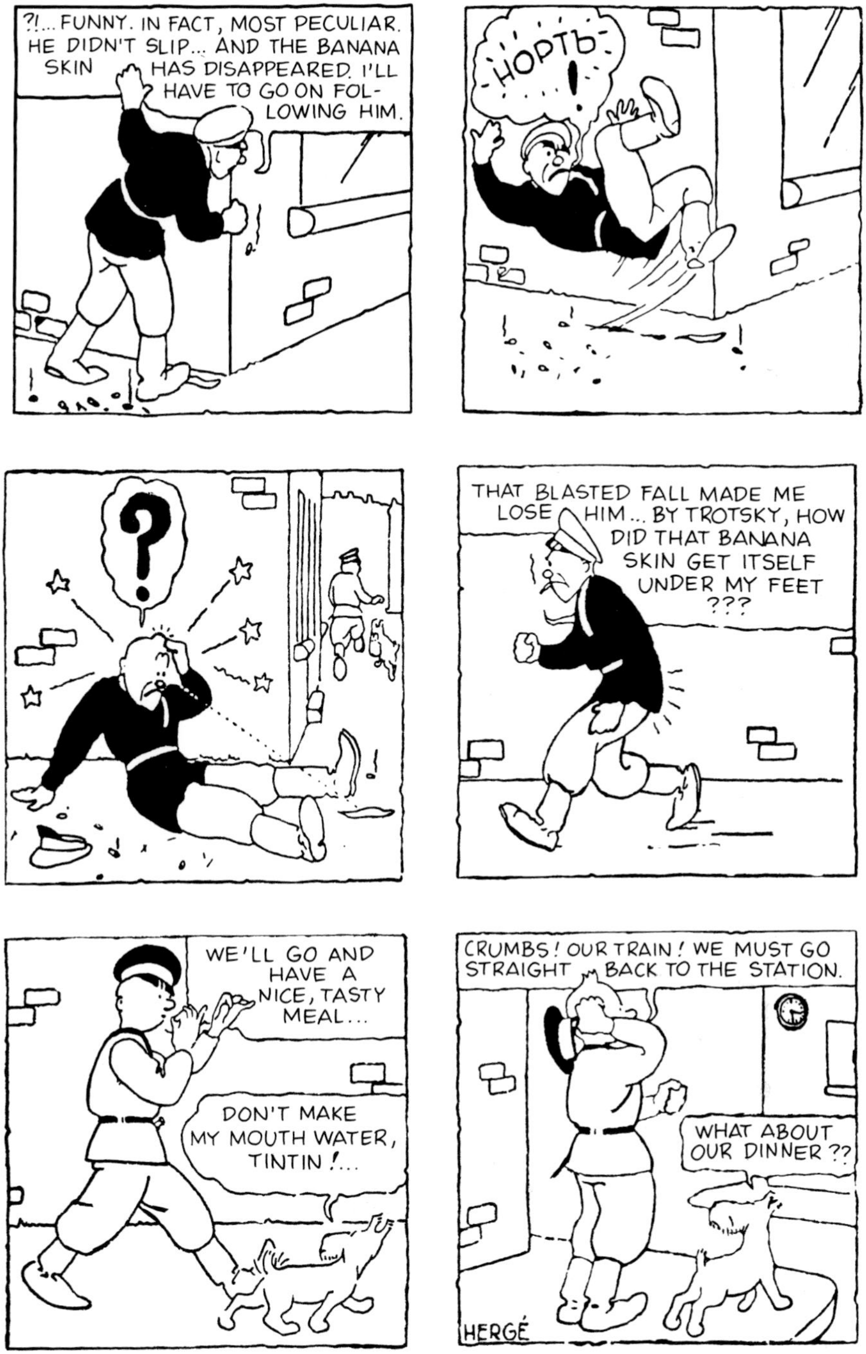
?!... FUNNY. IN FACT, MOST PECULIAR. HE DIDN'T SLIP... AND THE BANANA SKIN HAS DISAPPEARED. I'LL HAVE TO GO ON FOLLOWING HIM.
HOPTЬ
THAT BLASTED FALL MADE ME LOSE HIM... BY TROTSKY, HOW DID THAT BANANA SKIN GET ITSELF UNDER MY FEET ???
WE'LL GO AND HAVE A NICE, TASTY MEAL...
DON'T MAKE MY MOUTH WATER, TINTIN!...
CRUMBS! OUR TRAIN! WE MUST GO STRAIGHT BACK TO THE STATION.
WHAT ABOUT OUR DINNER ??
HERGÉ

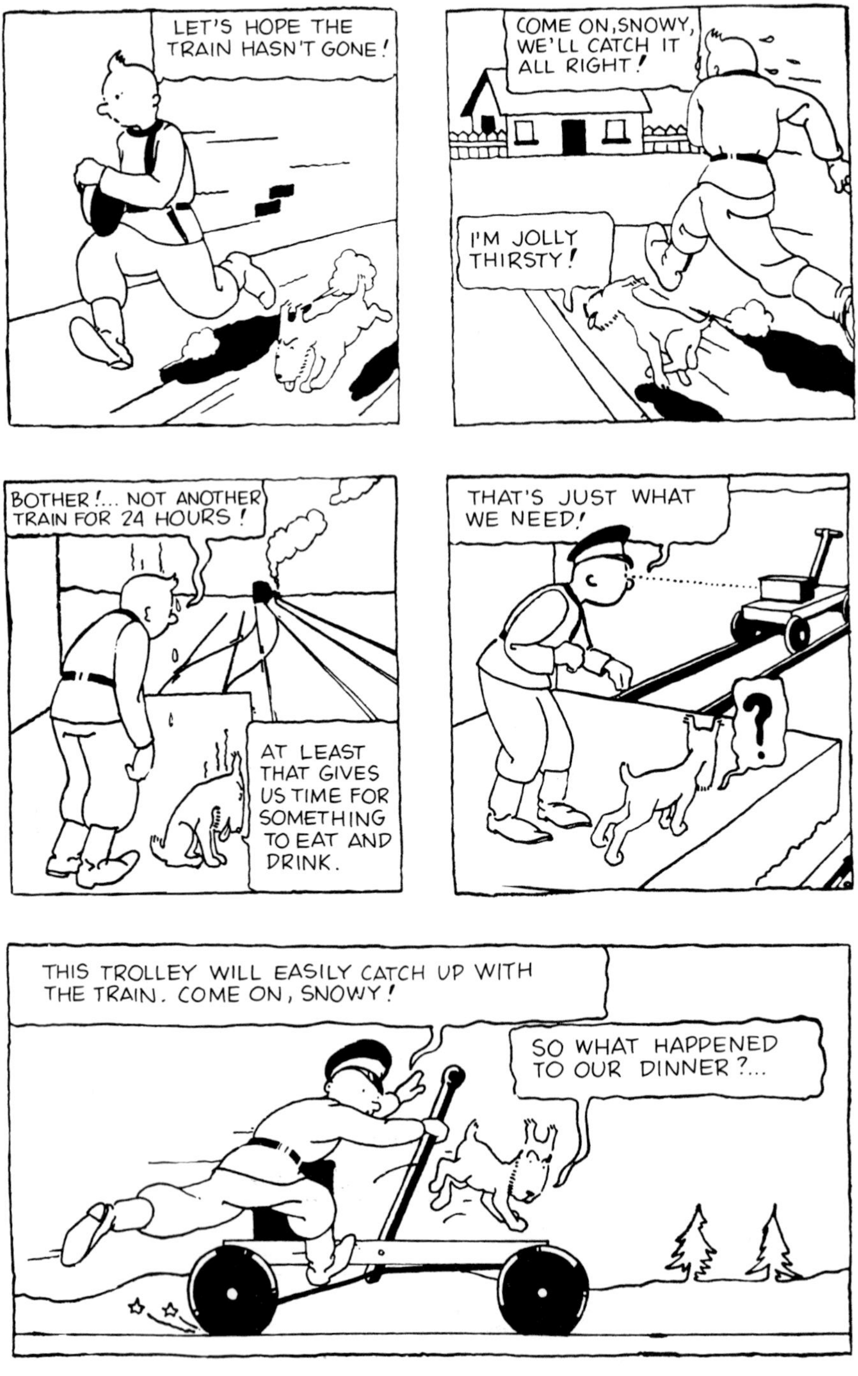

LET'S HOPE THE TRAIN HASN'T GONE!
COME ON, SNOWY, WE'LL CATCH IT ALL RIGHT!
I'M JOLLY THIRSTY!
BOTHER!... NOT ANOTHER TRAIN FOR 24 HOURS!
AT LEAST THAT GIVES US TIME FOR SOMETHING TO EAT AND DRINK.
THAT'S JUST WHAT WE NEED!
?
THIS TROLLEY WILL EASILY CATCH UP WITH THE TRAIN. COME ON, SNOWY!
SO WHAT HAPPENED TO OUR DINNER?...

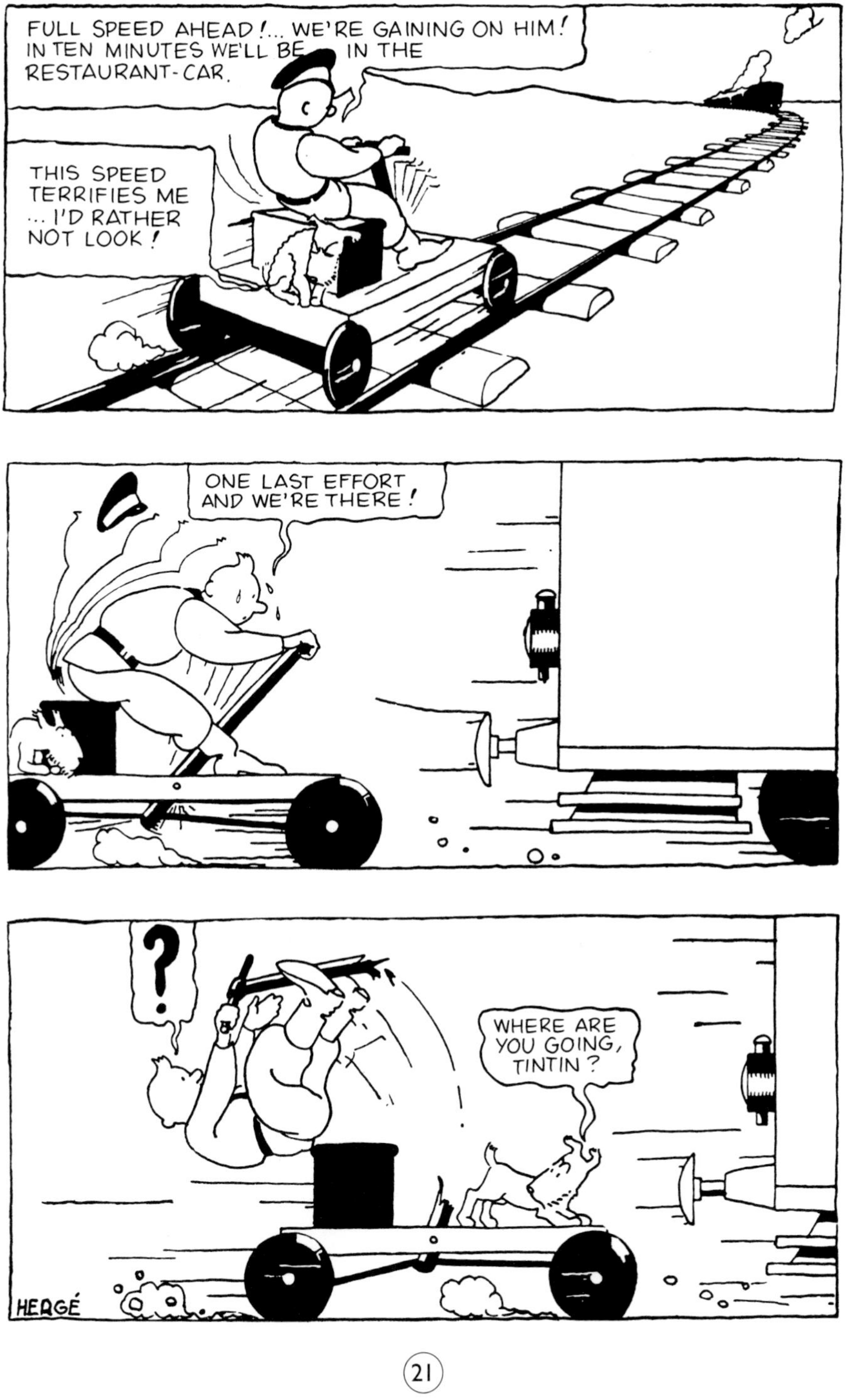
FULL SPEED AHEAD!... WE'RE GAINING ON HIM! IN TEN MINUTES WE'LL BE IN THE RESTAURANT-CAR.
THIS SPEED TERRIFIES ME ... I'D RATHER NOT LOOK!
ONE LAST EFFORT AND WE'RE THERE!
?
WHERE ARE YOU GOING, TINTIN?
HERGÉ

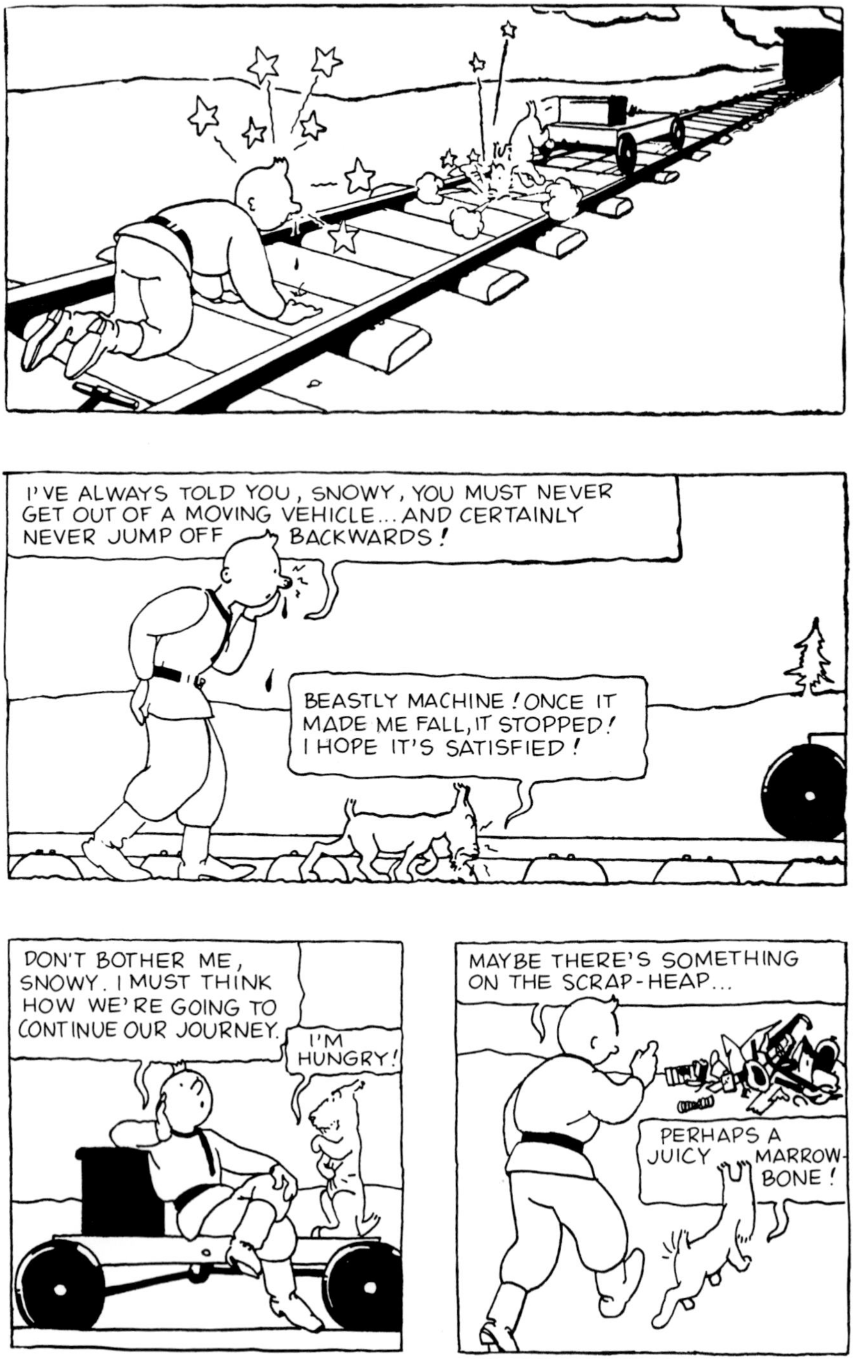
I'VE ALWAYS TOLD YOU, SNOWY, YOU MUST NEVER GET OUT OF A MOVING VEHICLE... AND CERTAINLY NEVER JUMP OFF BACKWARDS!
BEASTLY MACHINE! ONCE IT MADE ME FALL, IT STOPPED! I HOPE IT'S SATISFIED!
DON'T BOTHER ME, SNOWY. I MUST THINK HOW WE'RE GOING TO CONTINUE OUR JOURNEY.
I'M HUNGRY!
MAYBE THERE'S SOMETHING ON THE SCRAP-HEAP...
PERHAPS A JUICY MARROW-BONE!

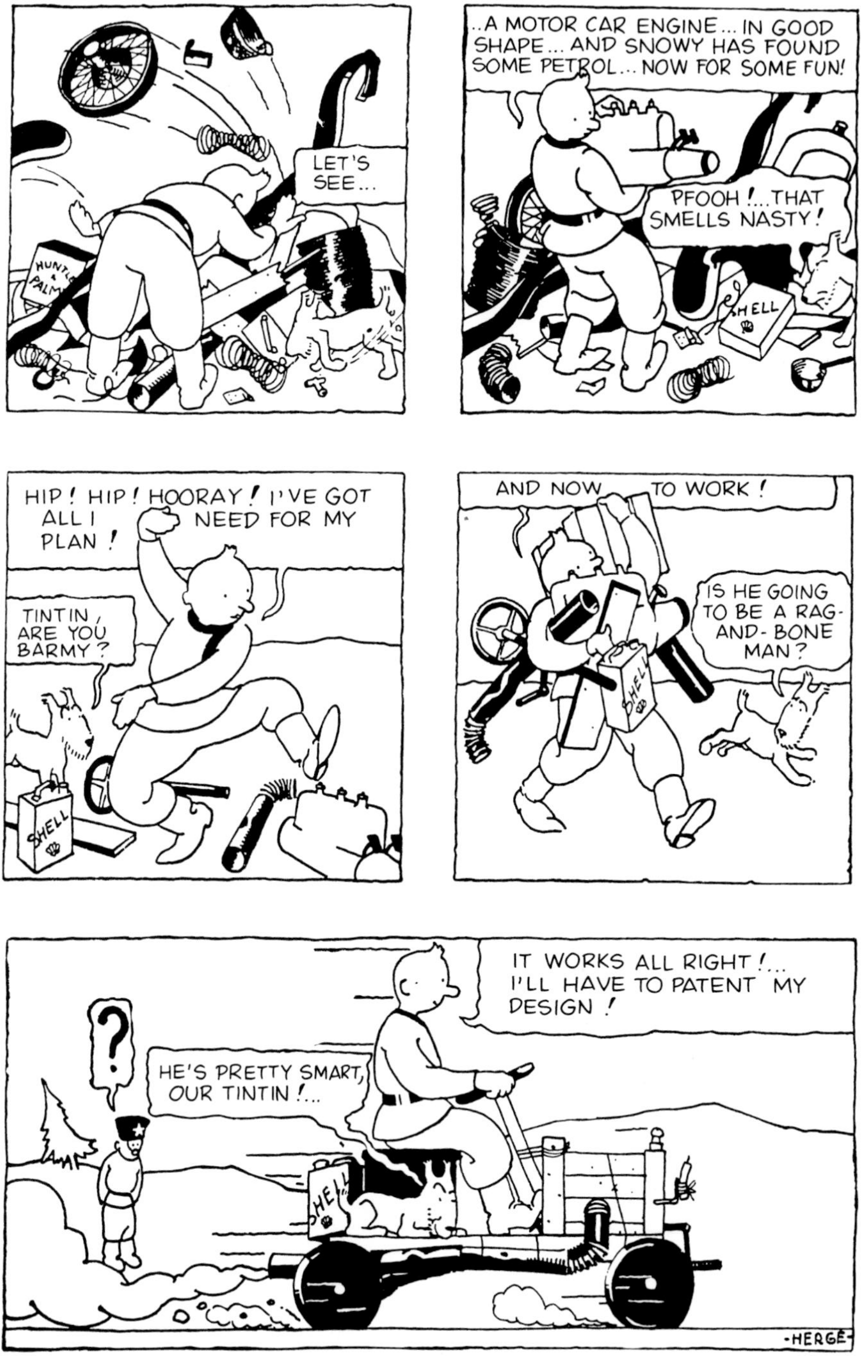
LET'S SEE...
..A MOTOR CAR ENGINE... IN GOOD SHAPE... AND SNOWY HAS FOUND SOME PETROL... NOW FOR SOME FUN!
PFOOH!... THAT SMELLS NASTY!
SHELL
HIP! HIP! HOORAY! I'VE GOT ALL I NEED FOR MY PLAN!
TINTIN, ARE YOU BARMY?
SHELL
AND NOW TO WORK!
IS HE GOING TO BE A RAG-AND-BONE MAN?
SHELL
IT WORKS ALL RIGHT!... I'LL HAVE TO PATENT MY DESIGN!
HE'S PRETTY SMART, OUR TINTIN!...
?
SHELL
-HERGÉ-

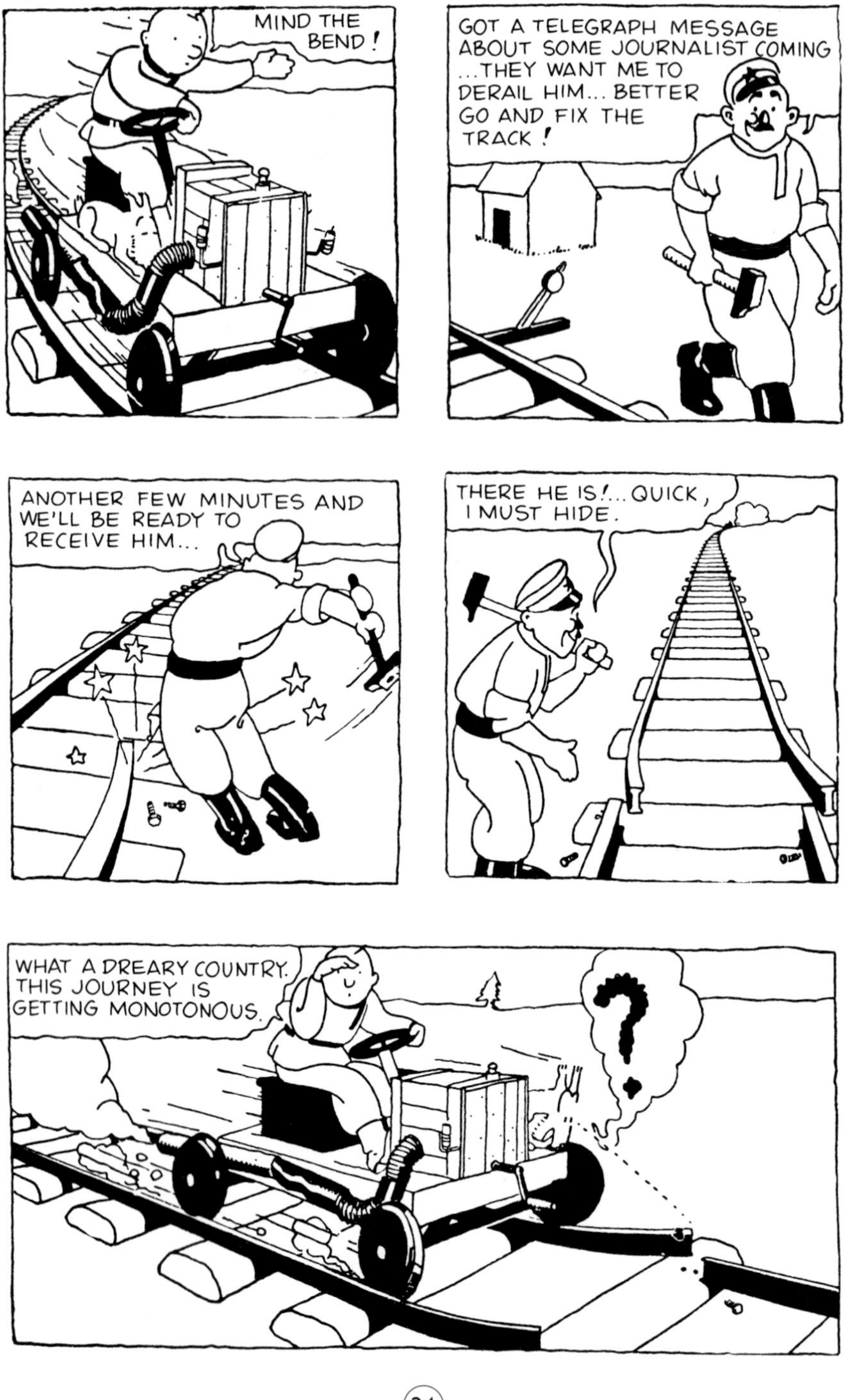
MIND THE BEND!
GOT A TELEGRAPH MESSAGE ABOUT SOME JOURNALIST COMING ...THEY WANT ME TO DERAIL HIM... BETTER GO AND FIX THE TRACK!
ANOTHER FEW MINUTES AND WE'LL BE READY TO RECEIVE HIM...
THERE HE IS!...QUICK, I MUST HIDE.
WHAT A DREARY COUNTRY. THIS JOURNEY IS GETTING MONOTONOUS.
?

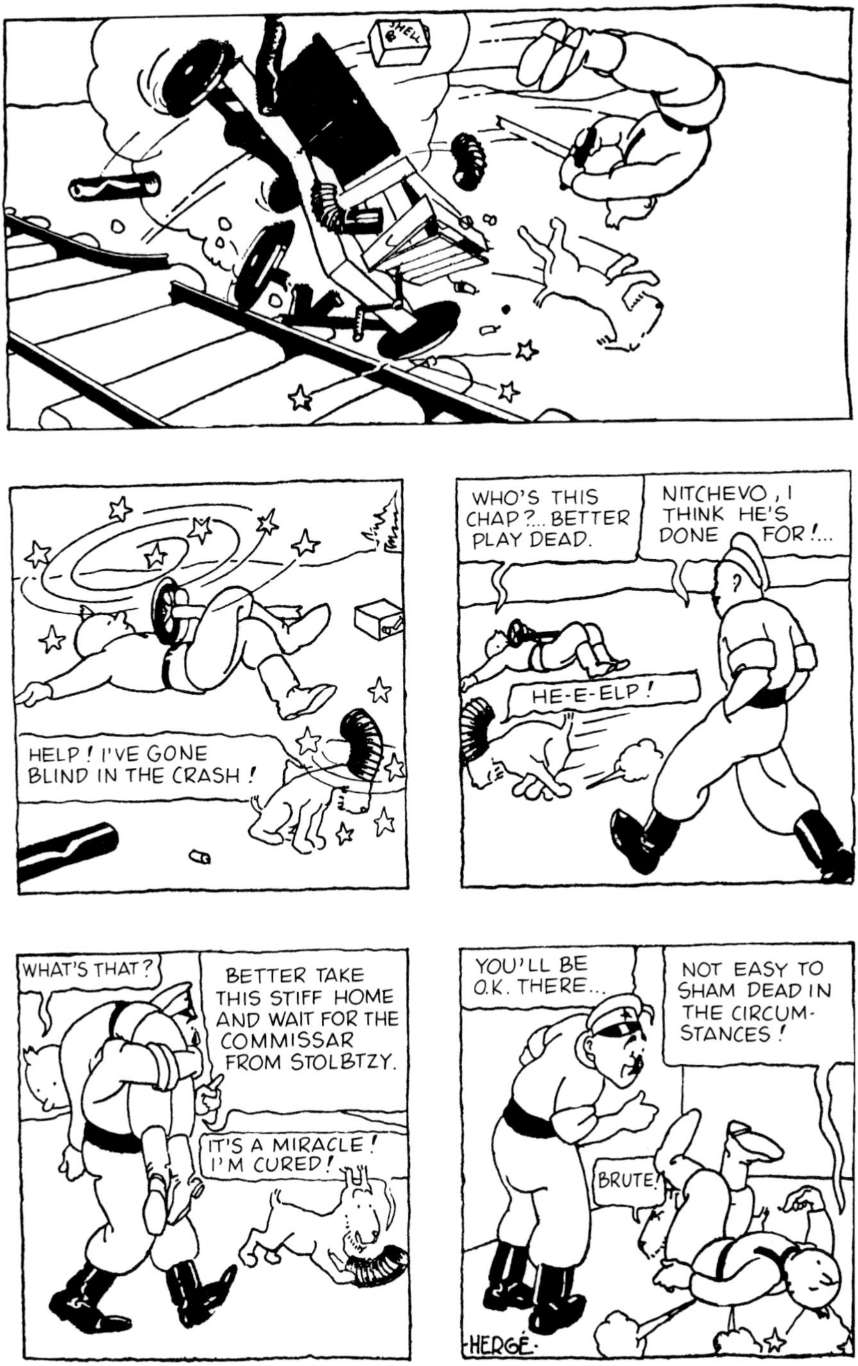
SHELL
HELP! I'VE GONE BLIND IN THE CRASH!
WHO'S THIS CHAP?... BETTER PLAY DEAD.
NITCHEVO, I THINK HE'S DONE FOR!...
HE-E-ELP!
WHAT'S THAT?
BETTER TAKE THIS STIFF HOME AND WAIT FOR THE COMMISSAR FROM STOLBTZY.
IT'S A MIRACLE! I'M CURED!
YOU'LL BE O.K. THERE...
NOT EASY TO SHAM DEAD IN THE CIRCUMSTANCES!
BRUTE!
HERGÉ

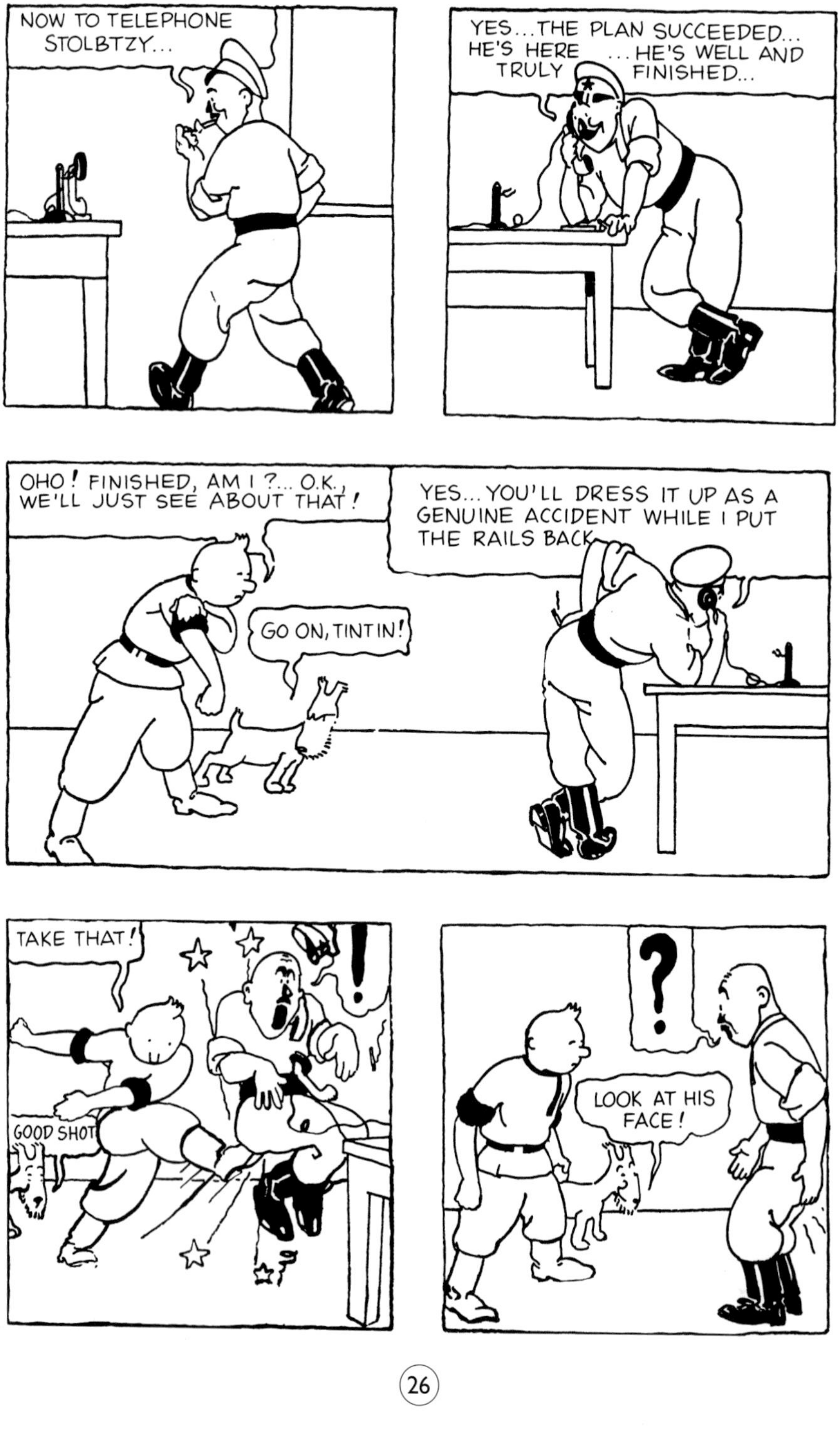
NOW TO TELEPHONE STOLBTZY...
YES...THE PLAN SUCCEEDED... HE'S HERE ...HE'S WELL AND TRULY FINISHED...
OHO! FINISHED, AM I?... O.K., WE'LL JUST SEE ABOUT THAT!
YES... YOU'LL DRESS IT UP AS A GENUINE ACCIDENT WHILE I PUT THE RAILS BACK
GO ON, TINTIN!
TAKE THAT!
!
GOOD SHOT
?
LOOK AT HIS FACE!

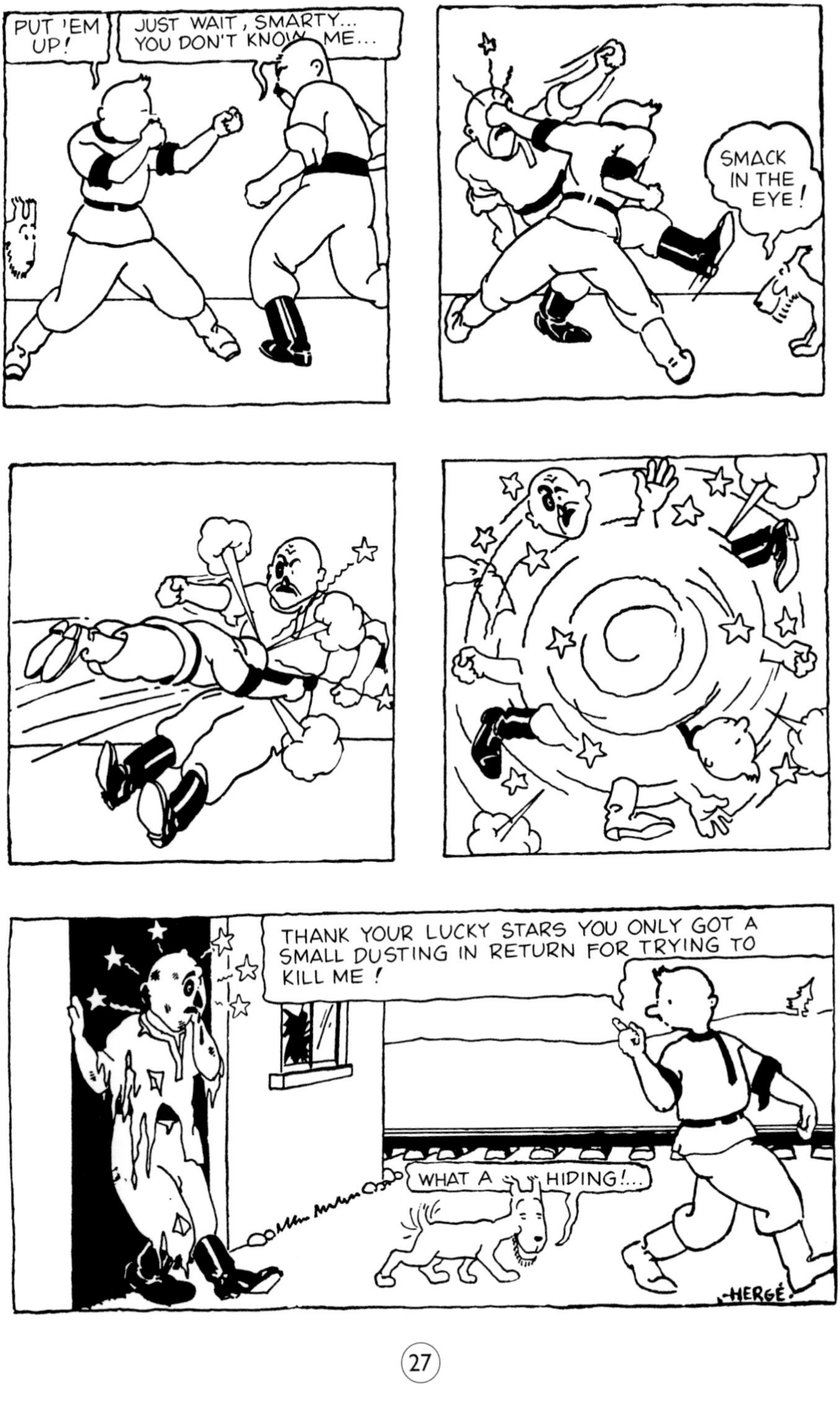
PUT 'EM UP!
JUST WAIT, SMARTY... YOU DON'T KNOW ME...
SMACK IN THE EYE!
THANK YOUR LUCKY STARS YOU ONLY GOT A SMALL DUSTING IN RETURN FOR TRYING TO KILL ME!
WHAT A HIDING!...
HERGÉ

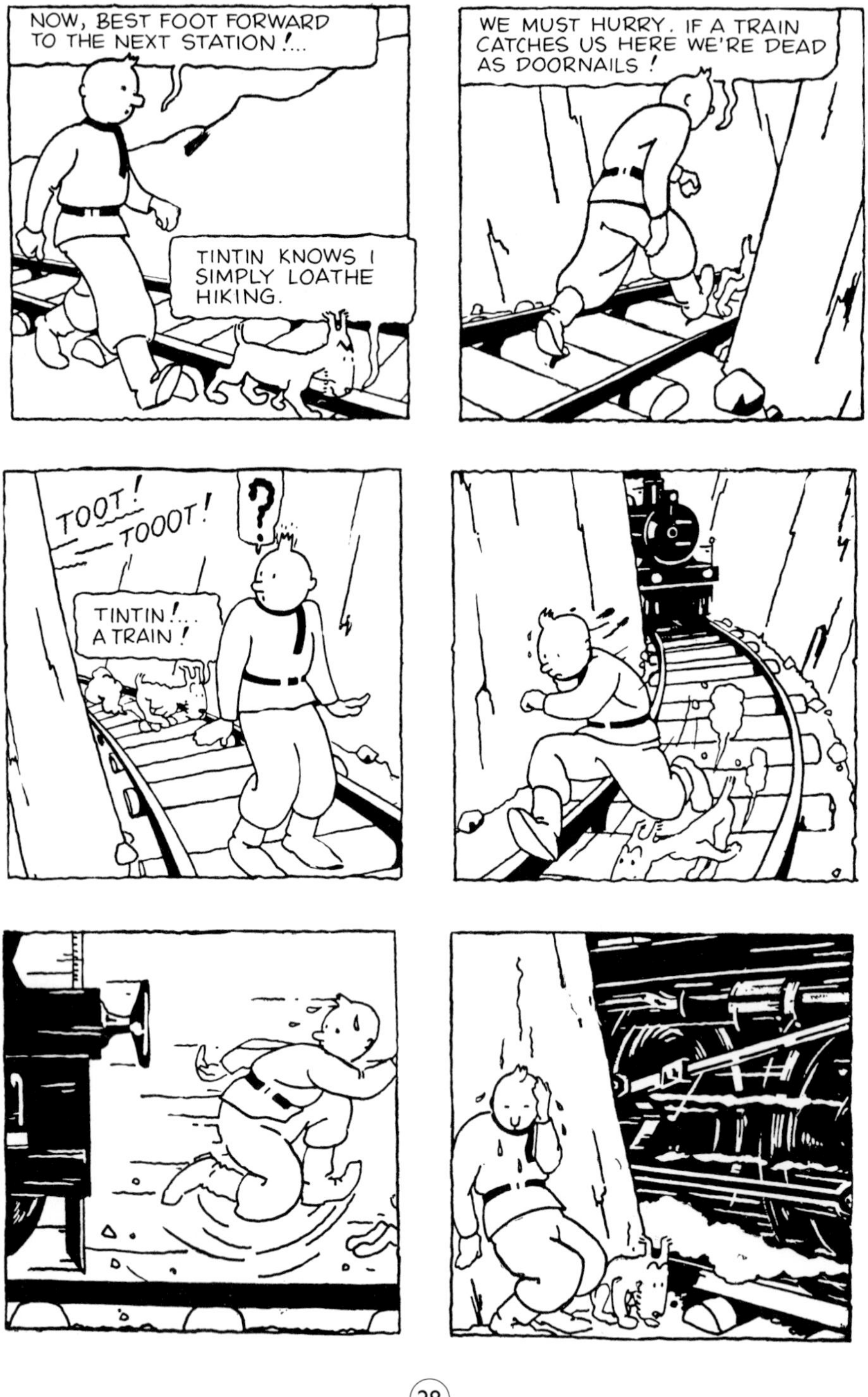

NOW, BEST FOOT FORWARD TO THE NEXT STATION!...
TINTIN KNOWS I SIMPLY LOATHE HIKING.
WE MUST HURRY. IF A TRAIN CATCHES US HERE WE'RE DEAD AS DOORNAILS!
TOOT! TOOOT!
?
TINTIN!... A TRAIN!

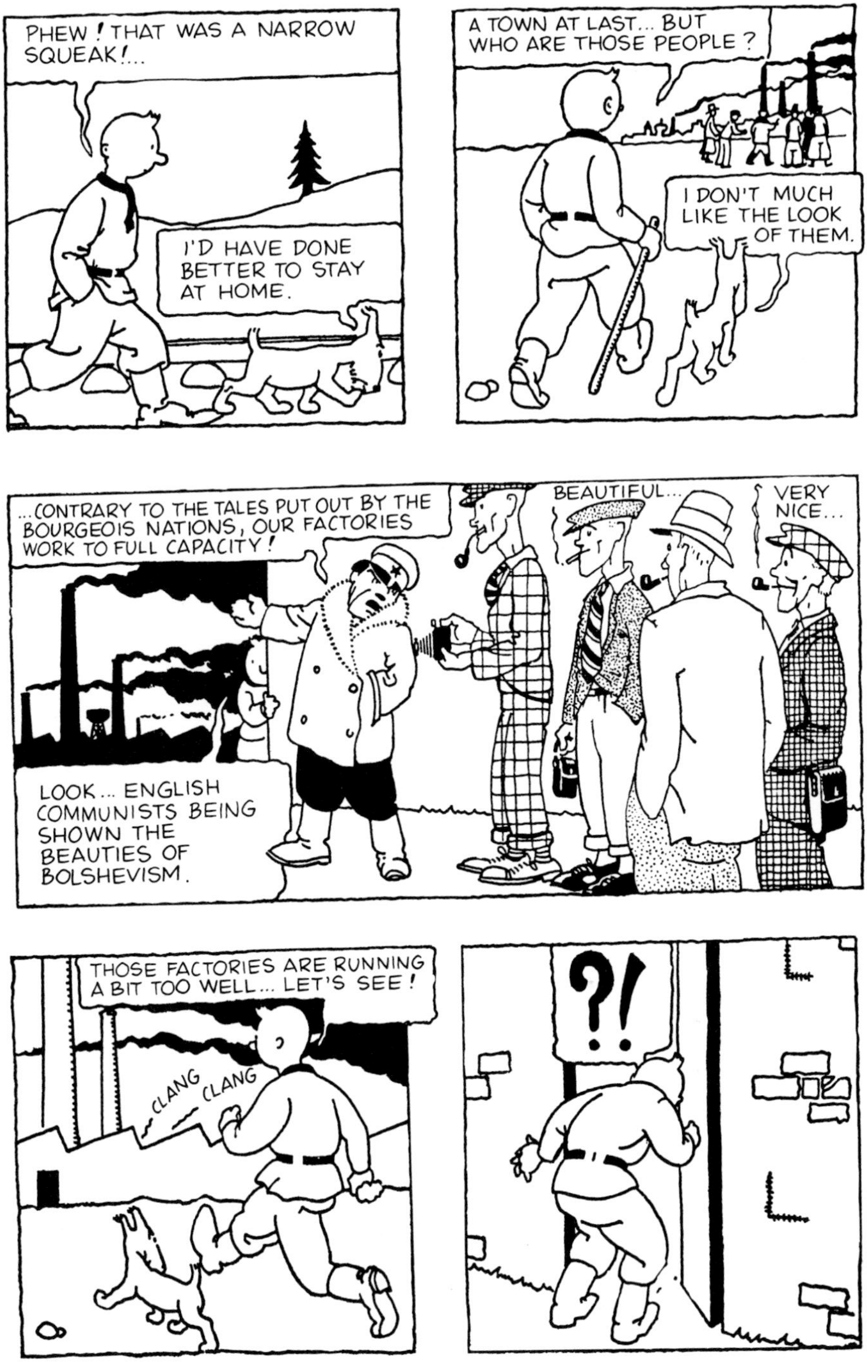
PHEW! THAT WAS A NARROW SQUEAK!...
I'D HAVE DONE BETTER TO STAY AT HOME.
A TOWN AT LAST... BUT WHO ARE THOSE PEOPLE?
I DON'T MUCH LIKE THE LOOK OF THEM.
...CONTRARY TO THE TALES PUT OUT BY THE BOURGEOIS NATIONS, OUR FACTORIES WORK TO FULL CAPACITY!
BEAUTIFUL...
VERY NICE...
LOOK... ENGLISH COMMUNISTS BEING SHOWN THE BEAUTIES OF BOLSHEVISM.
THOSE FACTORIES ARE RUNNING A BIT TOO WELL... LET'S SEE!
CLANG
CLANG
?!

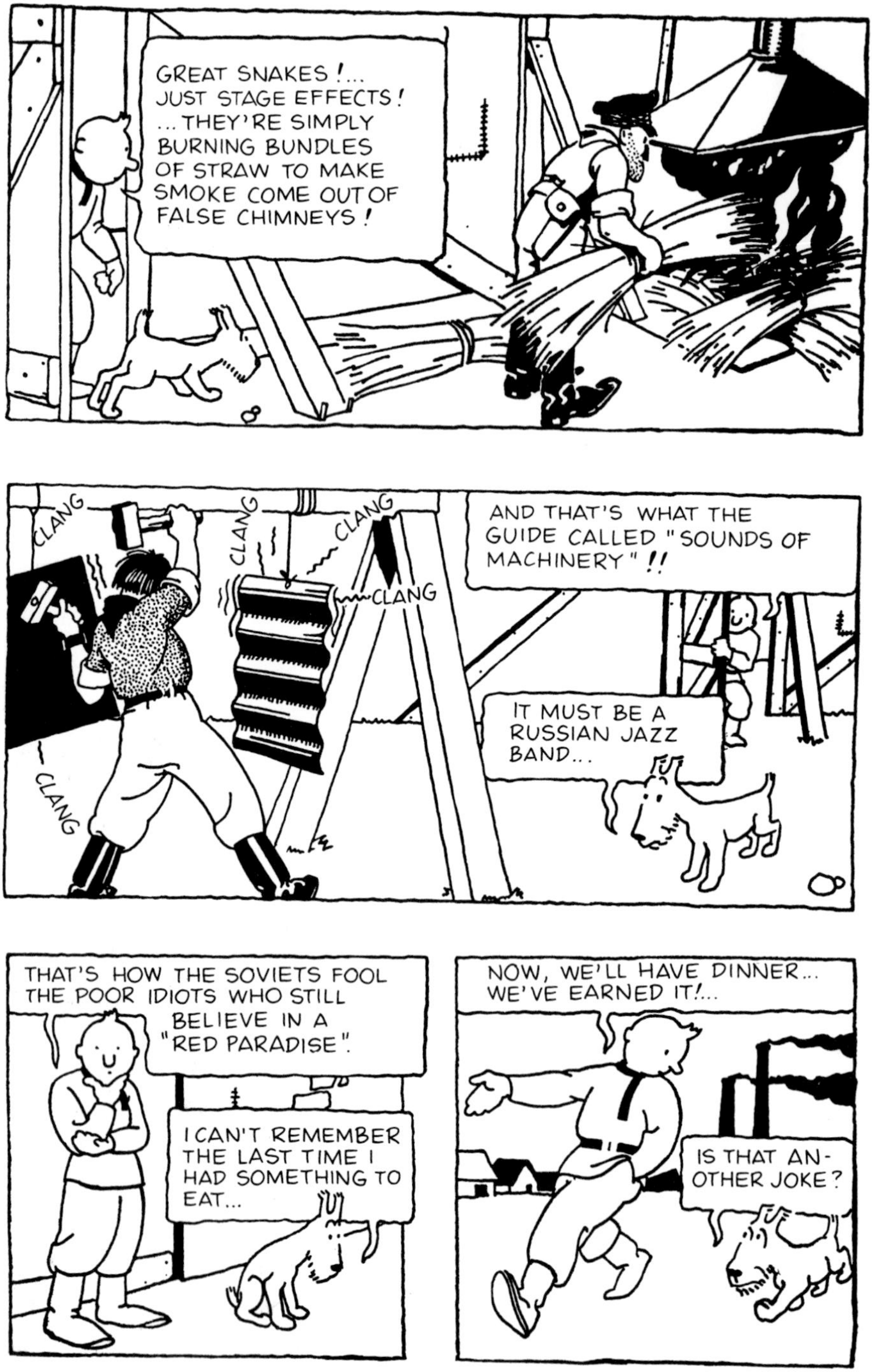

GREAT SNAKES!... JUST STAGE EFFECTS! ...THEY'RE SIMPLY BURNING BUNDLES OF STRAW TO MAKE SMOKE COME OUT OF FALSE CHIMNEYS!
CLANG
CLANG
CLANG
CLANG
CLANG
AND THAT'S WHAT THE GUIDE CALLED "SOUNDS OF MACHINERY"!!
IT MUST BE A RUSSIAN JAZZ BAND...
THAT'S HOW THE SOVIETS FOOL THE POOR IDIOTS WHO STILL BELIEVE IN A "RED PARADISE".
I CAN'T REMEMBER THE LAST TIME I HAD SOMETHING TO EAT...
NOW, WE'LL HAVE DINNER... WE'VE EARNED IT!...
IS THAT ANOTHER JOKE?

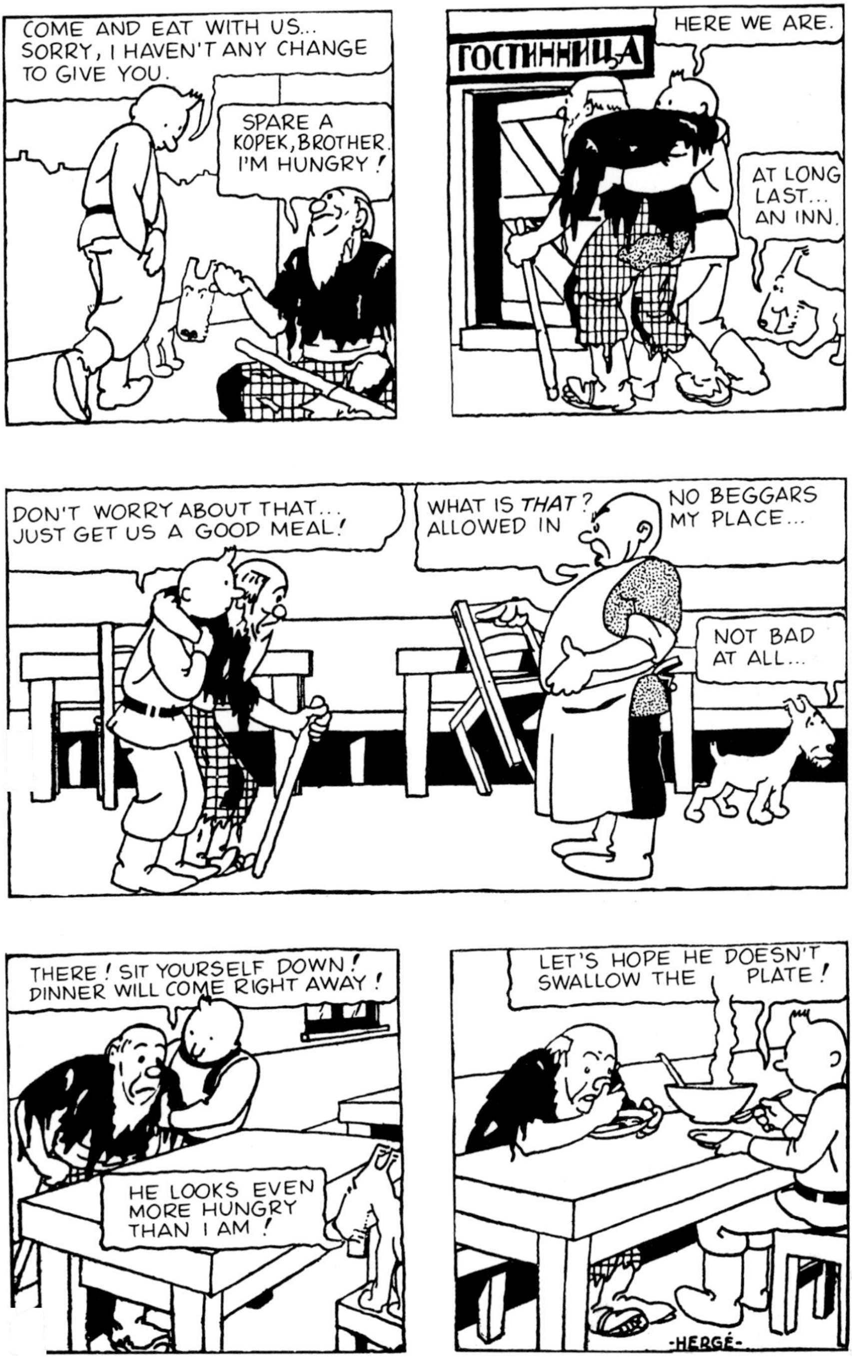
COME AND EAT WITH US... SORRY, I HAVEN'T ANY CHANGE TO GIVE YOU.
SPARE A KOPEK, BROTHER. I'M HUNGRY!
ГОСТИННИЦА
HERE WE ARE.
AT LONG LAST... AN INN.
DON'T WORRY ABOUT THAT... JUST GET US A GOOD MEAL!
WHAT IS *THAT*? NO BEGGARS ALLOWED IN MY PLACE...
NOT BAD AT ALL...
THERE! SIT YOURSELF DOWN! DINNER WILL COME RIGHT AWAY!
HE LOOKS EVEN MORE HUNGRY THAN I AM!
LET'S HOPE HE DOESN'T SWALLOW THE PLATE!
-HERGÉ-

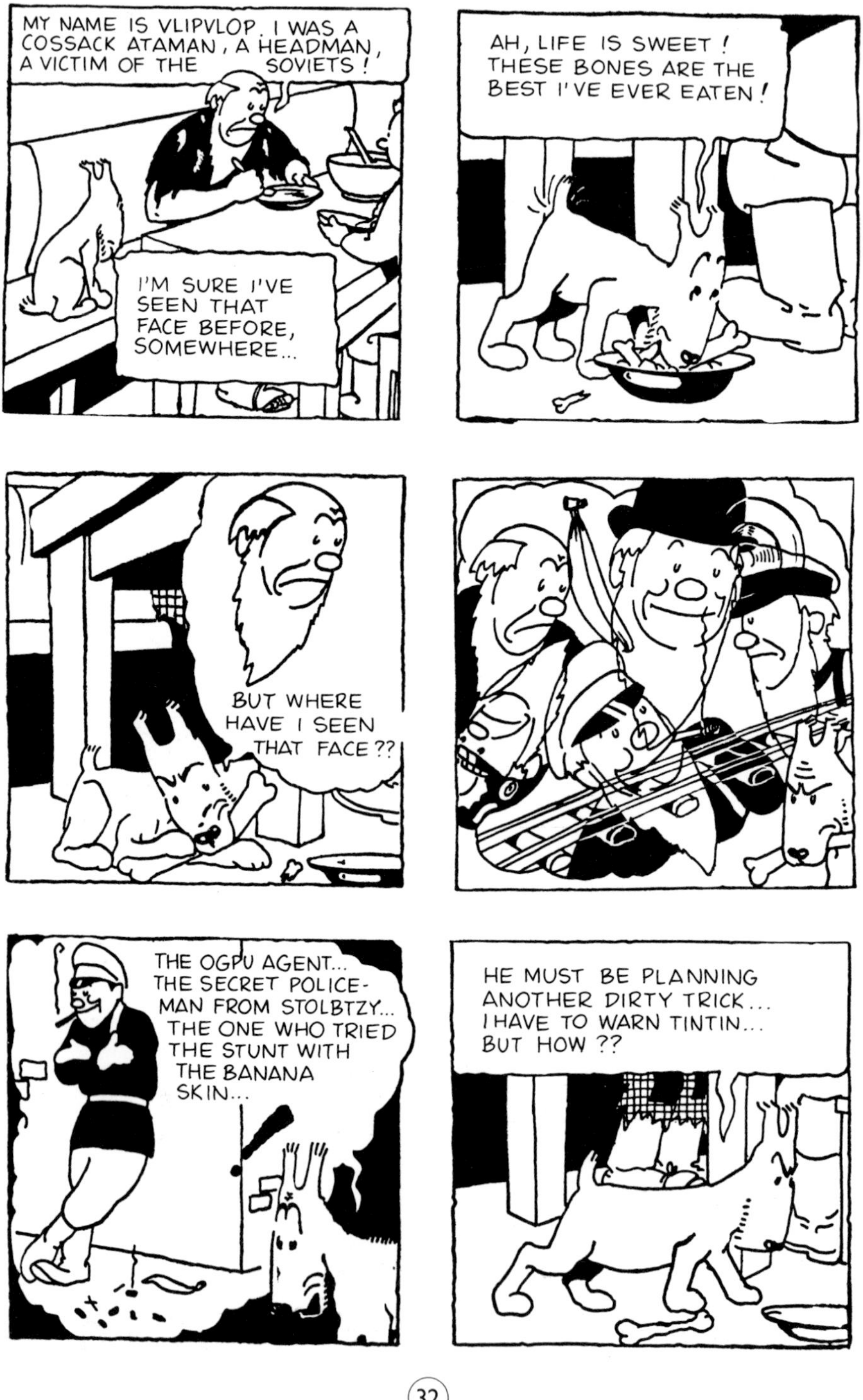
MY NAME IS VLIPVLOP. I WAS A COSSACK ATAMAN, A HEADMAN, A VICTIM OF THE SOVIETS!
I'M SURE I'VE SEEN THAT FACE BEFORE, SOMEWHERE...
AH, LIFE IS SWEET! THESE BONES ARE THE BEST I'VE EVER EATEN!
BUT WHERE HAVE I SEEN THAT FACE??
THE OGPU AGENT... THE SECRET POLICEMAN FROM STOLBTZY... THE ONE WHO TRIED THE STUNT WITH THE BANANA SKIN...
HE MUST BE PLANNING ANOTHER DIRTY TRICK... I HAVE TO WARN TINTIN... BUT HOW??

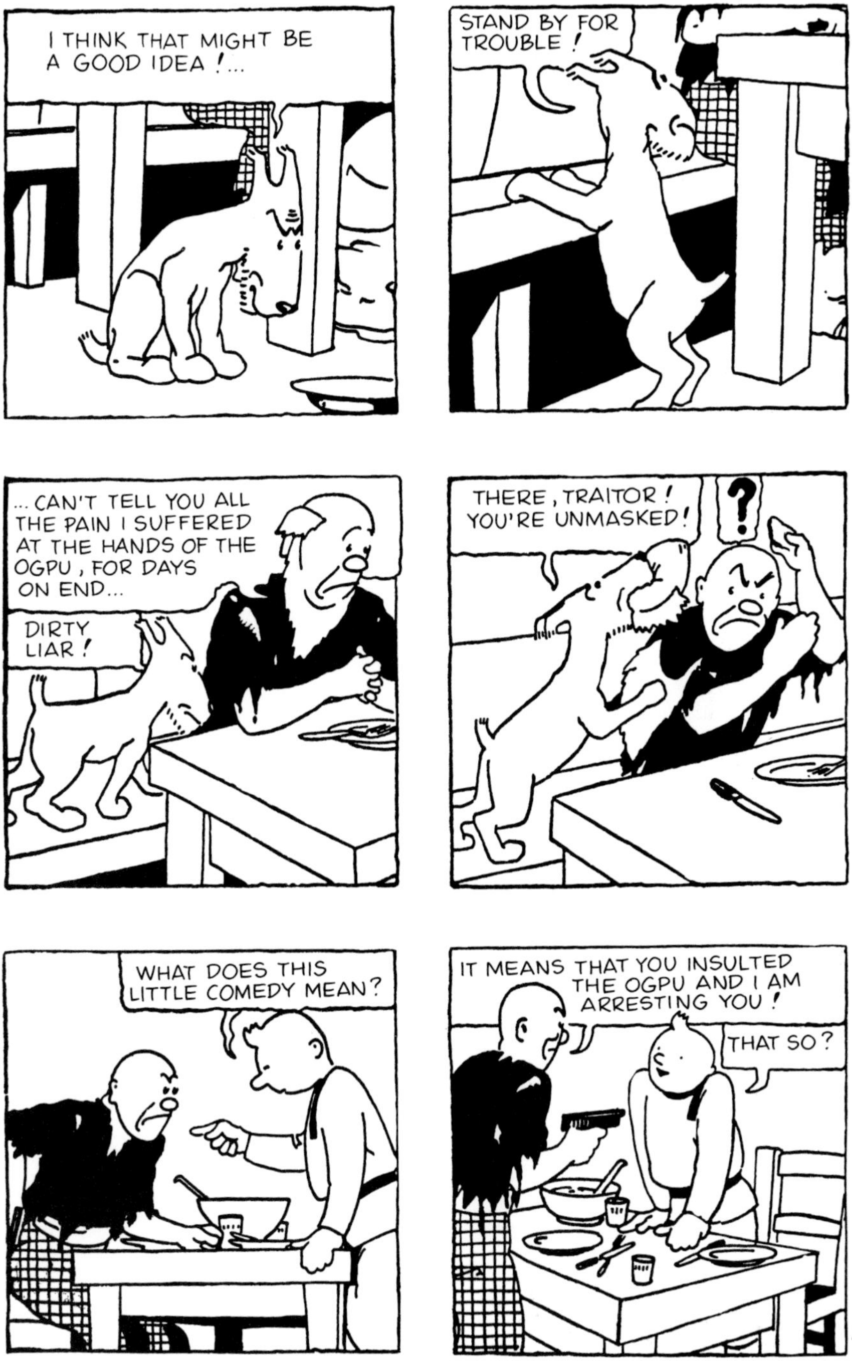
I THINK THAT MIGHT BE A GOOD IDEA !...
STAND BY FOR TROUBLE !
... CAN'T TELL YOU ALL THE PAIN I SUFFERED AT THE HANDS OF THE OGPU , FOR DAYS ON END...
DIRTY LIAR !
THERE, TRAITOR ! YOU'RE UNMASKED !
?
WHAT DOES THIS LITTLE COMEDY MEAN ?
IT MEANS THAT YOU INSULTED THE OGPU AND I AM ARRESTING YOU !
THAT SO ?

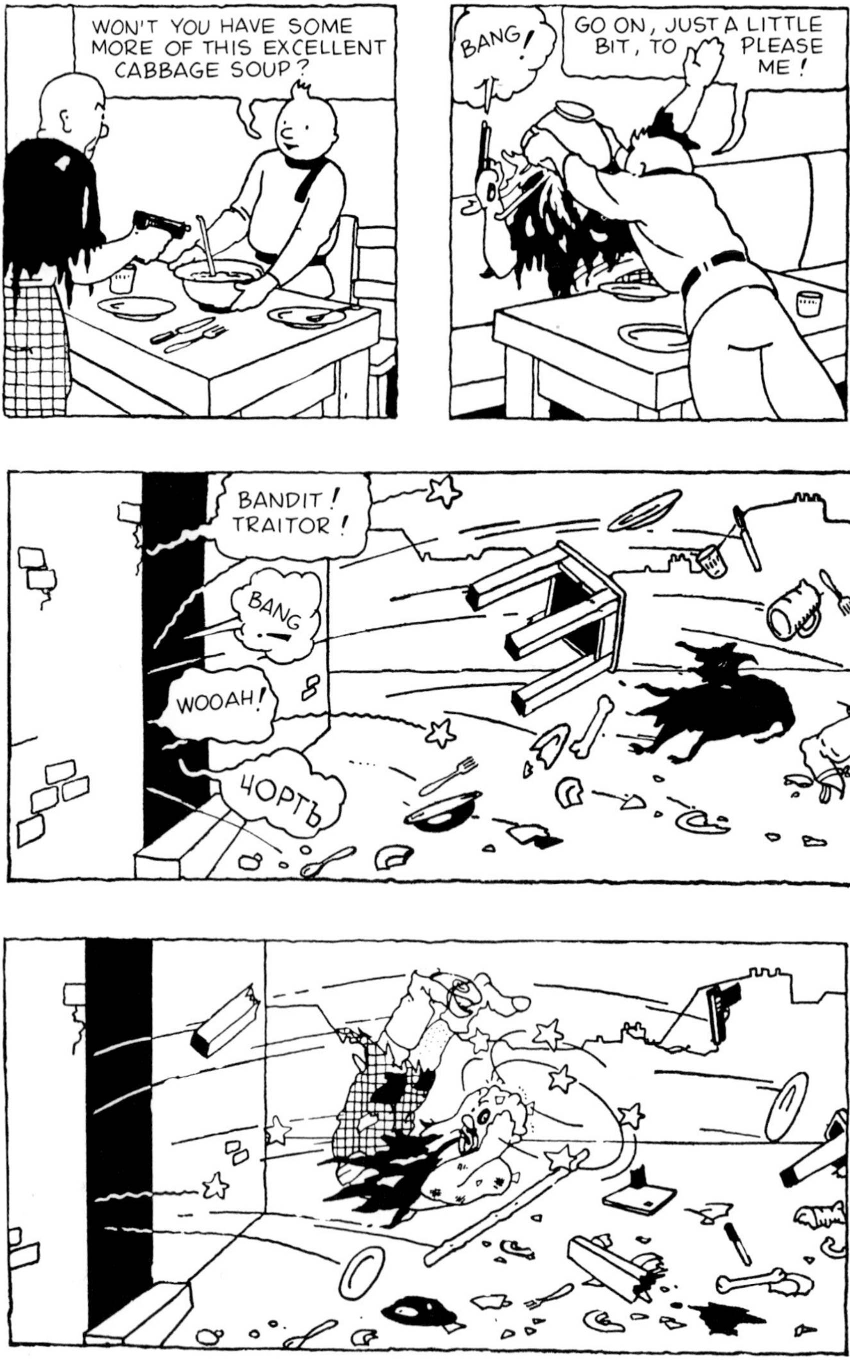
WON'T YOU HAVE SOME MORE OF THIS EXCELLENT CABBAGE SOUP?
BANG!
GO ON, JUST A LITTLE BIT, TO PLEASE ME!
BANDIT! TRAITOR!
BANG
WOOAH!
ЧОРТЪ

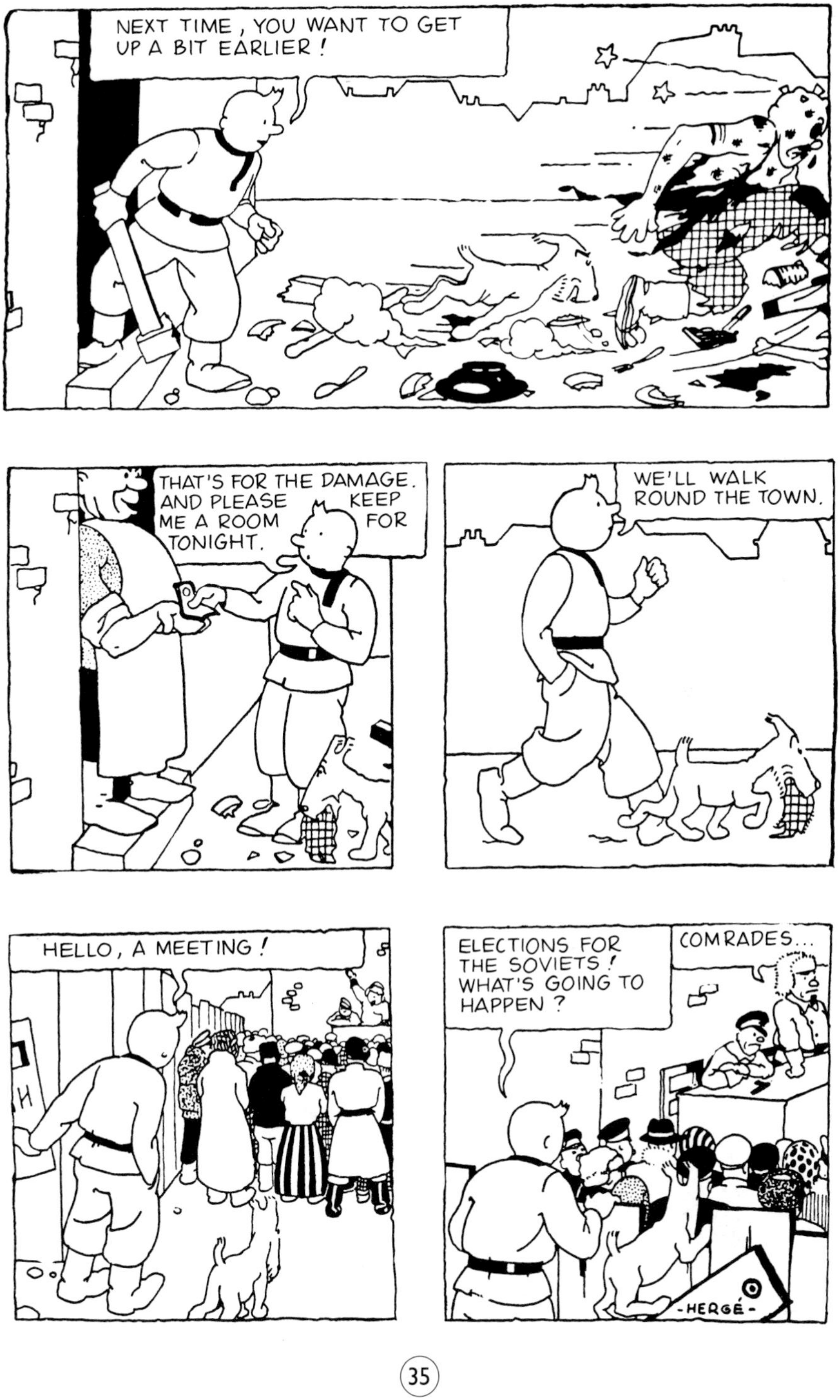
NEXT TIME, YOU WANT TO GET UP A BIT EARLIER!
THAT'S FOR THE DAMAGE. AND PLEASE KEEP ME A ROOM FOR TONIGHT.
WE'LL WALK ROUND THE TOWN.
HELLO, A MEETING!
ELECTIONS FOR THE SOVIETS! WHAT'S GOING TO HAPPEN?
COMRADES...
-HERGÉ-

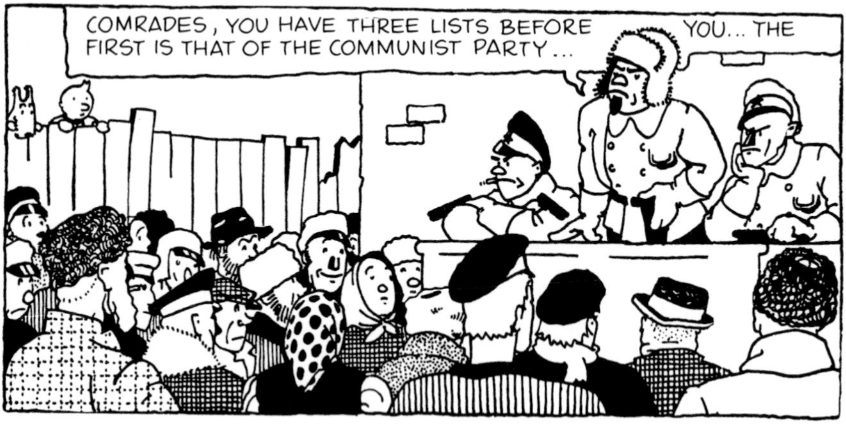
COMRADES, YOU HAVE THREE LISTS BEFORE YOU... THE FIRST IS THAT OF THE COMMUNIST PARTY...

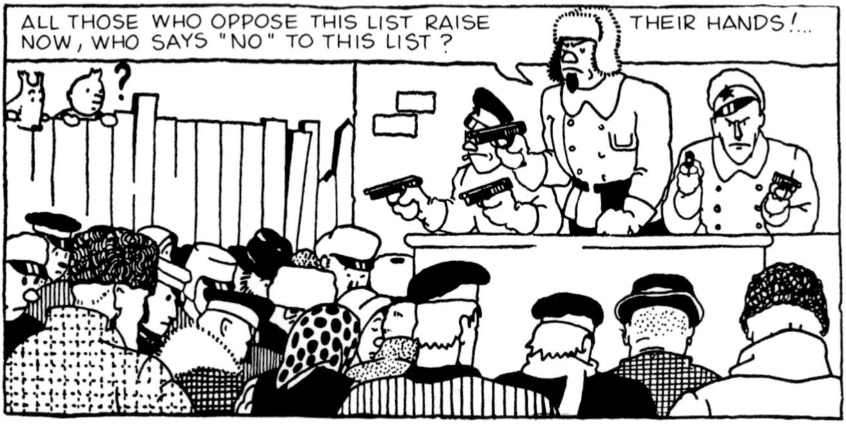
ALL THOSE WHO OPPOSE THIS LIST RAISE THEIR HANDS!... NOW, WHO SAYS "NO" TO THIS LIST?
?

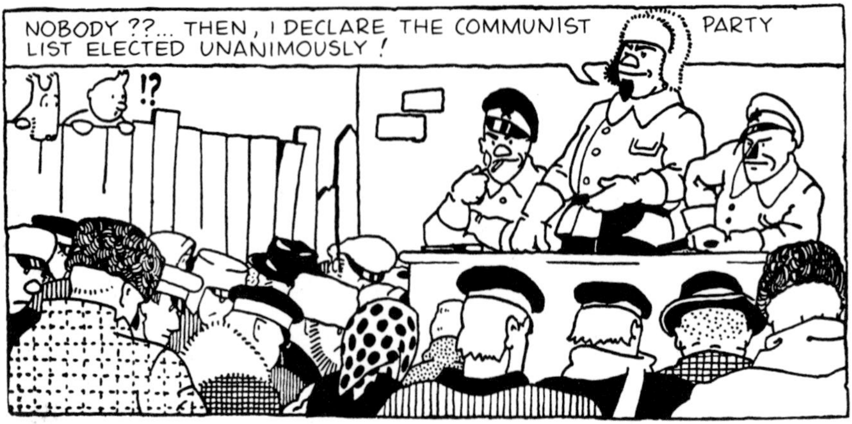
NOBODY??... THEN, I DECLARE THE COMMUNIST PARTY LIST ELECTED UNANIMOUSLY!
!?

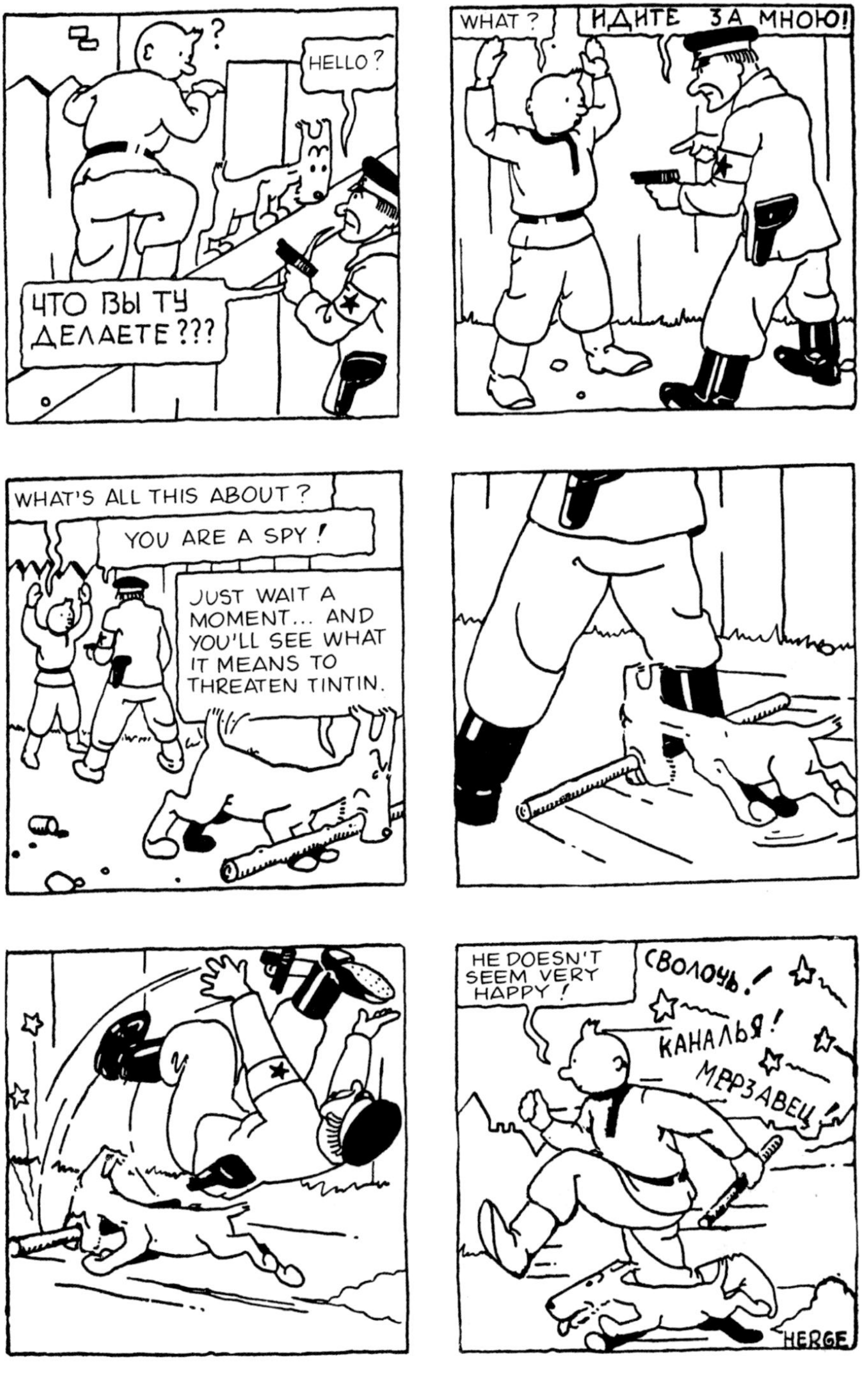
HELLO?
ЧТО ВЫ ТУ ДЕЛАЕТЕ???
WHAT?
ИДИТЕ ЗА МНОЮ!
WHAT'S ALL THIS ABOUT?
YOU ARE A SPY!
JUST WAIT A MOMENT... AND YOU'LL SEE WHAT IT MEANS TO THREATEN TINTIN.
HE DOESN'T SEEM VERY HAPPY!
СВОЛОЧЬ!
КАНАЛЬЯ!
МЕРЗАВЕЦ!
HERGE

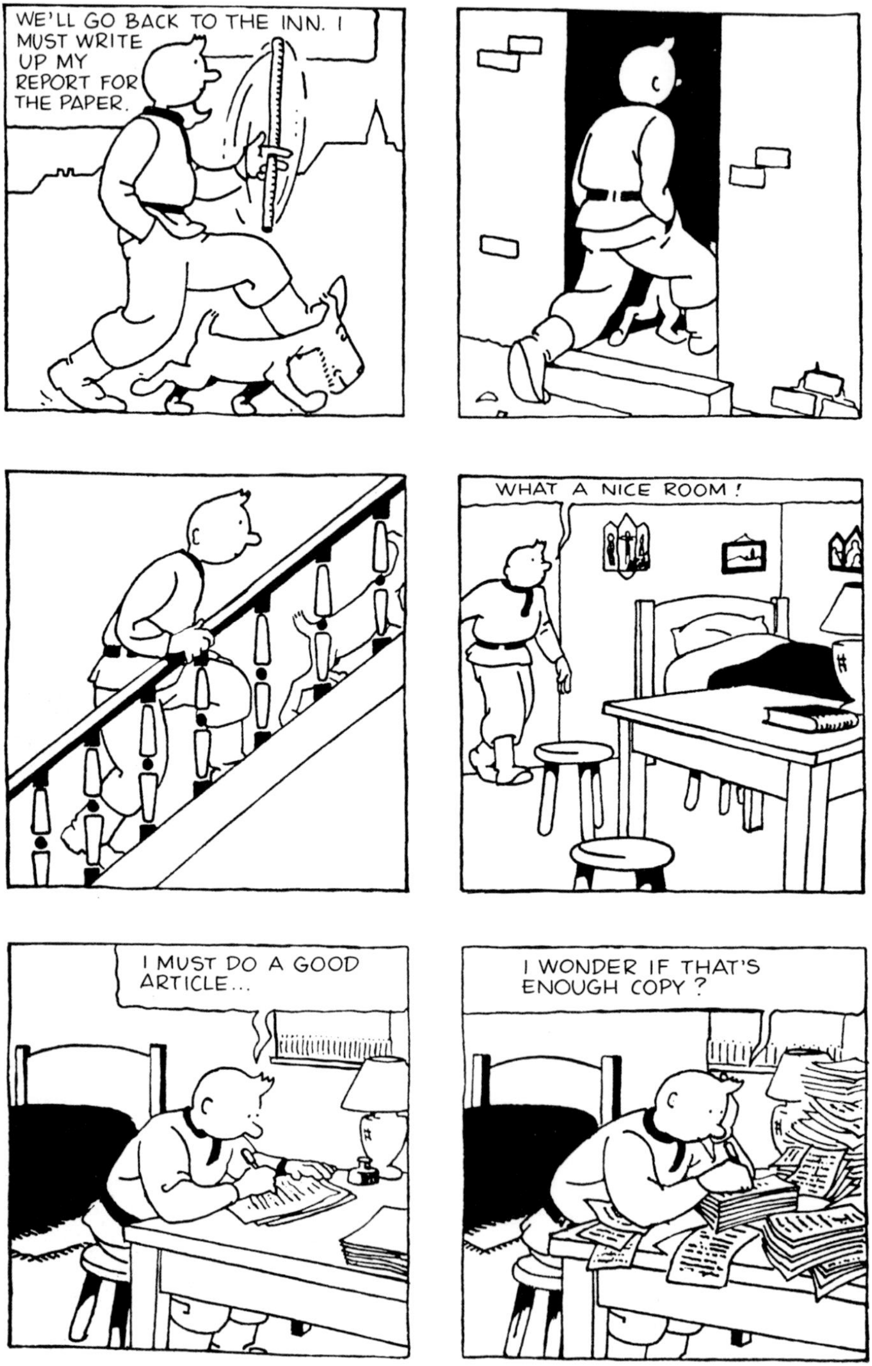
WE'LL GO BACK TO THE INN. I MUST WRITE UP MY REPORT FOR THE PAPER.
WHAT A NICE ROOM !
I MUST DO A GOOD ARTICLE...
I WONDER IF THAT'S ENOUGH COPY ?

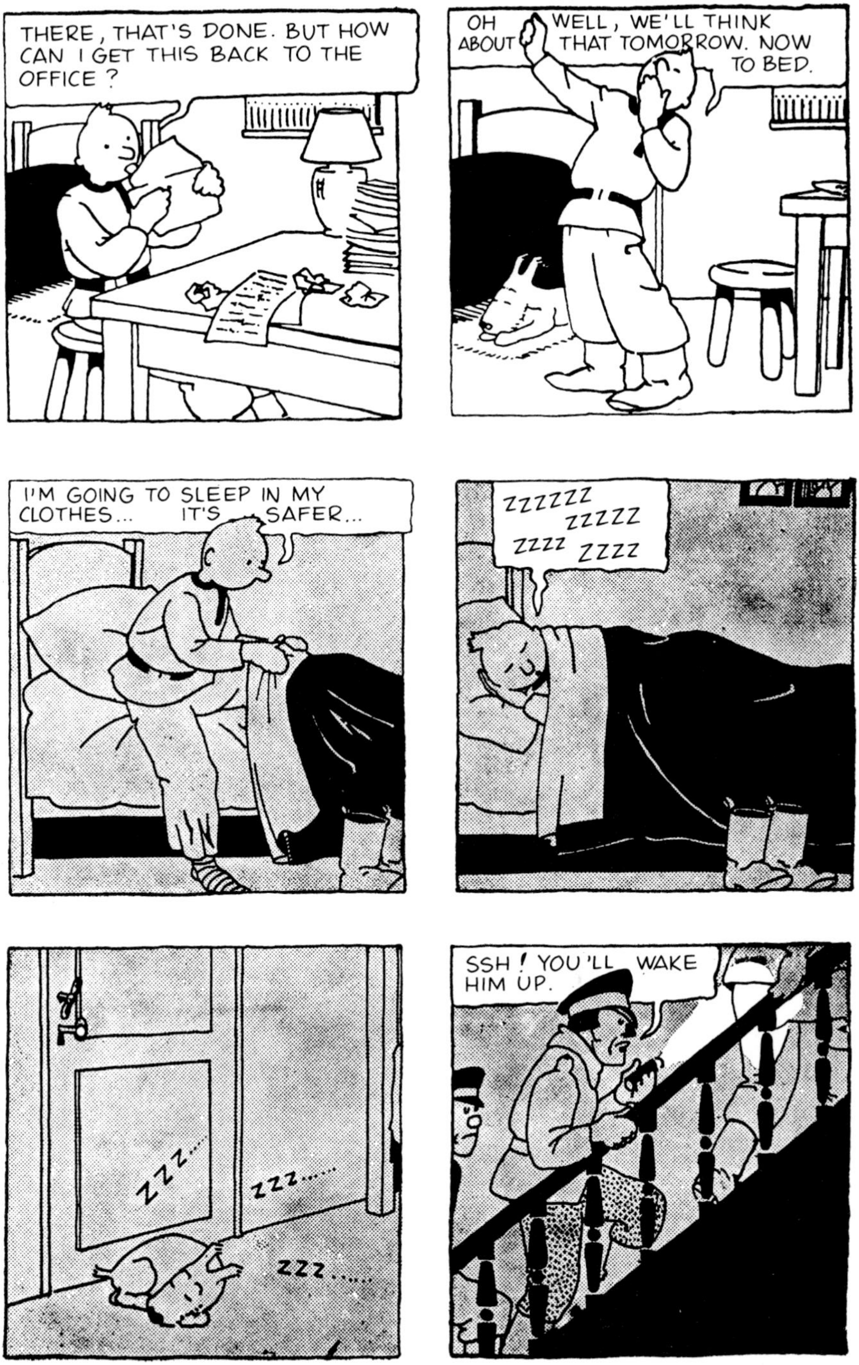
THERE, THAT'S DONE. BUT HOW CAN I GET THIS BACK TO THE OFFICE ?
OH WELL, WE'LL THINK ABOUT THAT TOMORROW. NOW TO BED.
I'M GOING TO SLEEP IN MY CLOTHES... IT'S ... SAFER...
ZZZZZZ ZZZZZ ZZZZ ZZZZ
ZZZ... ZZZ..... ZZZ.....
SSH ! YOU'LL WAKE HIM UP.

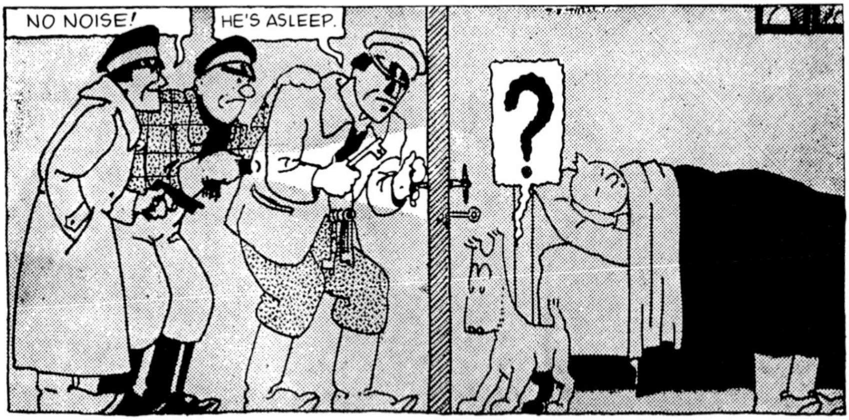
NO NOISE!
HE'S ASLEEP.
?

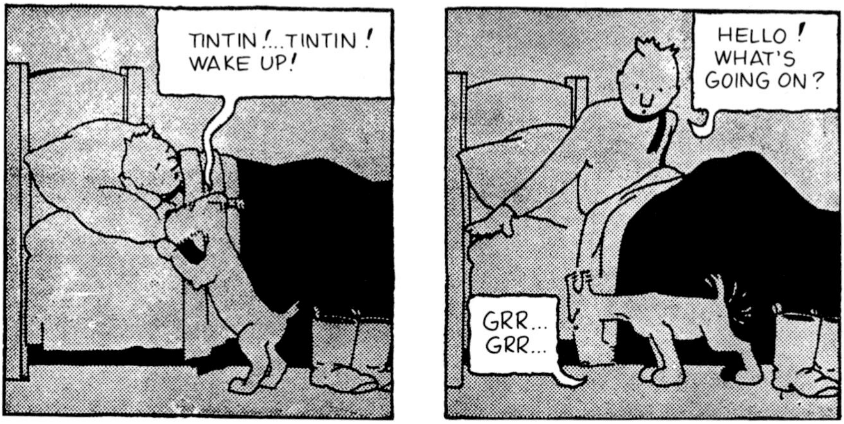
TINTIN!...TINTIN! WAKE UP!
HELLO! WHAT'S GOING ON?
GRR... GRR...

36

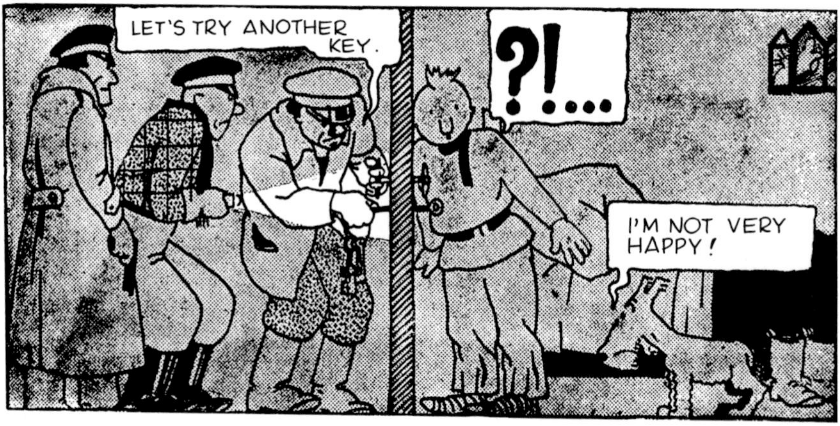
LET'S TRY ANOTHER KEY.
?!...
I'M NOT VERY HAPPY!

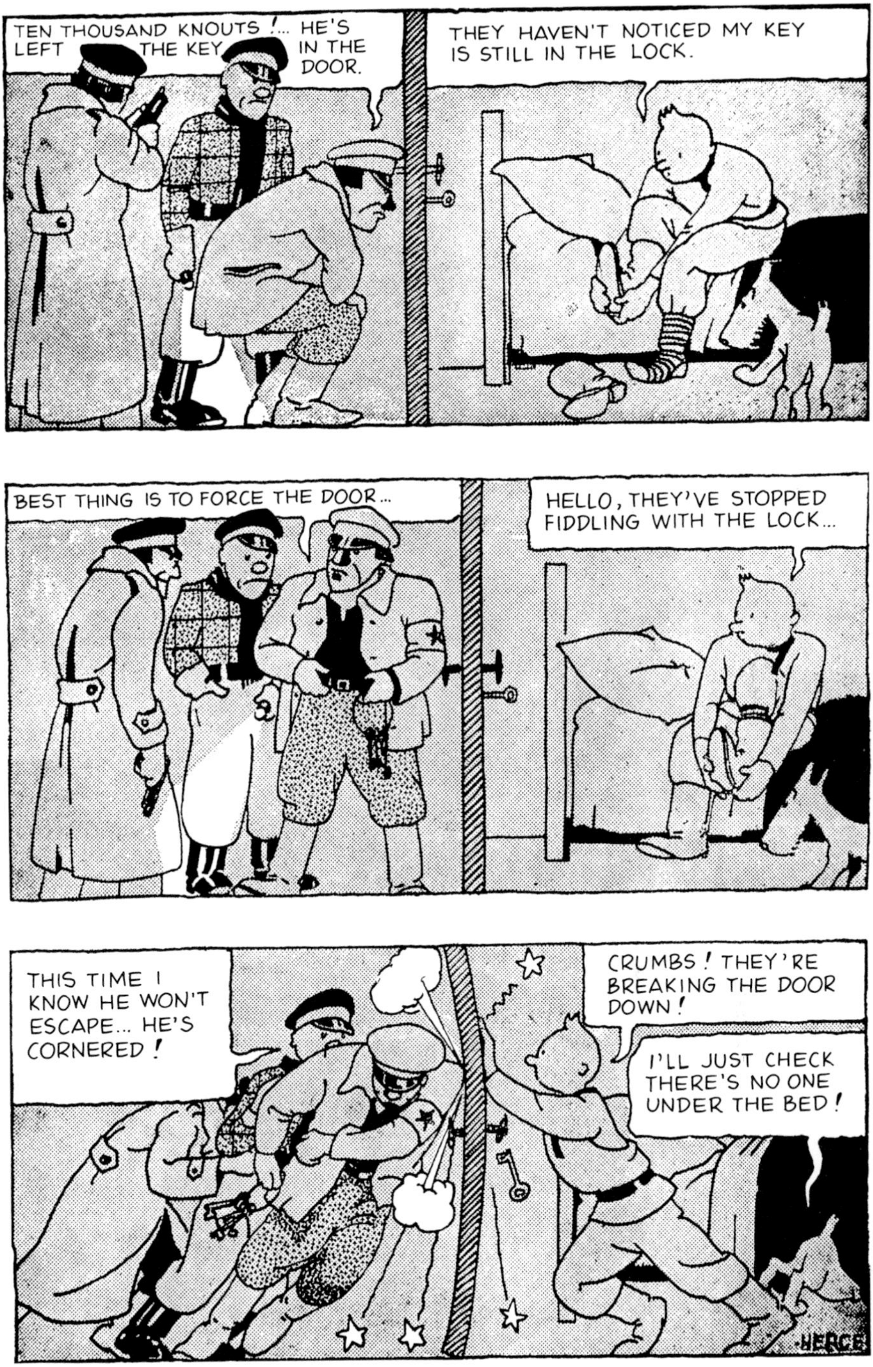
TEN THOUSAND KNOUTS !... HE'S LEFT THE KEY IN THE DOOR.
THEY HAVEN'T NOTICED MY KEY IS STILL IN THE LOCK.
BEST THING IS TO FORCE THE DOOR...
HELLO, THEY'VE STOPPED FIDDLING WITH THE LOCK...
THIS TIME I KNOW HE WON'T ESCAPE... HE'S CORNERED !
CRUMBS ! THEY'RE BREAKING THE DOOR DOWN !
I'LL JUST CHECK THERE'S NO ONE UNDER THE BED !
HERGE

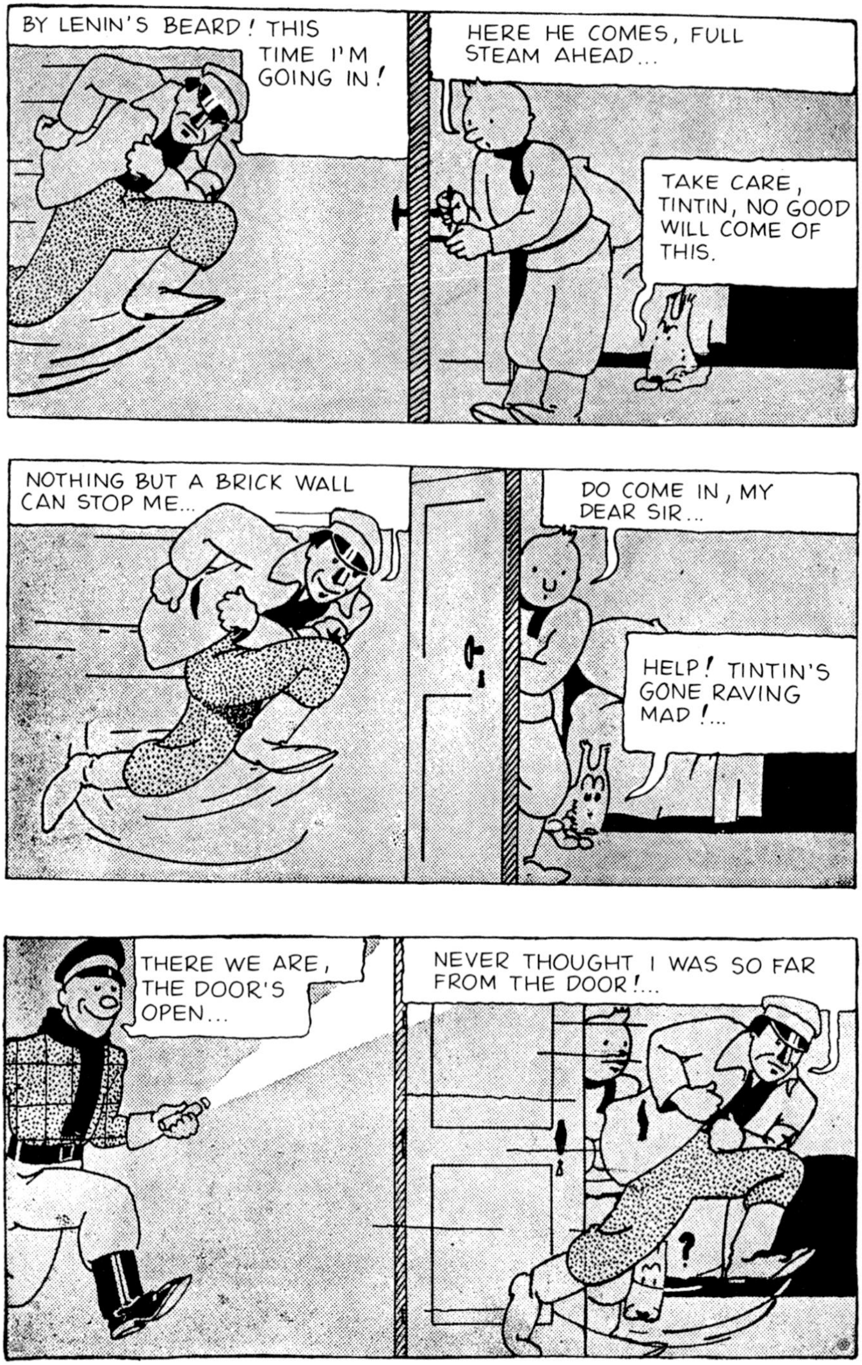
BY LENIN'S BEARD! THIS TIME I'M GOING IN!
HERE HE COMES, FULL STEAM AHEAD...
TAKE CARE, TINTIN, NO GOOD WILL COME OF THIS.
NOTHING BUT A BRICK WALL CAN STOP ME...
DO COME IN, MY DEAR SIR...
HELP! TINTIN'S GONE RAVING MAD!...
THERE WE ARE, THE DOOR'S OPEN...
NEVER THOUGHT I WAS SO FAR FROM THE DOOR!...
?

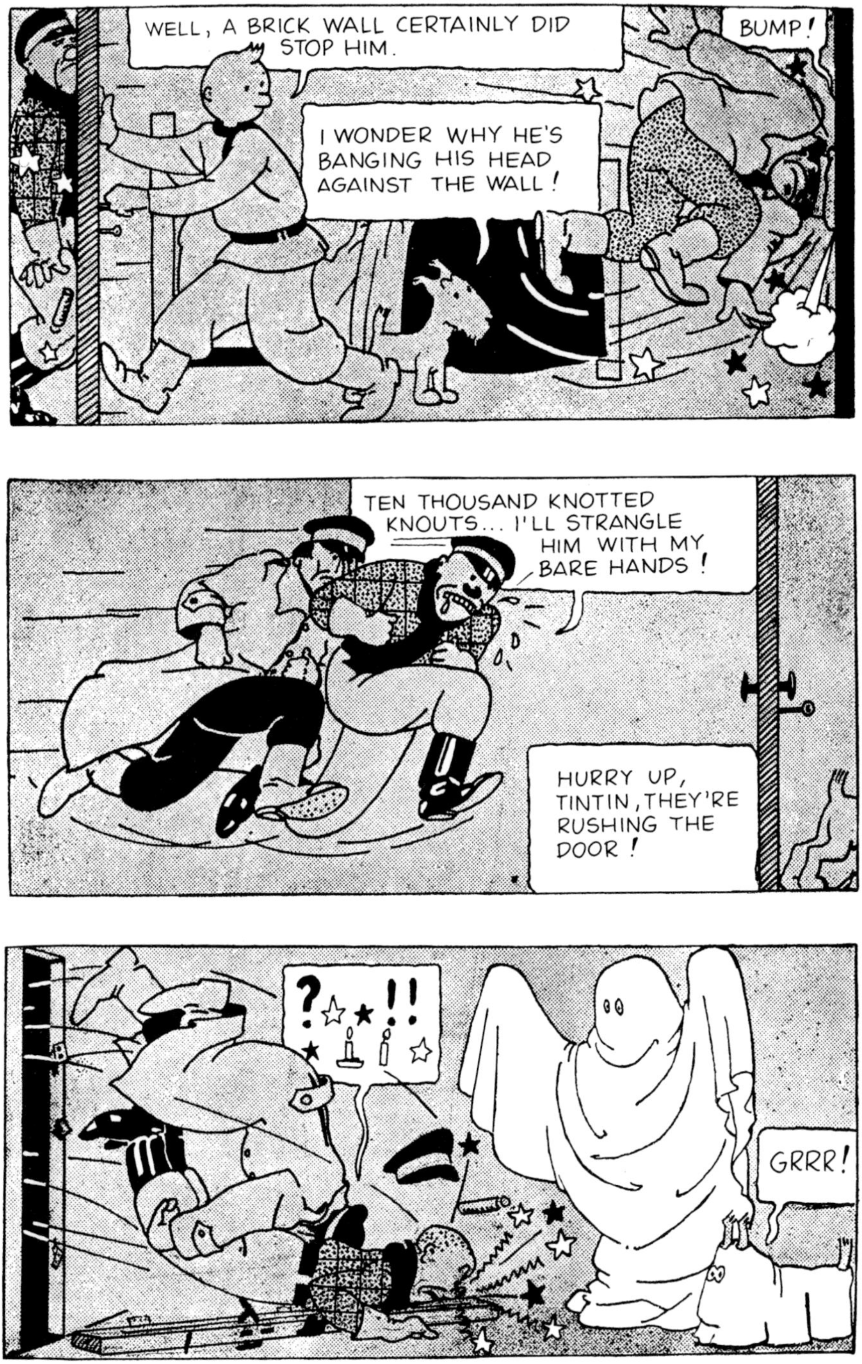
WELL, A BRICK WALL CERTAINLY DID STOP HIM.
BUMP!
I WONDER WHY HE'S BANGING HIS HEAD AGAINST THE WALL!
TEN THOUSAND KNOTTED KNOUTS... I'LL STRANGLE HIM WITH MY BARE HANDS!
HURRY UP, TINTIN, THEY'RE RUSHING THE DOOR!
?!!
GRRR!

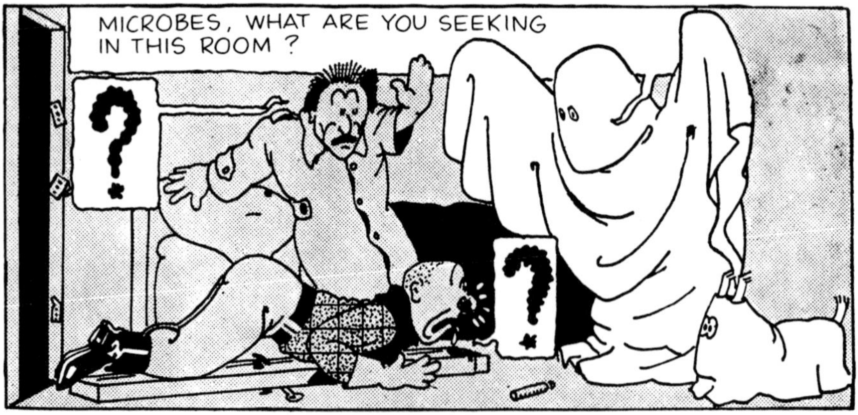
MICROBES, WHAT ARE YOU SEEKING IN THIS ROOM ?

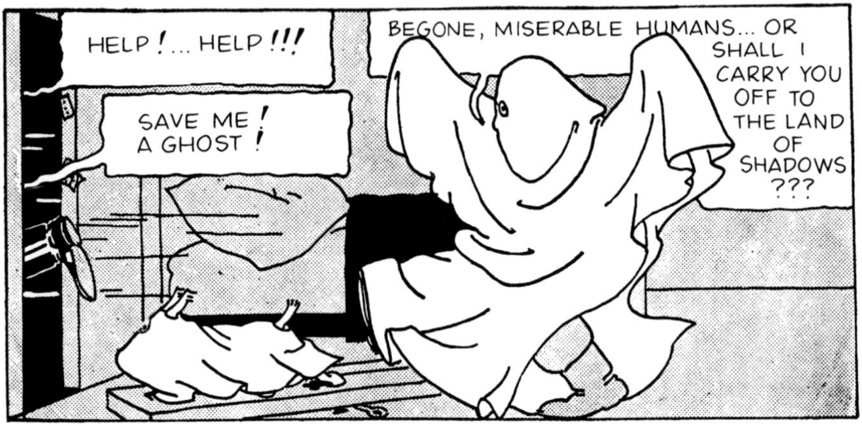
HELP !... HELP !!!
SAVE ME ! A GHOST !
BEGONE, MISERABLE HUMANS... OR SHALL I CARRY YOU OFF TO THE LAND OF SHADOWS ???

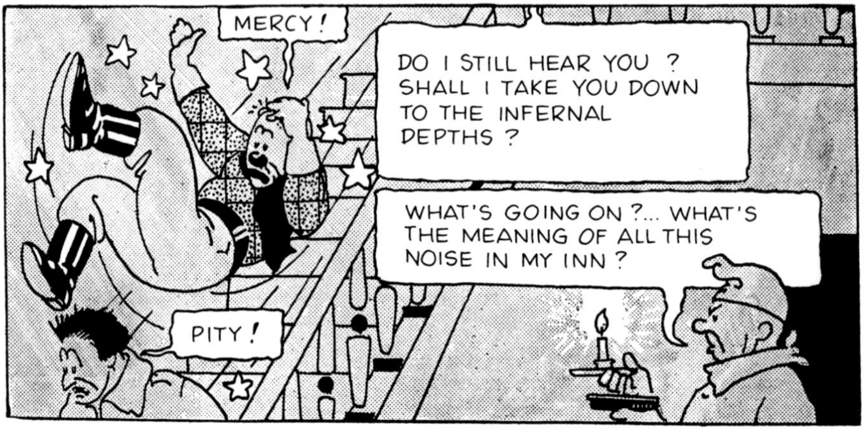
MERCY !
DO I STILL HEAR YOU ? SHALL I TAKE YOU DOWN TO THE INFERNAL DEPTHS ?
WHAT'S GOING ON ?... WHAT'S THE MEANING OF ALL THIS NOISE IN MY INN ?
PITY !

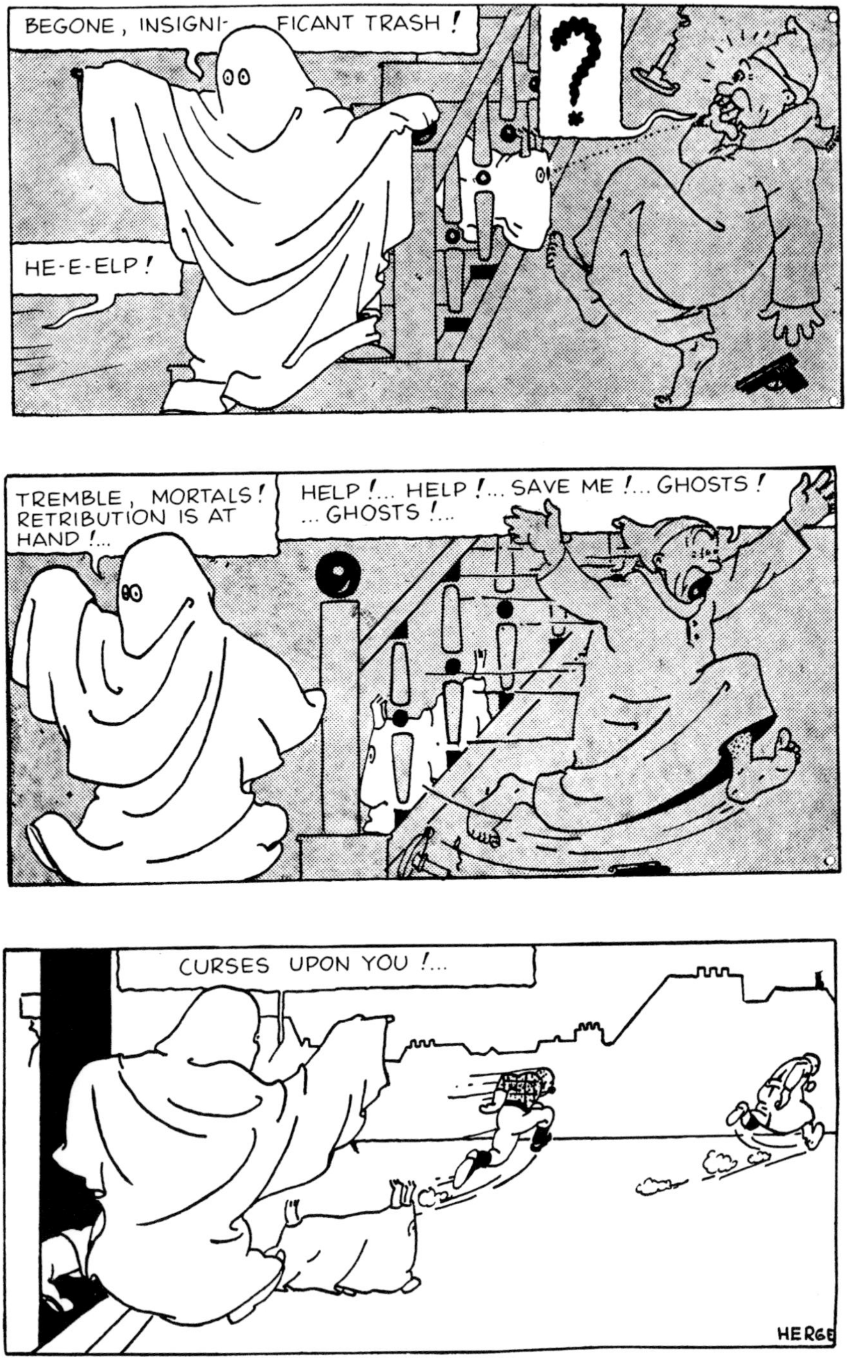
BEGONE, INSIGNI- FICANT TRASH!
HE-E-ELP!
TREMBLE, MORTALS! RETRIBUTION IS AT HAND!...
HELP!... HELP!... SAVE ME!... GHOSTS! ... GHOSTS!...
CURSES UPON YOU!...
HERGE

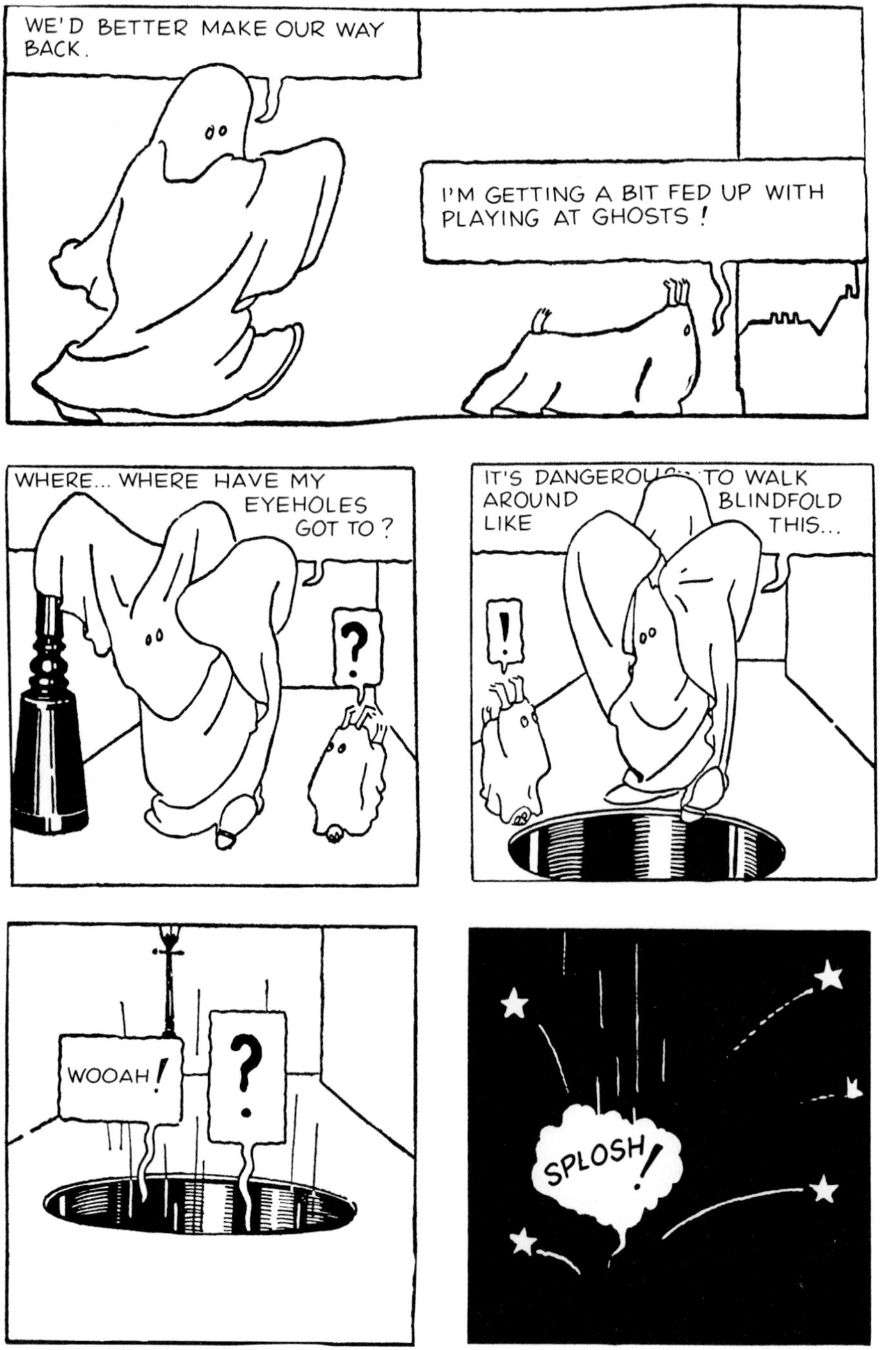
WE'D BETTER MAKE OUR WAY BACK.
I'M GETTING A BIT FED UP WITH PLAYING AT GHOSTS !
WHERE... WHERE HAVE MY EYEHOLES GOT TO ?
?
IT'S DANGEROUS TO WALK AROUND BLINDFOLD LIKE THIS...
!
WOOAH !
?
SPLOSH !

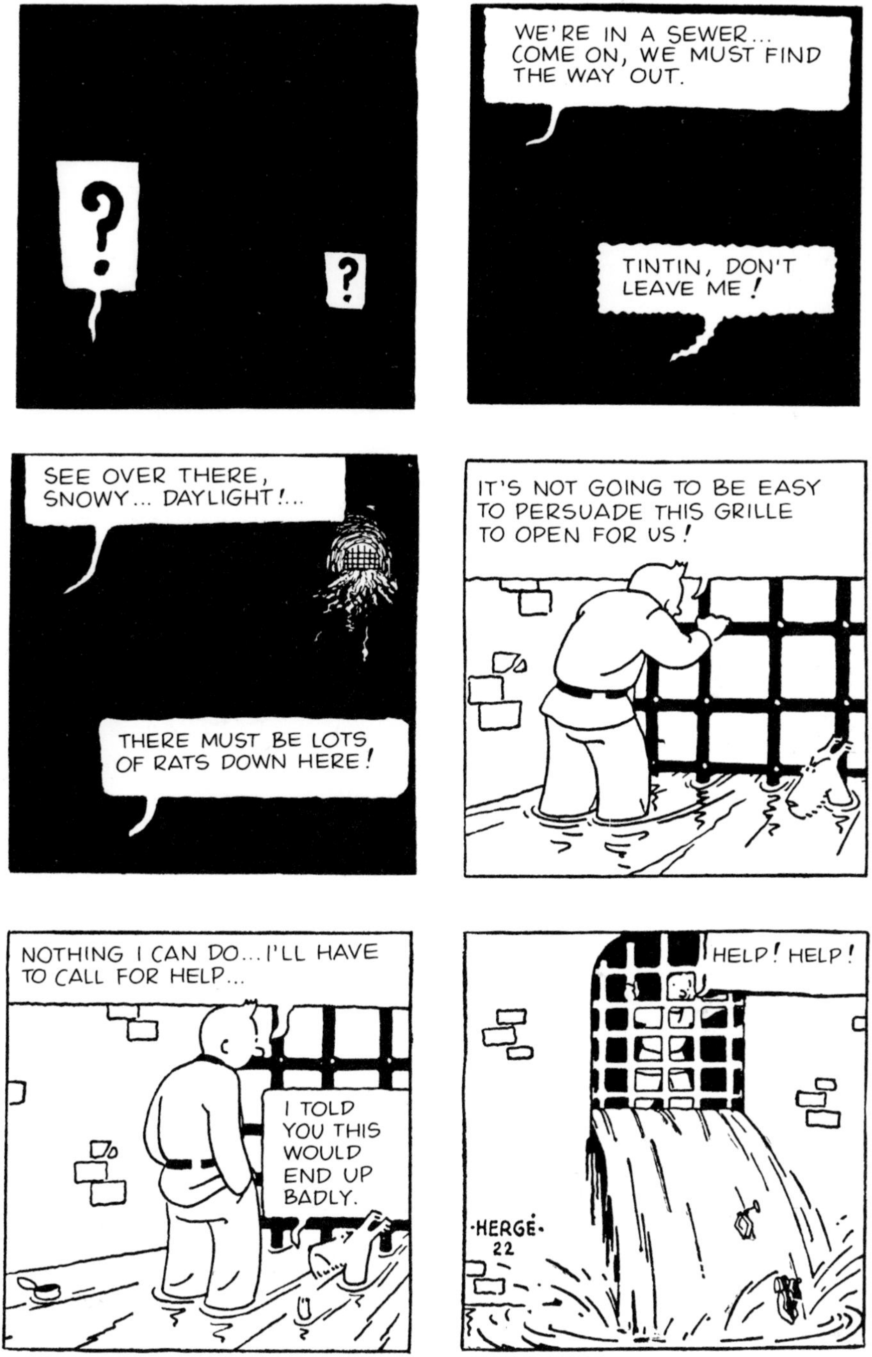
?
?
WE'RE IN A SEWER... COME ON, WE MUST FIND THE WAY OUT.
TINTIN, DON'T LEAVE ME!
SEE OVER THERE, SNOWY... DAYLIGHT!...
THERE MUST BE LOTS OF RATS DOWN HERE!
IT'S NOT GOING TO BE EASY TO PERSUADE THIS GRILLE TO OPEN FOR US!
NOTHING I CAN DO... I'LL HAVE TO CALL FOR HELP...
I TOLD YOU THIS WOULD END UP BADLY.
HELP! HELP!
·HERGÉ·
22

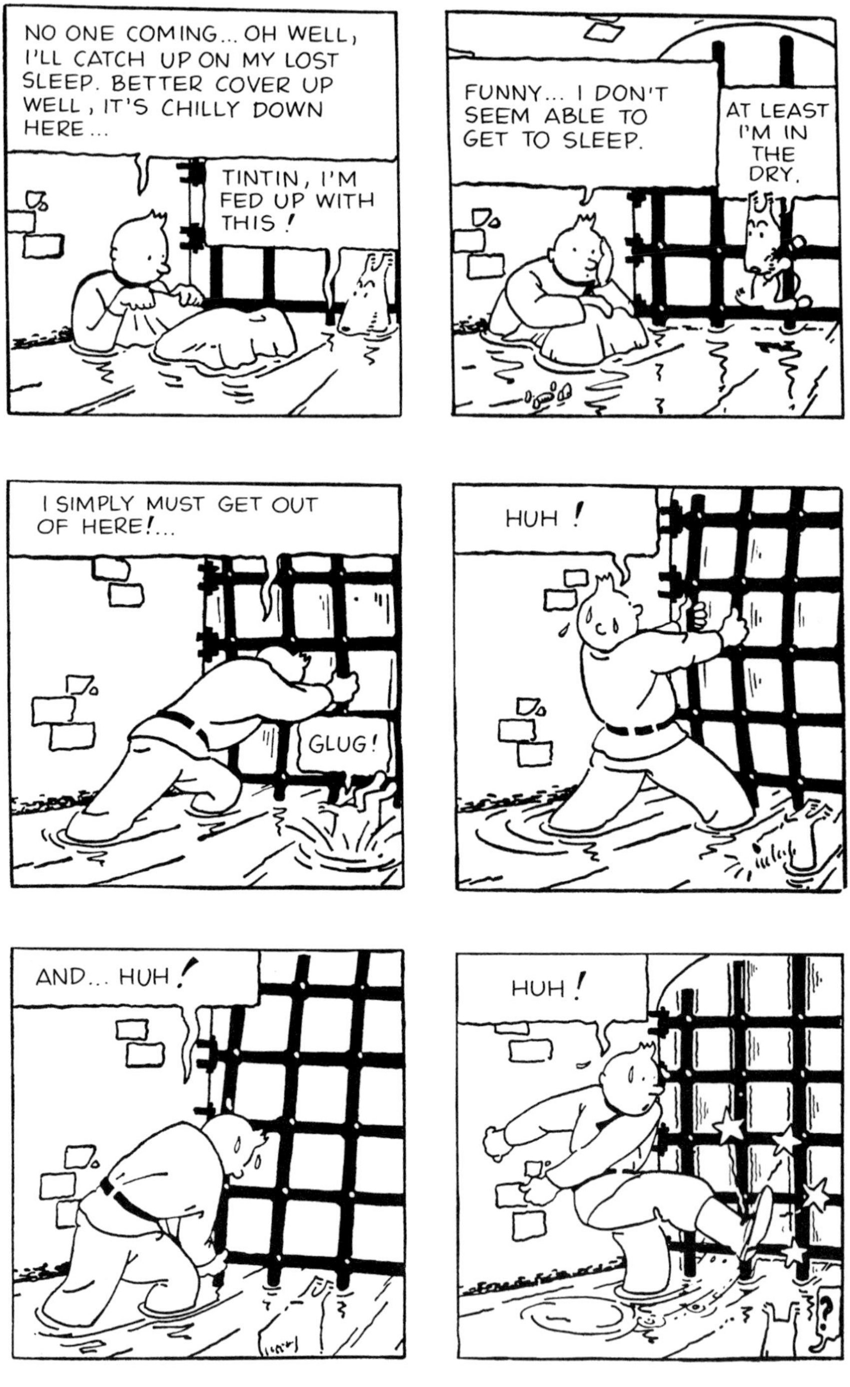
NO ONE COMING... OH WELL, I'LL CATCH UP ON MY LOST SLEEP. BETTER COVER UP WELL, IT'S CHILLY DOWN HERE...
TINTIN, I'M FED UP WITH THIS!
FUNNY... I DON'T SEEM ABLE TO GET TO SLEEP.
AT LEAST I'M IN THE DRY.
I SIMPLY MUST GET OUT OF HERE!...
GLUG!
HUH!
AND... HUH!
HUH!

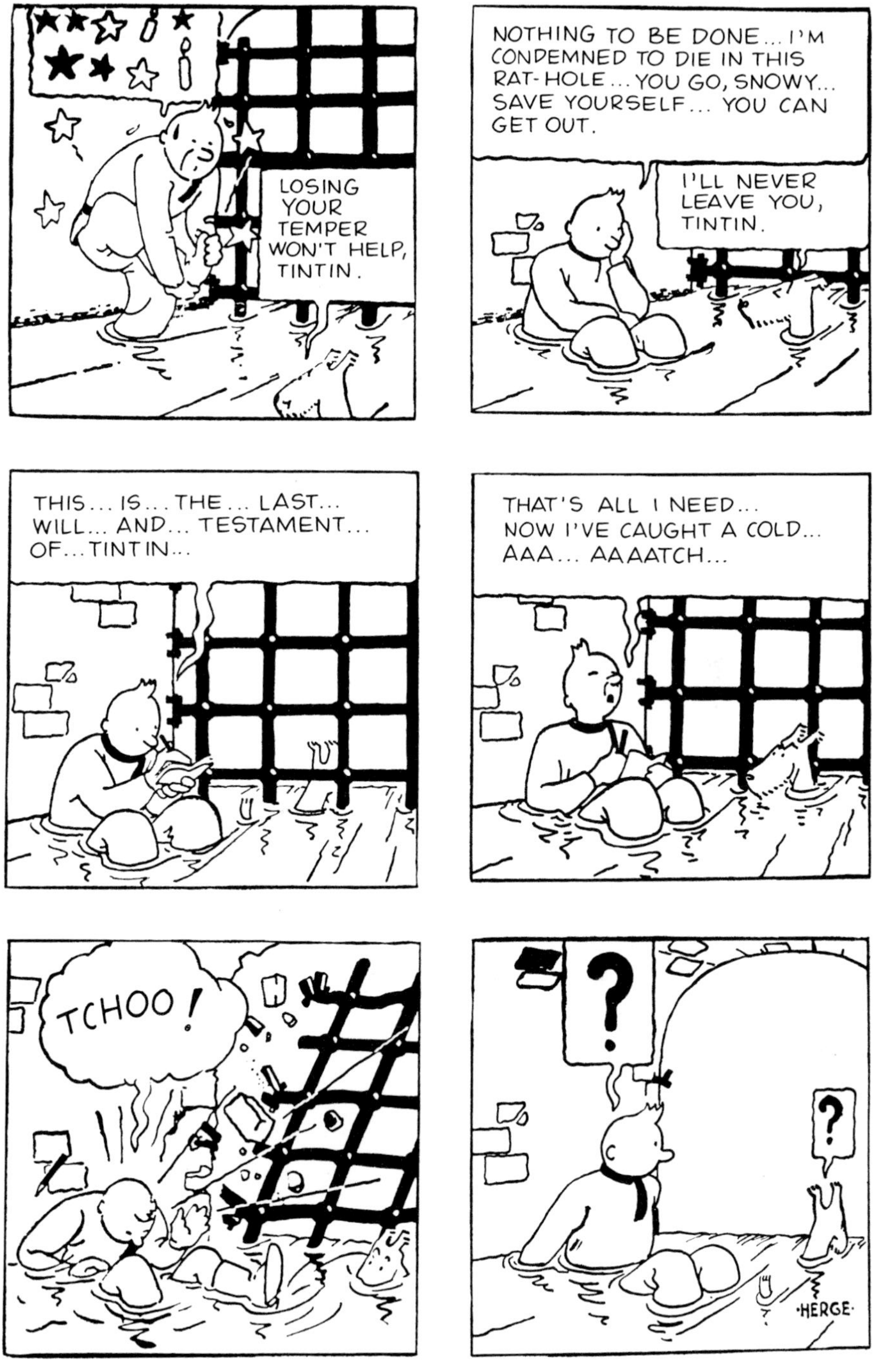
LOSING YOUR TEMPER WON'T HELP, TINTIN.
NOTHING TO BE DONE... I'M CONDEMNED TO DIE IN THIS RAT-HOLE... YOU GO, SNOWY... SAVE YOURSELF... YOU CAN GET OUT.
I'LL NEVER LEAVE YOU, TINTIN.
THIS... IS... THE... LAST... WILL... AND... TESTAMENT... OF... TINTIN...
THAT'S ALL I NEED... NOW I'VE CAUGHT A COLD... AAA... AAAATCH...
TCHOO!
?
?
·HERGE·

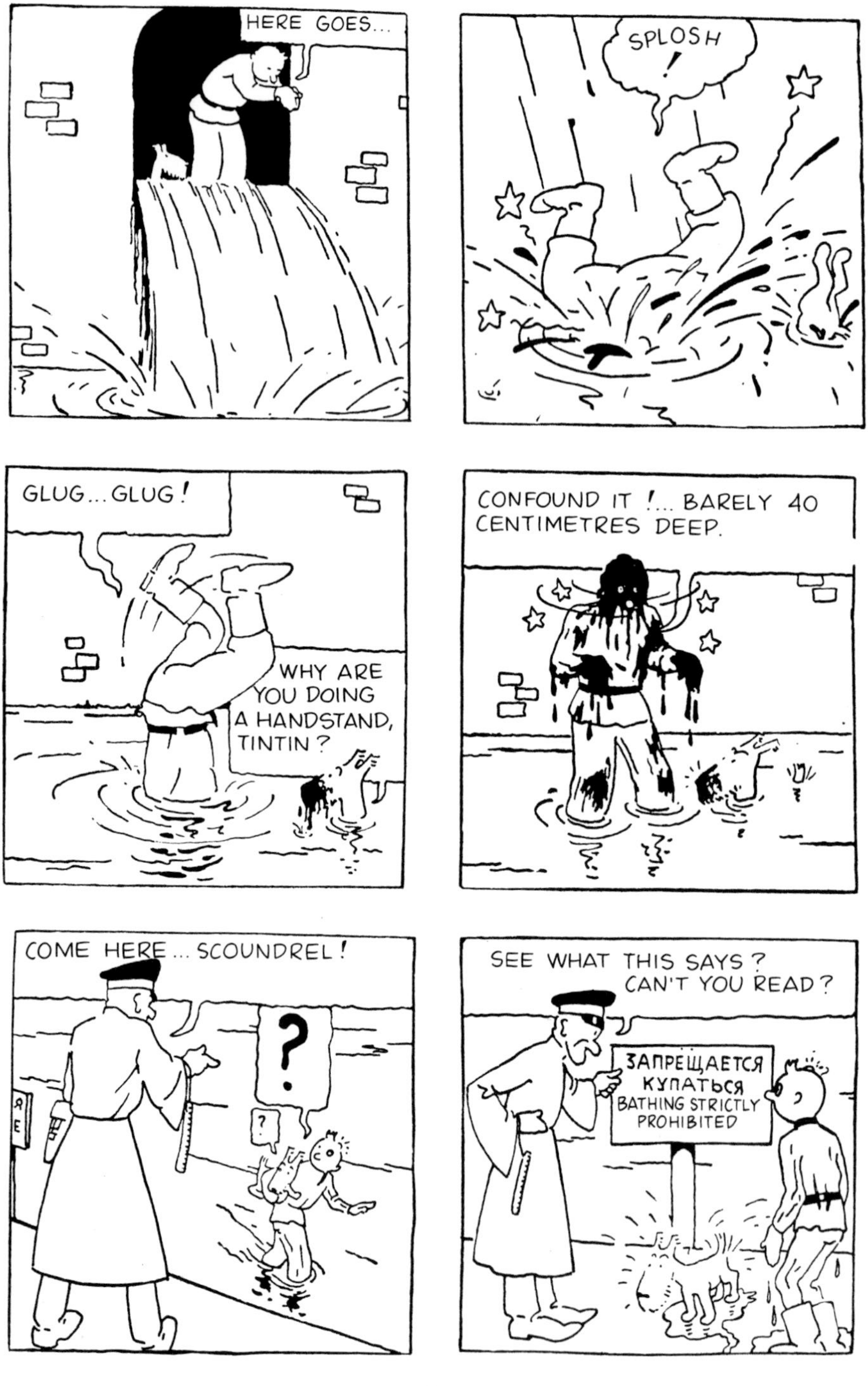
HERE GOES...
SPLOSH!
GLUG...GLUG!
WHY ARE YOU DOING A HANDSTAND, TINTIN?
CONFOUND IT!... BARELY 40 CENTIMETRES DEEP.
COME HERE... SCOUNDREL!
?
?
SEE WHAT THIS SAYS? CAN'T YOU READ?
ЗАПРЕЩАЕТСЯ КУПАТЬСЯ
BATHING STRICTLY PROHIBITED

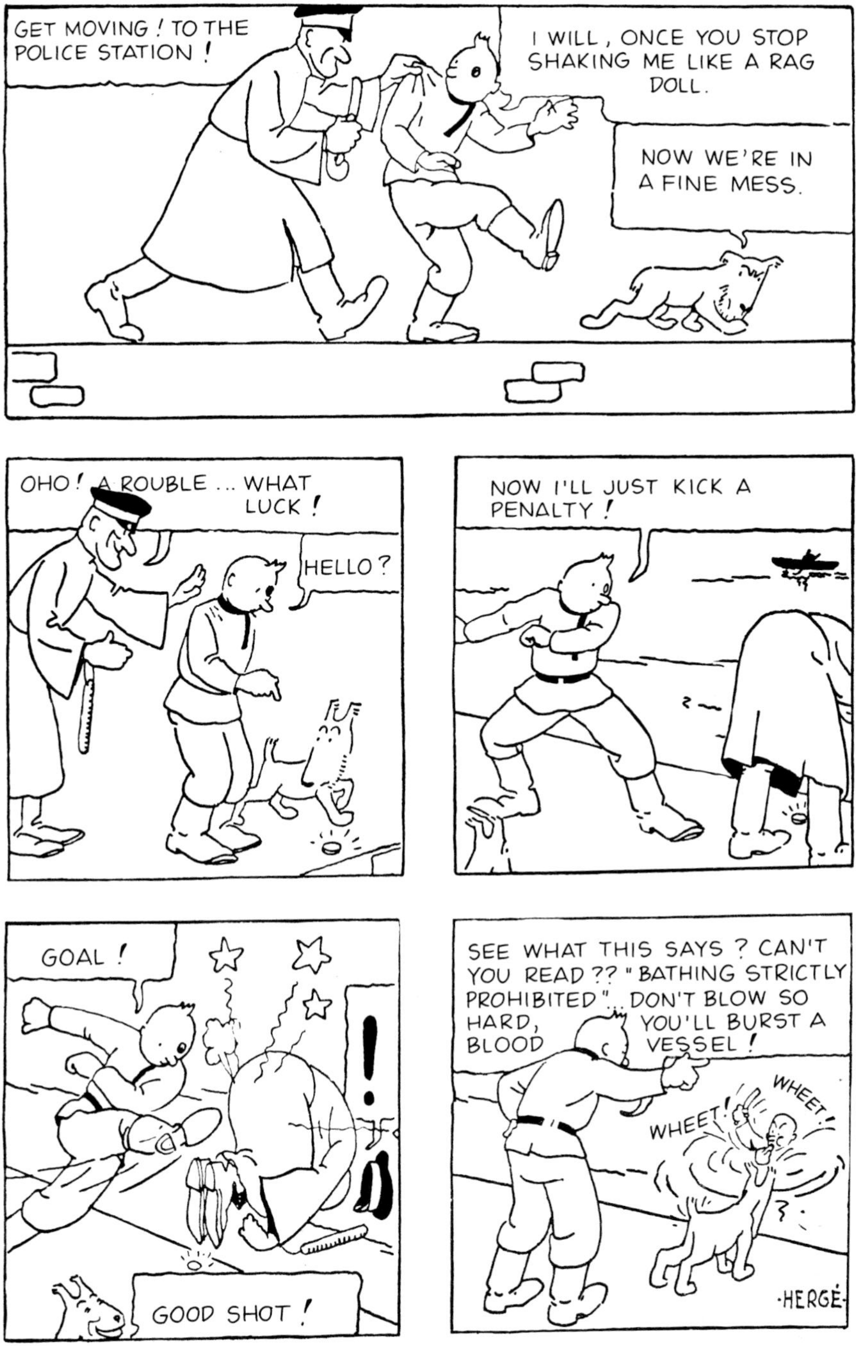
GET MOVING ! TO THE POLICE STATION !
I WILL, ONCE YOU STOP SHAKING ME LIKE A RAG DOLL.
NOW WE'RE IN A FINE MESS.
OHO ! A ROUBLE ... WHAT LUCK !
HELLO ?
NOW I'LL JUST KICK A PENALTY !
GOAL !
GOOD SHOT !
SEE WHAT THIS SAYS ? CAN'T YOU READ ?? "BATHING STRICTLY PROHIBITED"... DON'T BLOW SO HARD, YOU'LL BURST A BLOOD VESSEL !
WHEET !
WHEET !
·HERGÉ·

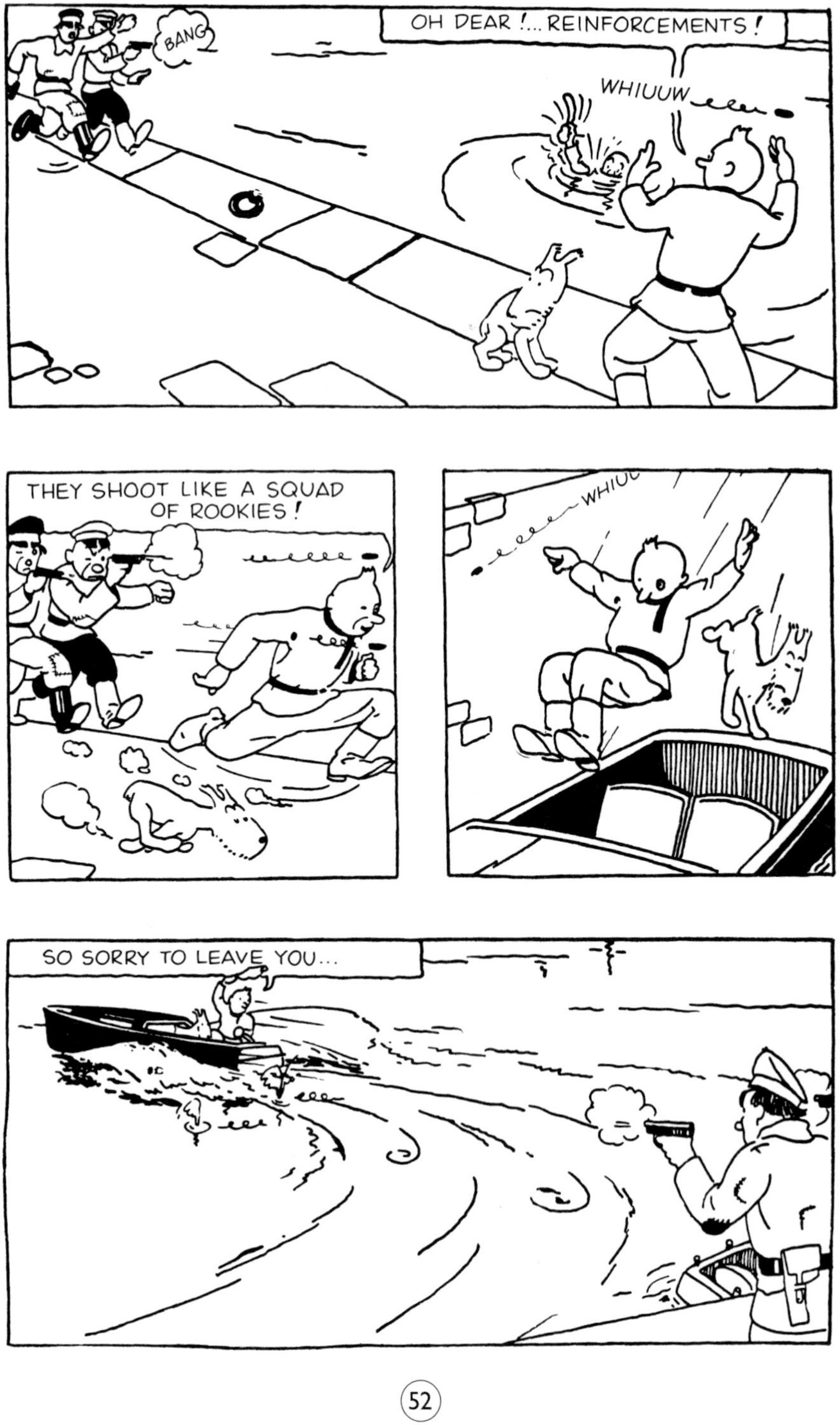
BANG
OH DEAR !... REINFORCEMENTS !
WHIUUW
THEY SHOOT LIKE A SQUAD OF ROOKIES !
WHIU
SO SORRY TO LEAVE YOU...

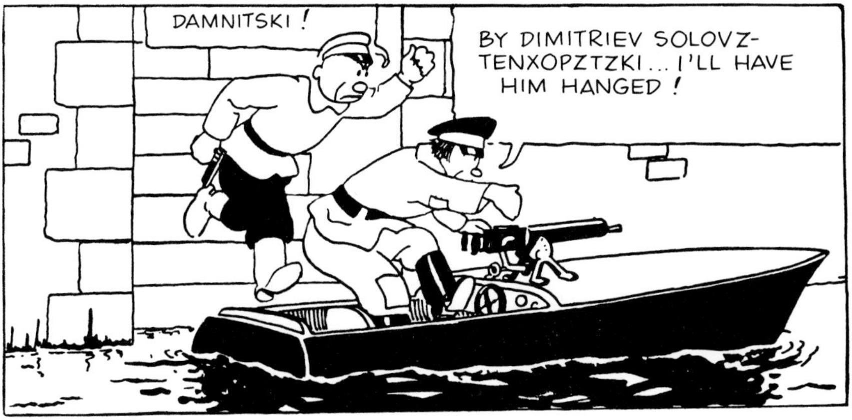
DAMNITSKI !
BY DIMITRIEV SOLOVZ-TENXOPZTZKI ... I'LL HAVE HIM HANGED !

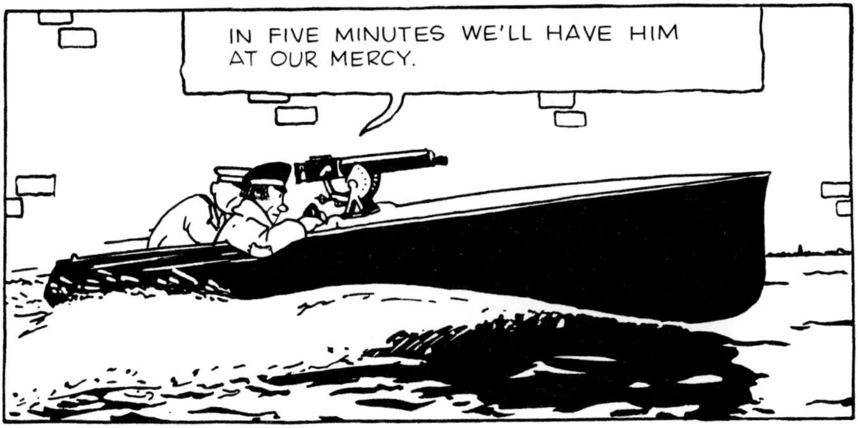
IN FIVE MINUTES WE'LL HAVE HIM AT OUR MERCY.

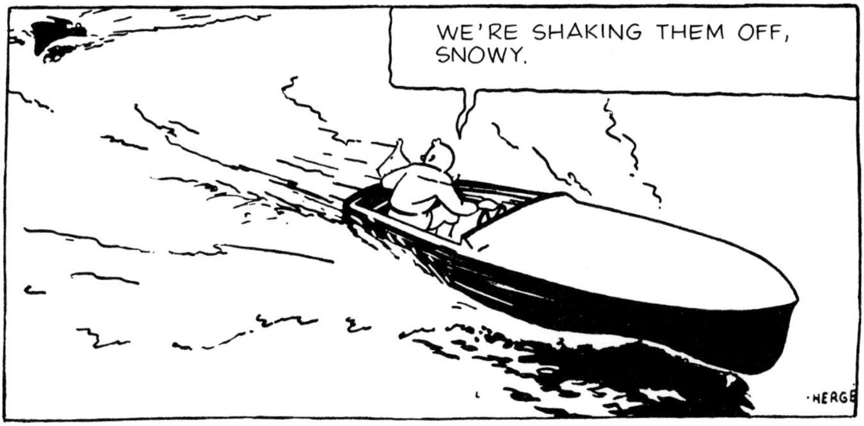
WE'RE SHAKING THEM OFF, SNOWY.
HERGÉ

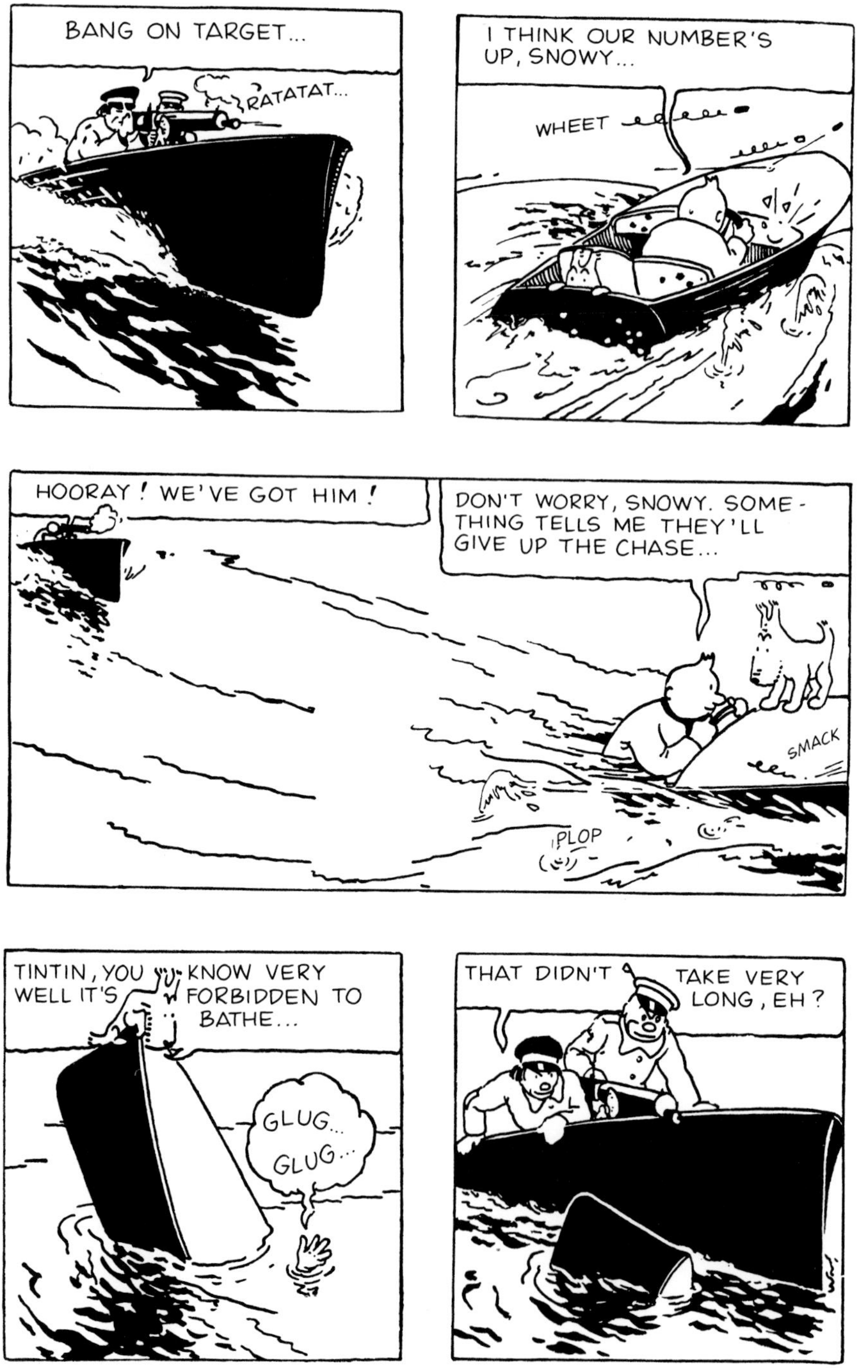
BANG ON TARGET...
RATATAT...
I THINK OUR NUMBER'S UP, SNOWY...
WHEET
HOORAY ! WE'VE GOT HIM !
DON'T WORRY, SNOWY. SOME-THING TELLS ME THEY'LL GIVE UP THE CHASE...
SMACK
PLOP
TINTIN, YOU KNOW VERY WELL IT'S FORBIDDEN TO BATHE...
GLUG... GLUG...
THAT DIDN'T TAKE VERY LONG, EH ?

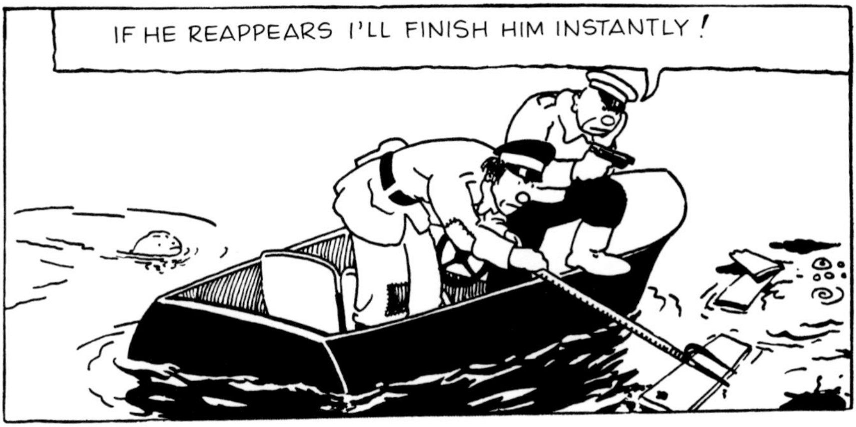
IF HE REAPPEARS I'LL FINISH HIM INSTANTLY !

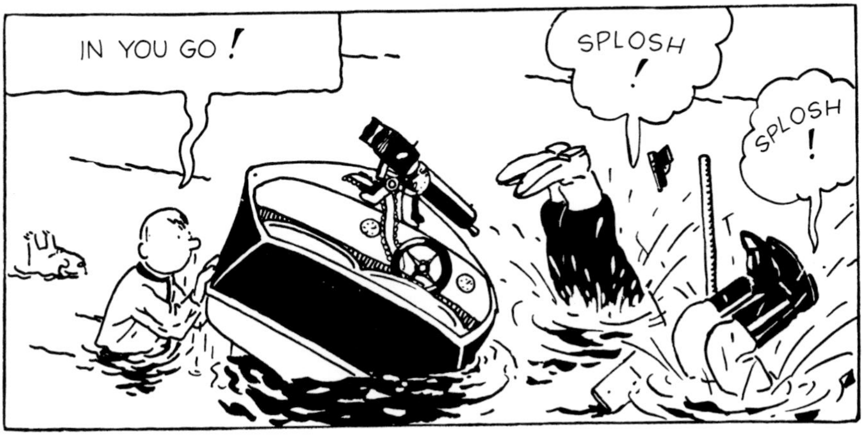
IN YOU GO !
SPLOSH !
SPLOSH !

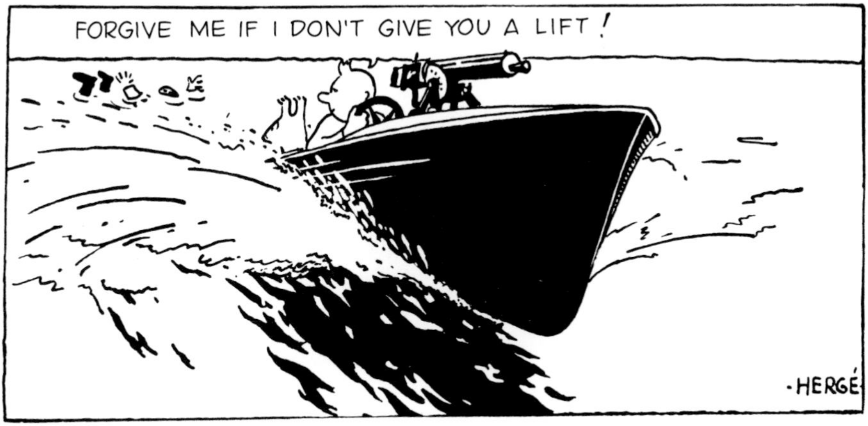
FORGIVE ME IF I DON'T GIVE YOU A LIFT !
·HERGÉ·

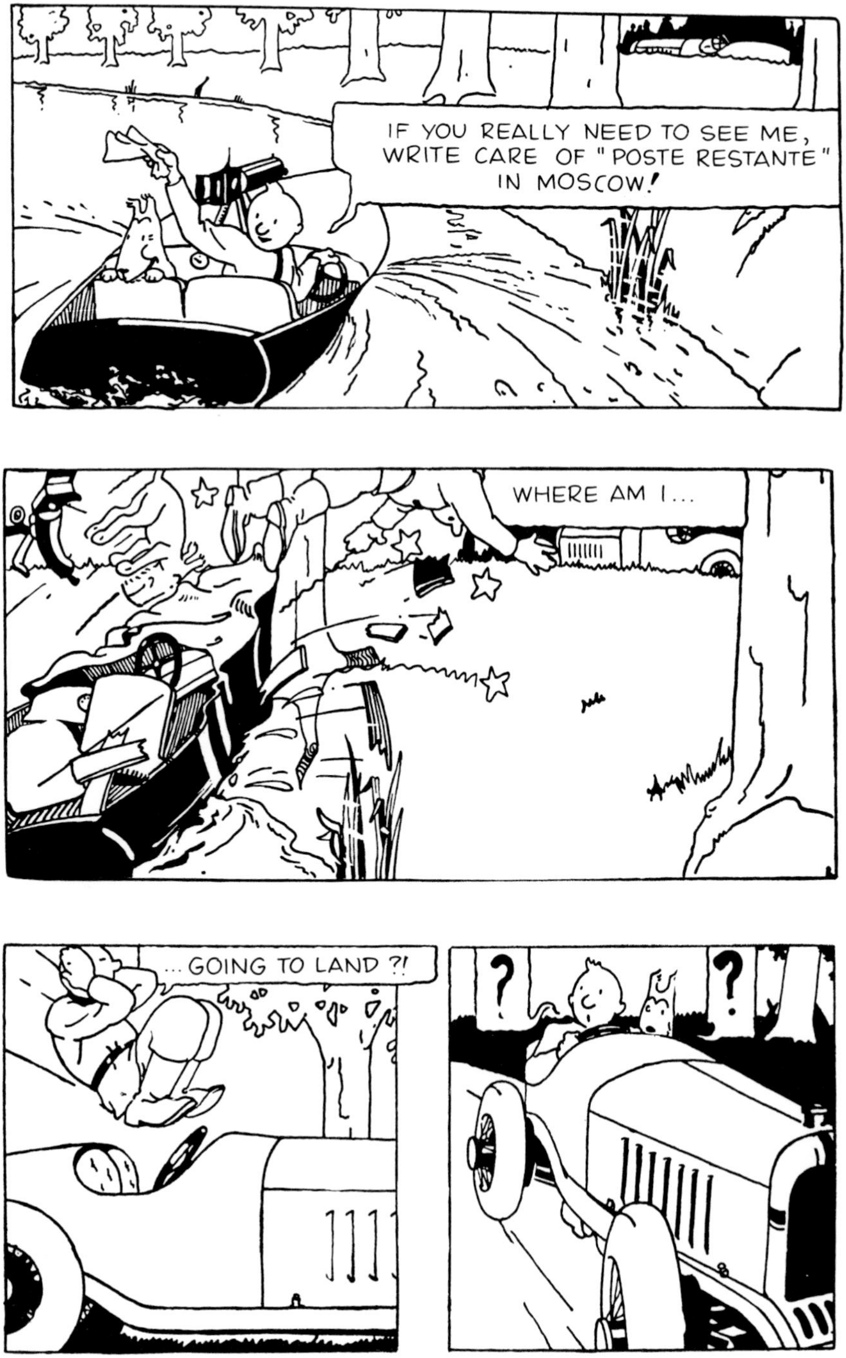
IF YOU REALLY NEED TO SEE ME, WRITE CARE OF "POSTE RESTANTE" IN MOSCOW!
WHERE AM I...
...GOING TO LAND ?!
?
?

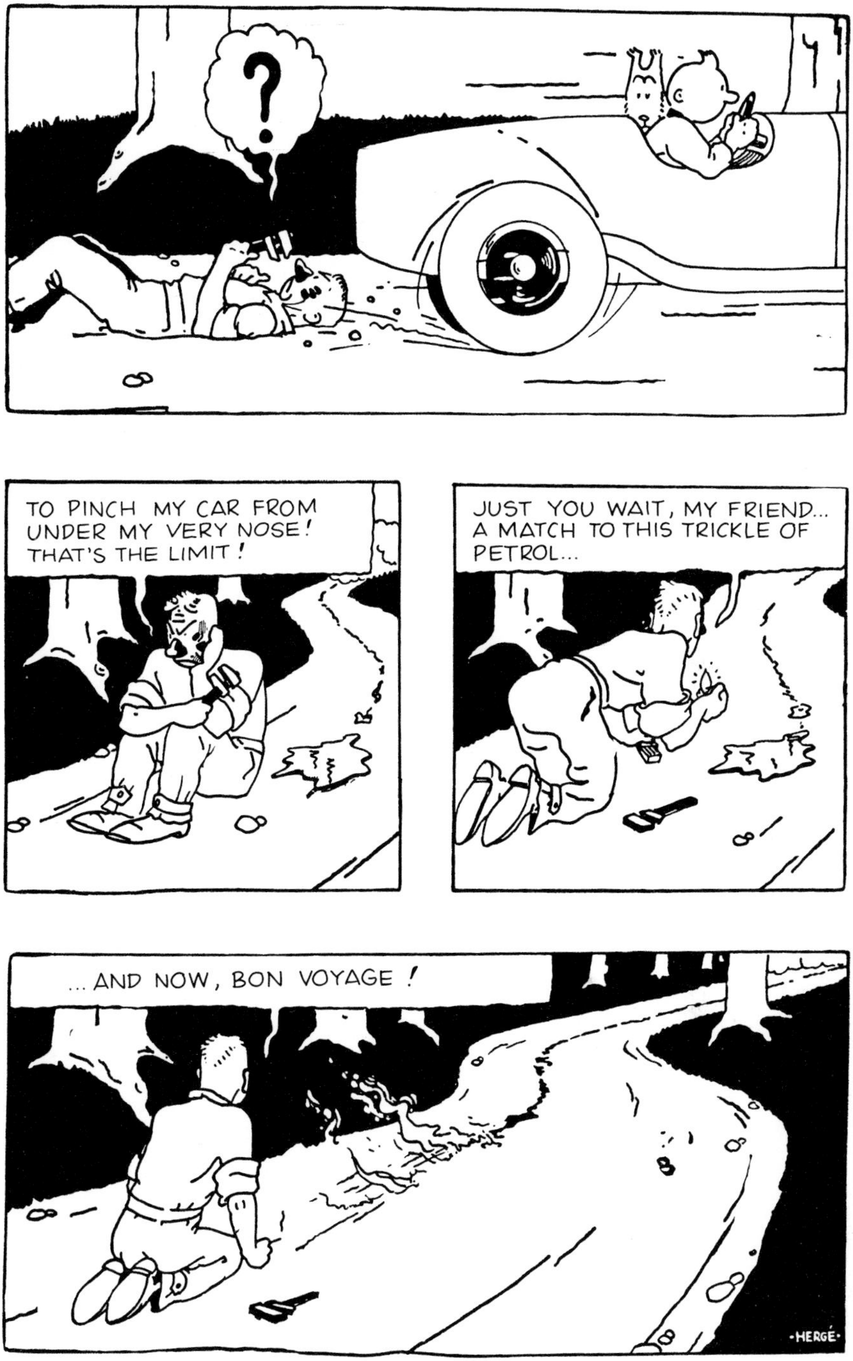
TO PINCH MY CAR FROM UNDER MY VERY NOSE! THAT'S THE LIMIT!
JUST YOU WAIT, MY FRIEND... A MATCH TO THIS TRICKLE OF PETROL...
... AND NOW, BON VOYAGE!
·HERGÉ·

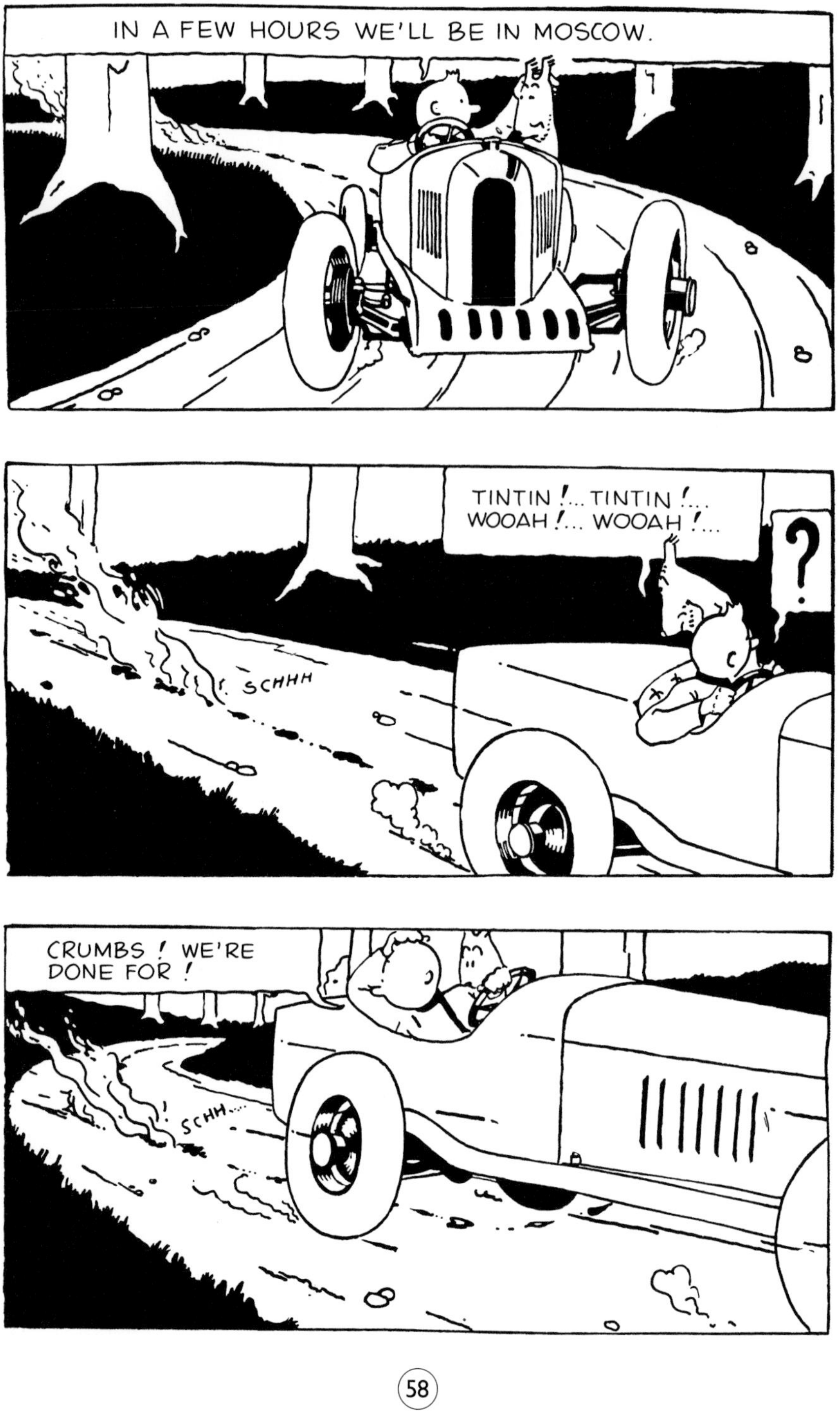
IN A FEW HOURS WE'LL BE IN MOSCOW.
TINTIN !... TINTIN !... WOOAH !... WOOAH !...
?
SCHHH
CRUMBS ! WE'RE DONE FOR !
SCHH...

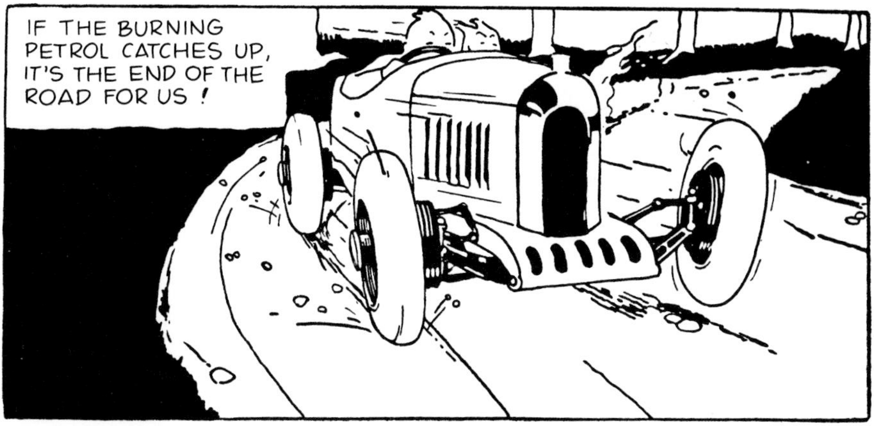
IF THE BURNING PETROL CATCHES UP, IT'S THE END OF THE ROAD FOR US !

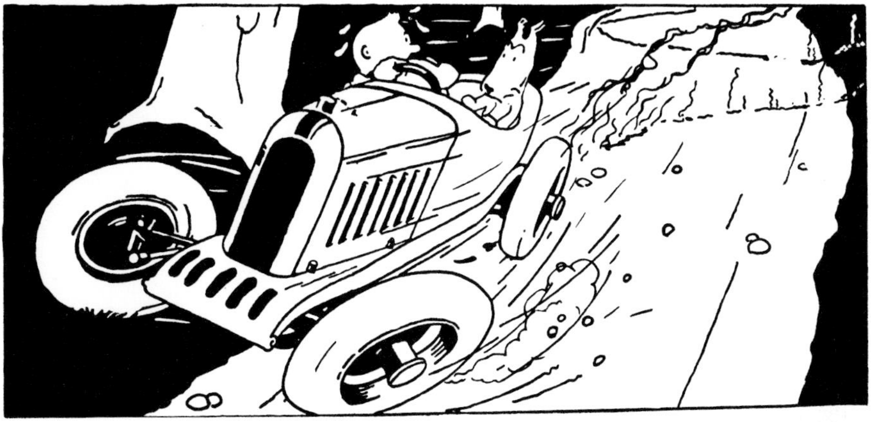

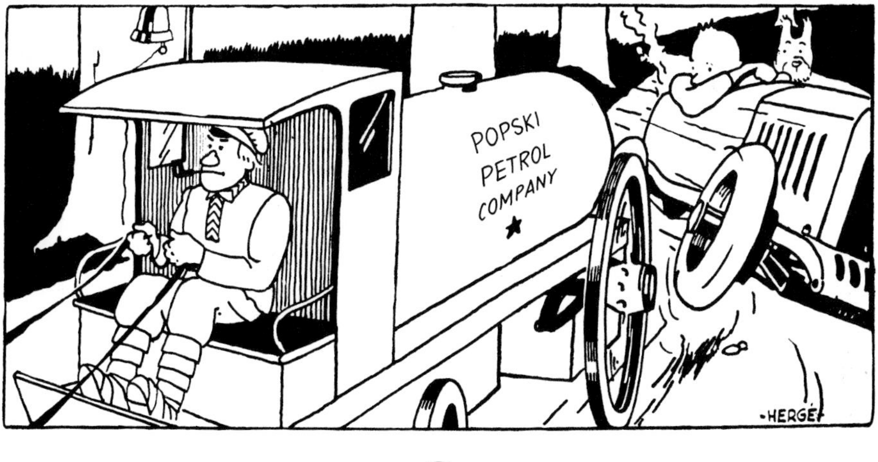
POPSKI
PETROL
COMPANY
-HERGÉ-

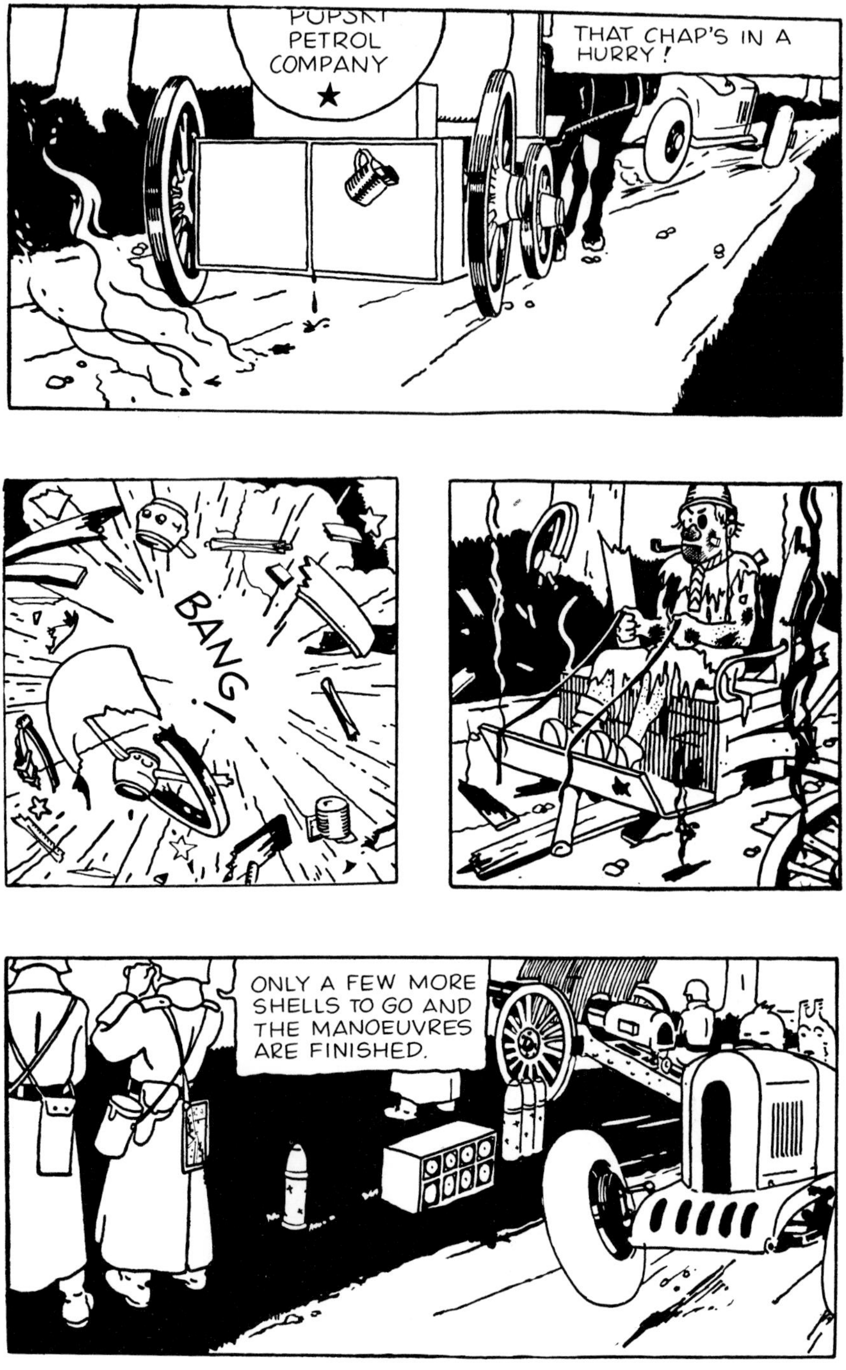
PUPSKI
PETROL
COMPANY
THAT CHAP'S IN A HURRY!
BANG!
ONLY A FEW MORE SHELLS TO GO AND THE MANOEUVRES ARE FINISHED.

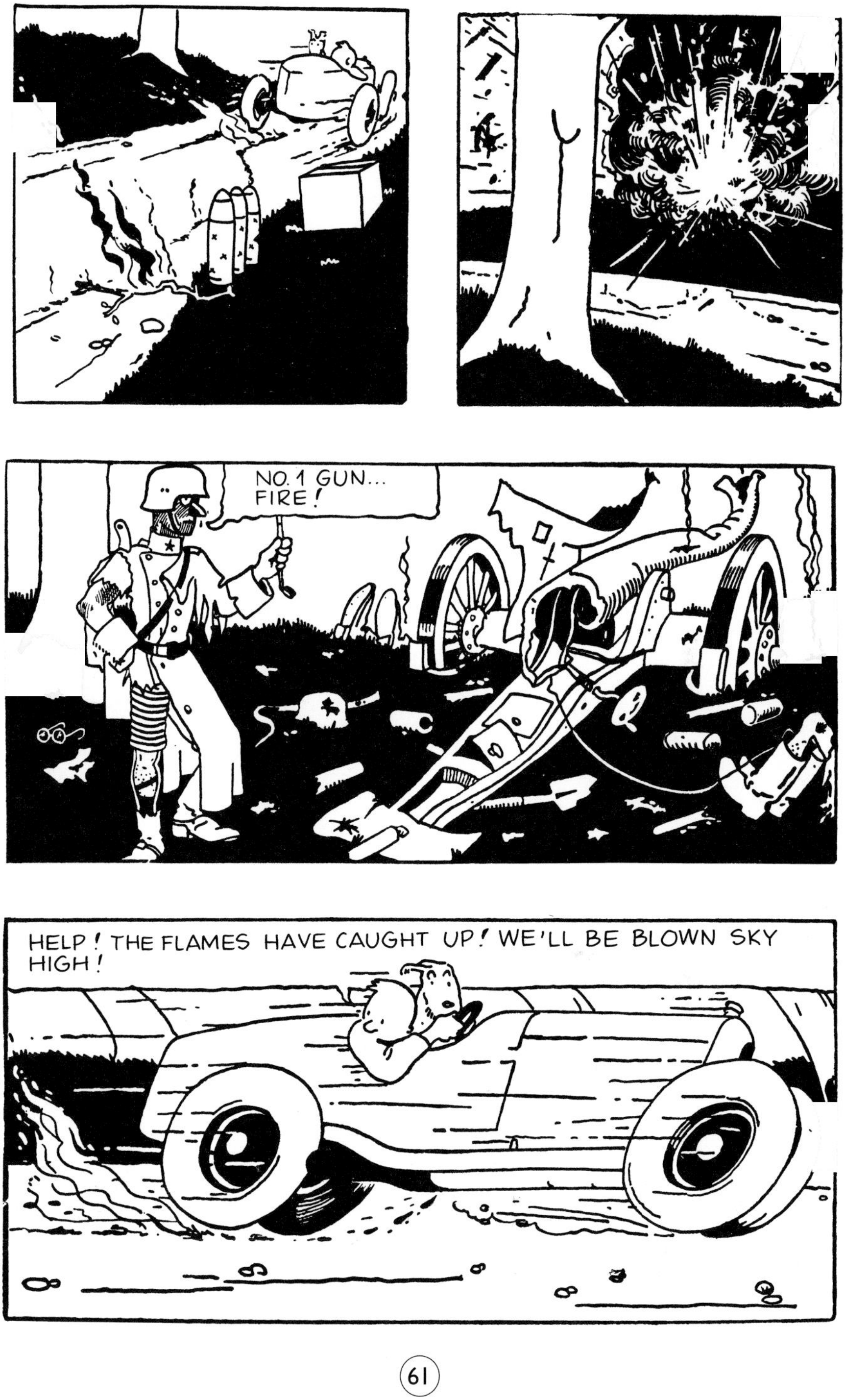
NO. 1 GUN...
FIRE!
HELP! THE FLAMES HAVE CAUGHT UP! WE'LL BE BLOWN SKY HIGH!

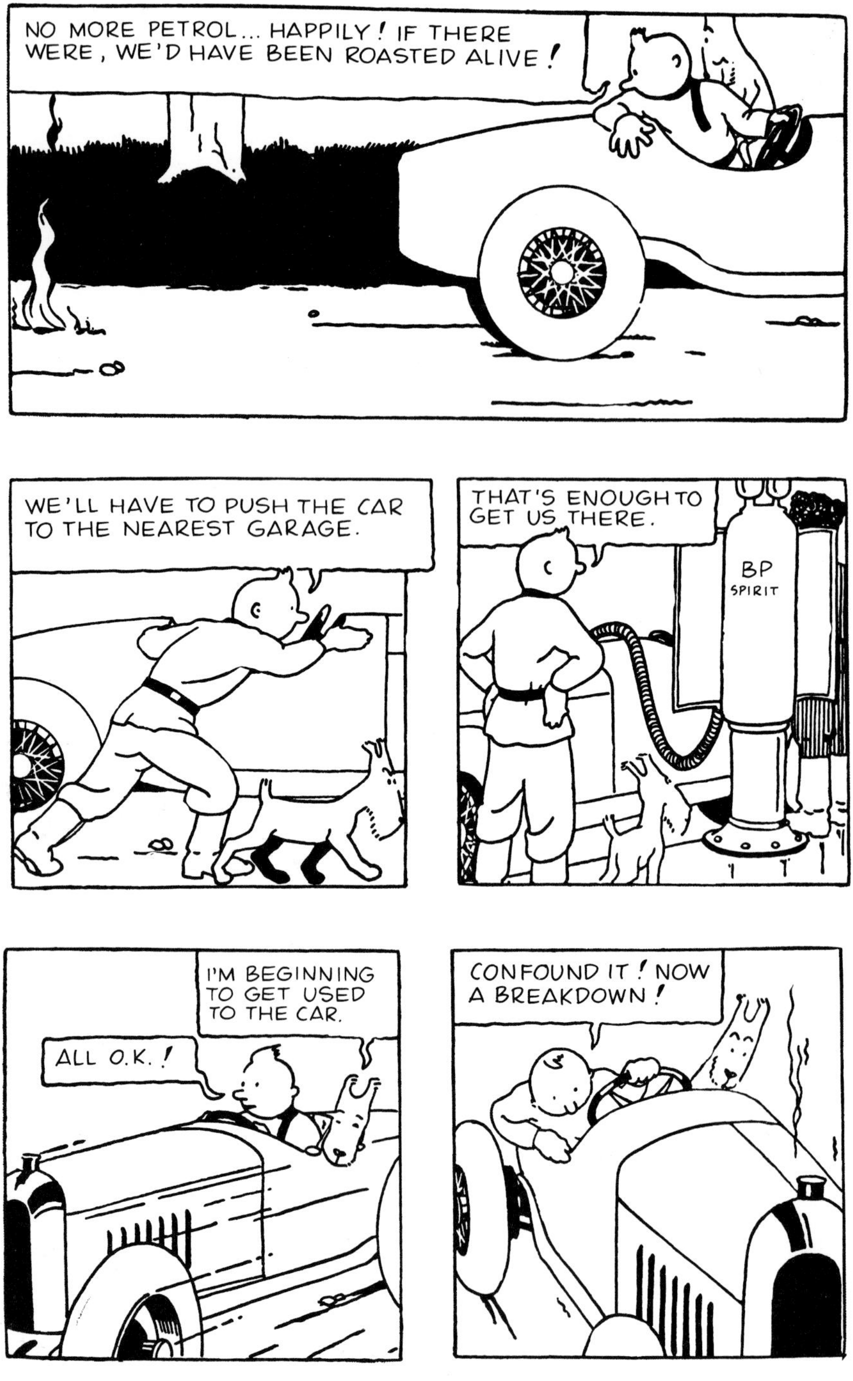
NO MORE PETROL... HAPPILY! IF THERE WERE, WE'D HAVE BEEN ROASTED ALIVE!
WE'LL HAVE TO PUSH THE CAR TO THE NEAREST GARAGE.
THAT'S ENOUGH TO GET US THERE.
BP SPIRIT
I'M BEGINNING TO GET USED TO THE CAR.
ALL O.K.!
CONFOUND IT! NOW A BREAKDOWN!

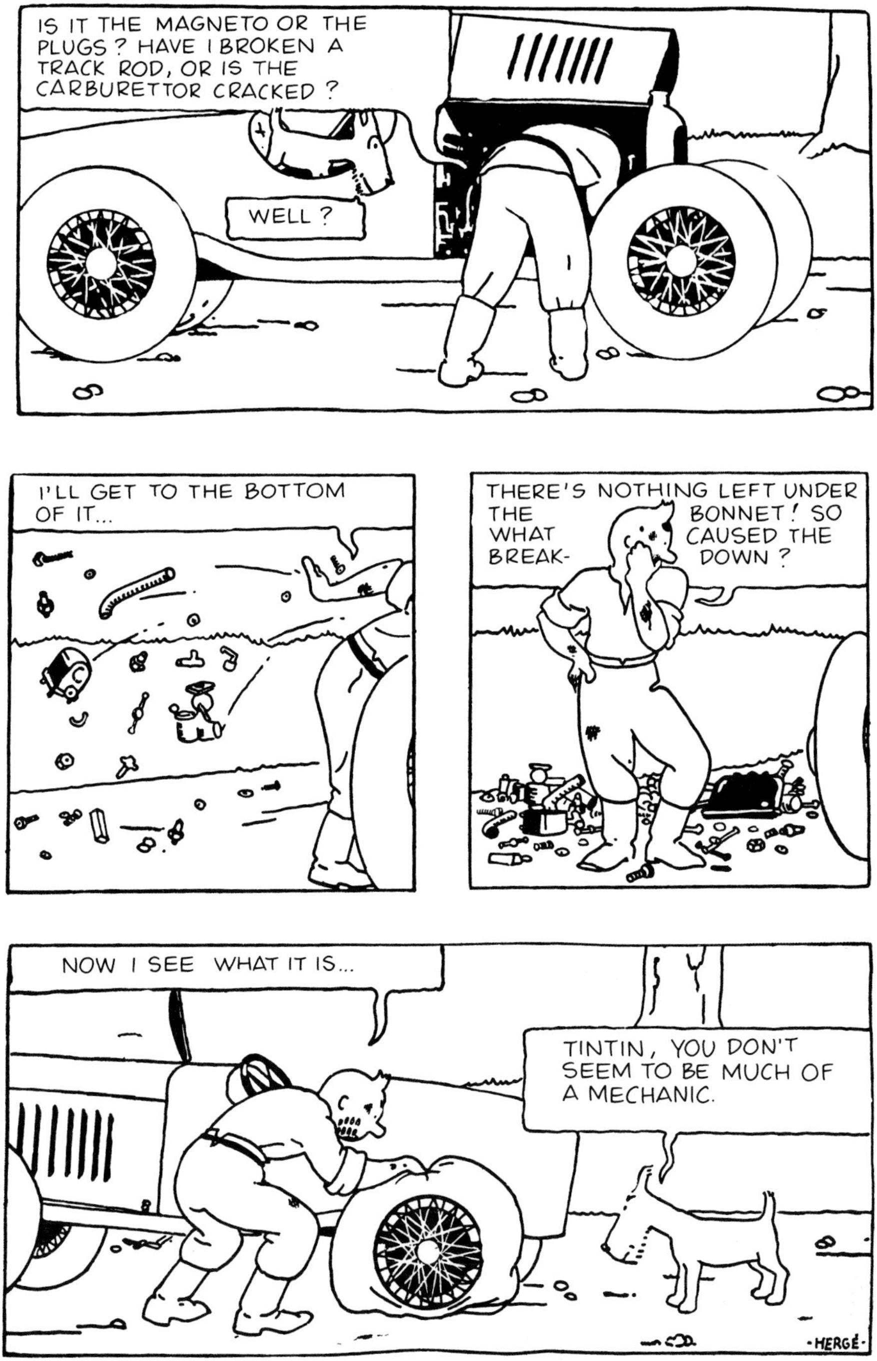
IS IT THE MAGNETO OR THE PLUGS? HAVE I BROKEN A TRACK ROD, OR IS THE CARBURETTOR CRACKED?
WELL?
I'LL GET TO THE BOTTOM OF IT...
THERE'S NOTHING LEFT UNDER THE BONNET! SO WHAT CAUSED THE BREAK-DOWN?
NOW I SEE WHAT IT IS...
TINTIN, YOU DON'T SEEM TO BE MUCH OF A MECHANIC.
-HERGÉ-

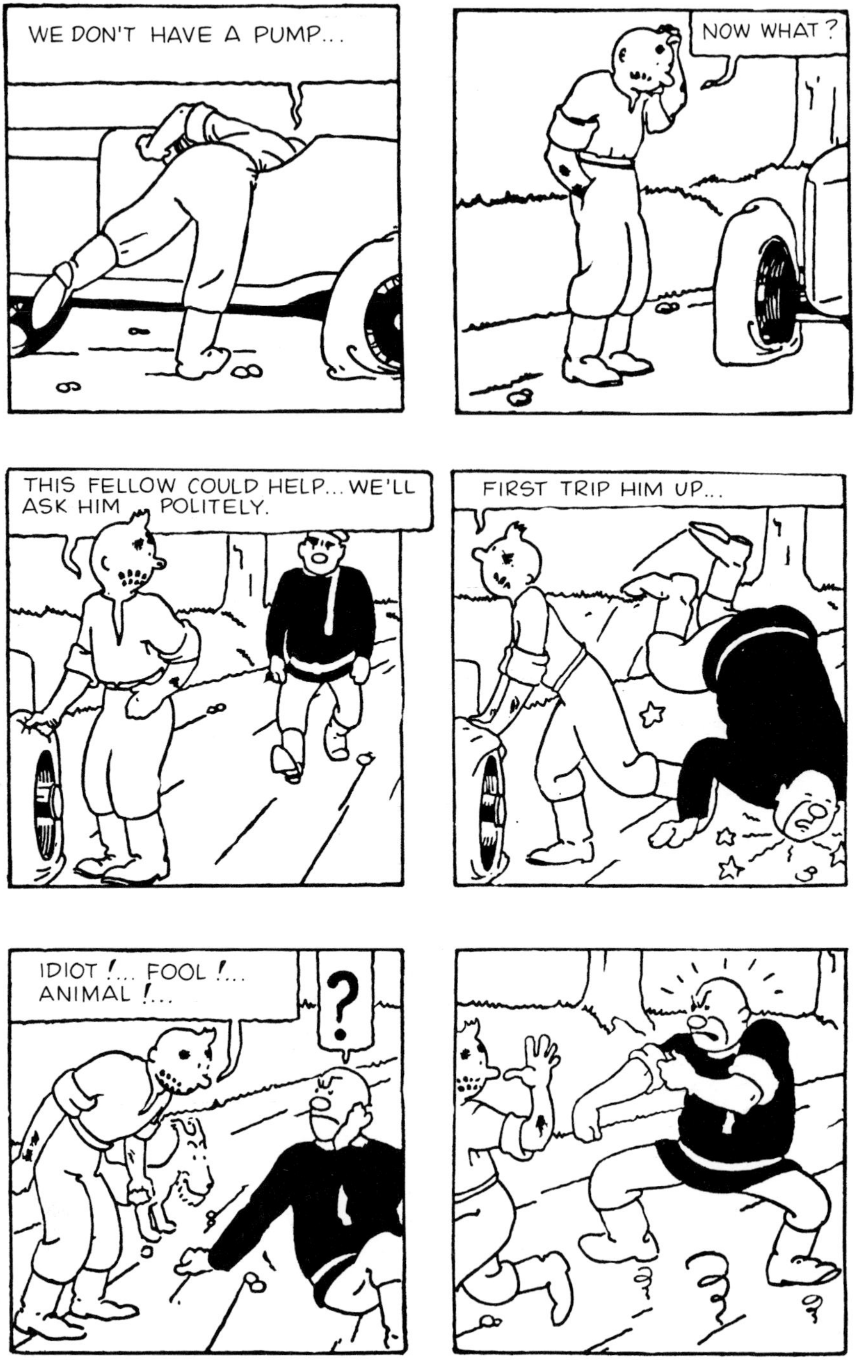
WE DON'T HAVE A PUMP...
NOW WHAT ?
THIS FELLOW COULD HELP... WE'LL ASK HIM ... POLITELY.
FIRST TRIP HIM UP...
IDIOT !... FOOL !... ANIMAL !...
?

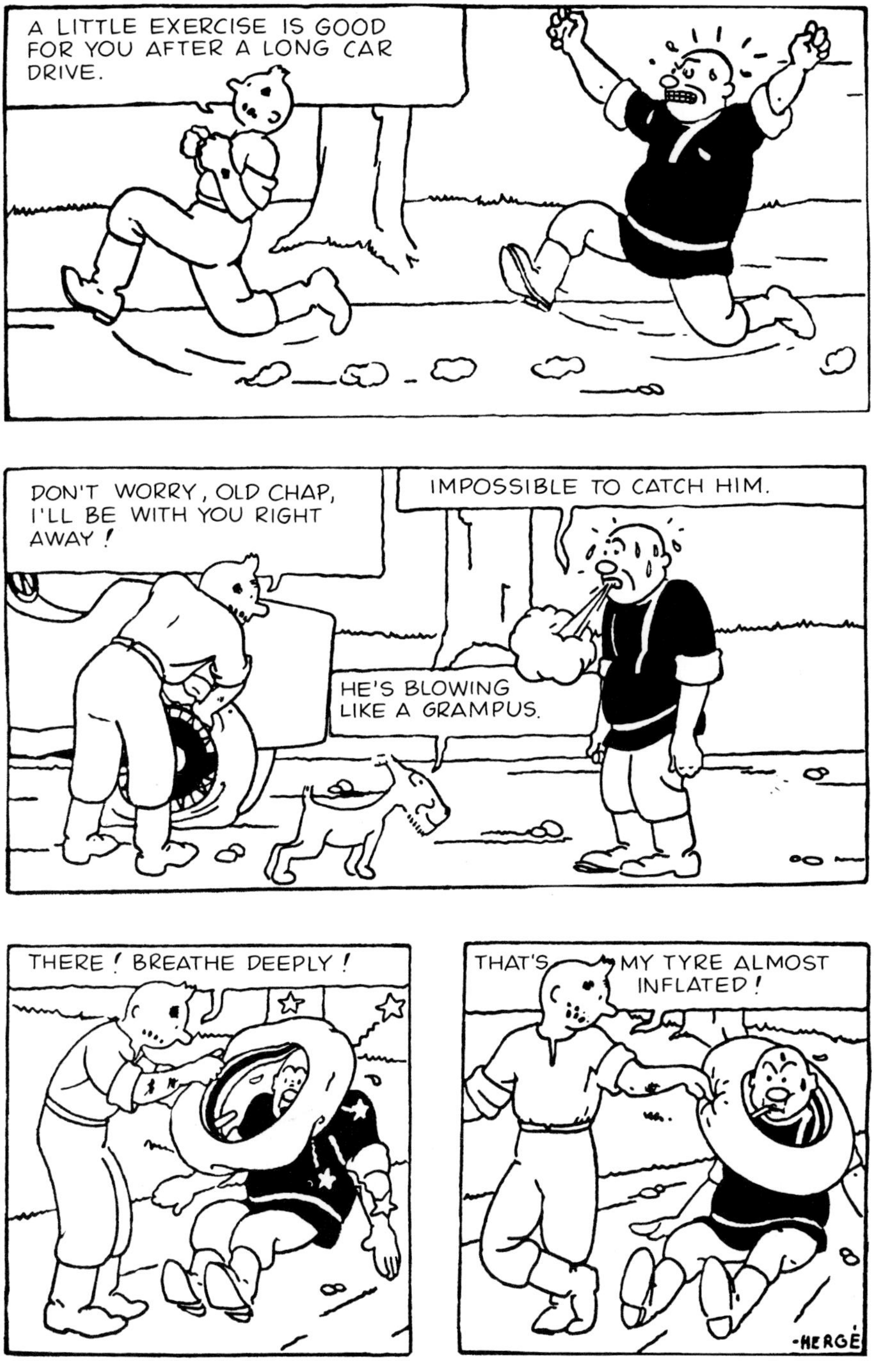
A LITTLE EXERCISE IS GOOD FOR YOU AFTER A LONG CAR DRIVE.
DON'T WORRY, OLD CHAP, I'LL BE WITH YOU RIGHT AWAY!
IMPOSSIBLE TO CATCH HIM.
HE'S BLOWING LIKE A GRAMPUS.
THERE! BREATHE DEEPLY!
THAT'S MY TYRE ALMOST INFLATED!
HERGÉ

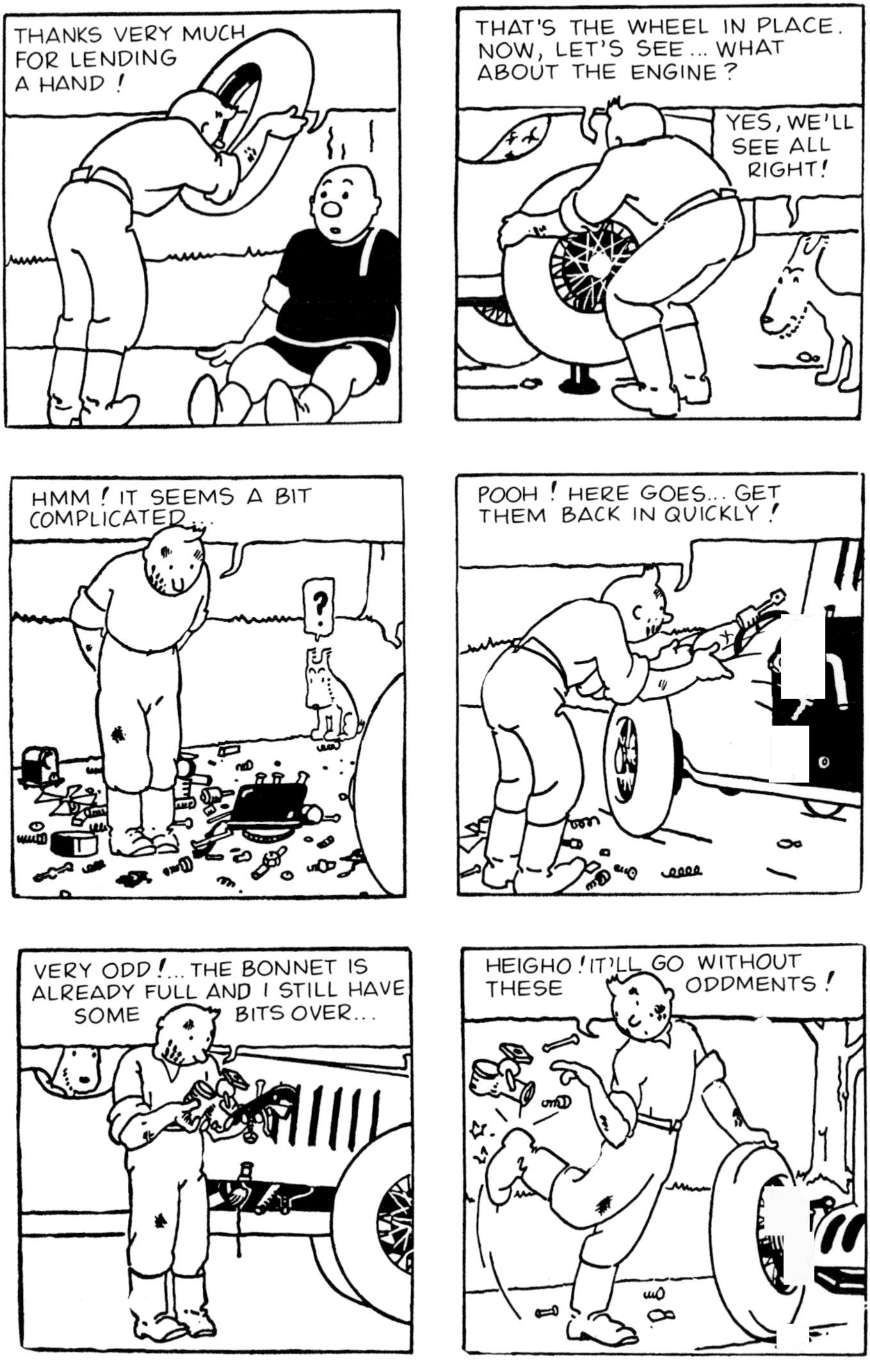
THANKS VERY MUCH FOR LENDING A HAND !
THAT'S THE WHEEL IN PLACE. NOW, LET'S SEE ... WHAT ABOUT THE ENGINE ?
YES, WE'LL SEE ALL RIGHT!
HMM ! IT SEEMS A BIT COMPLICATED...
?
POOH ! HERE GOES... GET THEM BACK IN QUICKLY !
VERY ODD !... THE BONNET IS ALREADY FULL AND I STILL HAVE SOME BITS OVER...
HEIGHO ! IT'LL GO WITHOUT THESE ODDMENTS !

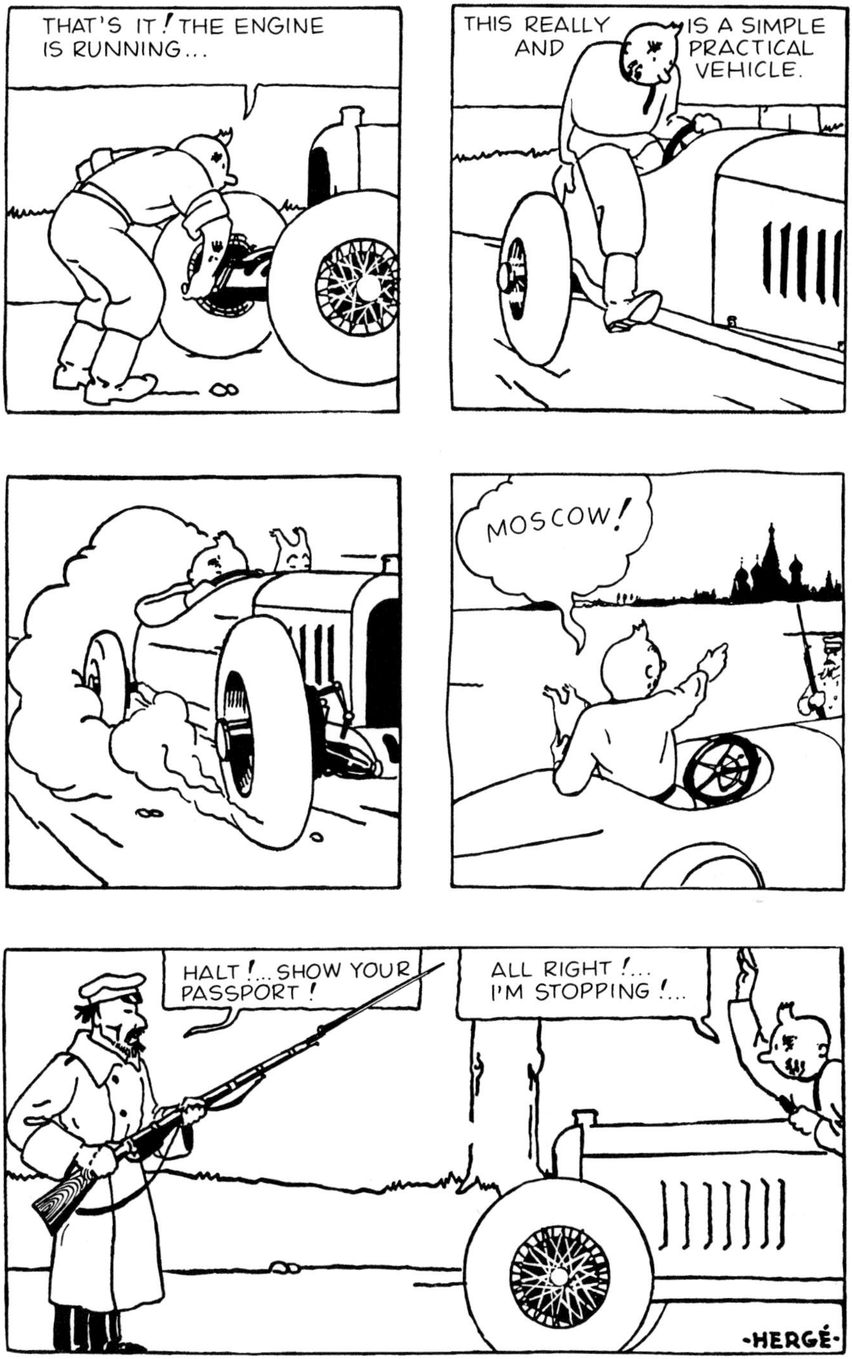
THAT'S IT! THE ENGINE IS RUNNING...
THIS REALLY IS A SIMPLE AND PRACTICAL VEHICLE.
MOSCOW!
HALT!... SHOW YOUR PASSPORT!
ALL RIGHT!... I'M STOPPING!...
-HERGÉ-

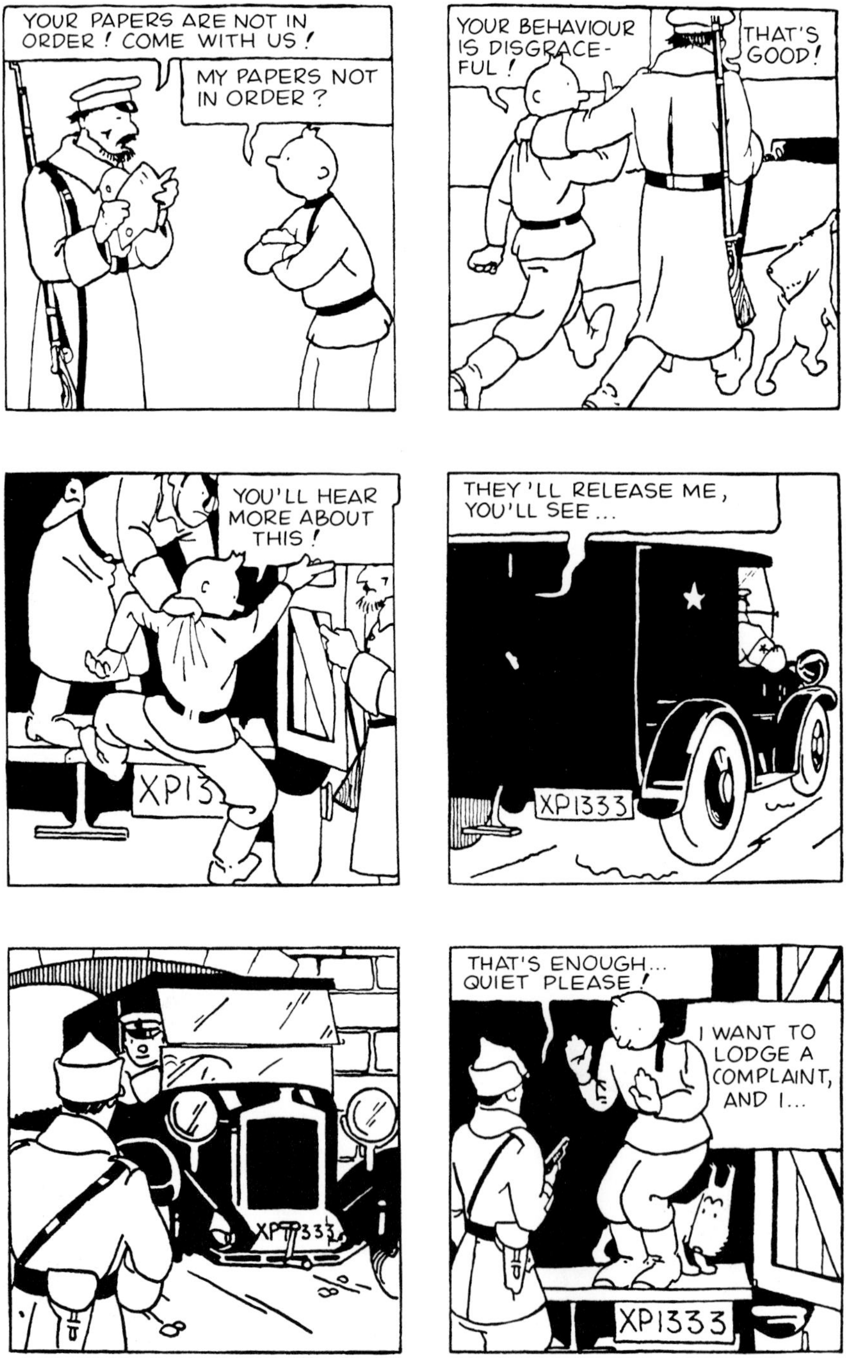

YOUR PAPERS ARE NOT IN ORDER ! COME WITH US !
MY PAPERS NOT IN ORDER ?
YOUR BEHAVIOUR IS DISGRACEFUL !
THAT'S GOOD !
YOU'LL HEAR MORE ABOUT THIS !
XP13
THEY'LL RELEASE ME, YOU'LL SEE ...
XP1333
XP1333
THAT'S ENOUGH... QUIET PLEASE !
I WANT TO LODGE A COMPLAINT, AND I...
XP1333

THERE ARE RATS IN HERE!

WHERE ARE WE?

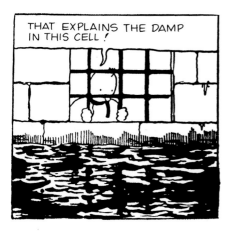

THAT EXPLAINS THE DAMP IN THIS CELL!

COME!... HURRY UP! THE PRISON GOVERNOR IS WAITING FOR YOU.

-HERGÉ-

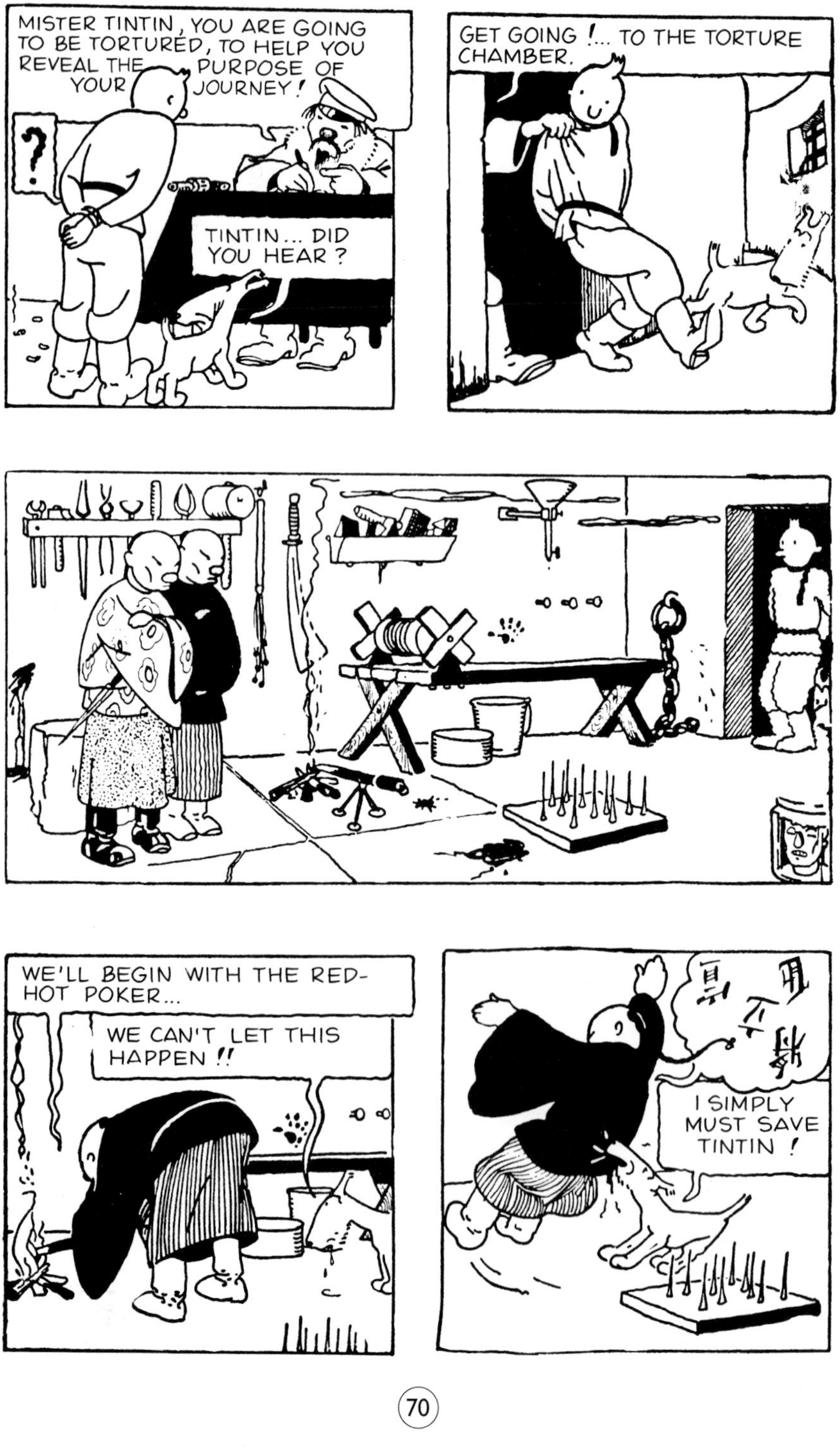
MISTER TINTIN, YOU ARE GOING TO BE TORTURED, TO HELP YOU REVEAL THE PURPOSE OF YOUR JOURNEY!
TINTIN... DID YOU HEAR?
GET GOING!... TO THE TORTURE CHAMBER.
WE'LL BEGIN WITH THE RED-HOT POKER...
WE CAN'T LET THIS HAPPEN!!
I SIMPLY MUST SAVE TINTIN!

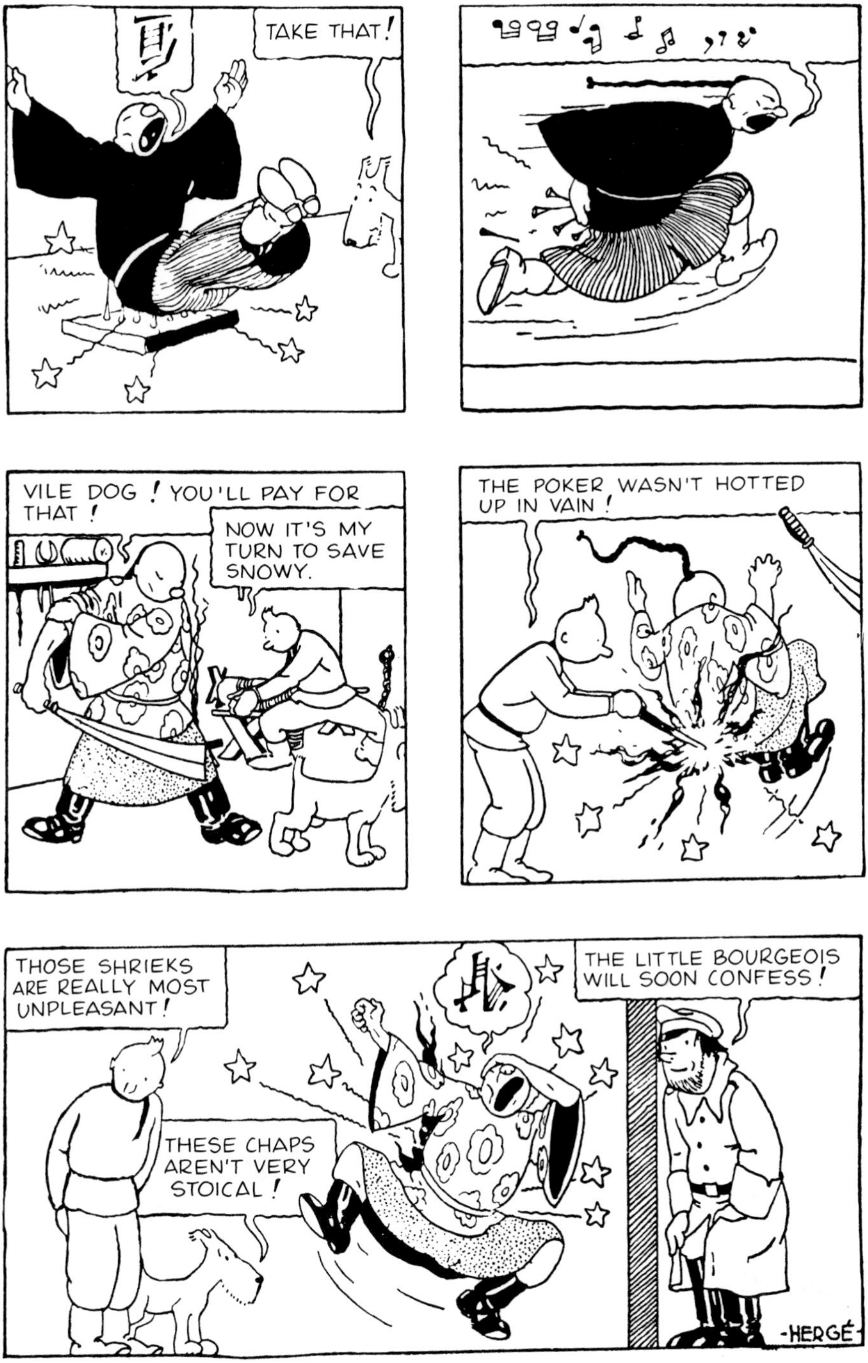
TAKE THAT!
VILE DOG! YOU'LL PAY FOR THAT!
NOW IT'S MY TURN TO SAVE SNOWY.
THE POKER WASN'T HOTTED UP IN VAIN!
THOSE SHRIEKS ARE REALLY MOST UNPLEASANT!
THE LITTLE BOURGEOIS WILL SOON CONFESS!
THESE CHAPS AREN'T VERY STOICAL!
-HERGÉ-

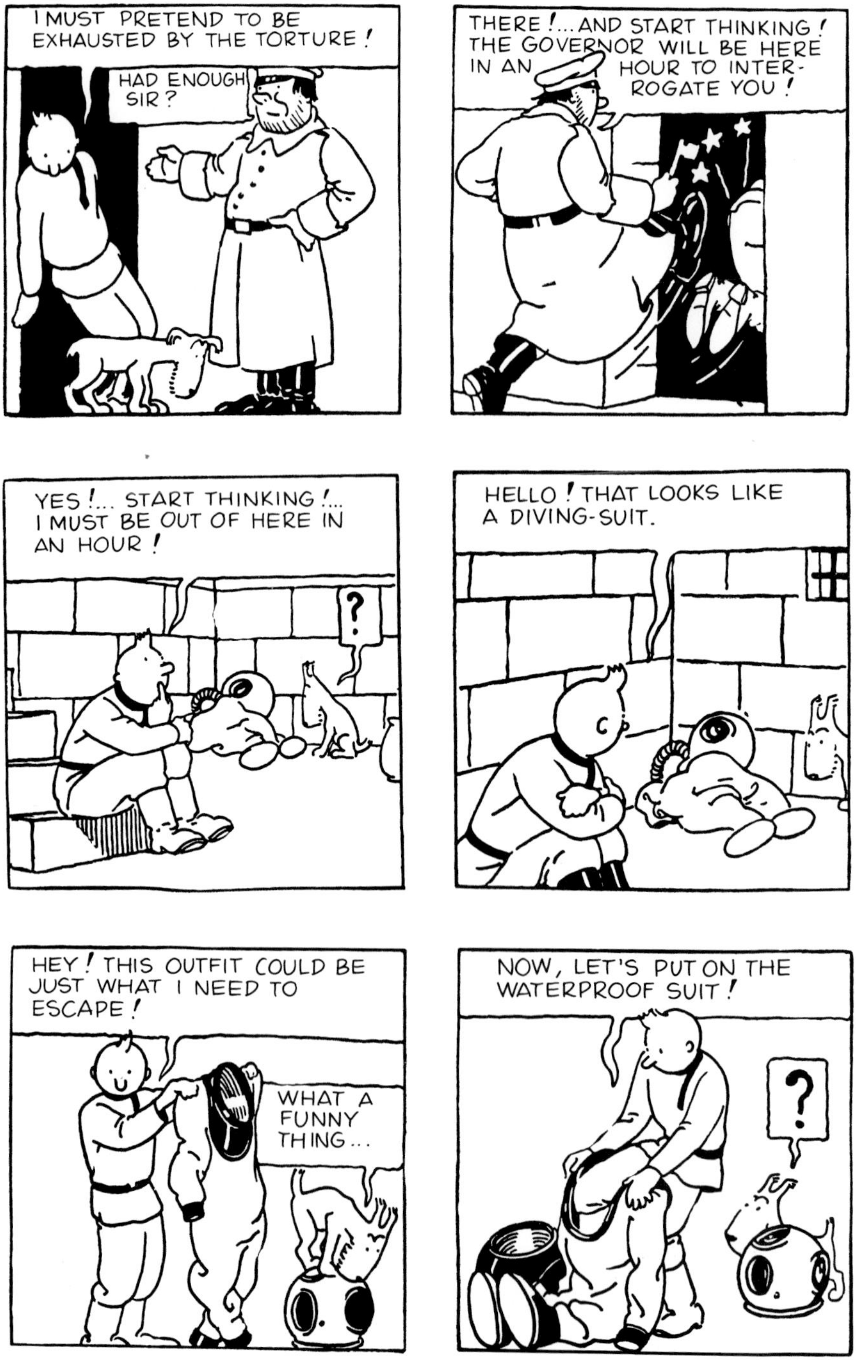
I MUST PRETEND TO BE EXHAUSTED BY THE TORTURE!
HAD ENOUGH SIR?
THERE!... AND START THINKING! THE GOVERNOR WILL BE HERE IN AN HOUR TO INTERROGATE YOU!
YES!... START THINKING!... I MUST BE OUT OF HERE IN AN HOUR!
?
HELLO! THAT LOOKS LIKE A DIVING-SUIT.
HEY! THIS OUTFIT COULD BE JUST WHAT I NEED TO ESCAPE!
WHAT A FUNNY THING...
NOW, LET'S PUT ON THE WATERPROOF SUIT!
?

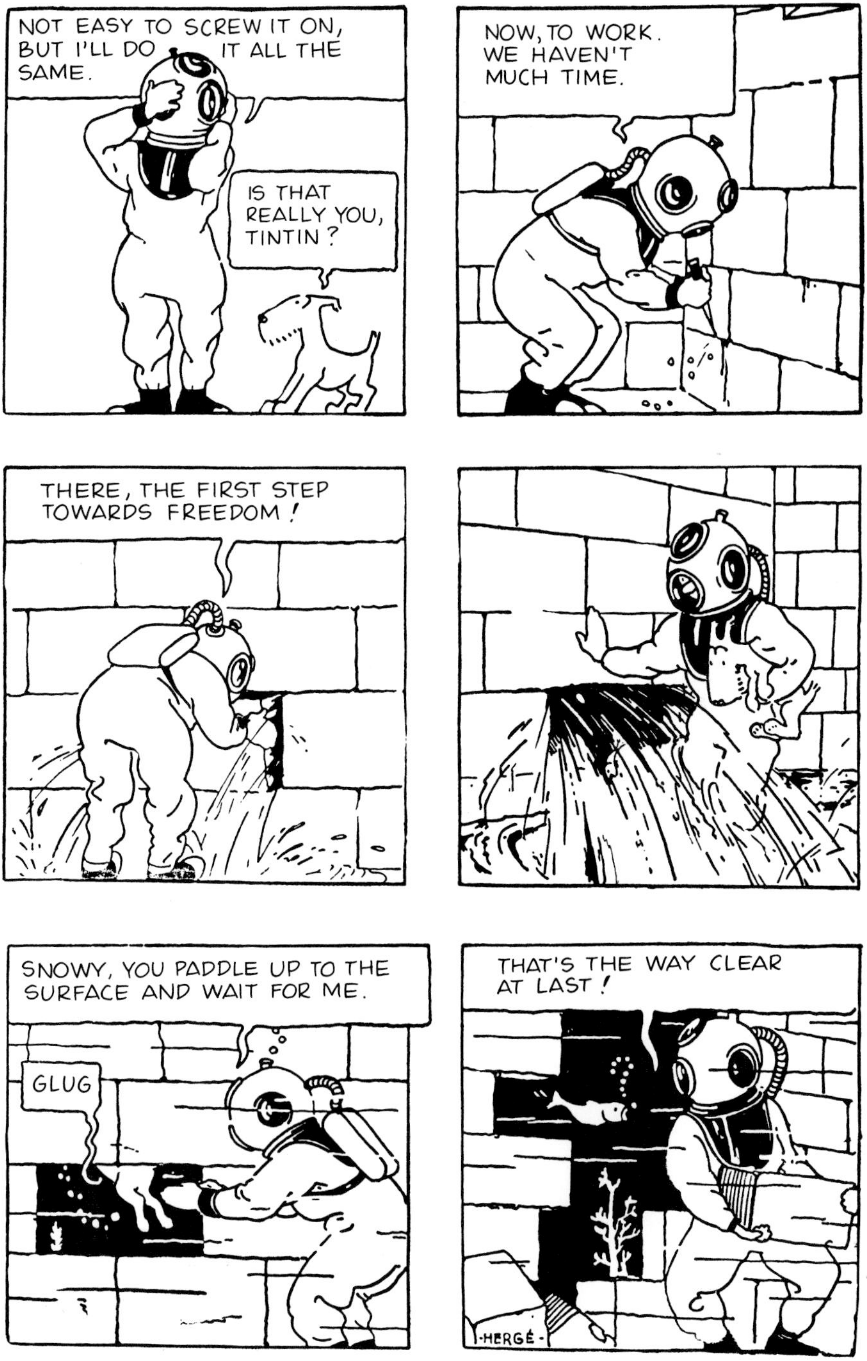
NOT EASY TO SCREW IT ON, BUT I'LL DO IT ALL THE SAME.
IS THAT REALLY YOU, TINTIN?
NOW, TO WORK. WE HAVEN'T MUCH TIME.
THERE, THE FIRST STEP TOWARDS FREEDOM!
SNOWY, YOU PADDLE UP TO THE SURFACE AND WAIT FOR ME.
GLUG
THAT'S THE WAY CLEAR AT LAST!
-HERGÉ-

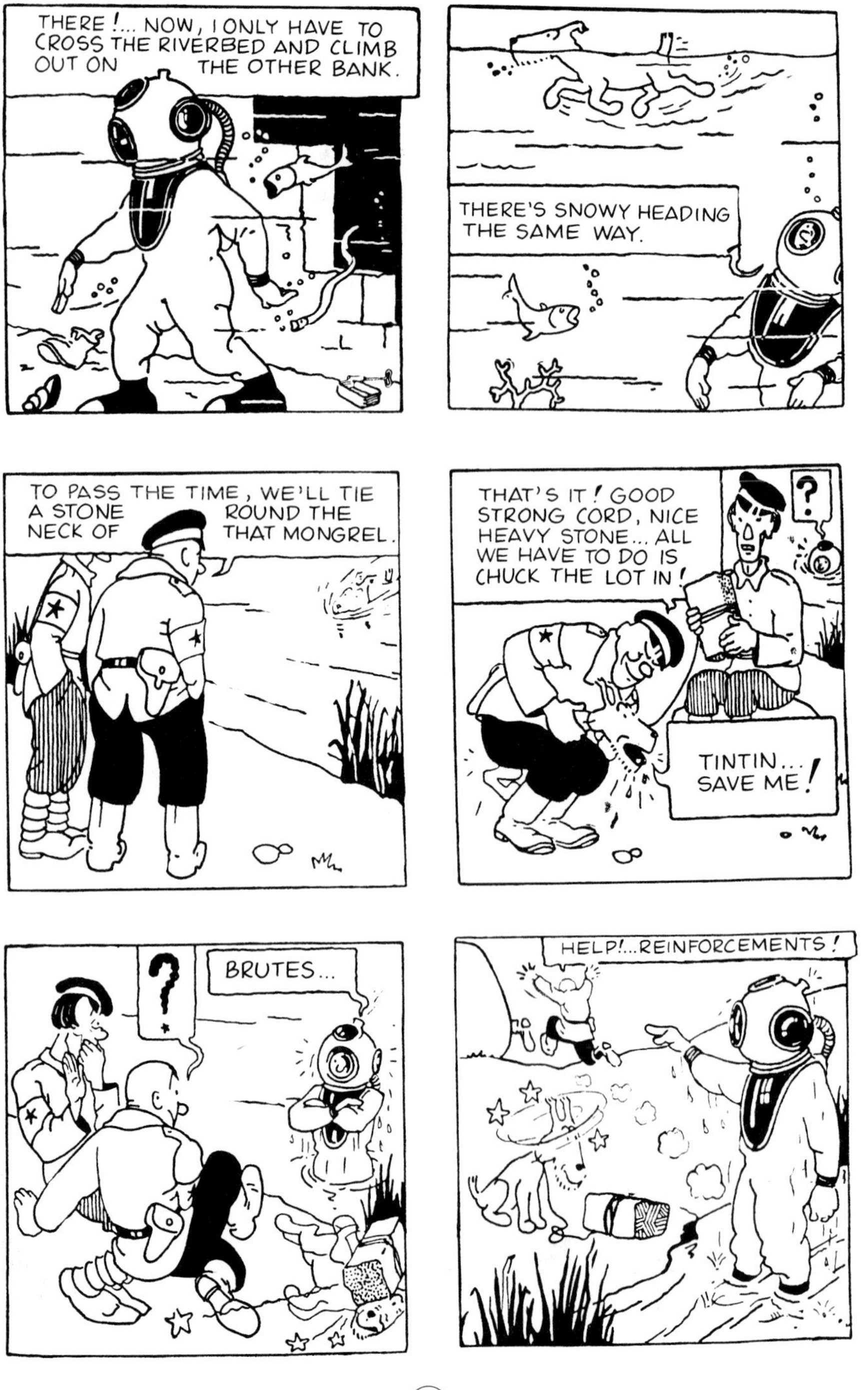
THERE!... NOW, I ONLY HAVE TO CROSS THE RIVERBED AND CLIMB OUT ON THE OTHER BANK.
THERE'S SNOWY HEADING THE SAME WAY.
TO PASS THE TIME, WE'LL TIE A STONE ROUND THE NECK OF THAT MONGREL.
THAT'S IT! GOOD STRONG CORD, NICE HEAVY STONE... ALL WE HAVE TO DO IS CHUCK THE LOT IN!
?
TINTIN... SAVE ME!
?
BRUTES...
HELP!...REINFORCEMENTS!

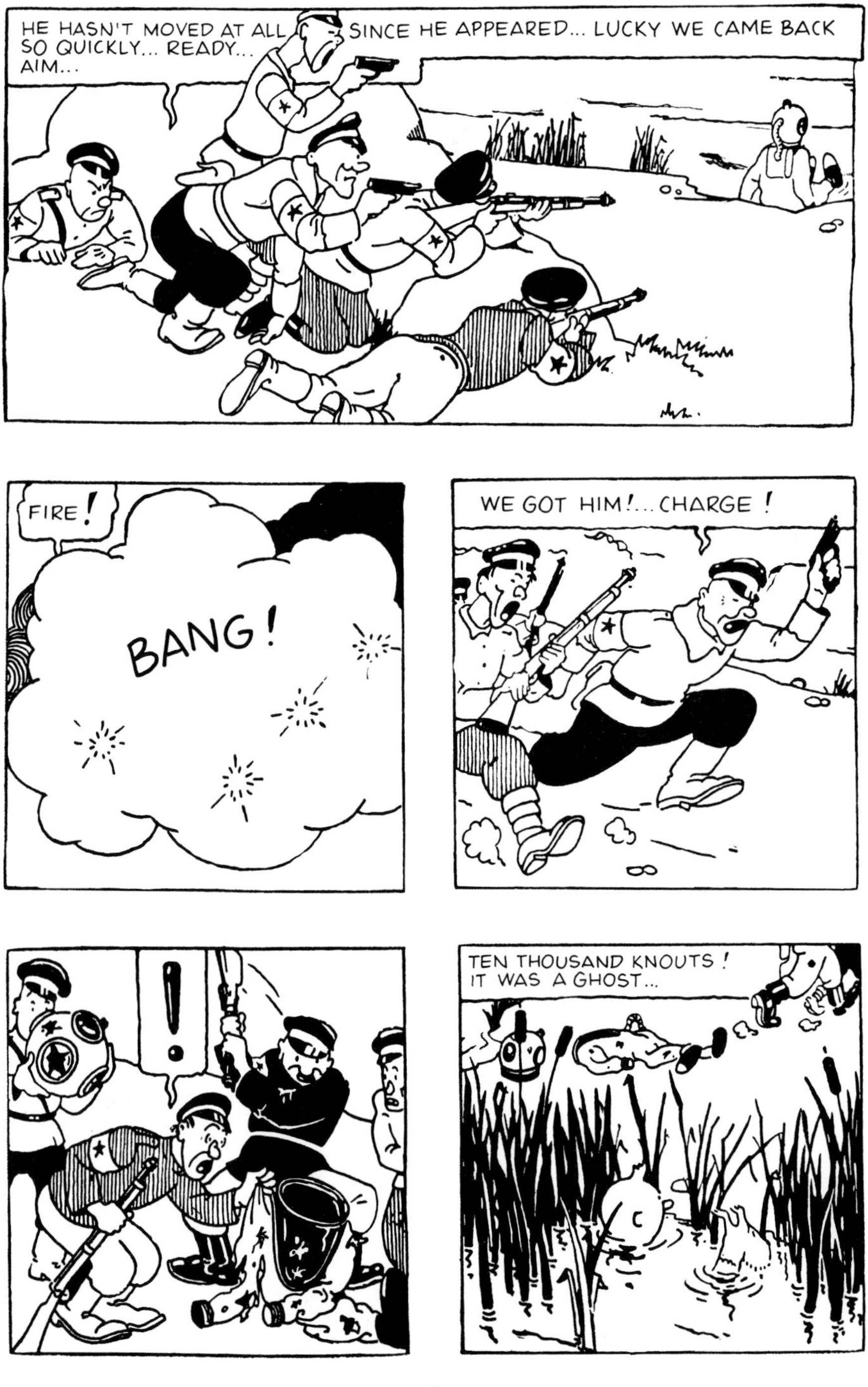
HE HASN'T MOVED AT ALL SINCE HE APPEARED... LUCKY WE CAME BACK SO QUICKLY... READY... AIM...
FIRE!
BANG!
WE GOT HIM!... CHARGE!
!
TEN THOUSAND KNOUTS! IT WAS A GHOST...

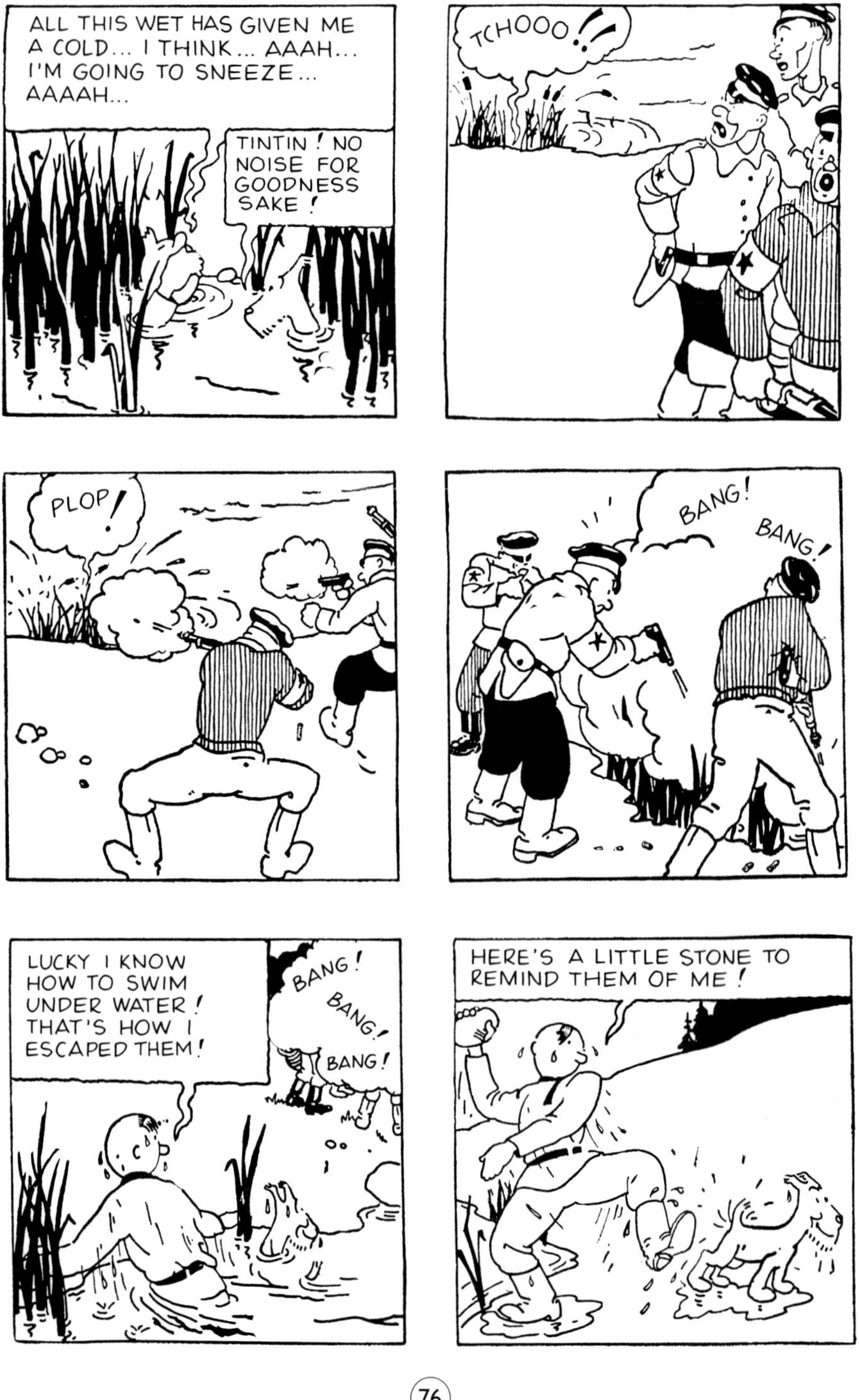

ALL THIS WET HAS GIVEN ME A COLD... I THINK... AAAH... I'M GOING TO SNEEZE... AAAAH...
TINTIN! NO NOISE FOR GOODNESS SAKE!
TCHOOO!!
PLOP!
BANG!
BANG!
LUCKY I KNOW HOW TO SWIM UNDER WATER! THAT'S HOW I ESCAPED THEM!
BANG!
BANG!
BANG!
HERE'S A LITTLE STONE TO REMIND THEM OF ME!

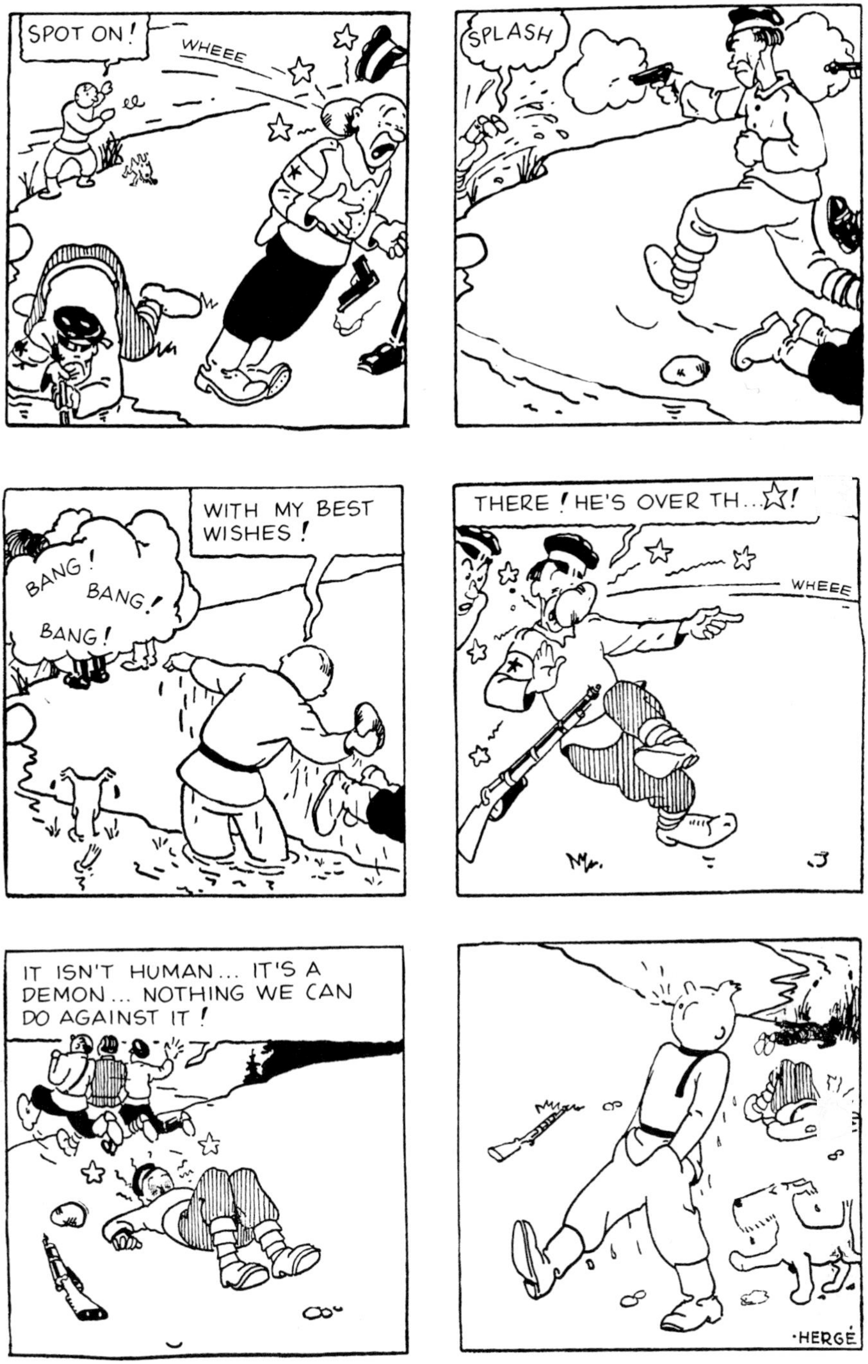
SPOT ON!
WHEEE
SPLASH
WITH MY BEST WISHES!
BANG!
BANG!
BANG!
THERE! HE'S OVER TH...☆!
WHEEE
IT ISN'T HUMAN... IT'S A DEMON... NOTHING WE CAN DO AGAINST IT!
HERGÉ

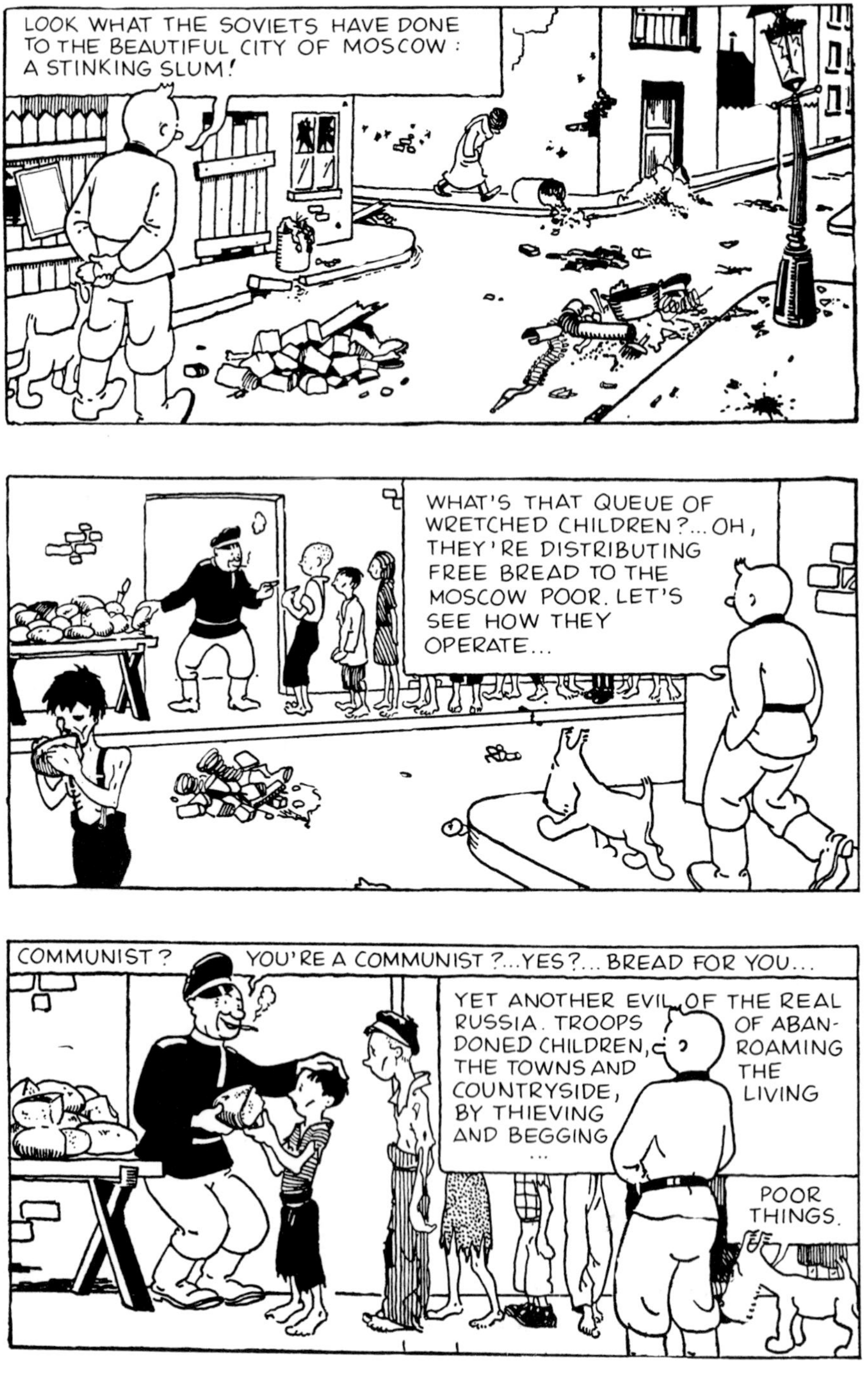
LOOK WHAT THE SOVIETS HAVE DONE TO THE BEAUTIFUL CITY OF MOSCOW : A STINKING SLUM!
WHAT'S THAT QUEUE OF WRETCHED CHILDREN?... OH, THEY'RE DISTRIBUTING FREE BREAD TO THE MOSCOW POOR. LET'S SEE HOW THEY OPERATE...
COMMUNIST?
YOU'RE A COMMUNIST?...YES?... BREAD FOR YOU...
YET ANOTHER EVIL OF THE REAL RUSSIA. TROOPS OF ABANDONED CHILDREN, ROAMING THE TOWNS AND COUNTRYSIDE, LIVING BY THIEVING AND BEGGING ...
POOR THINGS.

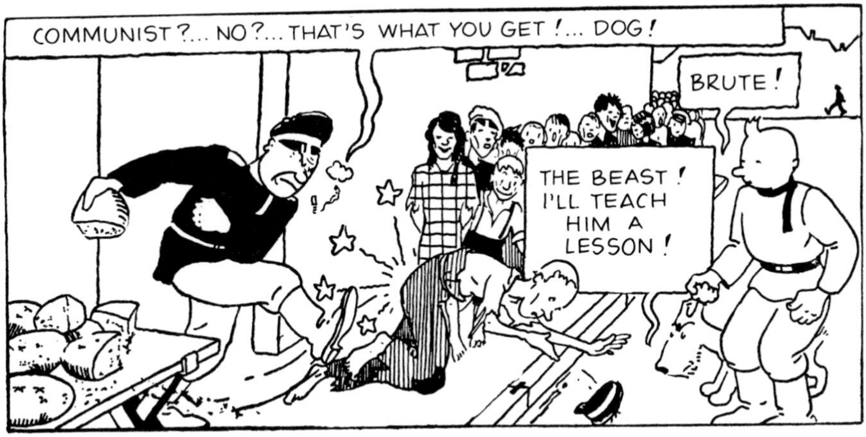
COMMUNIST?... NO?... THAT'S WHAT YOU GET!... DOG!
BRUTE!
THE BEAST! I'LL TEACH HIM A LESSON!

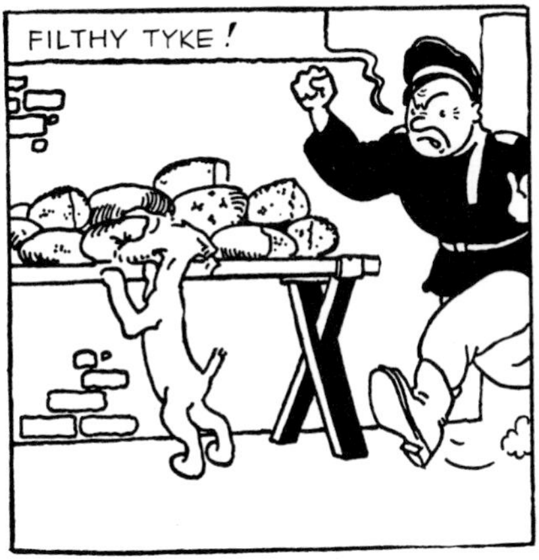
FILTHY TYKE!

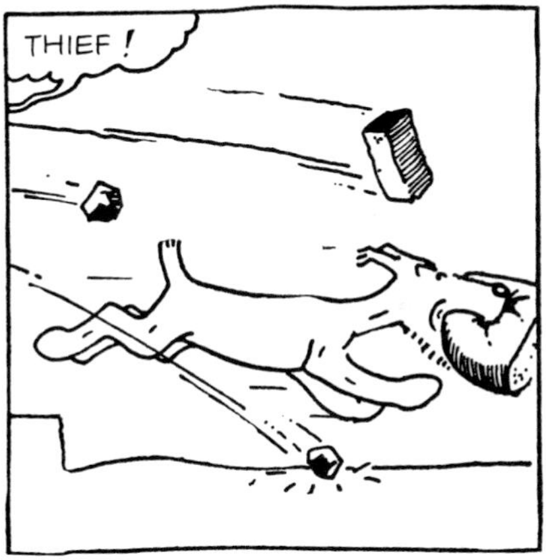
THIEF!

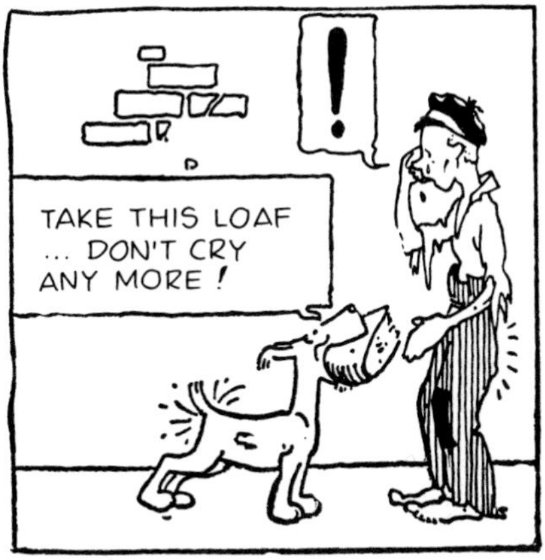
!
TAKE THIS LOAF ... DON'T CRY ANY MORE!

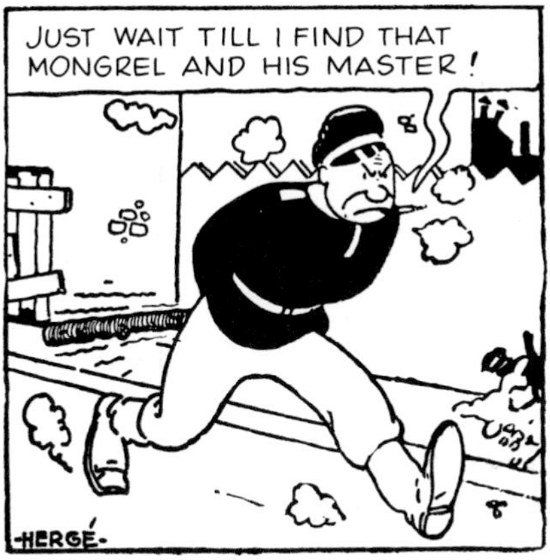
JUST WAIT TILL I FIND THAT MONGREL AND HIS MASTER!
-HERGÉ-

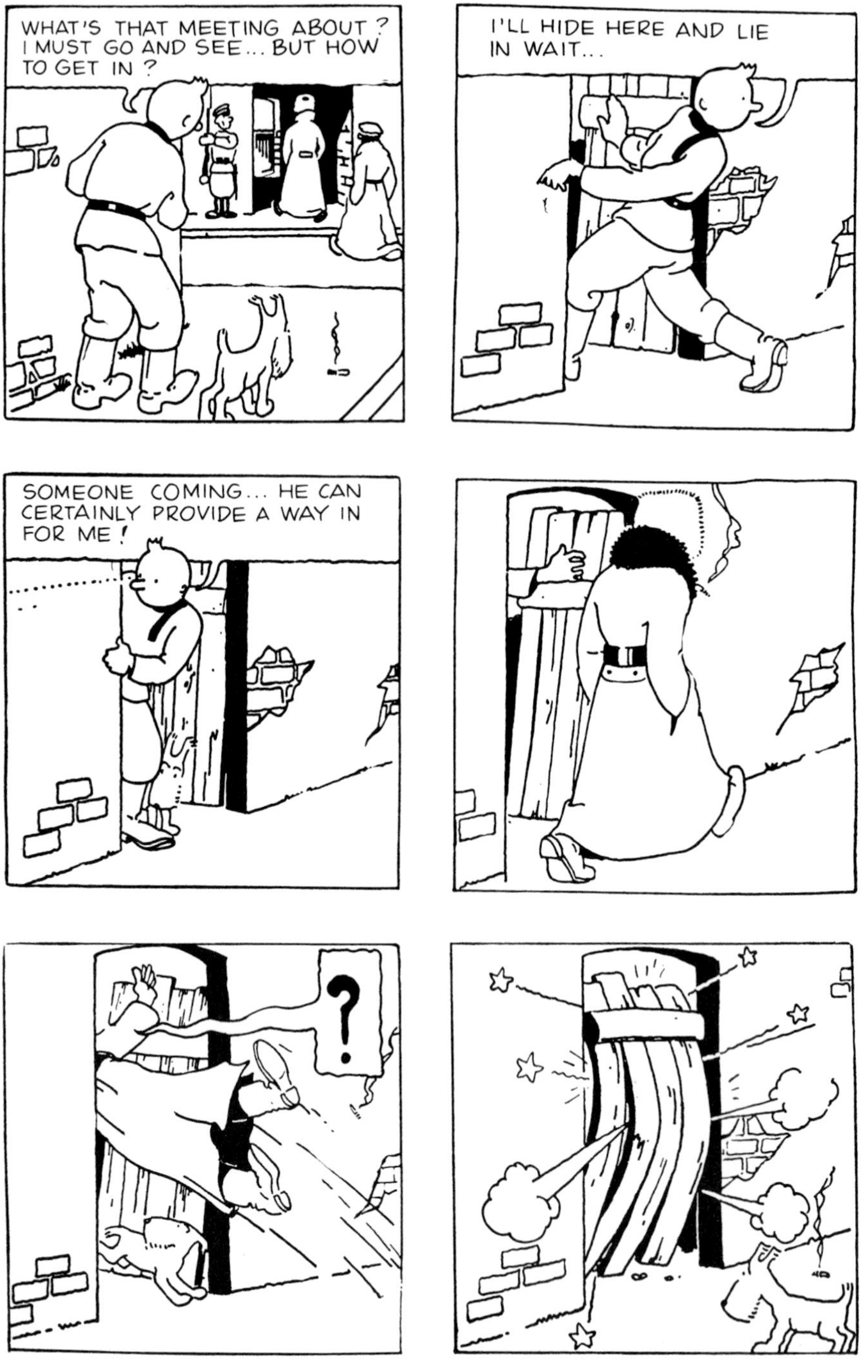
WHAT'S THAT MEETING ABOUT ? I MUST GO AND SEE... BUT HOW TO GET IN ?
I'LL HIDE HERE AND LIE IN WAIT...
SOMEONE COMING... HE CAN CERTAINLY PROVIDE A WAY IN FOR ME !
?

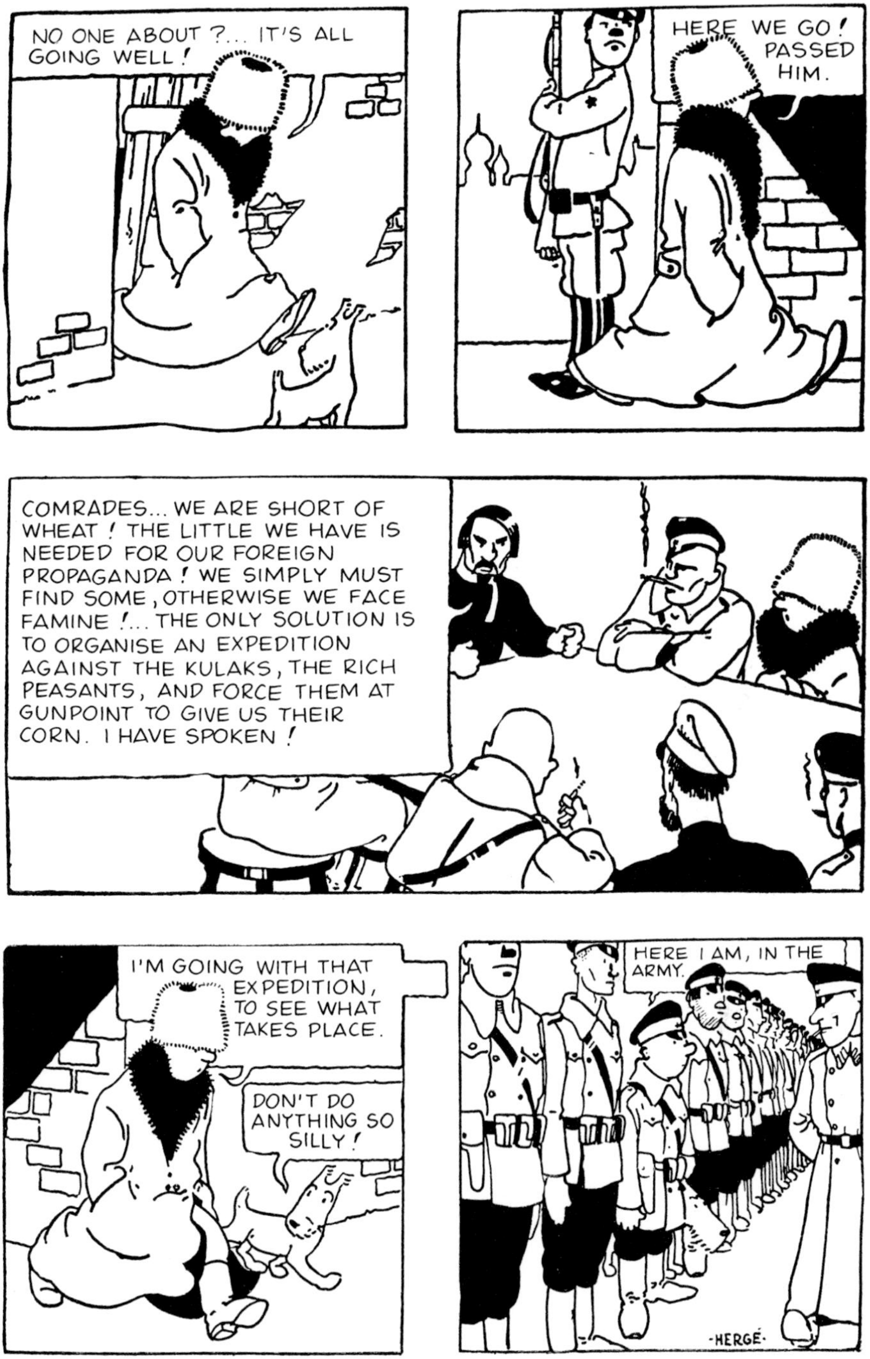
NO ONE ABOUT ?... IT'S ALL GOING WELL !
HERE WE GO ! PASSED HIM.
COMRADES... WE ARE SHORT OF WHEAT ! THE LITTLE WE HAVE IS NEEDED FOR OUR FOREIGN PROPAGANDA ! WE SIMPLY MUST FIND SOME, OTHERWISE WE FACE FAMINE !... THE ONLY SOLUTION IS TO ORGANISE AN EXPEDITION AGAINST THE KULAKS, THE RICH PEASANTS, AND FORCE THEM AT GUNPOINT TO GIVE US THEIR CORN. I HAVE SPOKEN !
I'M GOING WITH THAT EXPEDITION, TO SEE WHAT TAKES PLACE.
DON'T DO ANYTHING SO SILLY !
HERE I AM, IN THE ARMY.
HERGÉ

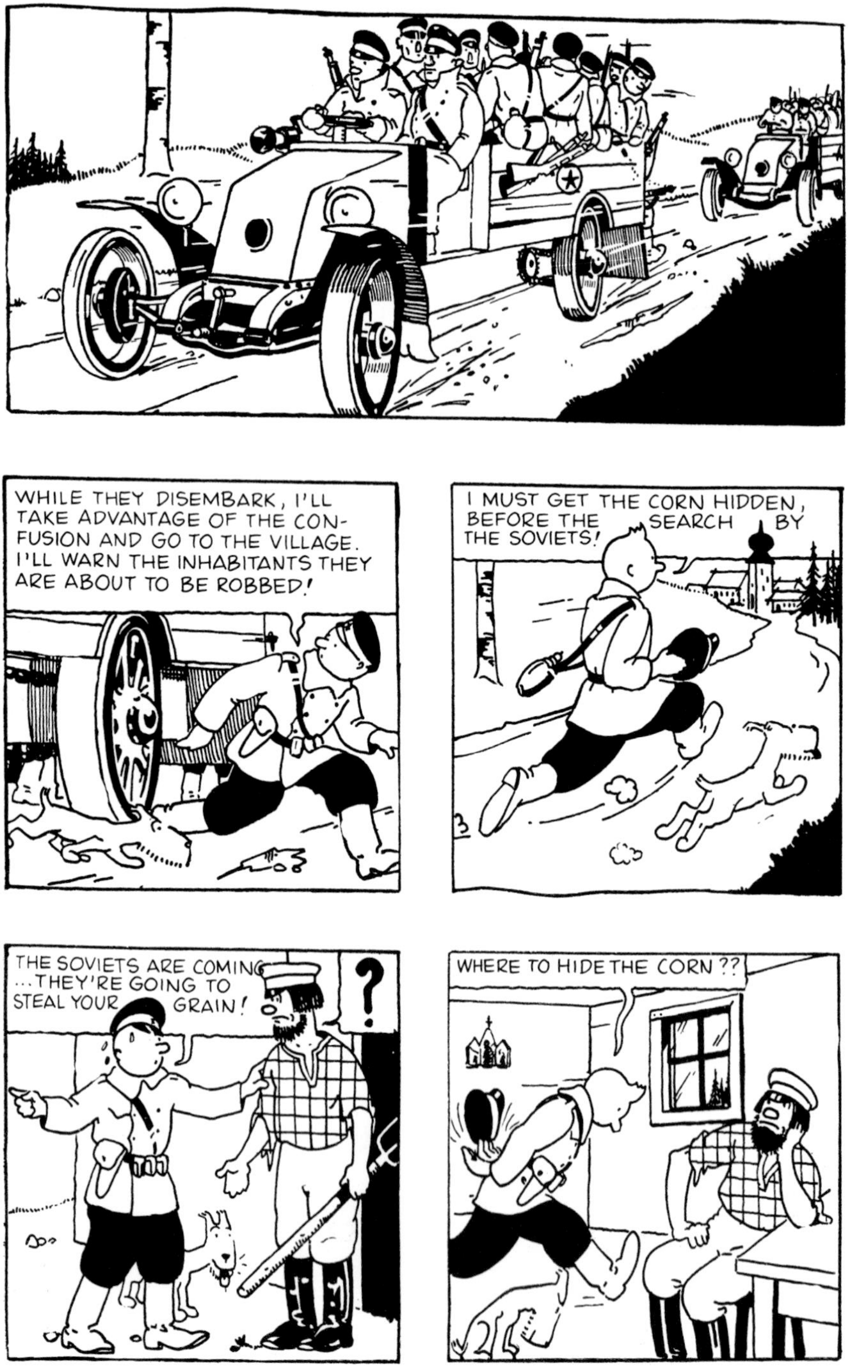
WHILE THEY DISEMBARK, I'LL TAKE ADVANTAGE OF THE CON-FUSION AND GO TO THE VILLAGE. I'LL WARN THE INHABITANTS THEY ARE ABOUT TO BE ROBBED!
I MUST GET THE CORN HIDDEN, BEFORE THE SEARCH BY THE SOVIETS!
THE SOVIETS ARE COMING ...THEY'RE GOING TO STEAL YOUR GRAIN!
?
WHERE TO HIDE THE CORN ??

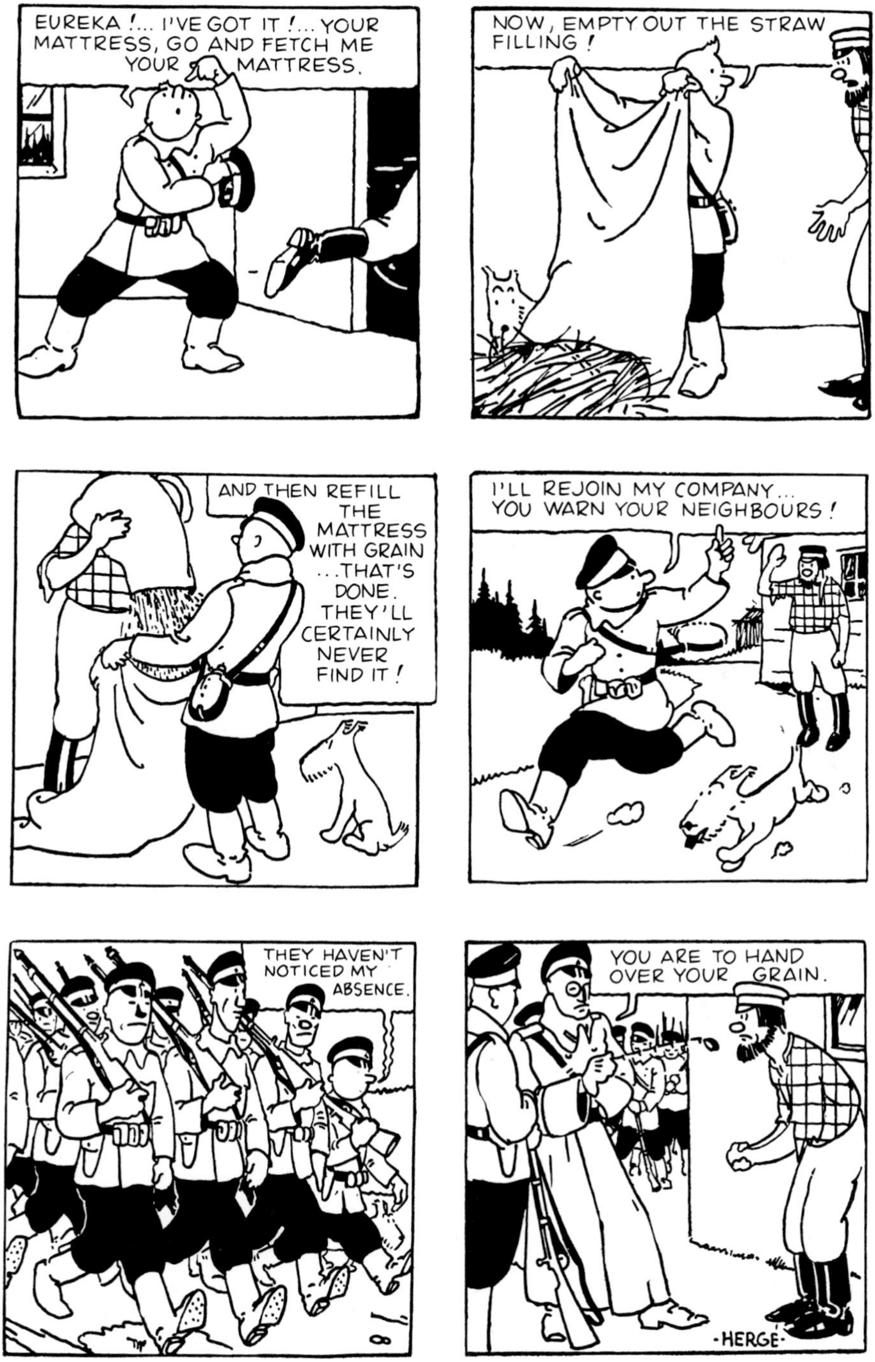
EUREKA !... I'VE GOT IT !... YOUR MATTRESS, GO AND FETCH ME YOUR MATTRESS.
NOW, EMPTY OUT THE STRAW FILLING !
AND THEN REFILL THE MATTRESS WITH GRAIN ...THAT'S DONE. THEY'LL CERTAINLY NEVER FIND IT !
I'LL REJOIN MY COMPANY... YOU WARN YOUR NEIGHBOURS !
THEY HAVEN'T NOTICED MY ABSENCE.
YOU ARE TO HAND OVER YOUR GRAIN.
-HERGE-

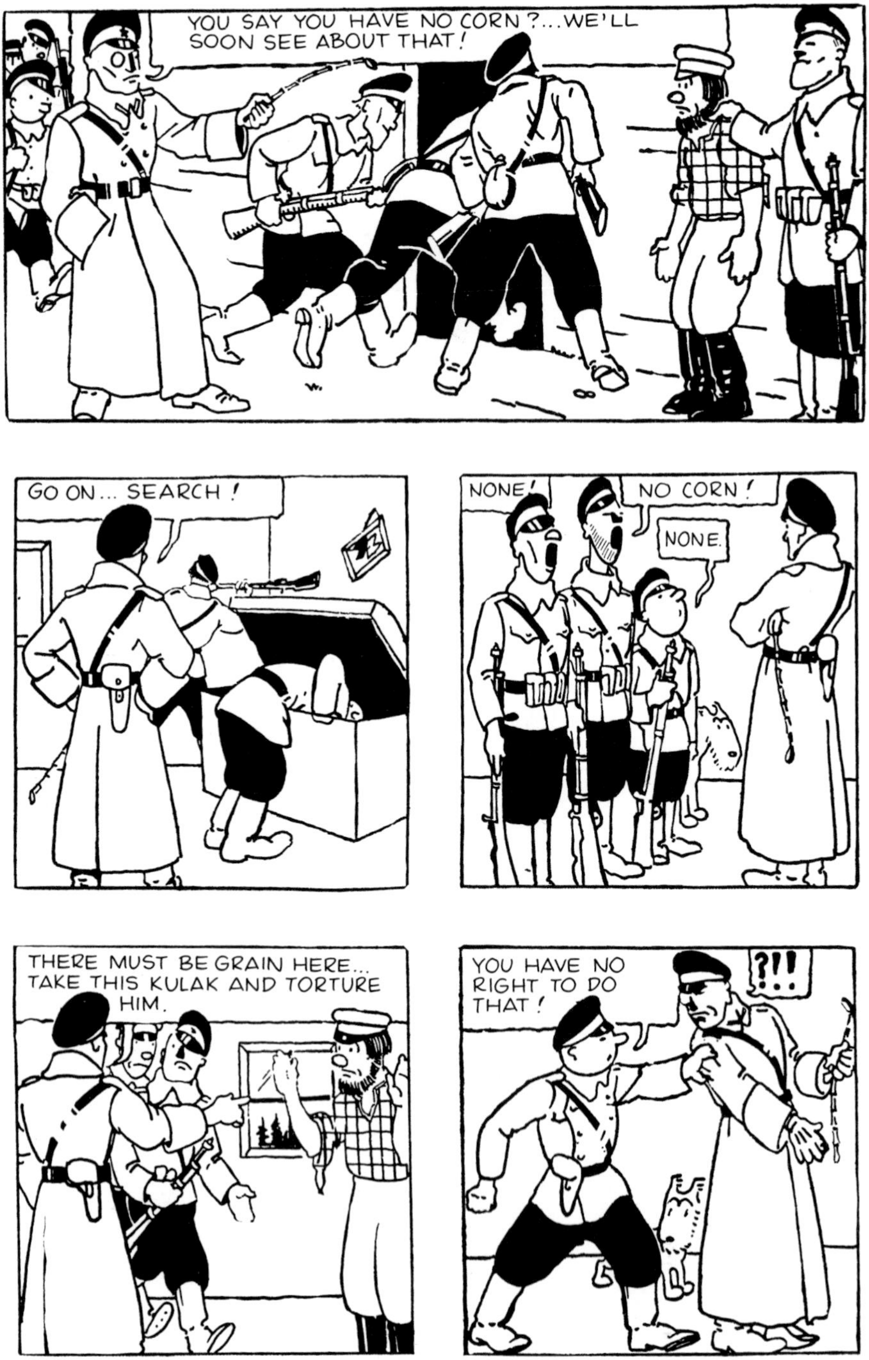
YOU SAY YOU HAVE NO CORN ?... WE'LL SOON SEE ABOUT THAT !
GO ON... SEARCH !
NONE !
NO CORN !
NONE.
THERE MUST BE GRAIN HERE... TAKE THIS KULAK AND TORTURE HIM.
YOU HAVE NO RIGHT TO DO THAT !
?!!

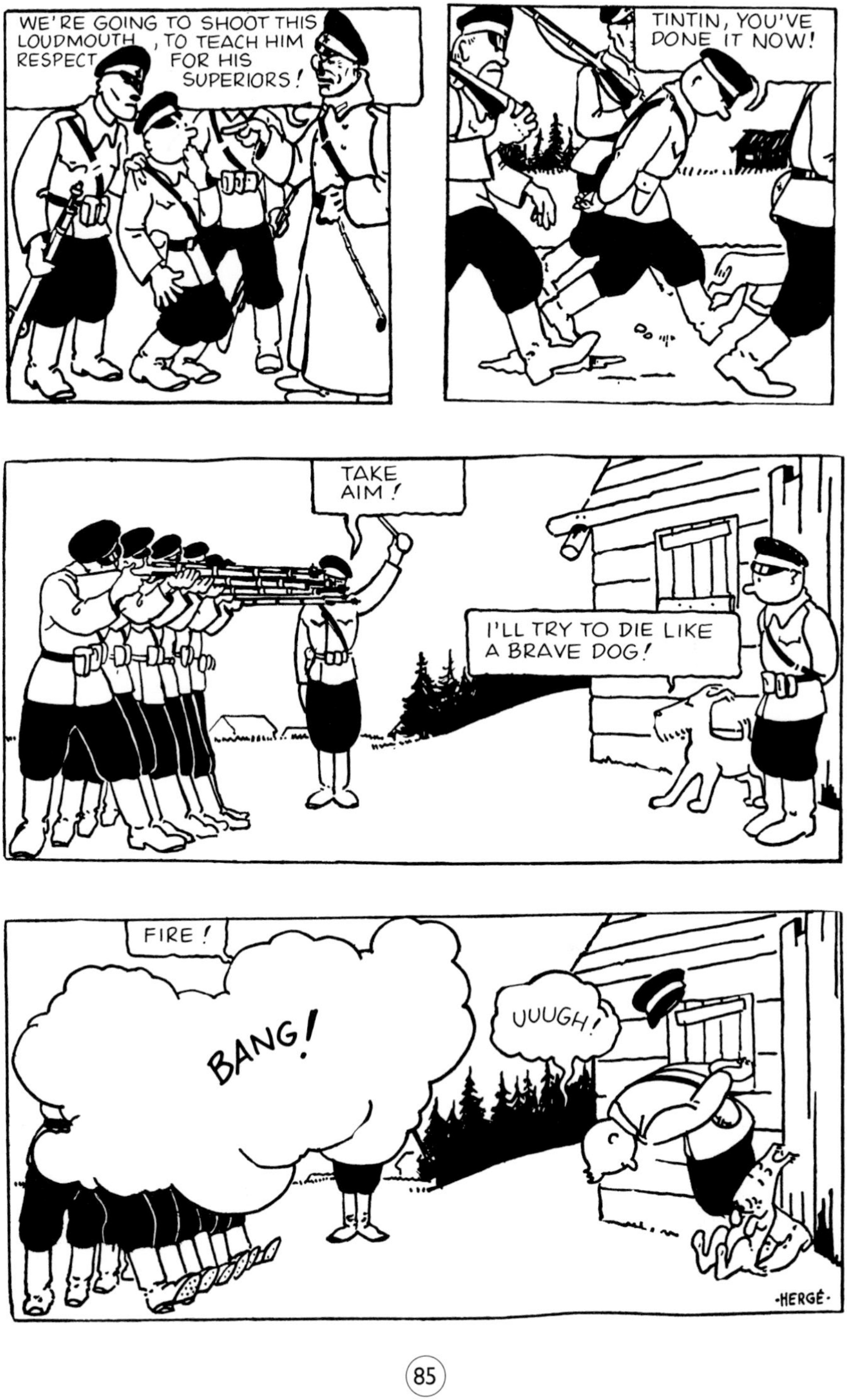
WE'RE GOING TO SHOOT THIS LOUDMOUTH, TO TEACH HIM RESPECT FOR HIS SUPERIORS!
TINTIN, YOU'VE DONE IT NOW!
TAKE AIM!
I'LL TRY TO DIE LIKE A BRAVE DOG!
FIRE!
BANG!
UUUGH!
-HERGÉ-

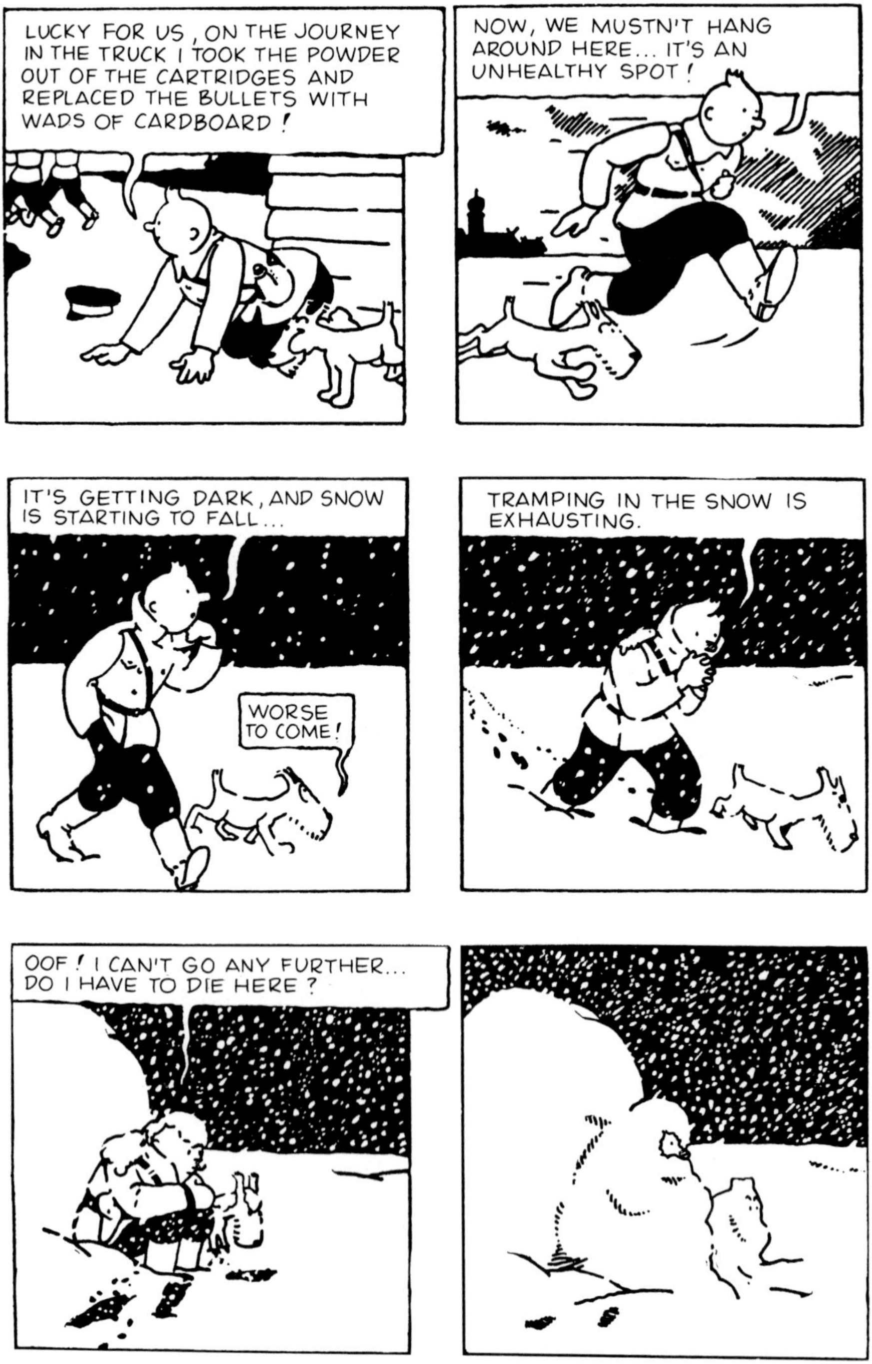
LUCKY FOR US, ON THE JOURNEY IN THE TRUCK I TOOK THE POWDER OUT OF THE CARTRIDGES AND REPLACED THE BULLETS WITH WADS OF CARDBOARD!
NOW, WE MUSTN'T HANG AROUND HERE... IT'S AN UNHEALTHY SPOT!
IT'S GETTING DARK, AND SNOW IS STARTING TO FALL...
WORSE TO COME!
TRAMPING IN THE SNOW IS EXHAUSTING.
OOF! I CAN'T GO ANY FURTHER... DO I HAVE TO DIE HERE?

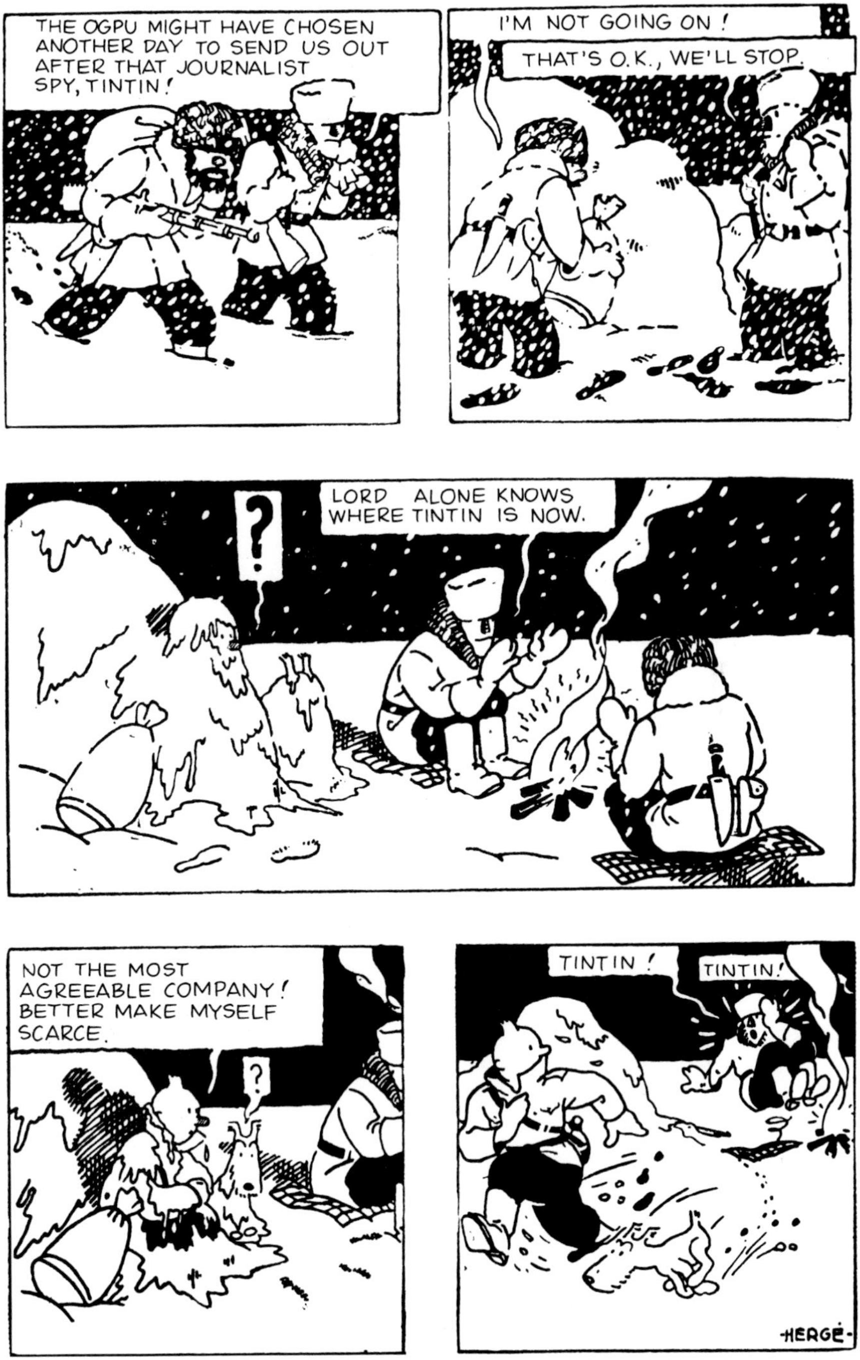
THE OGPU MIGHT HAVE CHOSEN ANOTHER DAY TO SEND US OUT AFTER THAT JOURNALIST SPY, TINTIN!
I'M NOT GOING ON!
THAT'S O.K., WE'LL STOP.
?
LORD ALONE KNOWS WHERE TINTIN IS NOW.
NOT THE MOST AGREEABLE COMPANY! BETTER MAKE MYSELF SCARCE.
?
TINTIN!
TINTIN!
HERGÉ

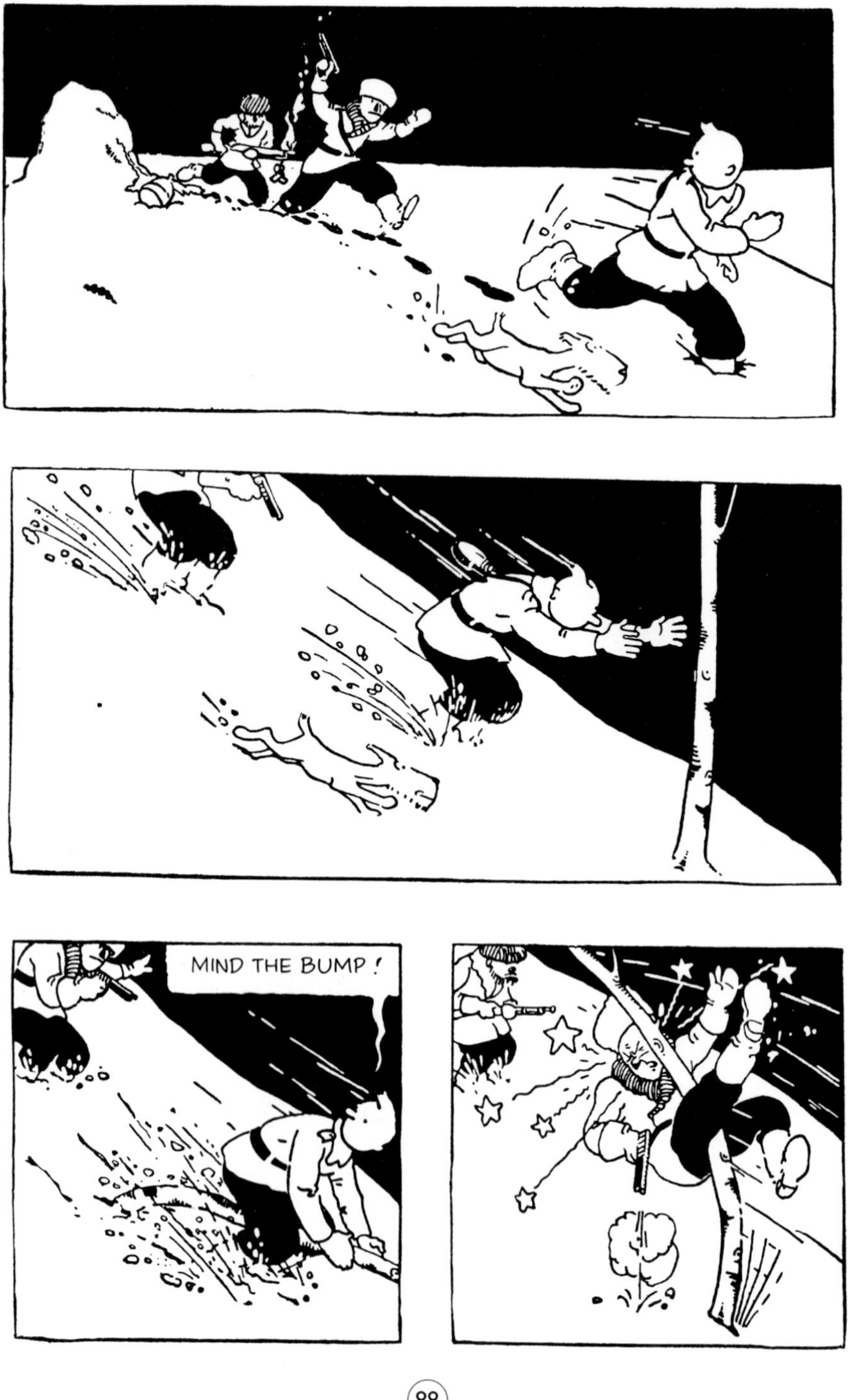
MIND THE BUMP !

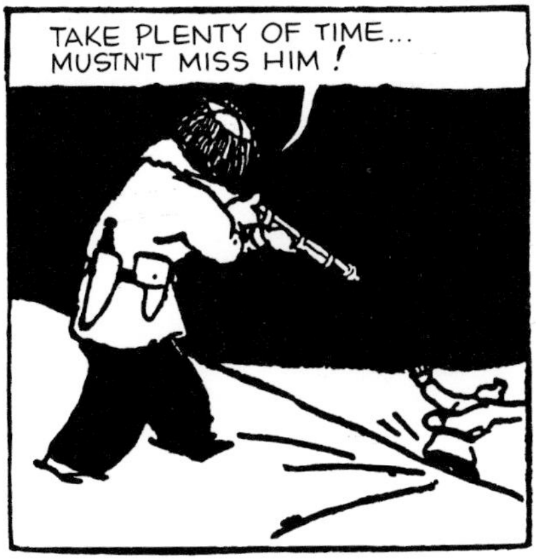
TAKE PLENTY OF TIME...
MUSTN'T MISS HIM!

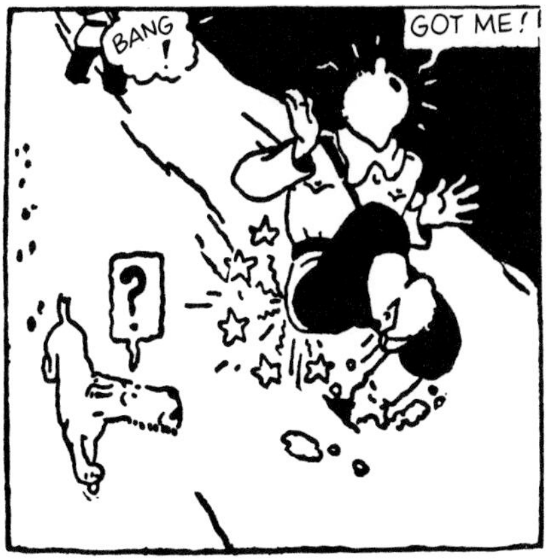
BANG!
GOT ME!
?

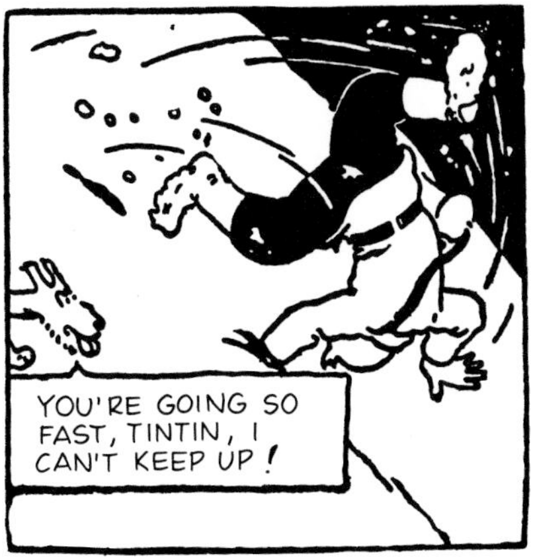
YOU'RE GOING SO FAST, TINTIN, I CAN'T KEEP UP!

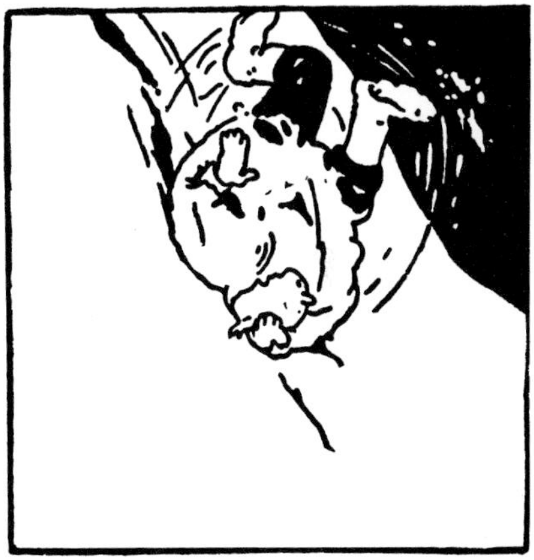

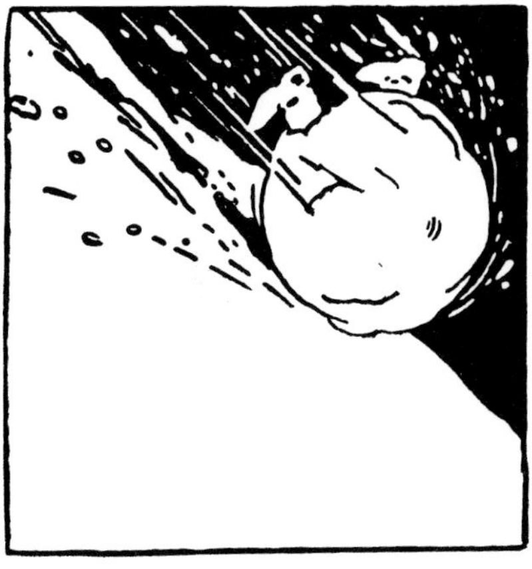

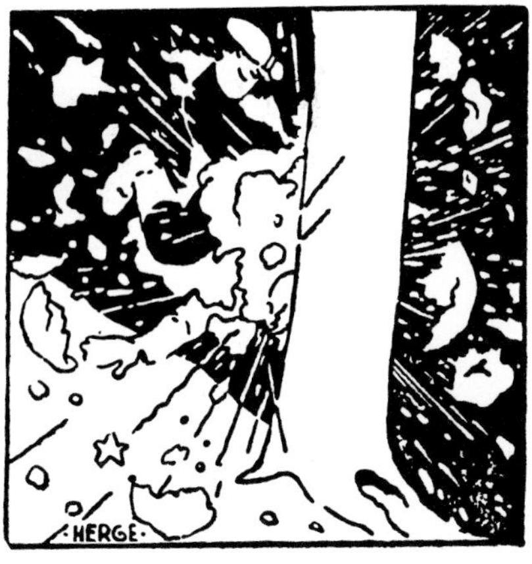
HERGE

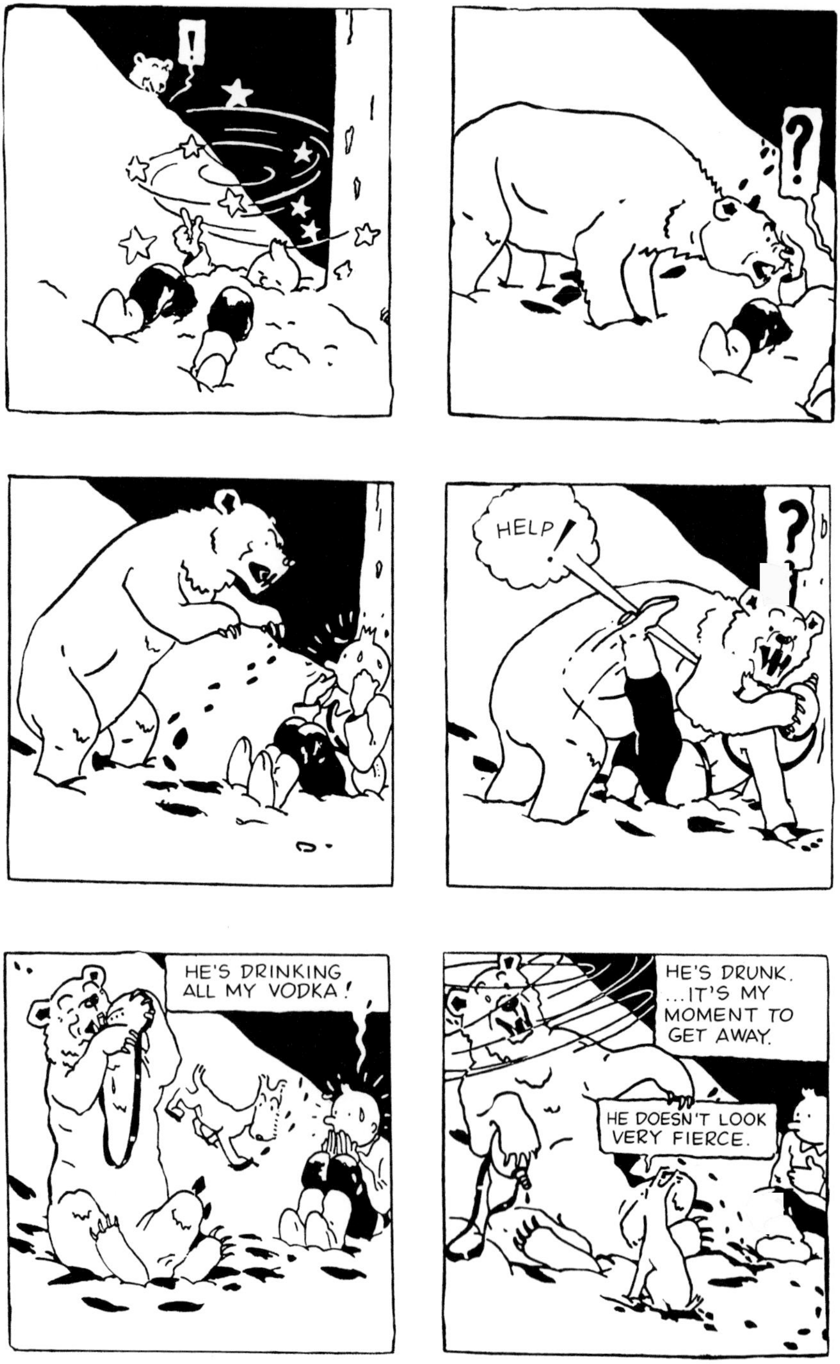
HELP!
HE'S DRINKING ALL MY VODKA!
HE'S DRUNK. ...IT'S MY MOMENT TO GET AWAY.
HE DOESN'T LOOK VERY FIERCE.

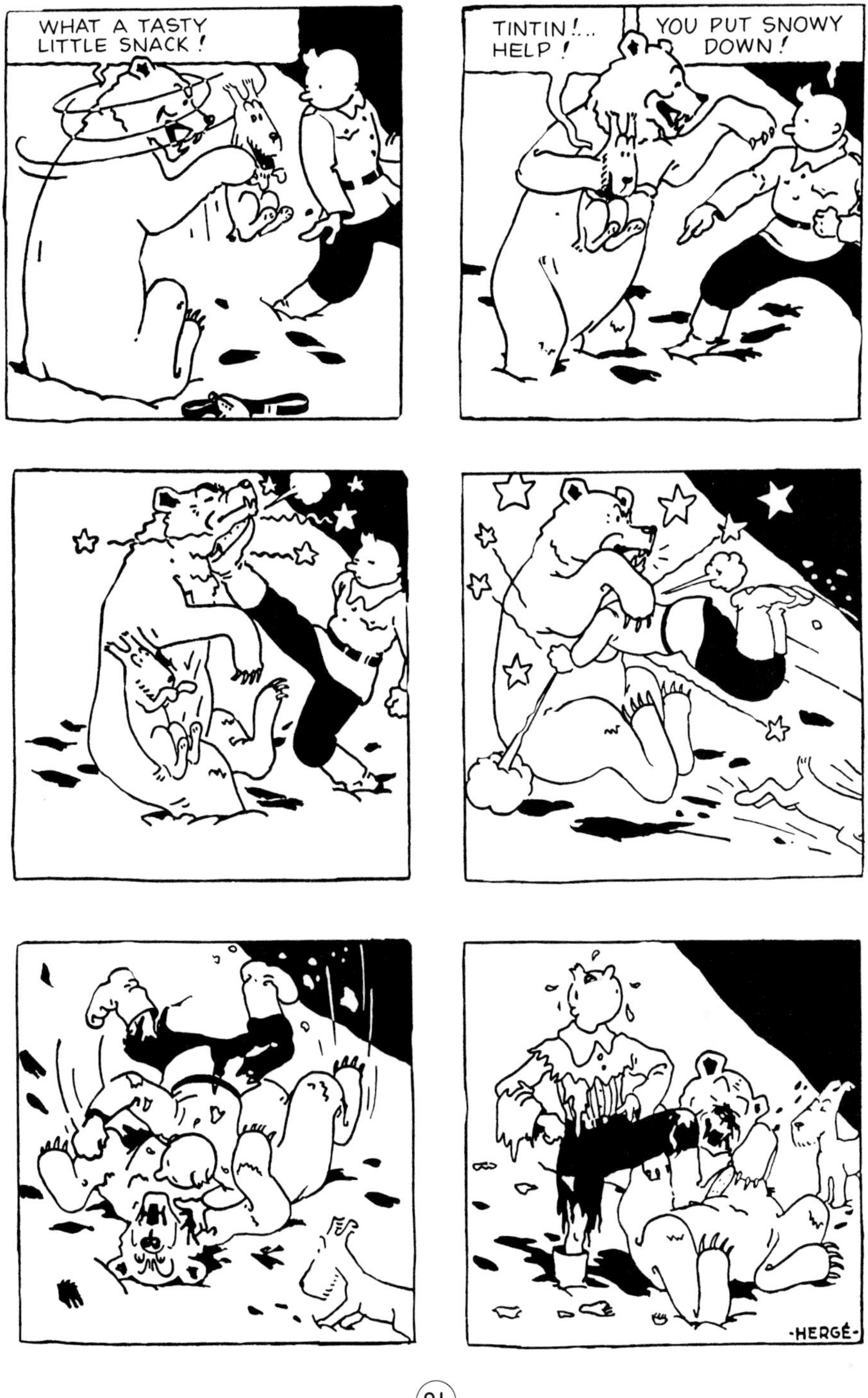
WHAT A TASTY LITTLE SNACK !
TINTIN !... HELP !
YOU PUT SNOWY DOWN !
-HERGÉ-

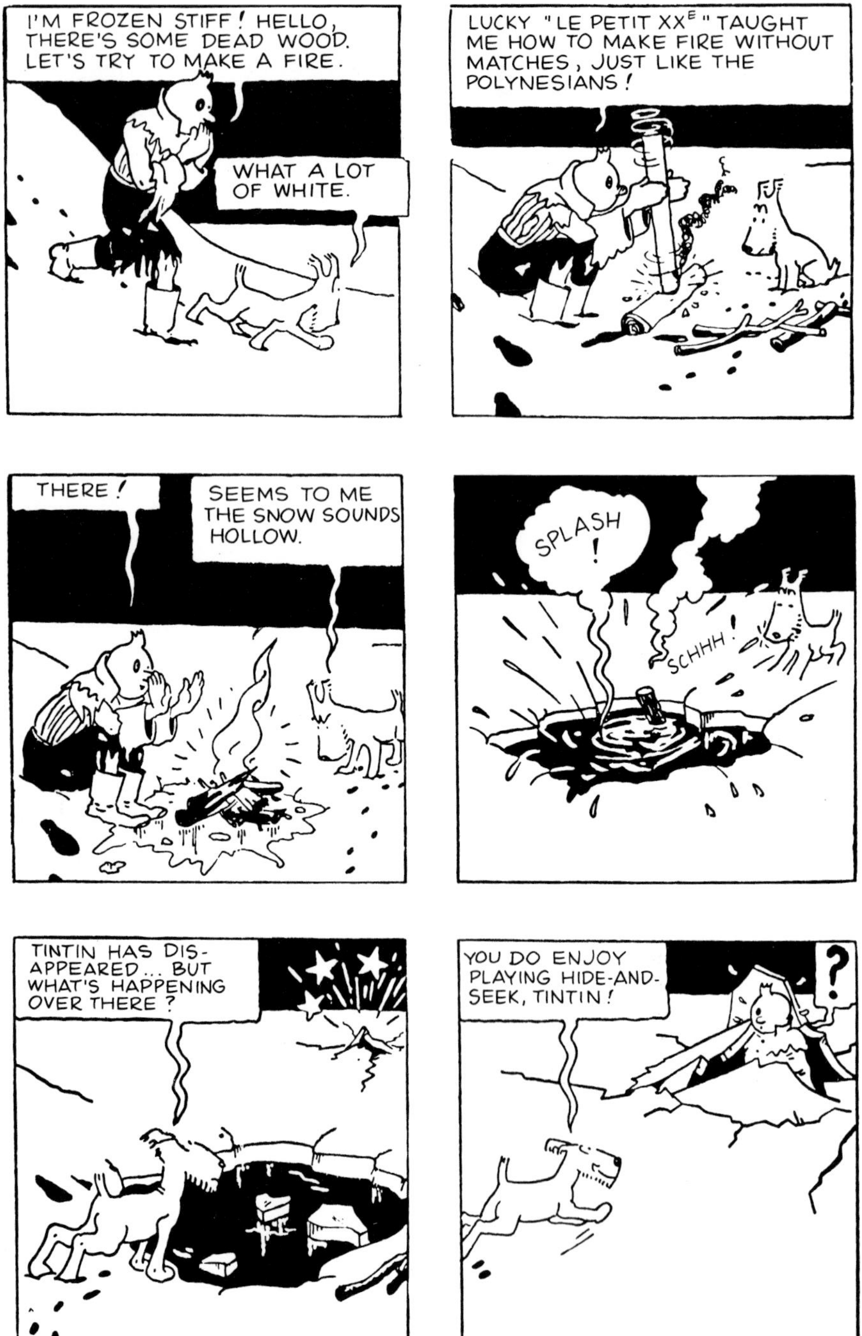

I'M FROZEN STIFF! HELLO, THERE'S SOME DEAD WOOD. LET'S TRY TO MAKE A FIRE.
WHAT A LOT OF WHITE.
LUCKY "LE PETIT XXE" TAUGHT ME HOW TO MAKE FIRE WITHOUT MATCHES, JUST LIKE THE POLYNESIANS!
THERE!
SEEMS TO ME THE SNOW SOUNDS HOLLOW.
SPLASH!
SCHHH!
TINTIN HAS DISAPPEARED... BUT WHAT'S HAPPENING OVER THERE?
YOU DO ENJOY PLAYING HIDE-AND-SEEK, TINTIN!
?

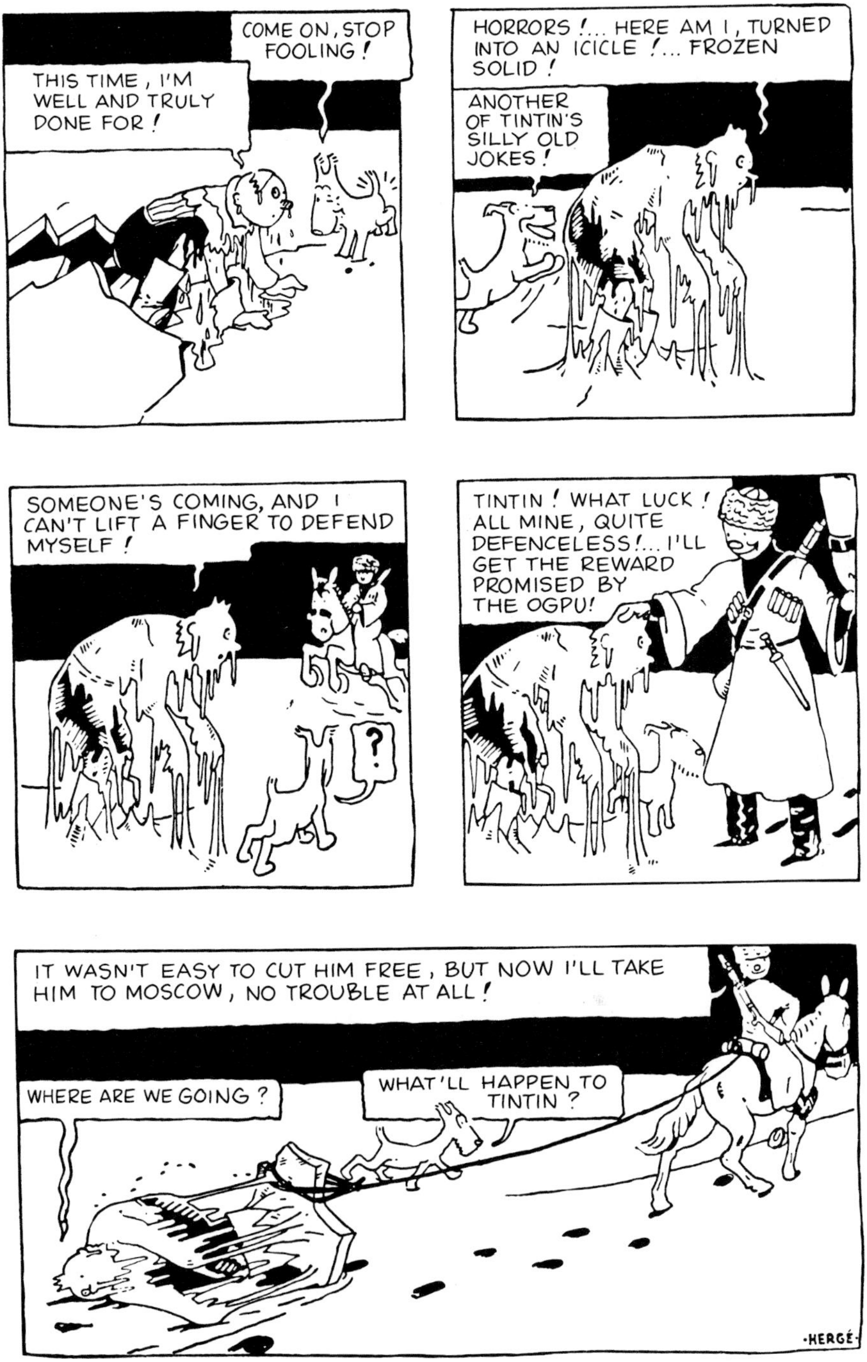
THIS TIME, I'M WELL AND TRULY DONE FOR!
COME ON, STOP FOOLING!
HORRORS!... HERE AM I, TURNED INTO AN ICICLE!... FROZEN SOLID!
ANOTHER OF TINTIN'S SILLY OLD JOKES!
SOMEONE'S COMING, AND I CAN'T LIFT A FINGER TO DEFEND MYSELF!
?
TINTIN! WHAT LUCK! ALL MINE, QUITE DEFENCELESS!... I'LL GET THE REWARD PROMISED BY THE OGPU!
IT WASN'T EASY TO CUT HIM FREE, BUT NOW I'LL TAKE HIM TO MOSCOW, NO TROUBLE AT ALL!
WHERE ARE WE GOING?
WHAT'LL HAPPEN TO TINTIN?
·HERGÉ·

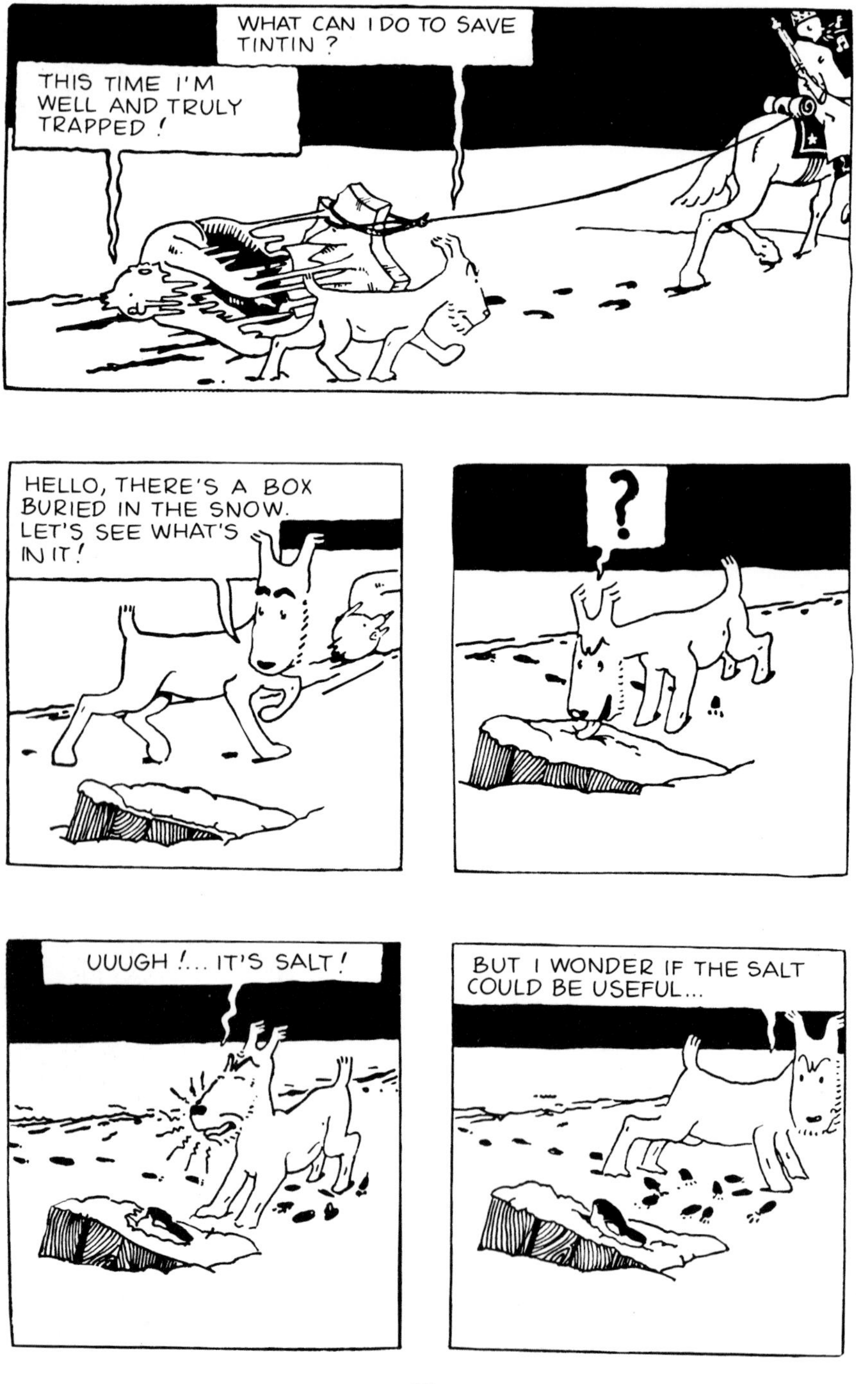
THIS TIME I'M WELL AND TRULY TRAPPED!
WHAT CAN I DO TO SAVE TINTIN?
HELLO, THERE'S A BOX BURIED IN THE SNOW. LET'S SEE WHAT'S IN IT!
?
UUUGH!... IT'S SALT!
BUT I WONDER IF THE SALT COULD BE USEFUL...

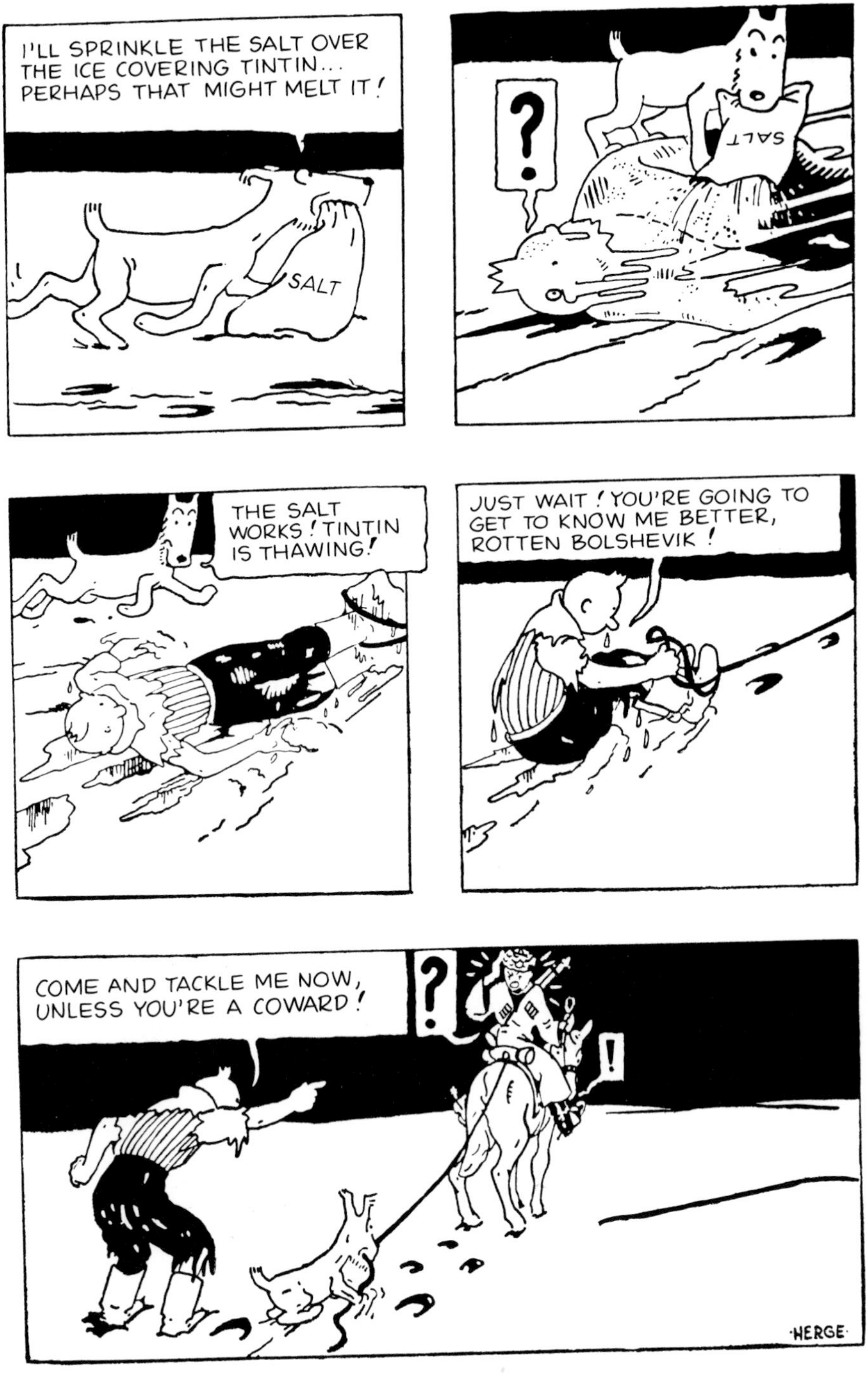
I'LL SPRINKLE THE SALT OVER THE ICE COVERING TINTIN... PERHAPS THAT MIGHT MELT IT!
SALT
?
SALT
THE SALT WORKS! TINTIN IS THAWING!
JUST WAIT! YOU'RE GOING TO GET TO KNOW ME BETTER, ROTTEN BOLSHEVIK!
COME AND TACKLE ME NOW, UNLESS YOU'RE A COWARD!
?
!
HERGE

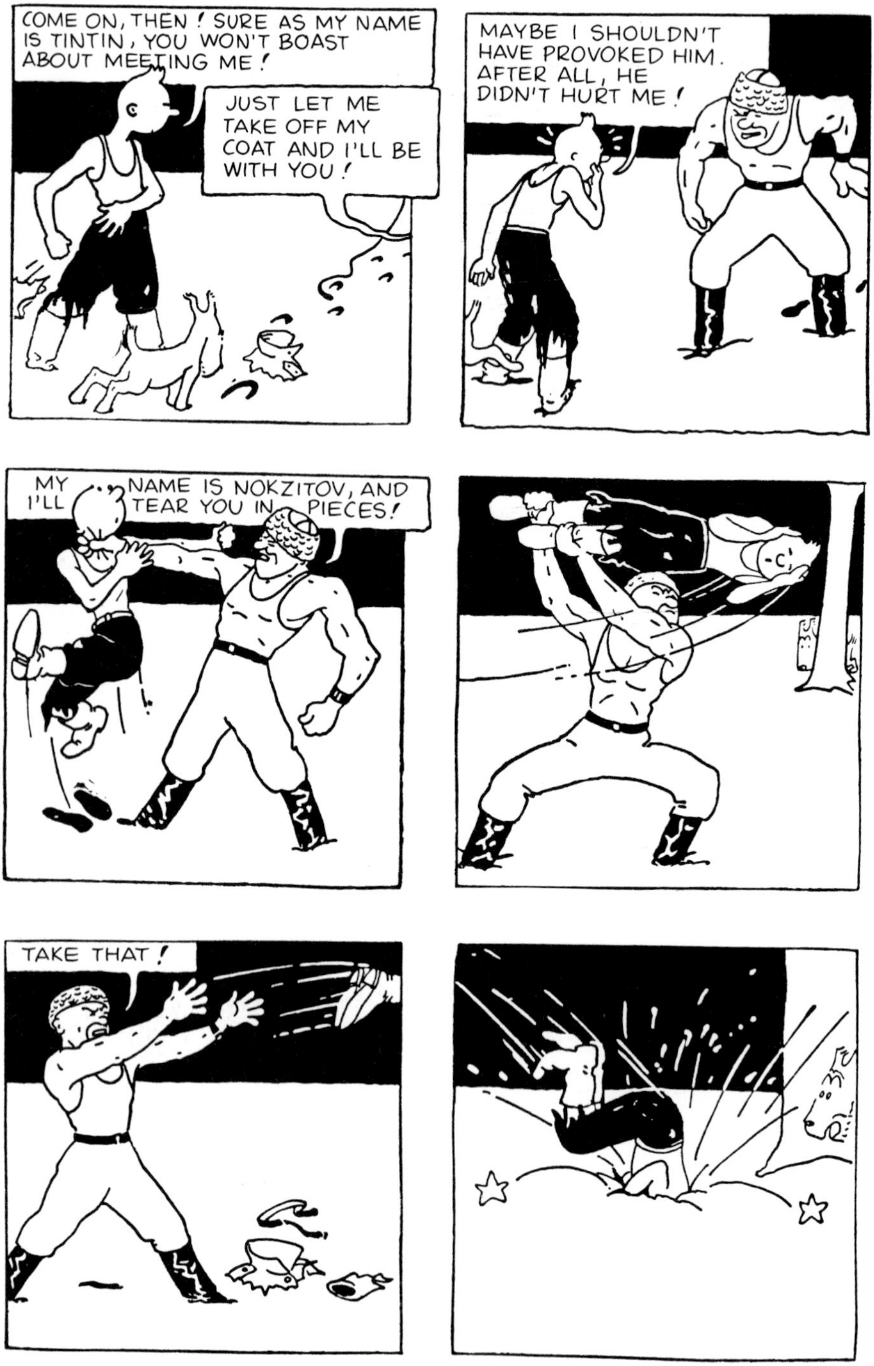
COME ON, THEN ! SURE AS MY NAME IS TINTIN, YOU WON'T BOAST ABOUT MEETING ME !
JUST LET ME TAKE OFF MY COAT AND I'LL BE WITH YOU !
MAYBE I SHOULDN'T HAVE PROVOKED HIM. AFTER ALL, HE DIDN'T HURT ME !
MY NAME IS NOKZITOV, AND I'LL TEAR YOU IN PIECES!
TAKE THAT !

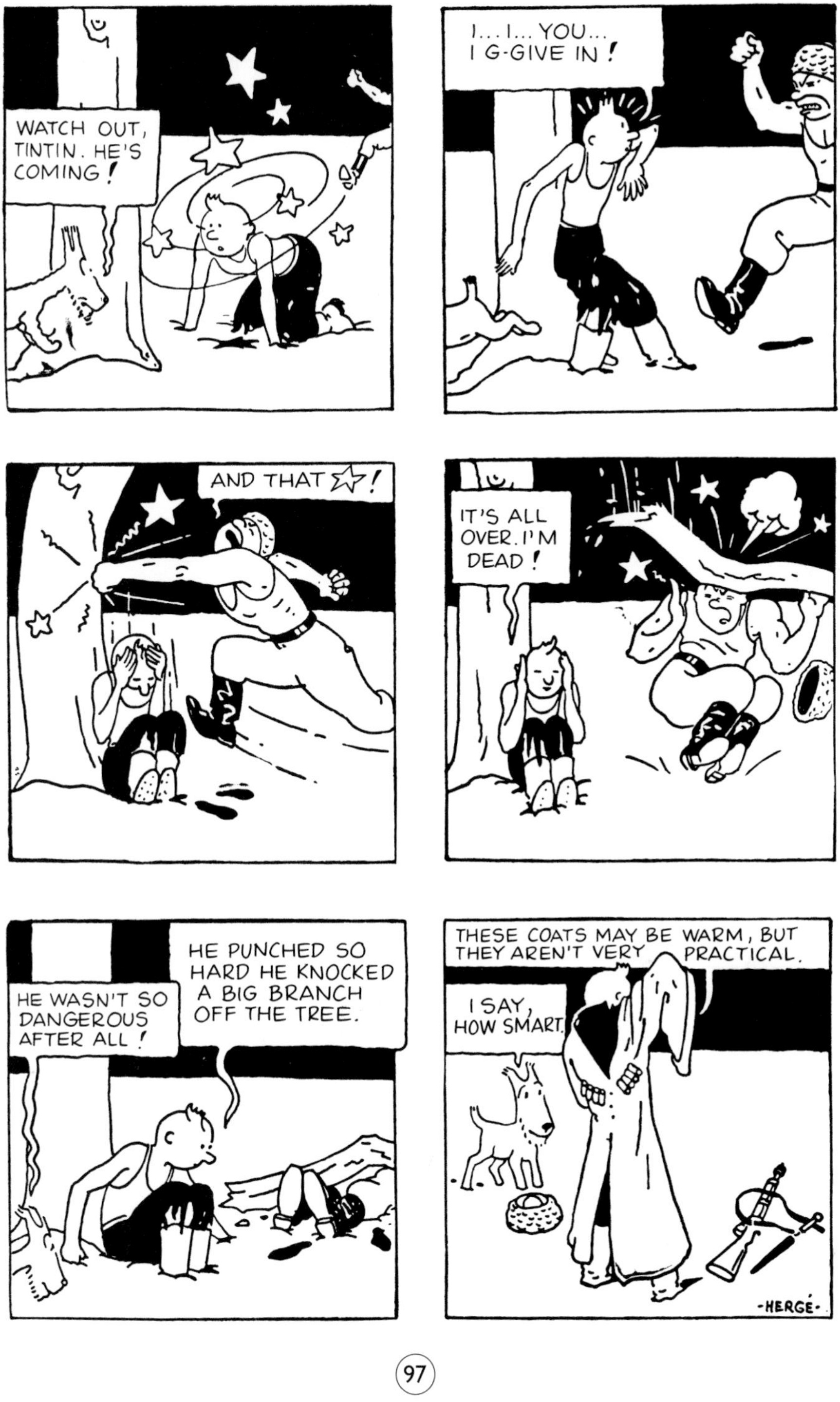
WATCH OUT, TINTIN. HE'S COMING!
I... I... YOU... I G-GIVE IN!
AND THAT ☆!
IT'S ALL OVER. I'M DEAD!
HE WASN'T SO DANGEROUS AFTER ALL!
HE PUNCHED SO HARD HE KNOCKED A BIG BRANCH OFF THE TREE.
THESE COATS MAY BE WARM, BUT THEY AREN'T VERY PRACTICAL.
I SAY, HOW SMART.
-HERGÉ-

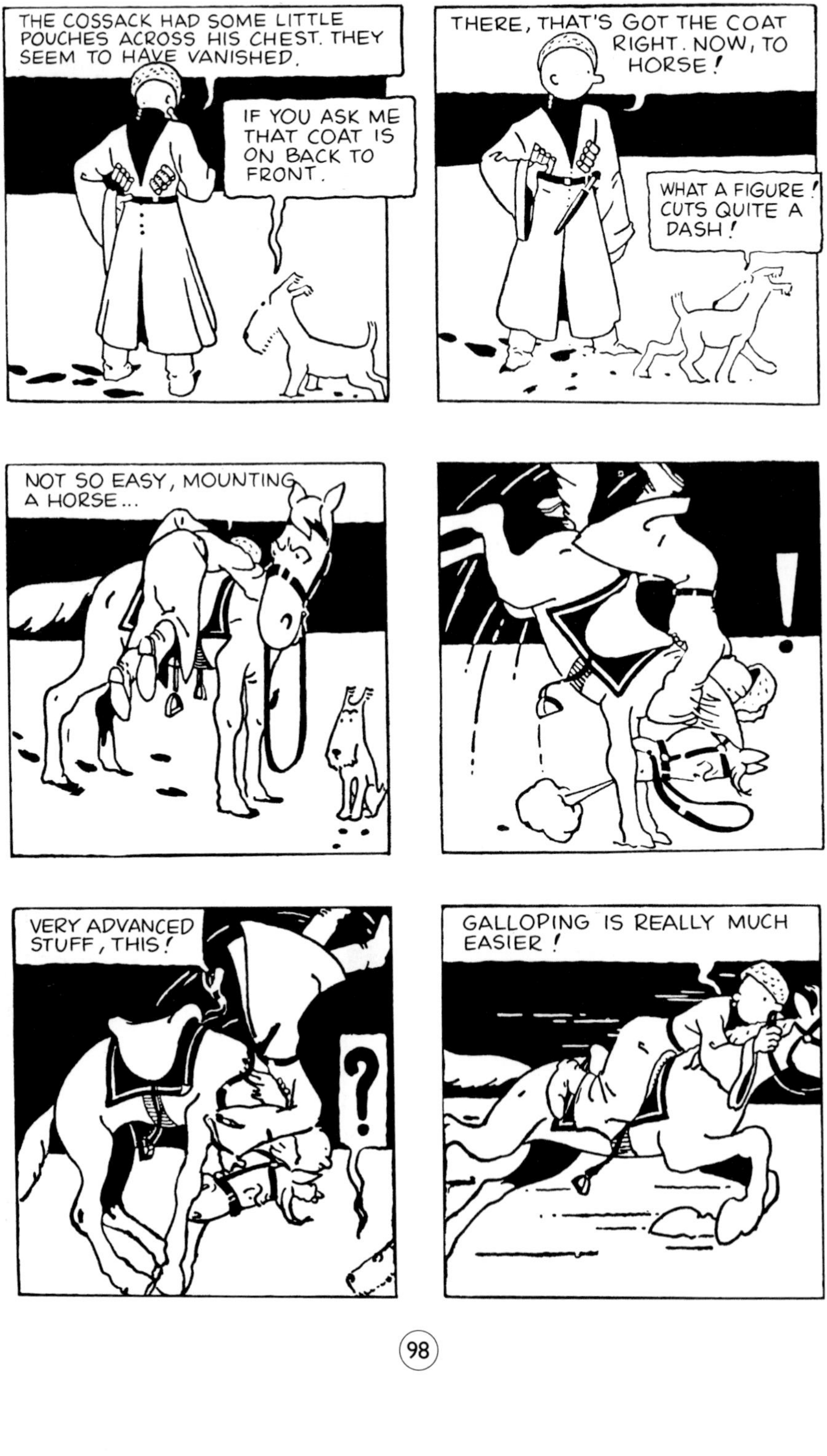
THE COSSACK HAD SOME LITTLE POUCHES ACROSS HIS CHEST. THEY SEEM TO HAVE VANISHED.
IF YOU ASK ME THAT COAT IS ON BACK TO FRONT.
THERE, THAT'S GOT THE COAT RIGHT. NOW, TO HORSE!
WHAT A FIGURE! CUTS QUITE A DASH!
NOT SO EASY, MOUNTING A HORSE...
!
VERY ADVANCED STUFF, THIS!
?
GALLOPING IS REALLY MUCH EASIER!

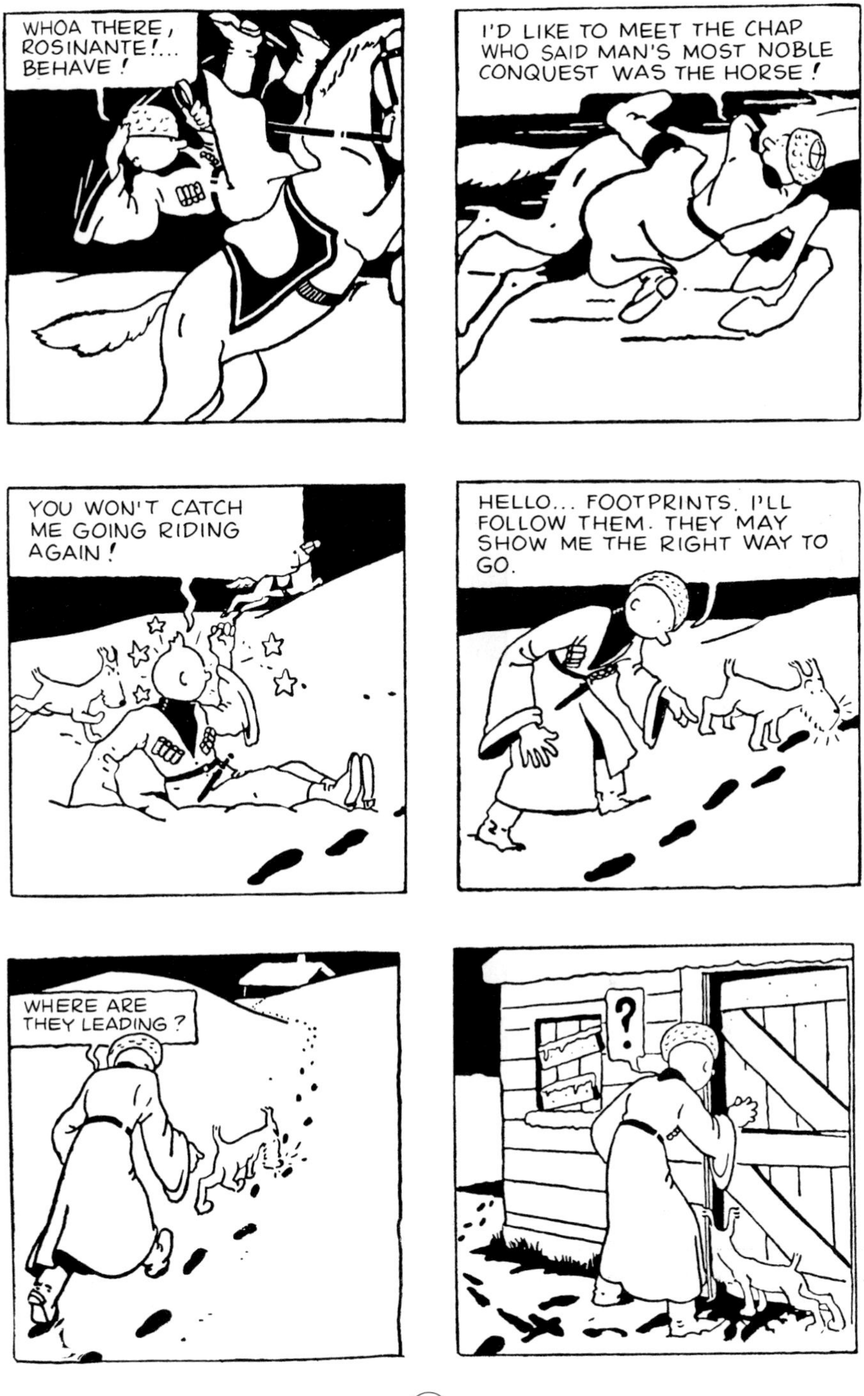
WHOA THERE, ROSINANTE!... BEHAVE!
I'D LIKE TO MEET THE CHAP WHO SAID MAN'S MOST NOBLE CONQUEST WAS THE HORSE!
YOU WON'T CATCH ME GOING RIDING AGAIN!
HELLO... FOOTPRINTS. I'LL FOLLOW THEM. THEY MAY SHOW ME THE RIGHT WAY TO GO.
WHERE ARE THEY LEADING?
?

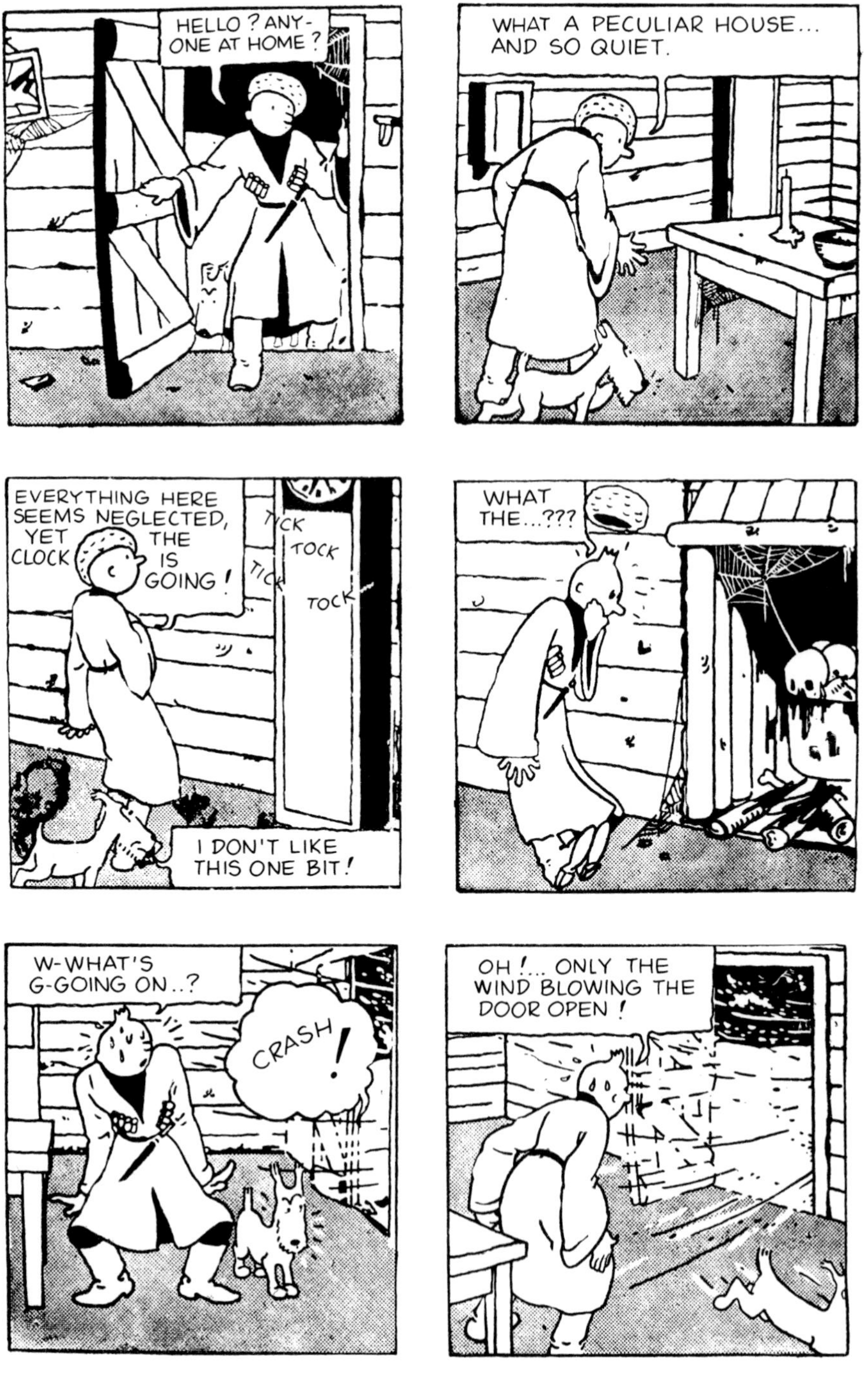
HELLO? ANY-ONE AT HOME?
WHAT A PECULIAR HOUSE... AND SO QUIET.
EVERYTHING HERE SEEMS NEGLECTED, YET THE CLOCK IS GOING!
TICK TOCK TICK TOCK
I DON'T LIKE THIS ONE BIT!
WHAT THE...???
W-WHAT'S G-GOING ON..?
CRASH!
OH!... ONLY THE WIND BLOWING THE DOOR OPEN!

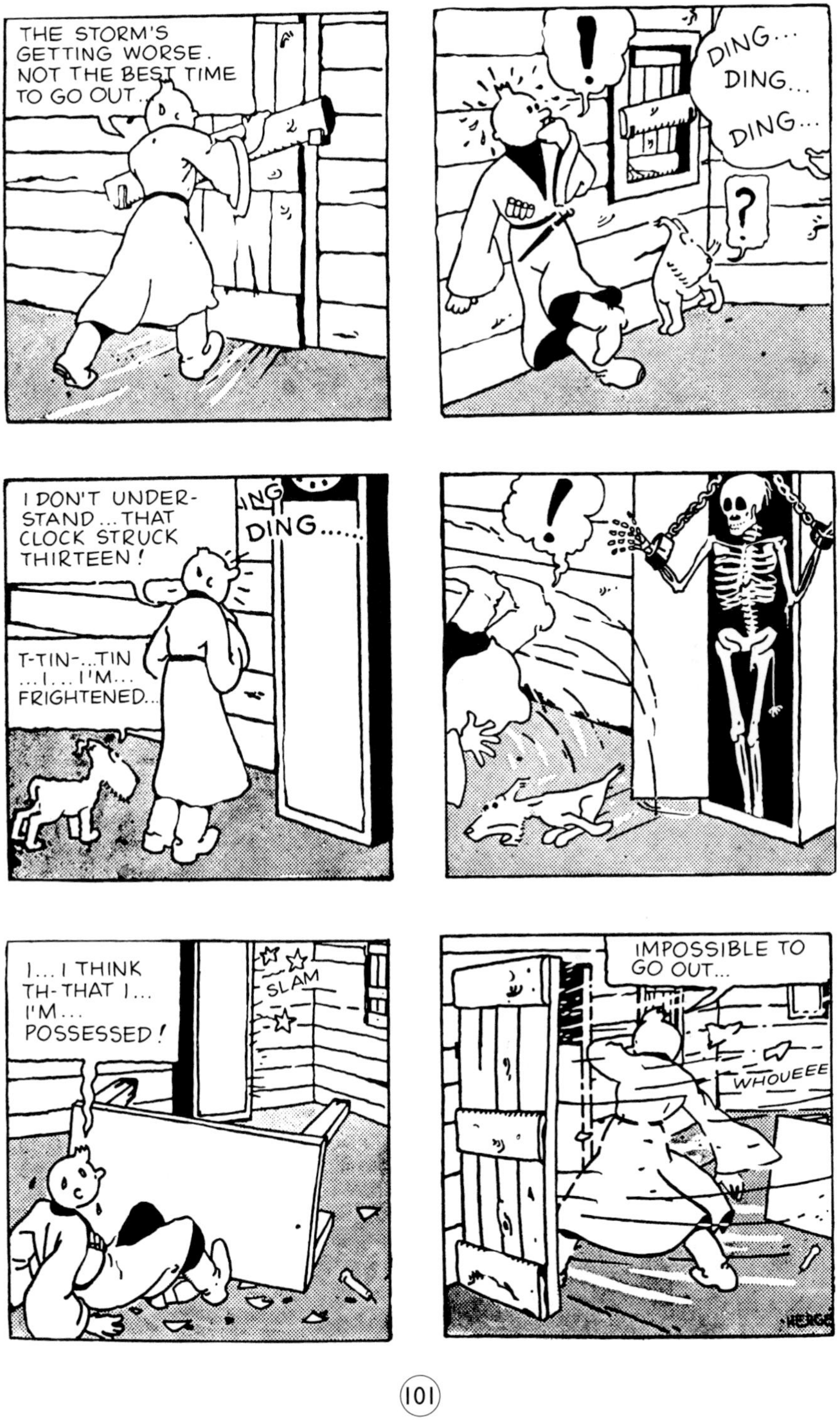

THE STORM'S GETTING WORSE. NOT THE BEST TIME TO GO OUT...
!
DING... DING... DING...
?
I DON'T UNDERSTAND... THAT CLOCK STRUCK THIRTEEN!
DING......
T-TIN-...TIN ...I... I'M... FRIGHTENED...
!
I... I THINK TH-THAT I... I'M... POSSESSED!
SLAM
IMPOSSIBLE TO GO OUT...
WHOUEEE
HERGÉ

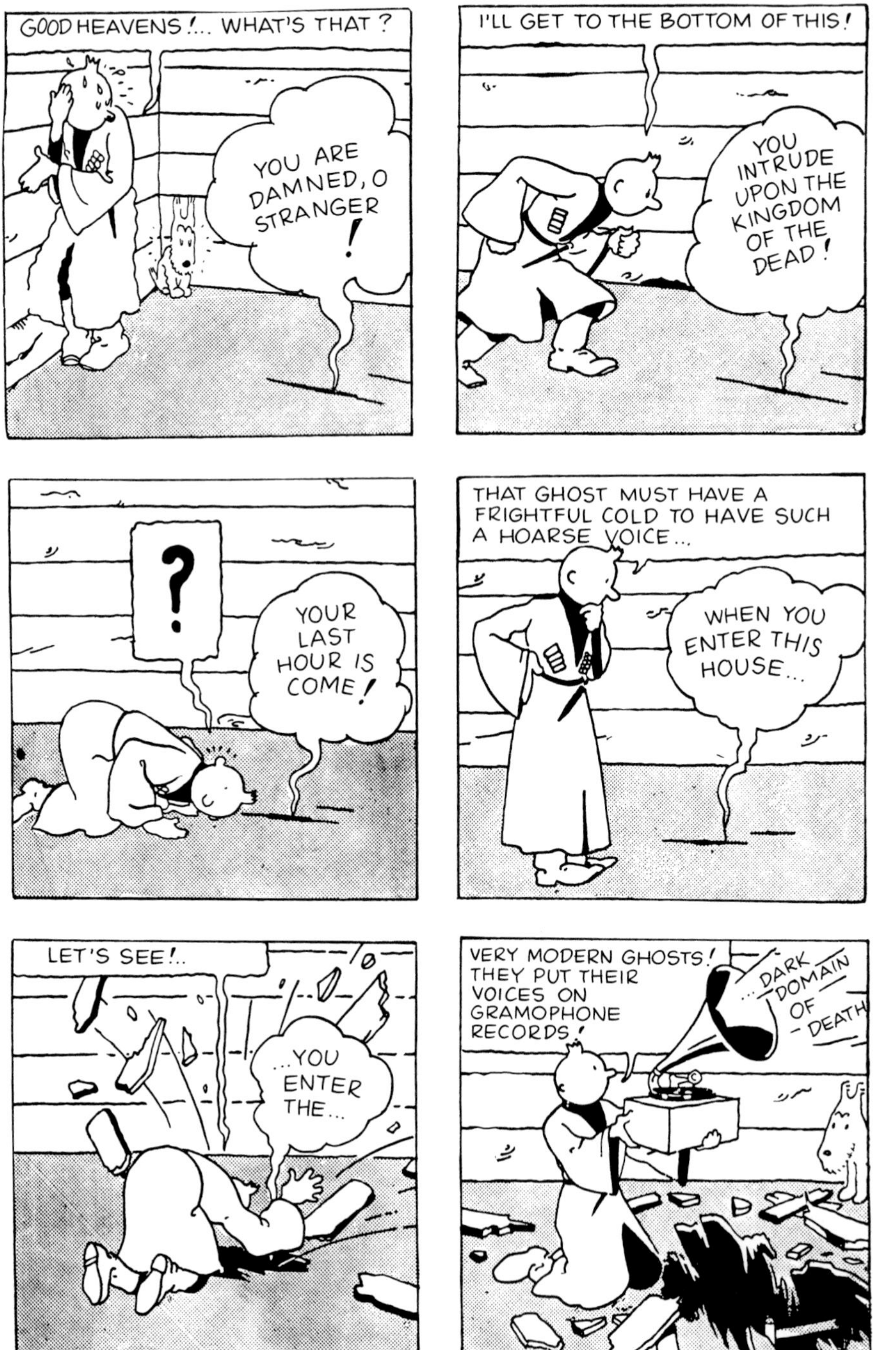
GOOD HEAVENS!... WHAT'S THAT?
YOU ARE DAMNED, O STRANGER!
I'LL GET TO THE BOTTOM OF THIS!
YOU INTRUDE UPON THE KINGDOM OF THE DEAD!
?
YOUR LAST HOUR IS COME!
THAT GHOST MUST HAVE A FRIGHTFUL COLD TO HAVE SUCH A HOARSE VOICE...
WHEN YOU ENTER THIS HOUSE...
LET'S SEE!..
...YOU ENTER THE...
VERY MODERN GHOSTS! THEY PUT THEIR VOICES ON GRAMOPHONE RECORDS!
...DARK DOMAIN OF DEATH

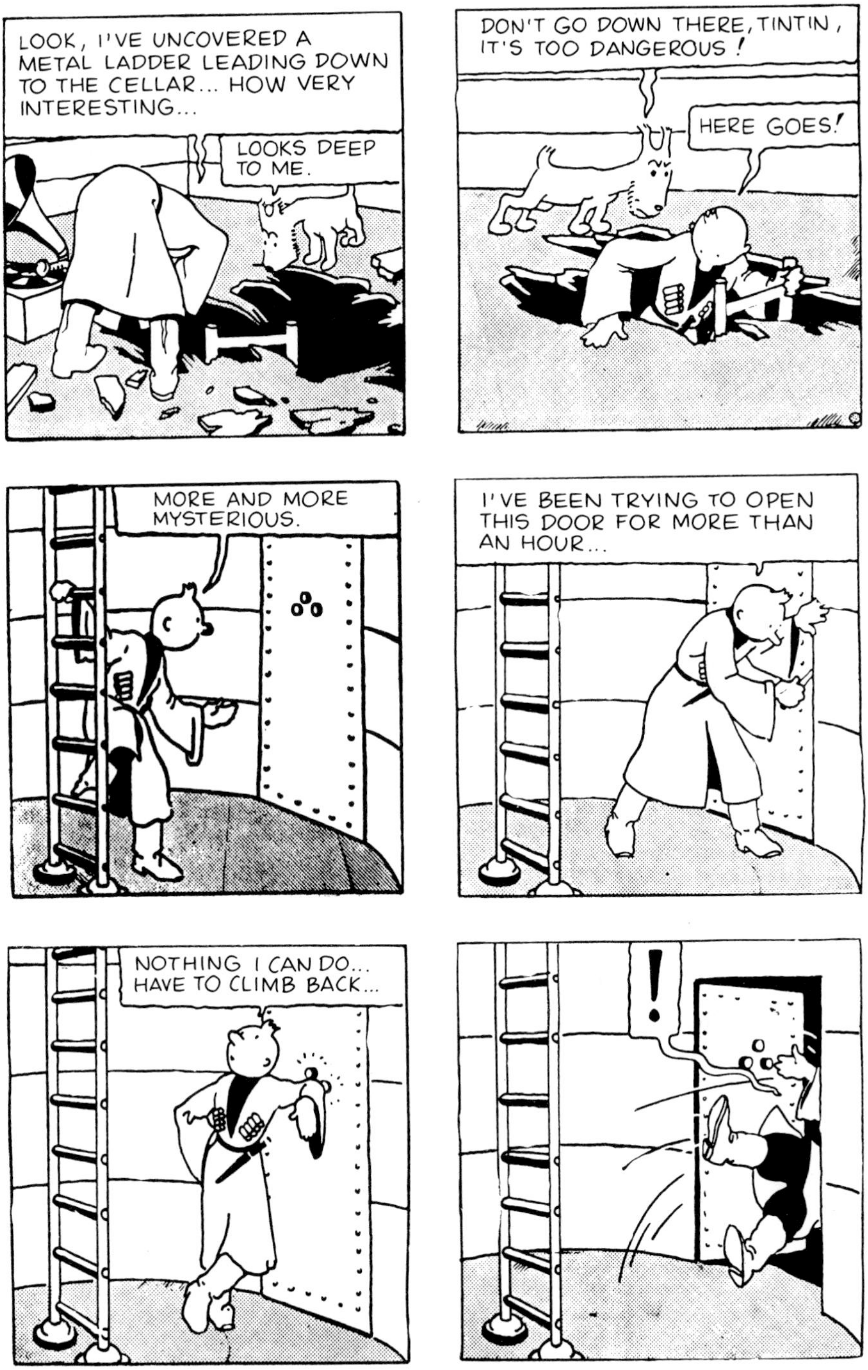
LOOK, I'VE UNCOVERED A METAL LADDER LEADING DOWN TO THE CELLAR... HOW VERY INTERESTING...
LOOKS DEEP TO ME.
DON'T GO DOWN THERE, TINTIN, IT'S TOO DANGEROUS!
HERE GOES!
MORE AND MORE MYSTERIOUS.
I'VE BEEN TRYING TO OPEN THIS DOOR FOR MORE THAN AN HOUR...
NOTHING I CAN DO... HAVE TO CLIMB BACK...
!

TAKE HIM TO OUR LEADER!

TIE HIM SECURELY, AND LEAVE US. I WANT TO TALK TO HIM.

WHERE AM I?

YOU'RE IN THE HIDEOUT WHERE LENIN, TROTSKY AND STALIN HAVE COLLECTED TOGETHER WEALTH STOLEN FROM THE PEOPLE! ALL AROUND THIS PLACE ARE IMMENSE, EMPTY STEPPES, ALMOST IMPASSABLE. BUT IF BY CHANCE A PEASANT WANDERED INTO THE HAUNTED ROOM WHICH COVERS THE ENTRANCE TO OUR VAULTS, HE'D BE FAR TOO SCARED TO PURSUE HIS INVESTIGATIONS.

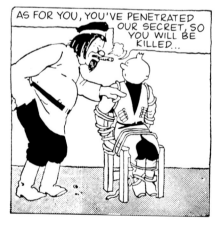

AS FOR YOU, YOU'VE PENETRATED OUR SECRET, SO YOU WILL BE KILLED...

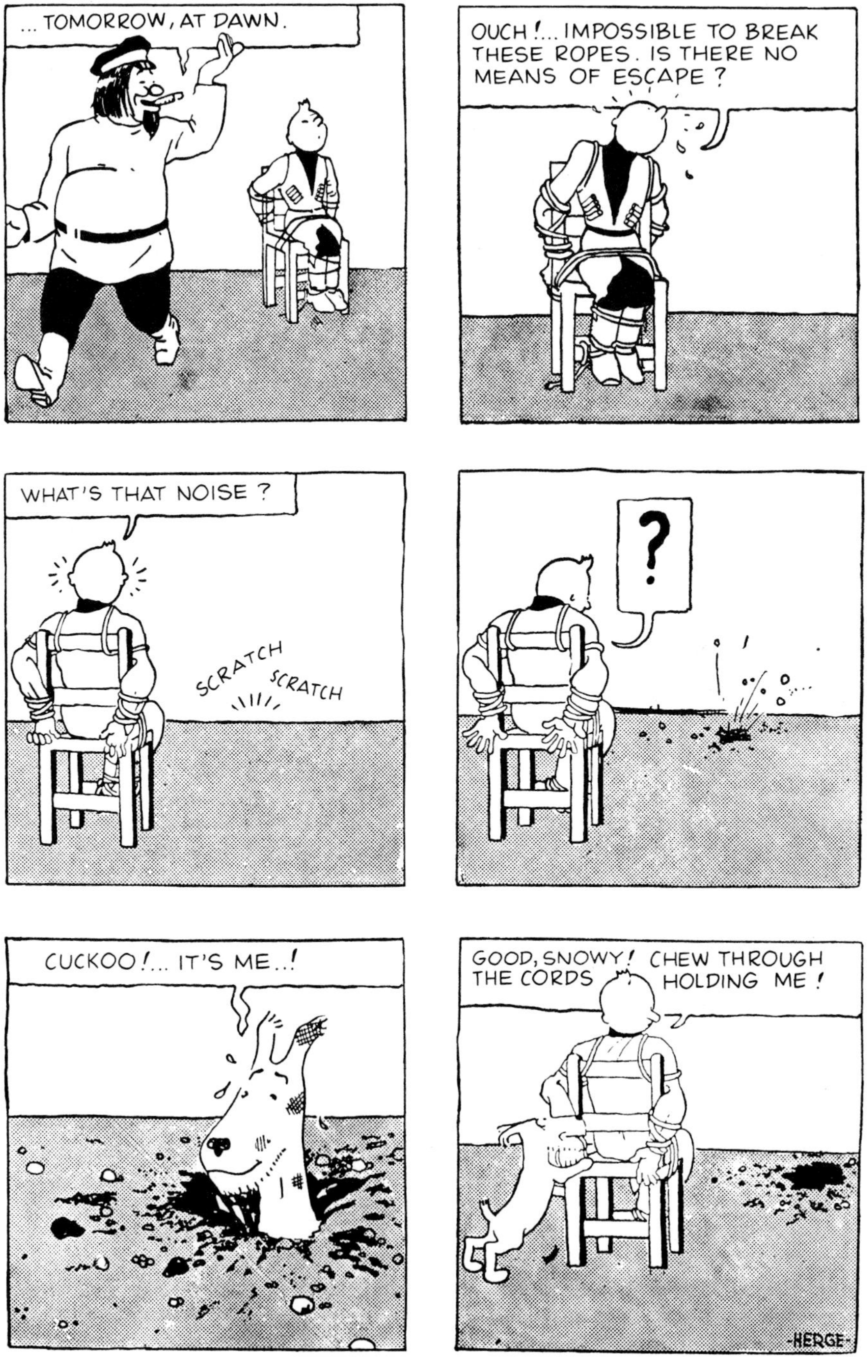

... TOMORROW, AT DAWN.
OUCH!... IMPOSSIBLE TO BREAK THESE ROPES. IS THERE NO MEANS OF ESCAPE?
WHAT'S THAT NOISE?
SCRATCH SCRATCH
?
CUCKOO!... IT'S ME..!
GOOD, SNOWY! CHEW THROUGH THE CORDS HOLDING ME!
HERGE

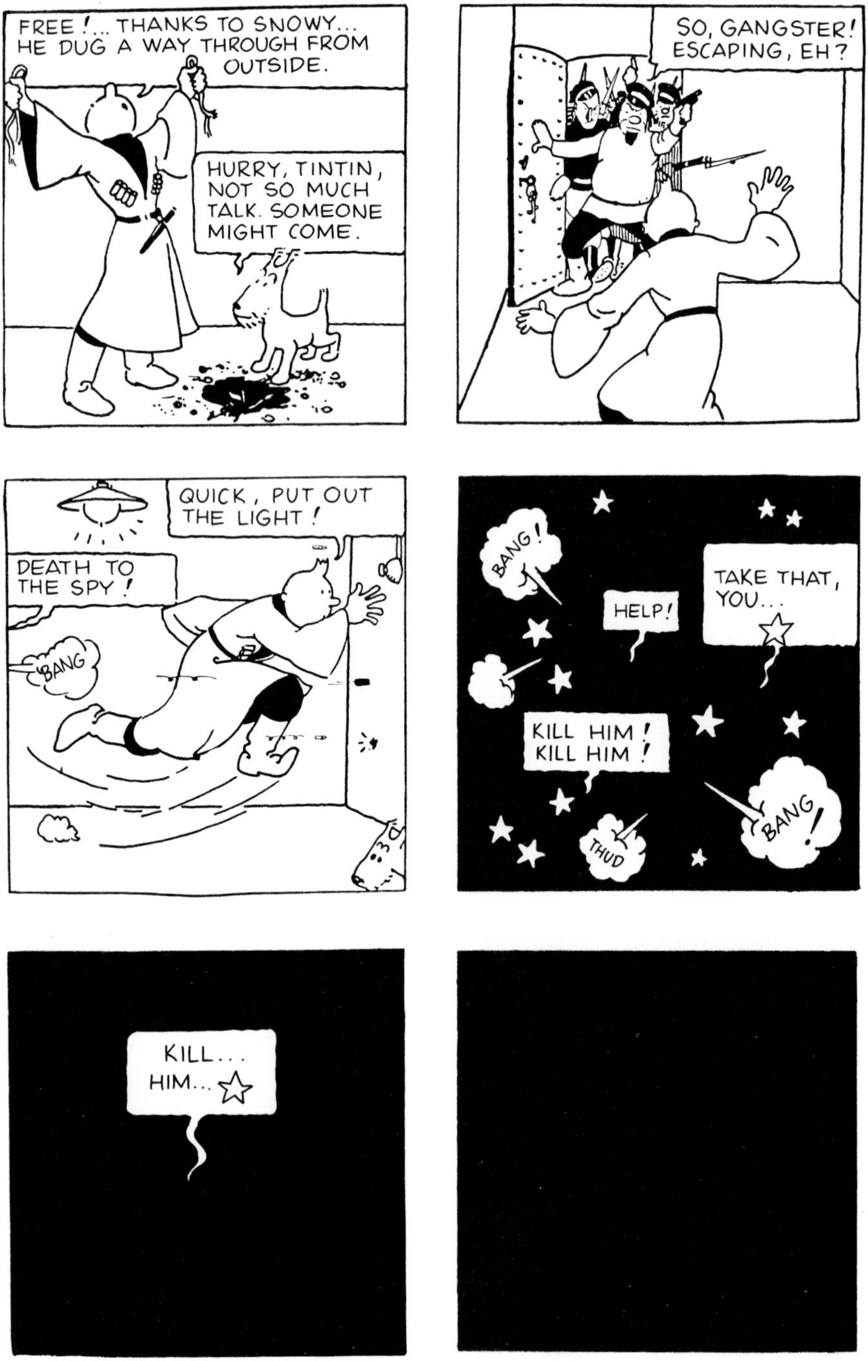
FREE !... THANKS TO SNOWY... HE DUG A WAY THROUGH FROM OUTSIDE.
HURRY, TINTIN, NOT SO MUCH TALK. SOMEONE MIGHT COME.
SO, GANGSTER! ESCAPING, EH?
QUICK, PUT OUT THE LIGHT!
DEATH TO THE SPY!
BANG
BANG!
HELP!
TAKE THAT, YOU...
KILL HIM! KILL HIM!
THUD
BANG!
KILL... HIM...

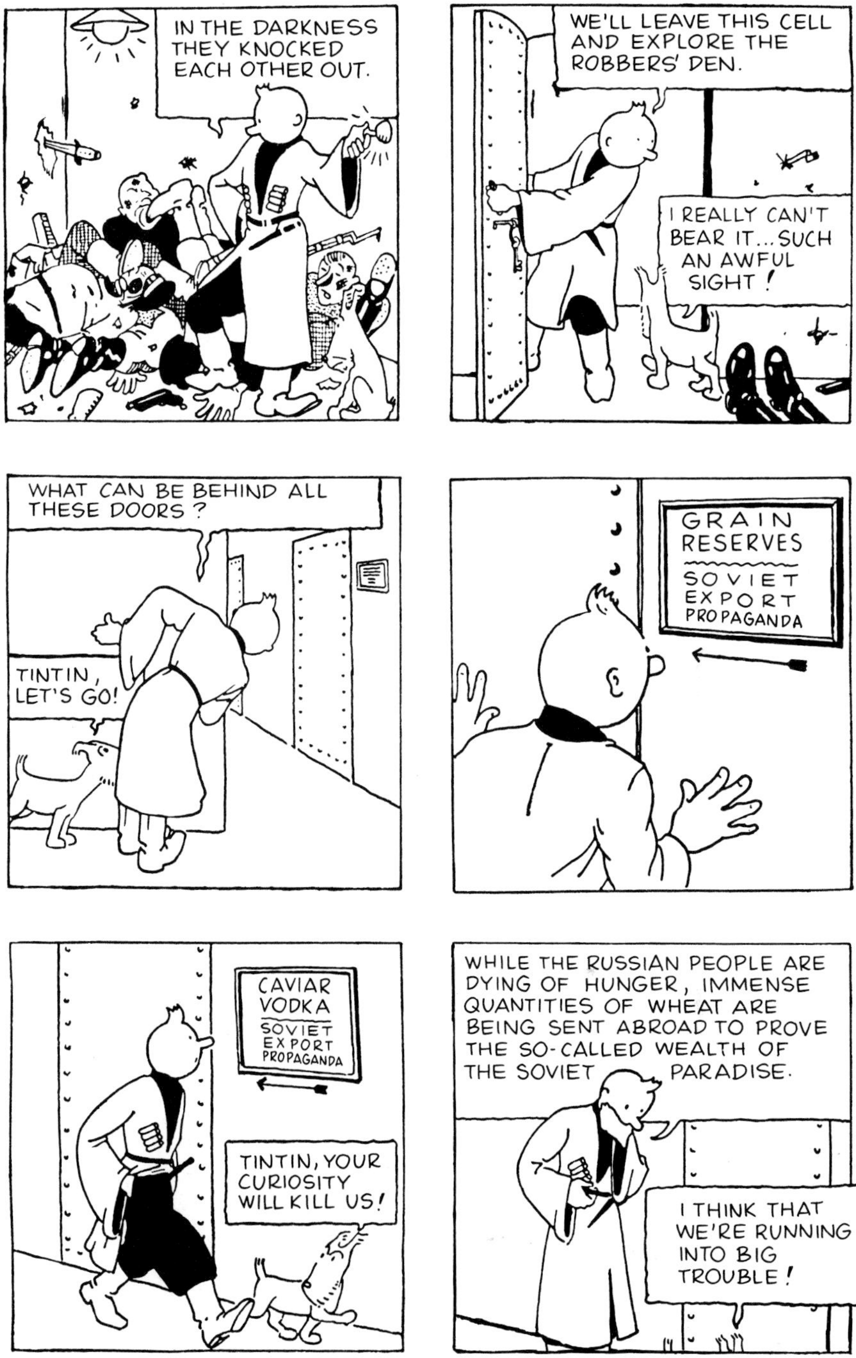
IN THE DARKNESS THEY KNOCKED EACH OTHER OUT.
WE'LL LEAVE THIS CELL AND EXPLORE THE ROBBERS' DEN.
I REALLY CAN'T BEAR IT... SUCH AN AWFUL SIGHT!
WHAT CAN BE BEHIND ALL THESE DOORS?
TINTIN, LET'S GO!
GRAIN RESERVES
SOVIET EXPORT PROPAGANDA
CAVIAR VODKA
SOVIET EXPORT PROPAGANDA
TINTIN, YOUR CURIOSITY WILL KILL US!
WHILE THE RUSSIAN PEOPLE ARE DYING OF HUNGER, IMMENSE QUANTITIES OF WHEAT ARE BEING SENT ABROAD TO PROVE THE SO-CALLED WEALTH OF THE SOVIET PARADISE.
I THINK THAT WE'RE RUNNING INTO BIG TROUBLE!

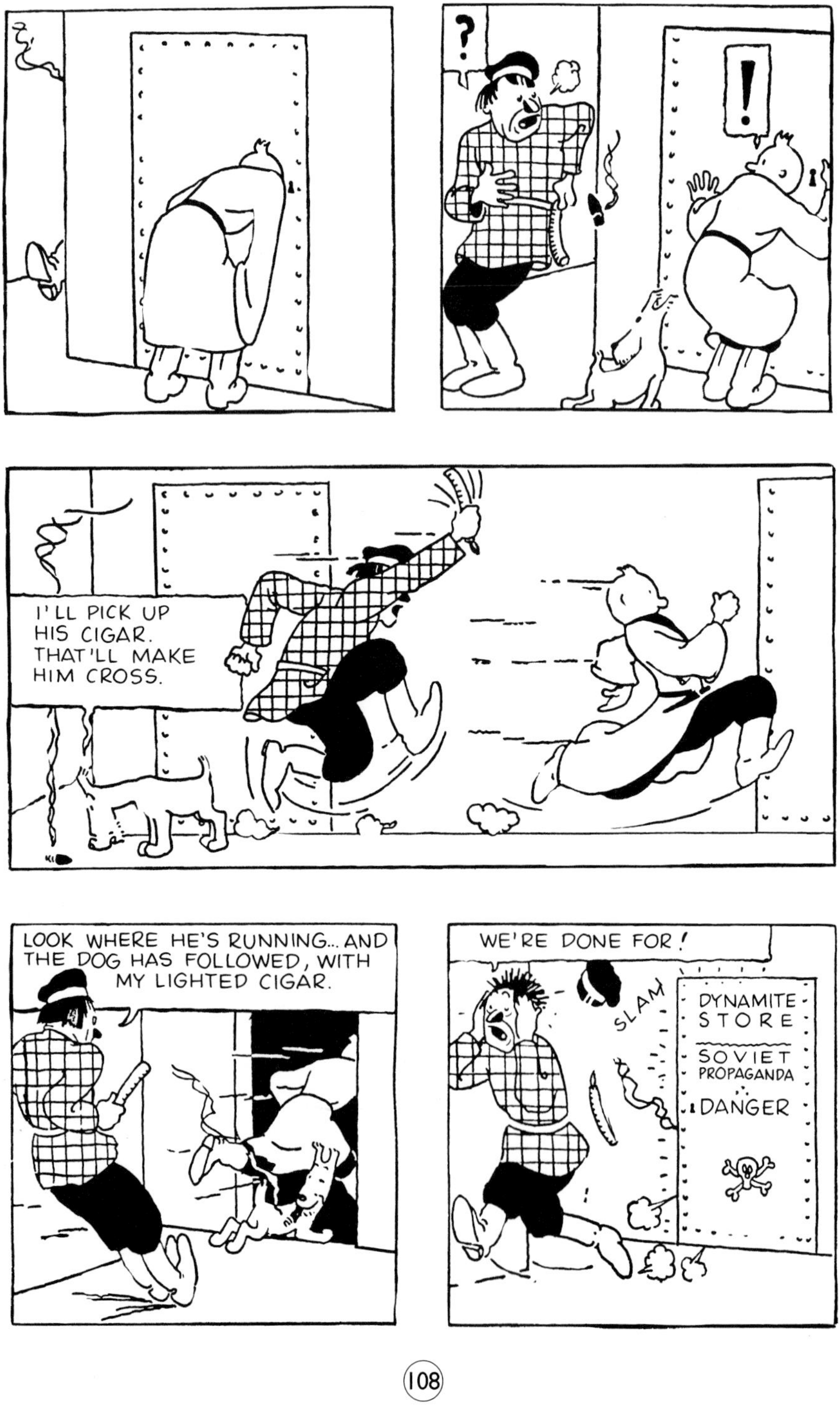
?
!
I'LL PICK UP HIS CIGAR. THAT'LL MAKE HIM CROSS.
LOOK WHERE HE'S RUNNING... AND THE DOG HAS FOLLOWED, WITH MY LIGHTED CIGAR.
WE'RE DONE FOR!
SLAM
DYNAMITE STORE
SOVIET PROPAGANDA
DANGER

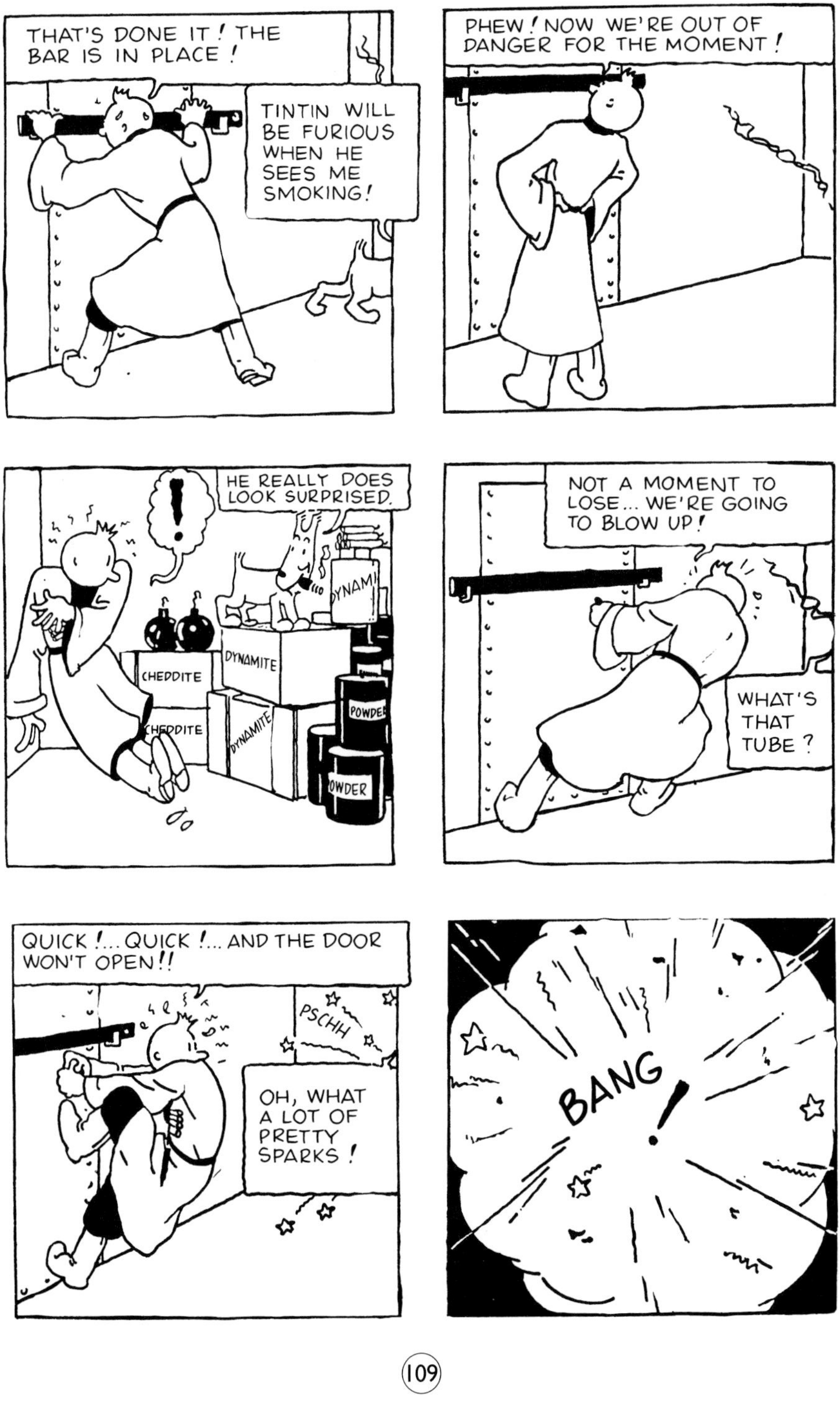
THAT'S DONE IT! THE BAR IS IN PLACE!
TINTIN WILL BE FURIOUS WHEN HE SEES ME SMOKING!
PHEW! NOW WE'RE OUT OF DANGER FOR THE MOMENT!
!
HE REALLY DOES LOOK SURPRISED.
CHEDDITE
CHEDDITE
DYNAMITE
DYNAMITE
POWDER
POWDER
NOT A MOMENT TO LOSE... WE'RE GOING TO BLOW UP!
WHAT'S THAT TUBE?
QUICK!... QUICK!... AND THE DOOR WON'T OPEN!!
PSCHH
OH, WHAT A LOT OF PRETTY SPARKS!
BANG!

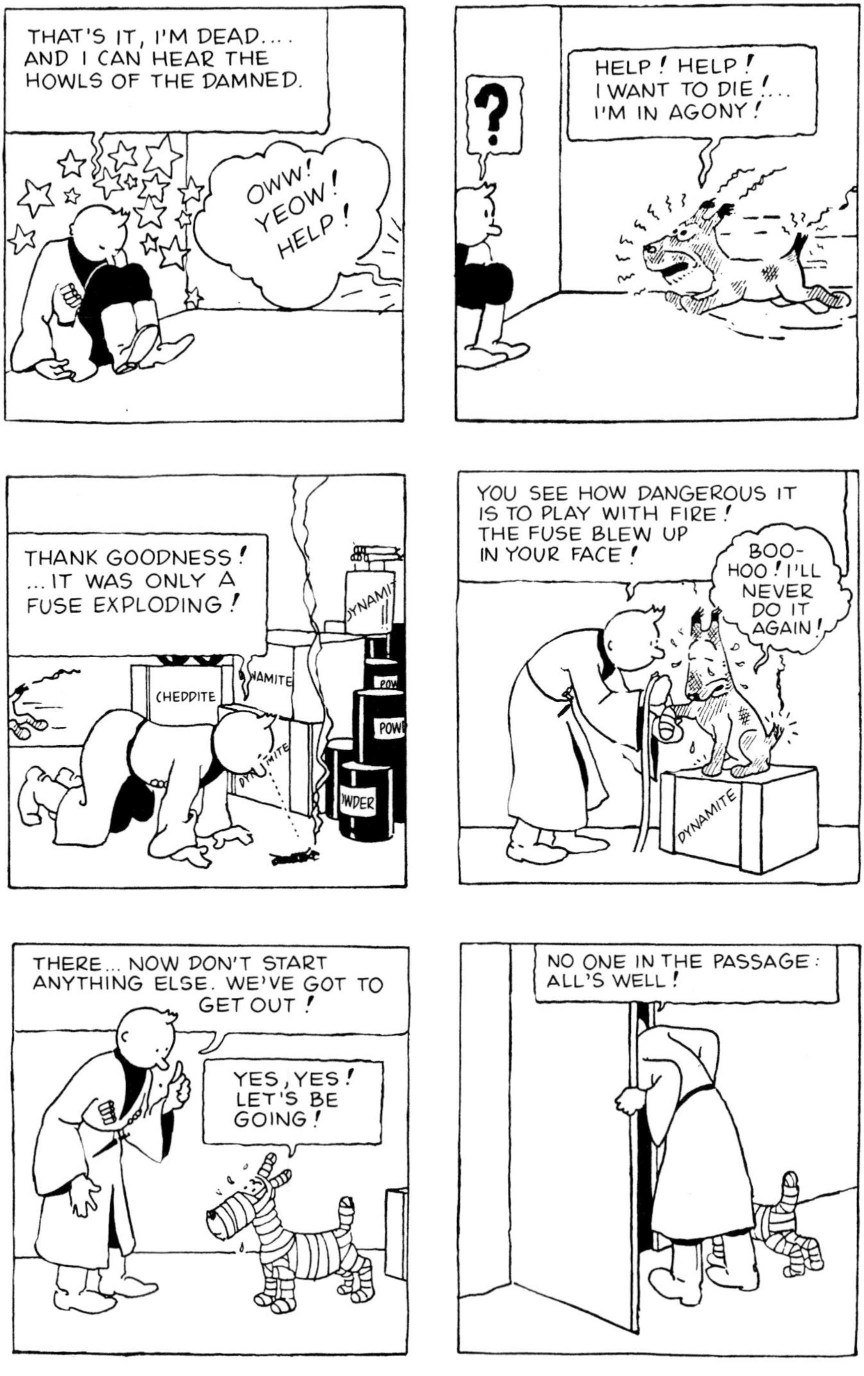
THAT'S IT, I'M DEAD.... AND I CAN HEAR THE HOWLS OF THE DAMNED.
OWW! YEOW! HELP!
?
HELP! HELP! I WANT TO DIE!... I'M IN AGONY!
THANK GOODNESS! ... IT WAS ONLY A FUSE EXPLODING!
CHEDDITE
YOU SEE HOW DANGEROUS IT IS TO PLAY WITH FIRE! THE FUSE BLEW UP IN YOUR FACE!
BOO-HOO! I'LL NEVER DO IT AGAIN!
DYNAMITE
THERE... NOW DON'T START ANYTHING ELSE. WE'VE GOT TO GET OUT!
YES, YES! LET'S BE GOING!
NO ONE IN THE PASSAGE: ALL'S WELL!

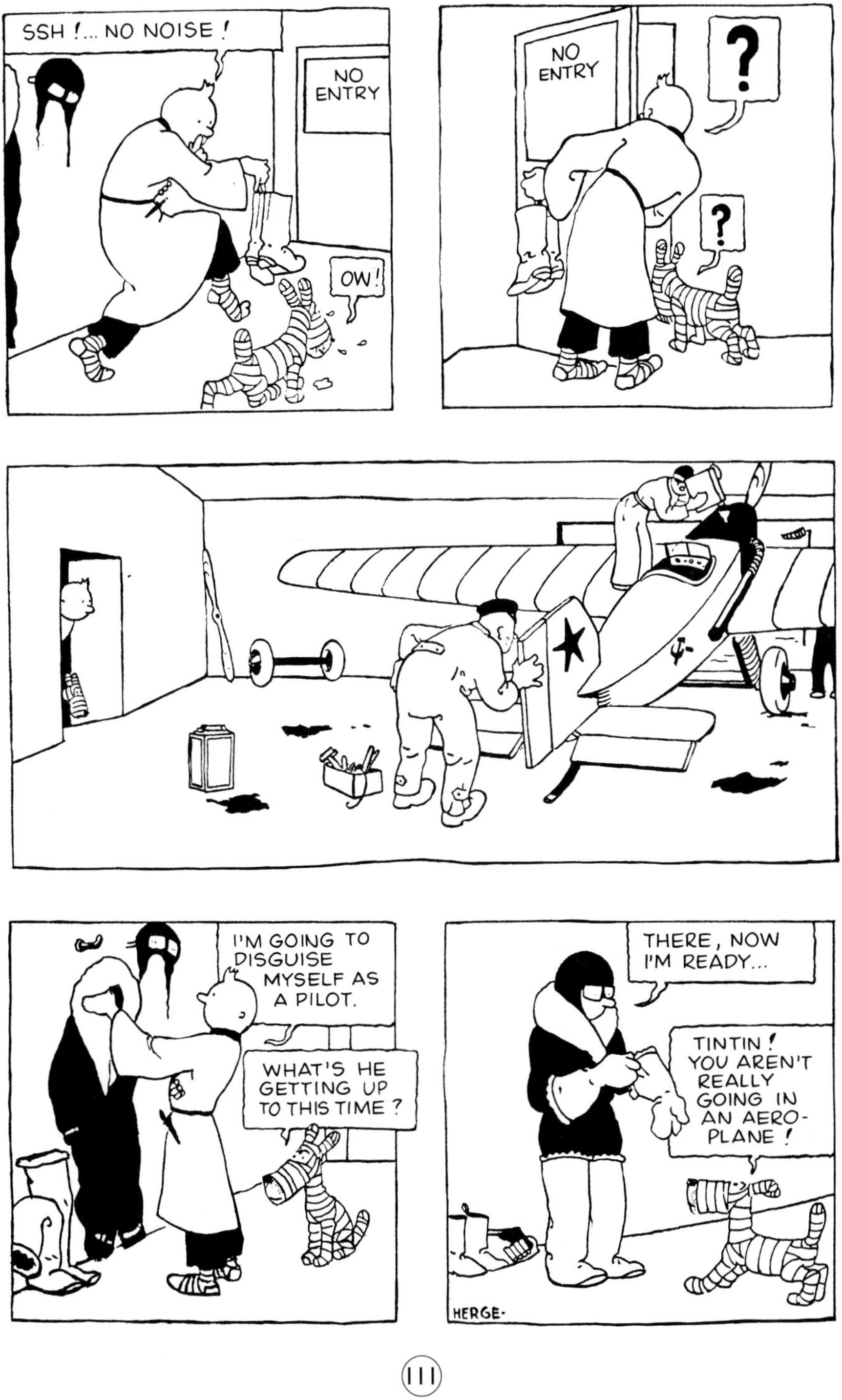
SSH !... NO NOISE !
NO ENTRY
OW !
NO ENTRY
?
?
I'M GOING TO DISGUISE MYSELF AS A PILOT.
WHAT'S HE GETTING UP TO THIS TIME ?
THERE, NOW I'M READY...
TINTIN ! YOU AREN'T REALLY GOING IN AN AERO-PLANE !
HERGE

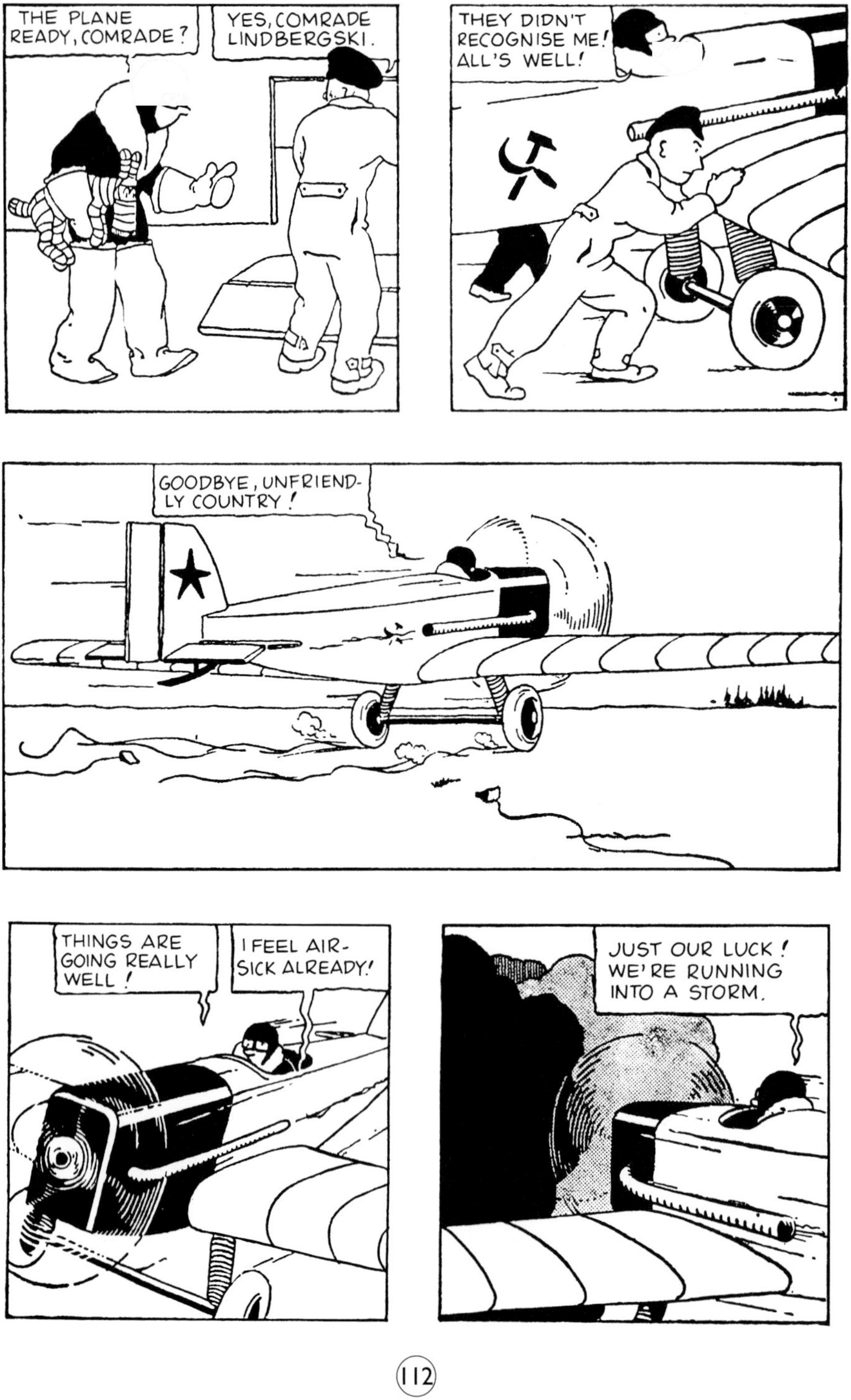
THE PLANE READY, COMRADE?
YES, COMRADE LINDBERGSKI.
THEY DIDN'T RECOGNISE ME! ALL'S WELL!
GOODBYE, UNFRIENDLY COUNTRY!
THINGS ARE GOING REALLY WELL!
I FEEL AIR-SICK ALREADY!
JUST OUR LUCK! WE'RE RUNNING INTO A STORM.

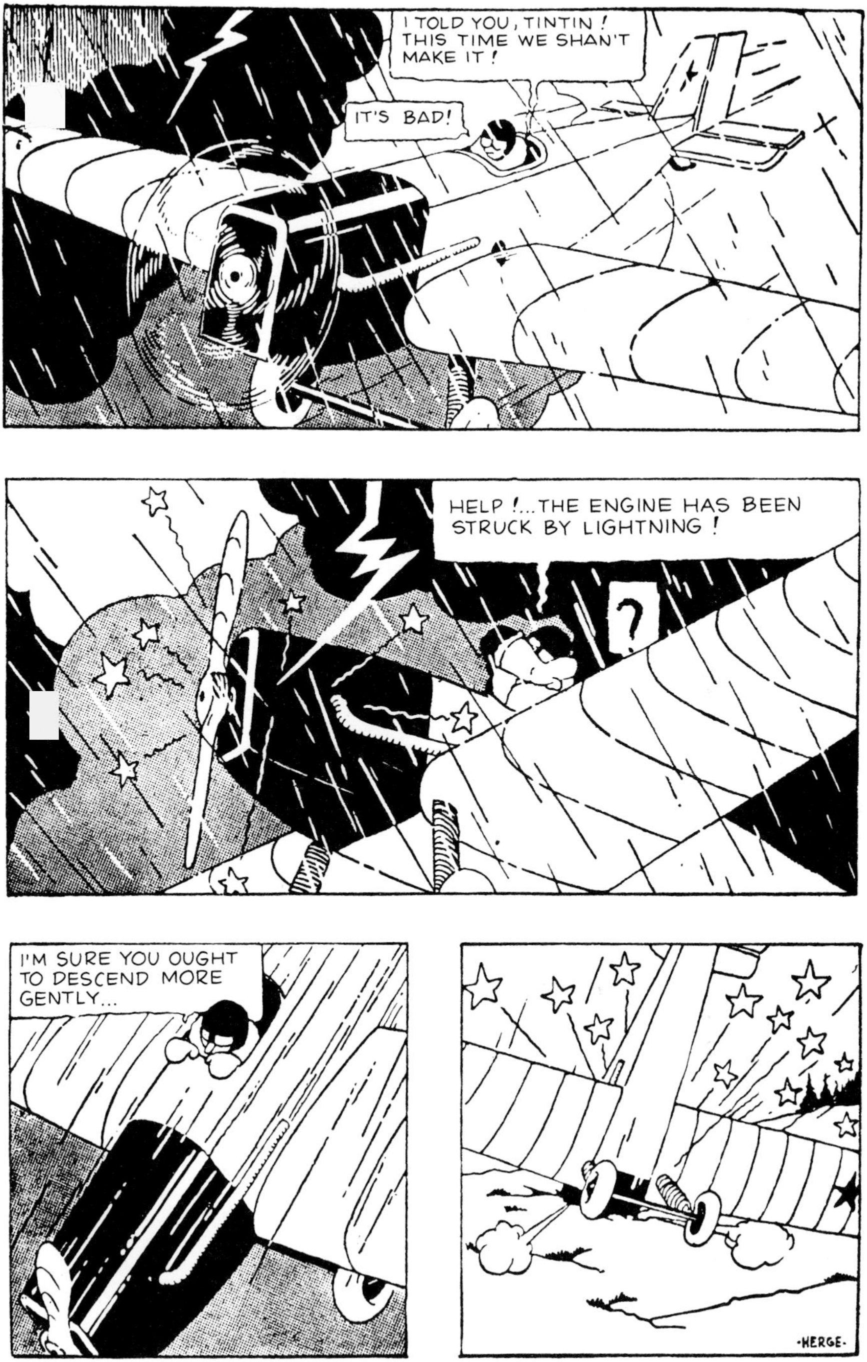
I TOLD YOU, TINTIN! THIS TIME WE SHAN'T MAKE IT!
IT'S BAD!
HELP!... THE ENGINE HAS BEEN STRUCK BY LIGHTNING!
?
I'M SURE YOU OUGHT TO DESCEND MORE GENTLY...
-HERGE-

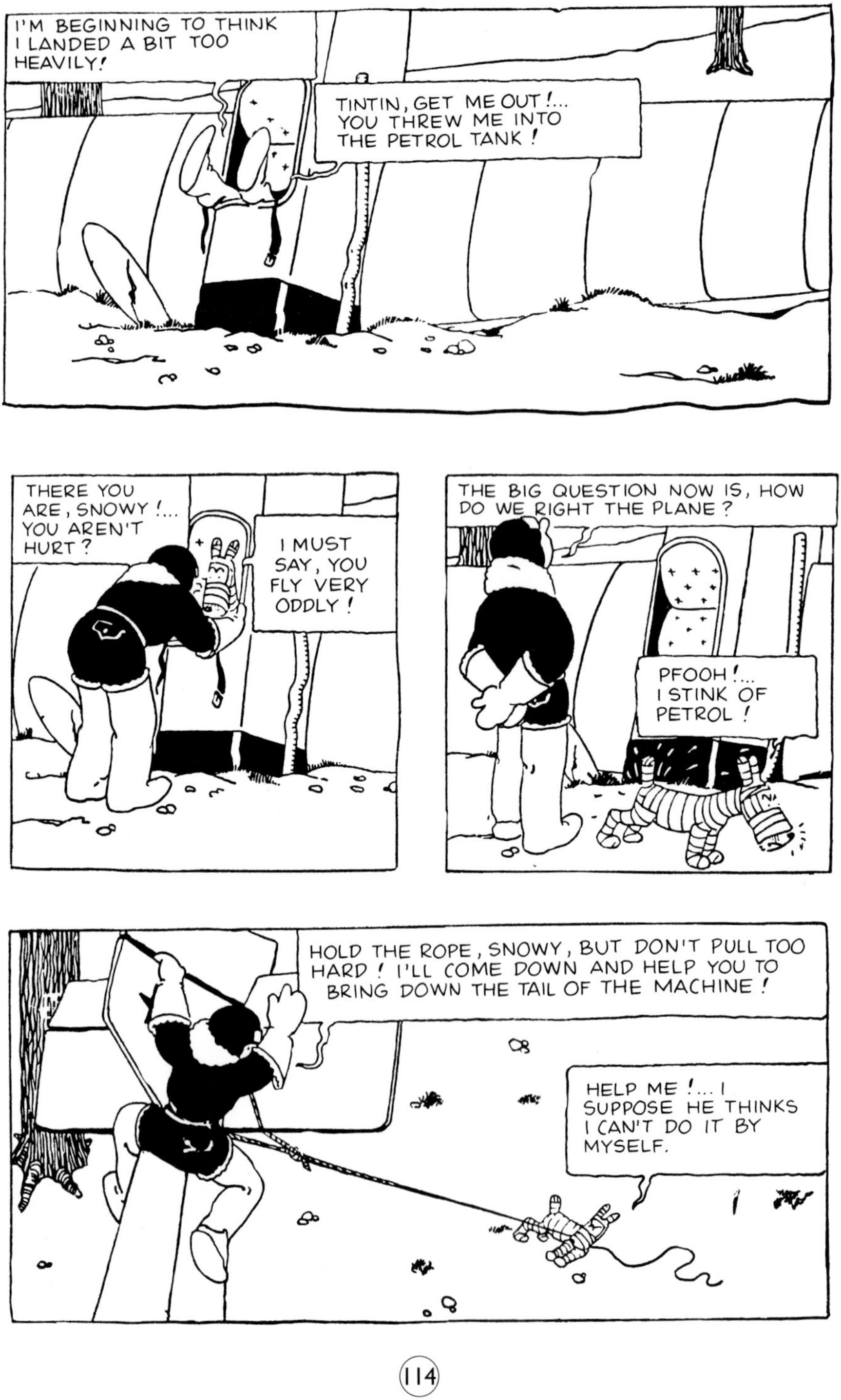

I'M BEGINNING TO THINK I LANDED A BIT TOO HEAVILY!
TINTIN, GET ME OUT!... YOU THREW ME INTO THE PETROL TANK!
THERE YOU ARE, SNOWY!... YOU AREN'T HURT?
I MUST SAY, YOU FLY VERY ODDLY!
THE BIG QUESTION NOW IS, HOW DO WE RIGHT THE PLANE?
PFOOH!... I STINK OF PETROL!
HOLD THE ROPE, SNOWY, BUT DON'T PULL TOO HARD! I'LL COME DOWN AND HELP YOU TO BRING DOWN THE TAIL OF THE MACHINE!
HELP ME!... I SUPPOSE HE THINKS I CAN'T DO IT BY MYSELF.

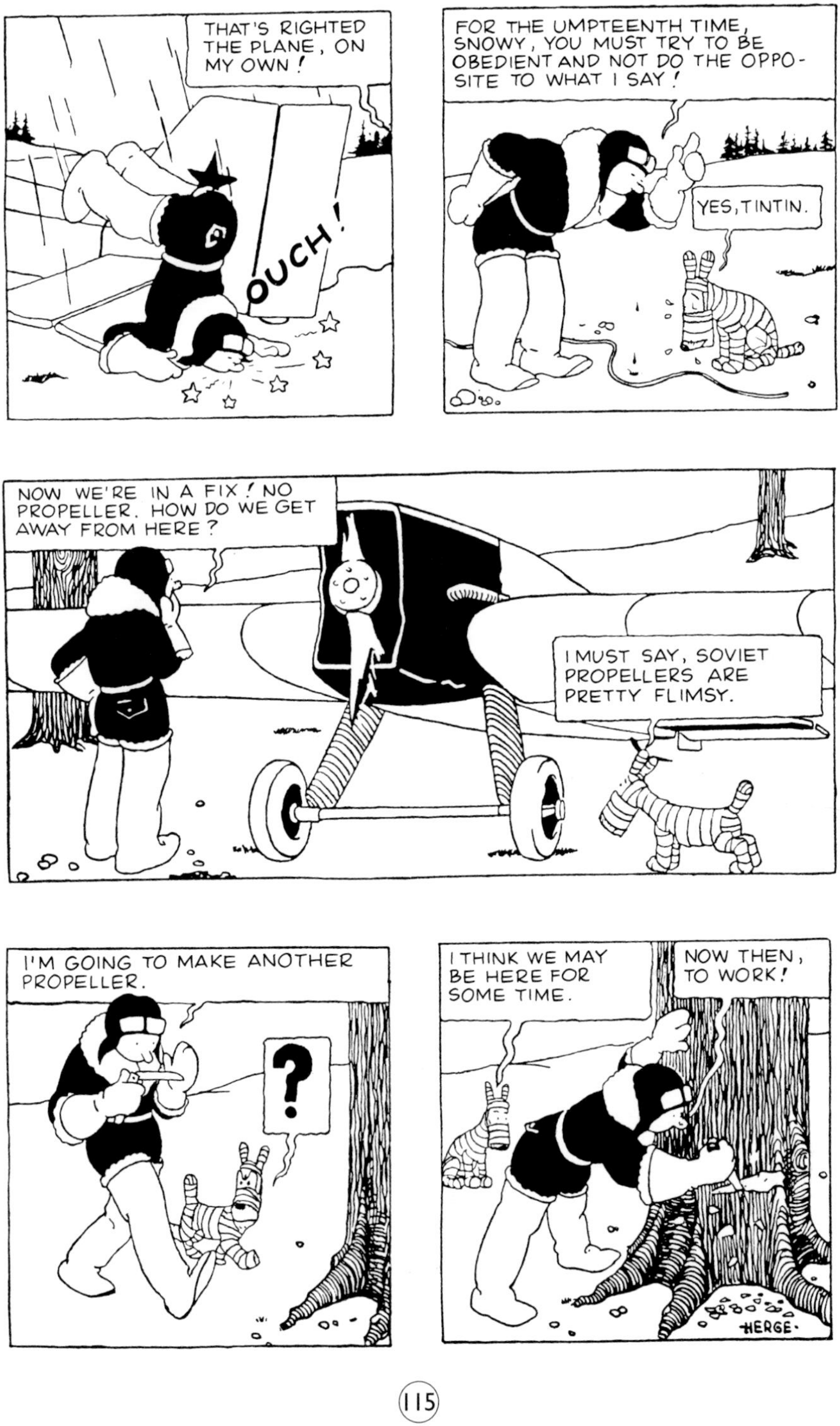
THAT'S RIGHTED THE PLANE, ON MY OWN!
OUCH!
FOR THE UMPTEENTH TIME, SNOWY, YOU MUST TRY TO BE OBEDIENT AND NOT DO THE OPPOSITE TO WHAT I SAY!
YES, TINTIN.
NOW WE'RE IN A FIX! NO PROPELLER. HOW DO WE GET AWAY FROM HERE?
I MUST SAY, SOVIET PROPELLERS ARE PRETTY FLIMSY.
I'M GOING TO MAKE ANOTHER PROPELLER.
?
I THINK WE MAY BE HERE FOR SOME TIME.
NOW THEN, TO WORK!
HERGE

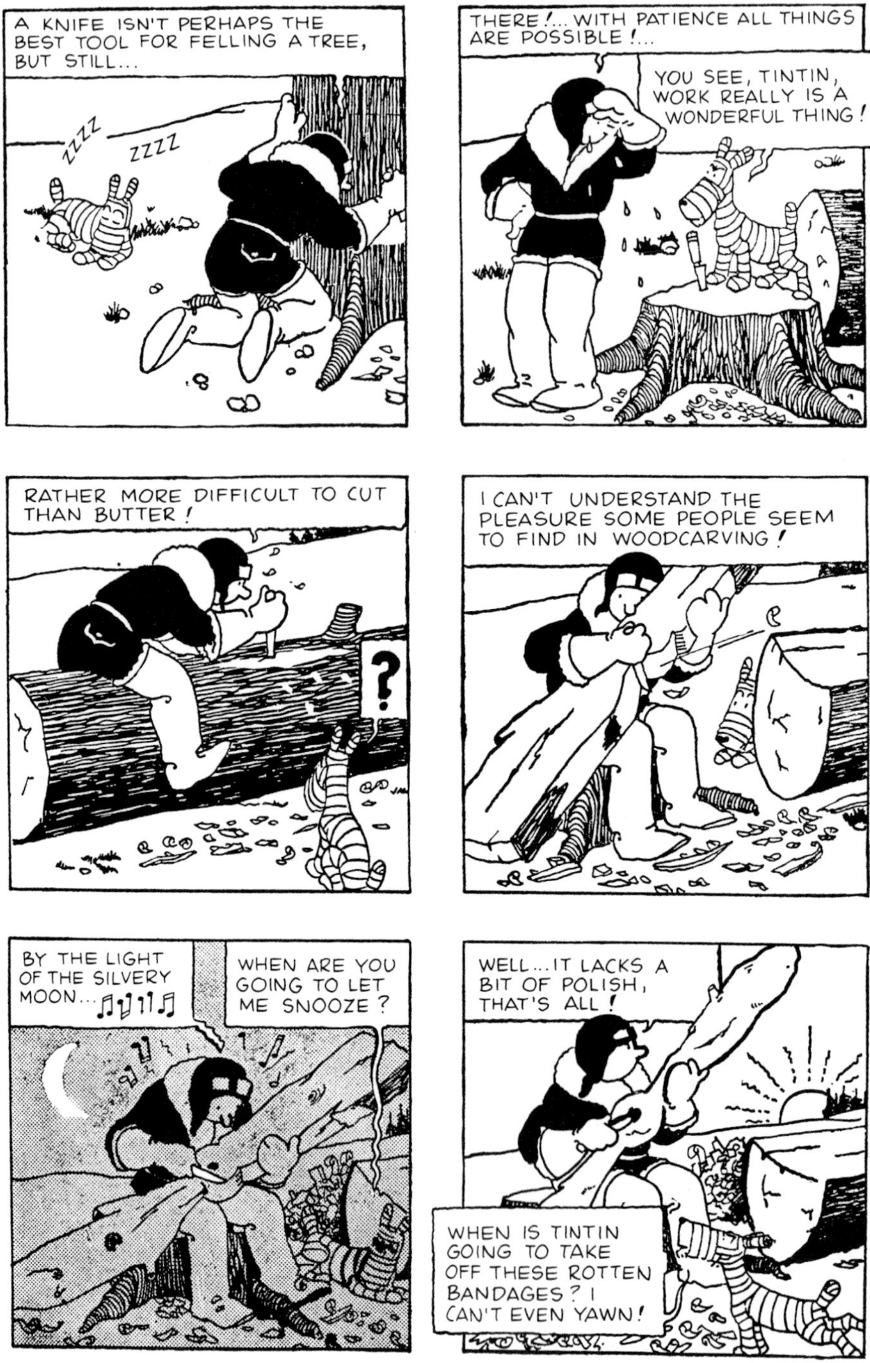
A KNIFE ISN'T PERHAPS THE BEST TOOL FOR FELLING A TREE, BUT STILL...
ZZZZ
ZZZZ
THERE!... WITH PATIENCE ALL THINGS ARE POSSIBLE!...
YOU SEE, TINTIN, WORK REALLY IS A WONDERFUL THING!
RATHER MORE DIFFICULT TO CUT THAN BUTTER!
?
I CAN'T UNDERSTAND THE PLEASURE SOME PEOPLE SEEM TO FIND IN WOODCARVING!
BY THE LIGHT OF THE SILVERY MOON...
WHEN ARE YOU GOING TO LET ME SNOOZE?
WELL... IT LACKS A BIT OF POLISH, THAT'S ALL!
WHEN IS TINTIN GOING TO TAKE OFF THESE ROTTEN BANDAGES? I CAN'T EVEN YAWN!

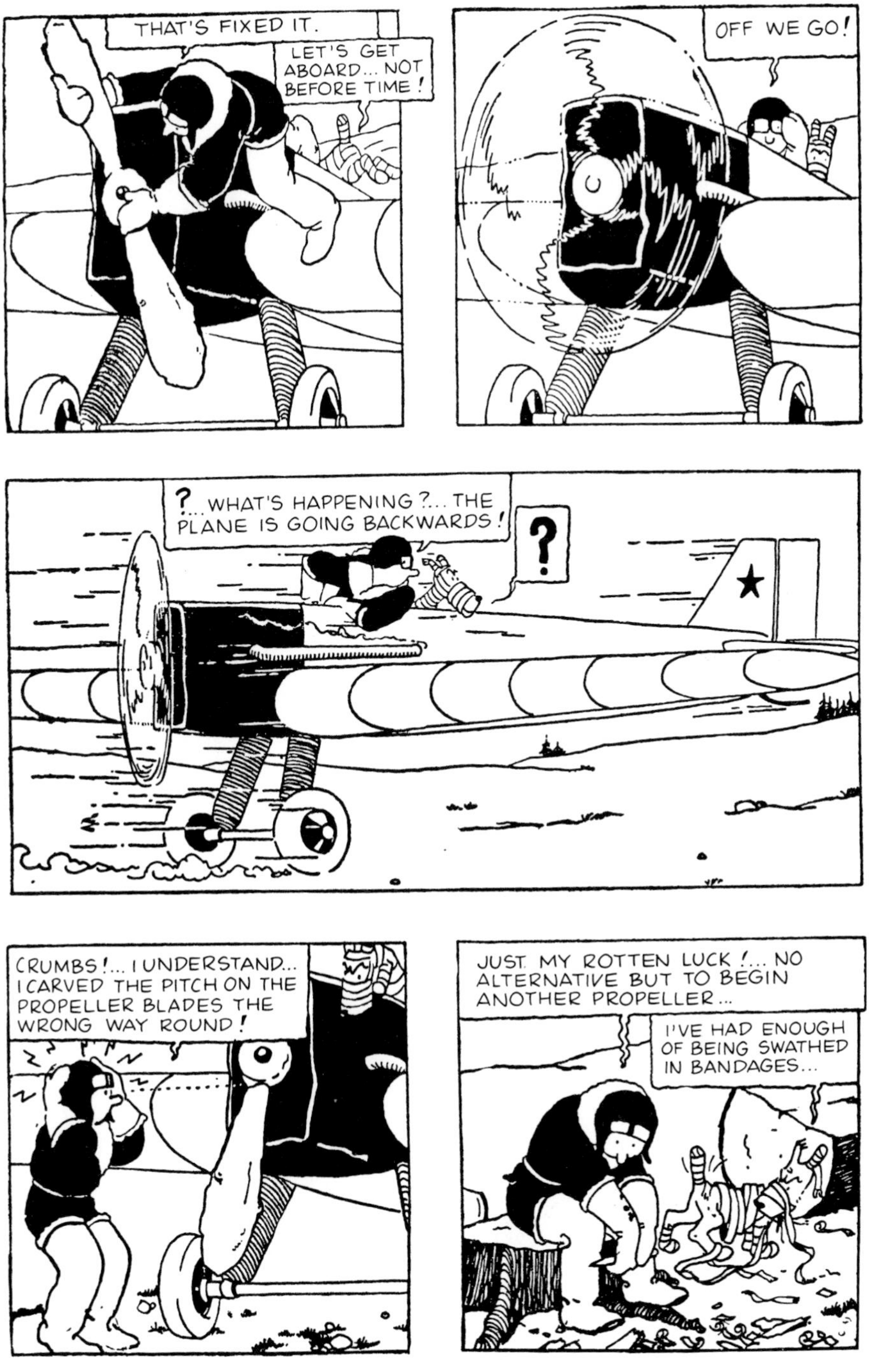
THAT'S FIXED IT.
LET'S GET ABOARD... NOT BEFORE TIME!
OFF WE GO!
?... WHAT'S HAPPENING?... THE PLANE IS GOING BACKWARDS!
?
CRUMBS!... I UNDERSTAND... I CARVED THE PITCH ON THE PROPELLER BLADES THE WRONG WAY ROUND!
JUST MY ROTTEN LUCK!... NO ALTERNATIVE BUT TO BEGIN ANOTHER PROPELLER...
I'VE HAD ENOUGH OF BEING SWATHED IN BANDAGES...

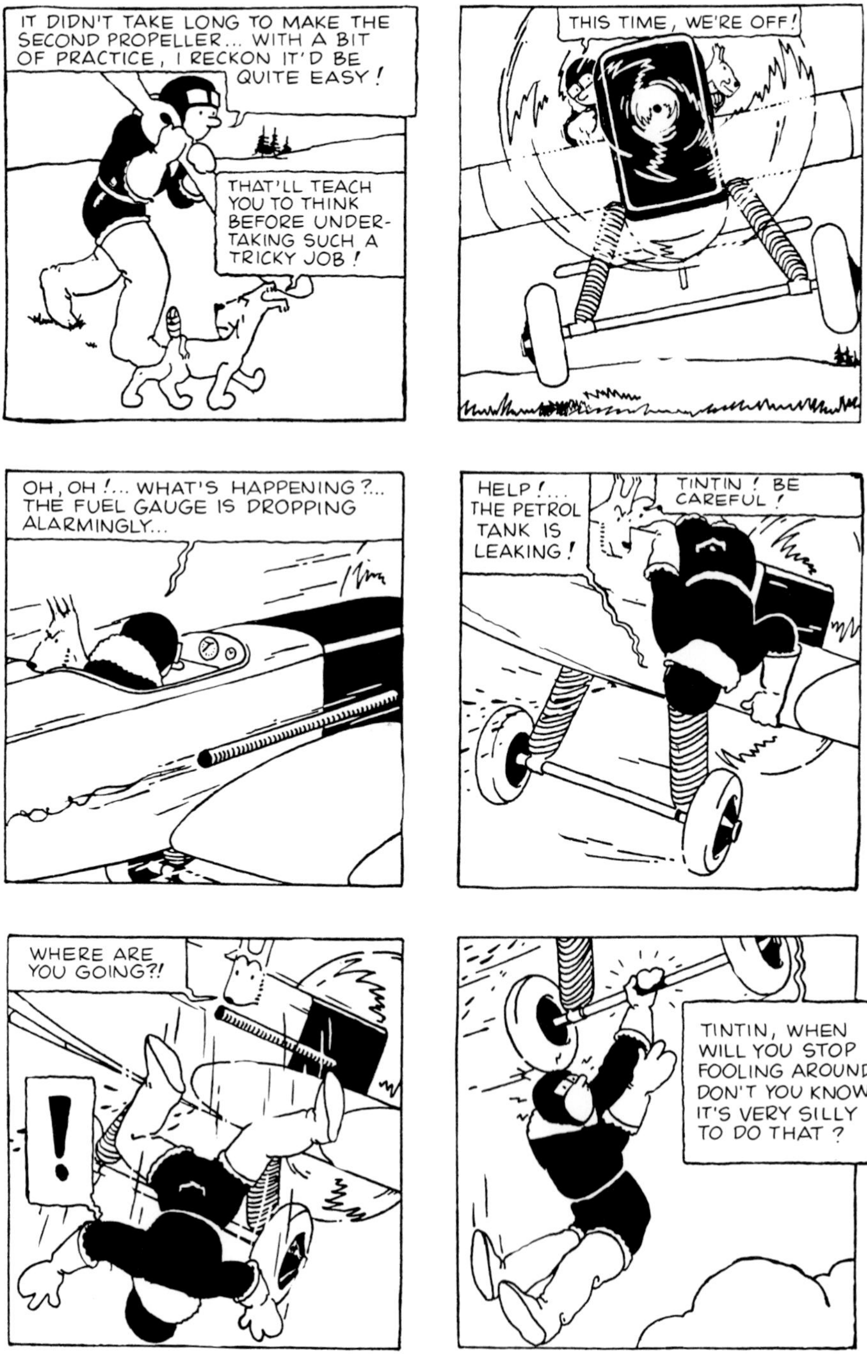
IT DIDN'T TAKE LONG TO MAKE THE SECOND PROPELLER... WITH A BIT OF PRACTICE, I RECKON IT'D BE QUITE EASY!
THAT'LL TEACH YOU TO THINK BEFORE UNDER-TAKING SUCH A TRICKY JOB!
THIS TIME, WE'RE OFF!
OH, OH!... WHAT'S HAPPENING?... THE FUEL GAUGE IS DROPPING ALARMINGLY...
HELP!... THE PETROL TANK IS LEAKING!
TINTIN! BE CAREFUL!
WHERE ARE YOU GOING?!
!
TINTIN, WHEN WILL YOU STOP FOOLING AROUND? DON'T YOU KNOW IT'S VERY SILLY TO DO THAT?

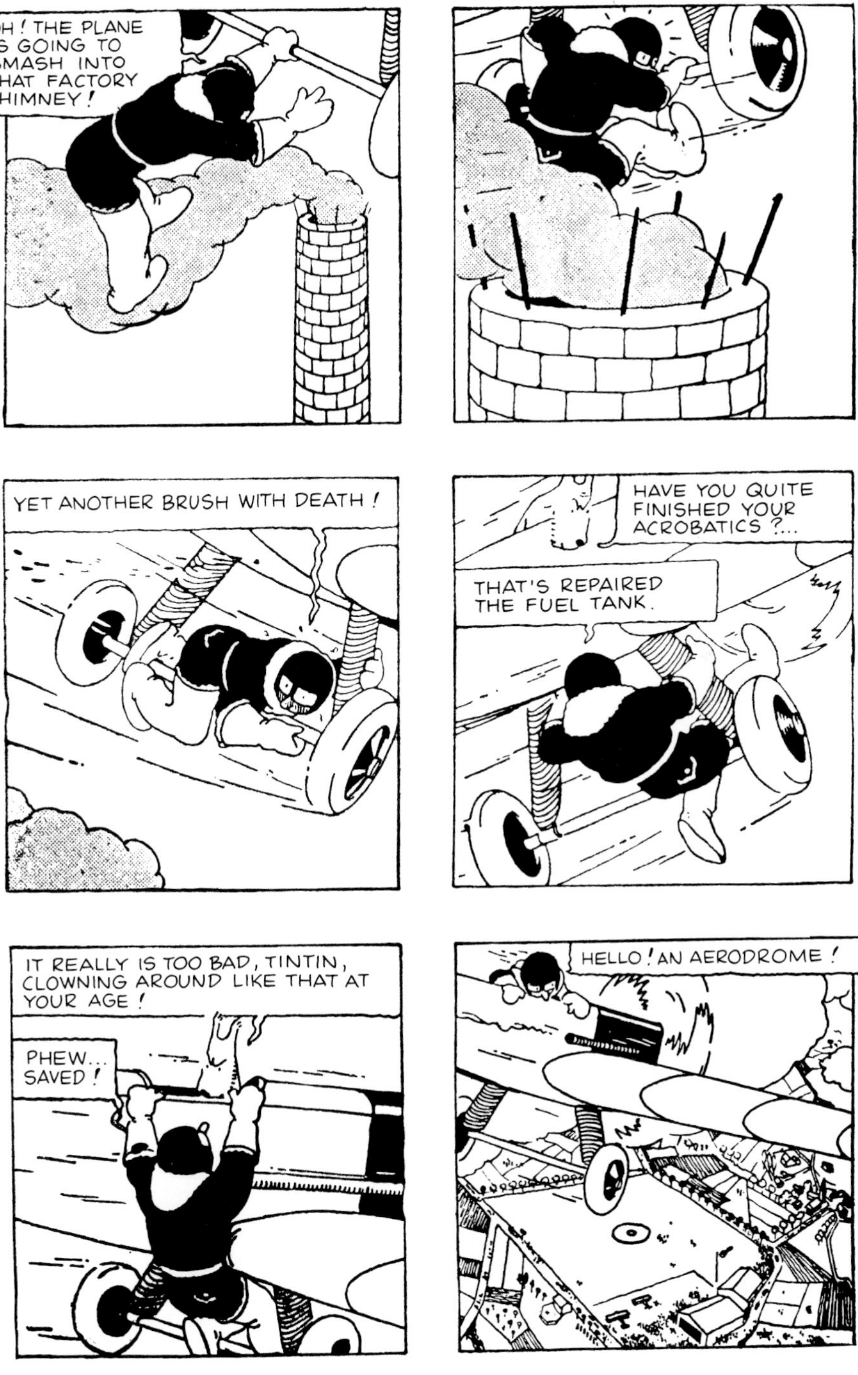

OH! THE PLANE IS GOING TO SMASH INTO THAT FACTORY CHIMNEY!
YET ANOTHER BRUSH WITH DEATH!
HAVE YOU QUITE FINISHED YOUR ACROBATICS?...
THAT'S REPAIRED THE FUEL TANK.
IT REALLY IS TOO BAD, TINTIN, CLOWNING AROUND LIKE THAT AT YOUR AGE!
PHEW... SAVED!
HELLO! AN AERODROME!

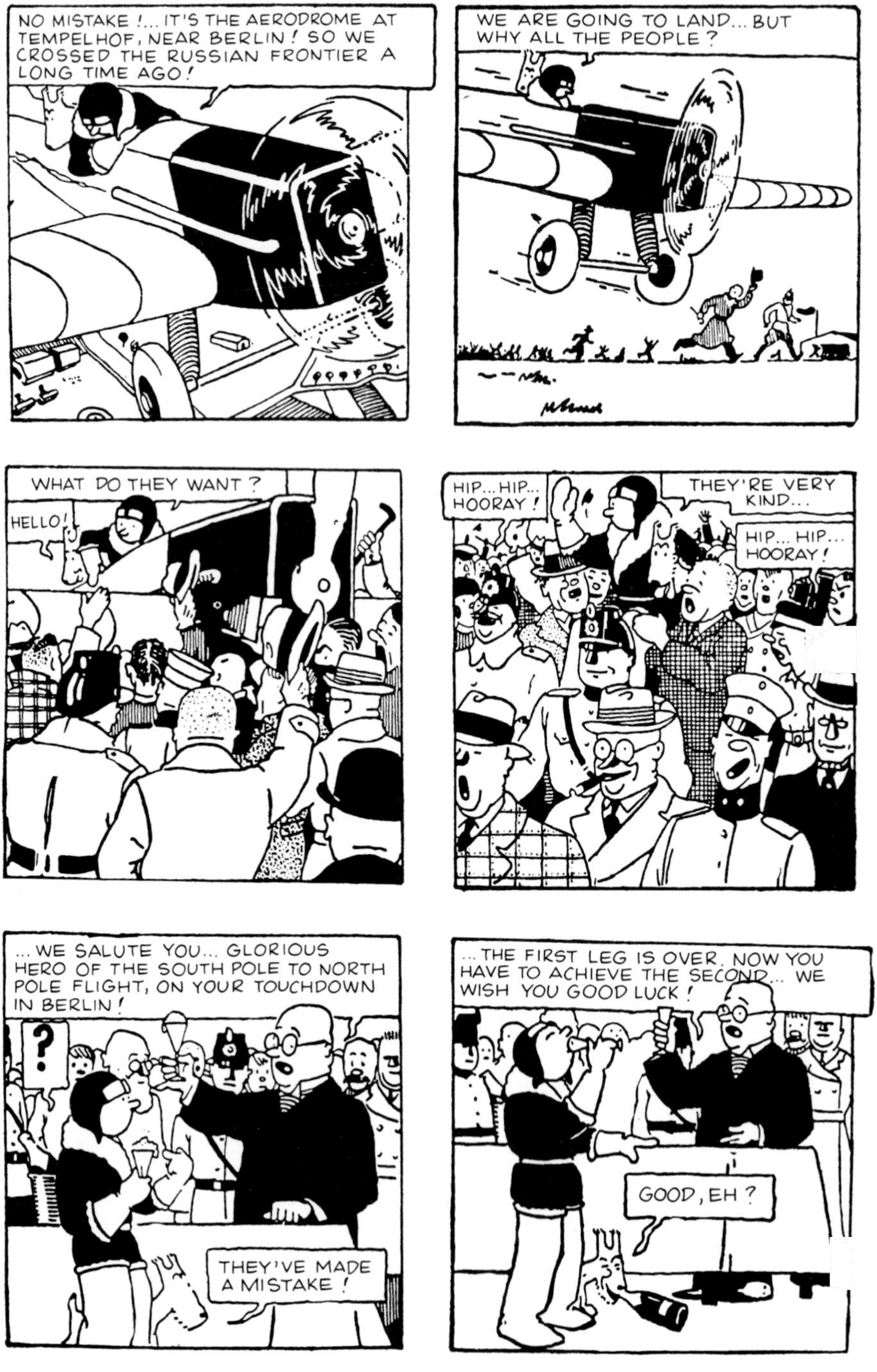
NO MISTAKE !... IT'S THE AERODROME AT TEMPELHOF, NEAR BERLIN ! SO WE CROSSED THE RUSSIAN FRONTIER A LONG TIME AGO !
WE ARE GOING TO LAND... BUT WHY ALL THE PEOPLE ?
WHAT DO THEY WANT ?
HELLO !
HIP... HIP... HOORAY !
THEY'RE VERY KIND...
HIP... HIP... HOORAY !
... WE SALUTE YOU... GLORIOUS HERO OF THE SOUTH POLE TO NORTH POLE FLIGHT, ON YOUR TOUCHDOWN IN BERLIN !
?
THEY'VE MADE A MISTAKE !
... THE FIRST LEG IS OVER. NOW YOU HAVE TO ACHIEVE THE SECOND... WE WISH YOU GOOD LUCK !
GOOD, EH ?

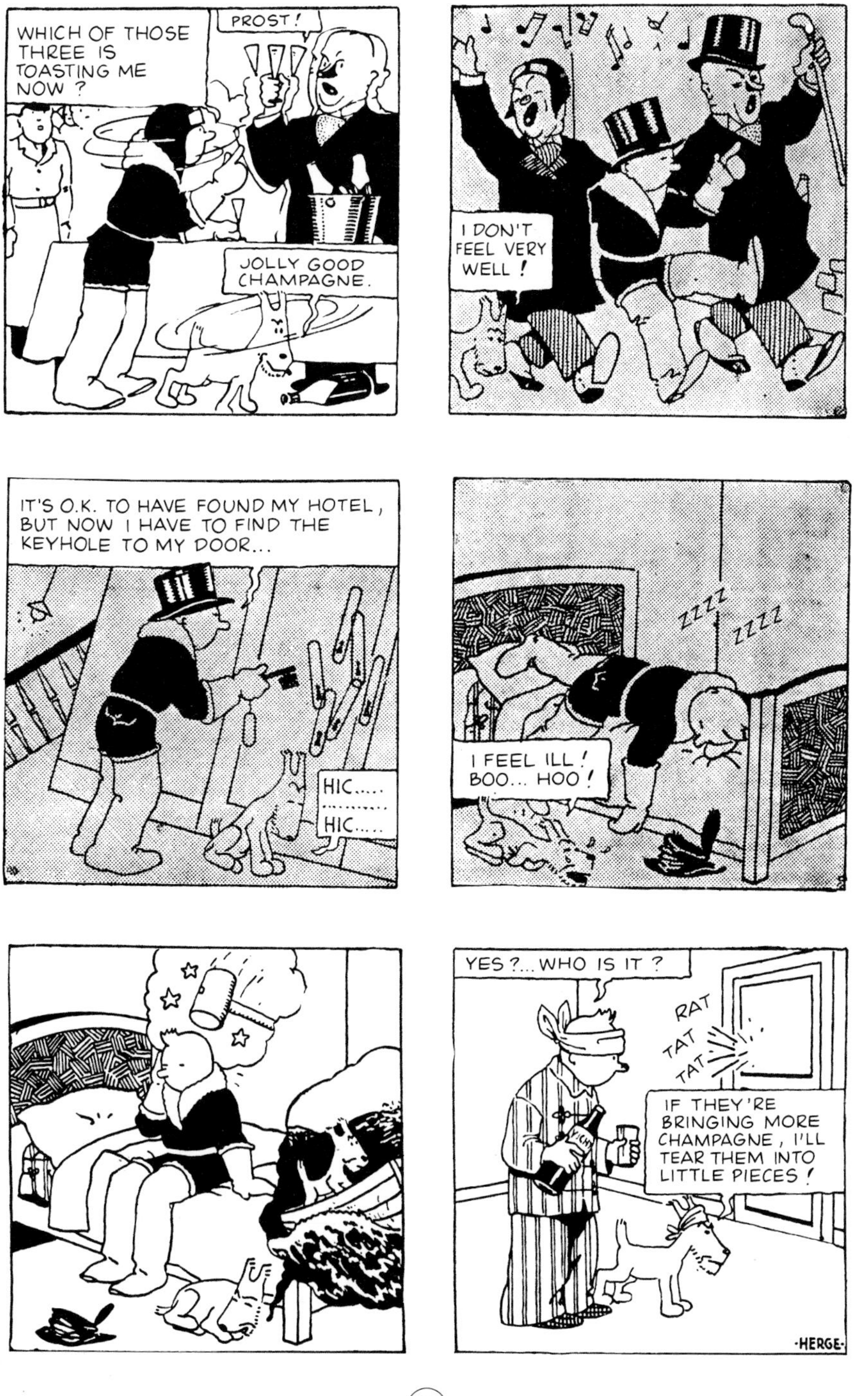
WHICH OF THOSE THREE IS TOASTING ME NOW ?
PROST !
JOLLY GOOD CHAMPAGNE.
I DON'T FEEL VERY WELL !
IT'S O.K. TO HAVE FOUND MY HOTEL , BUT NOW I HAVE TO FIND THE KEYHOLE TO MY DOOR...
HIC..... .... HIC.....
ZZZZ
ZZZZ
I FEEL ILL ! BOO... HOO !
YES ?... WHO IS IT ?
RAT TAT TAT
IF THEY'RE BRINGING MORE CHAMPAGNE , I'LL TEAR THEM INTO LITTLE PIECES !
·HERGE·

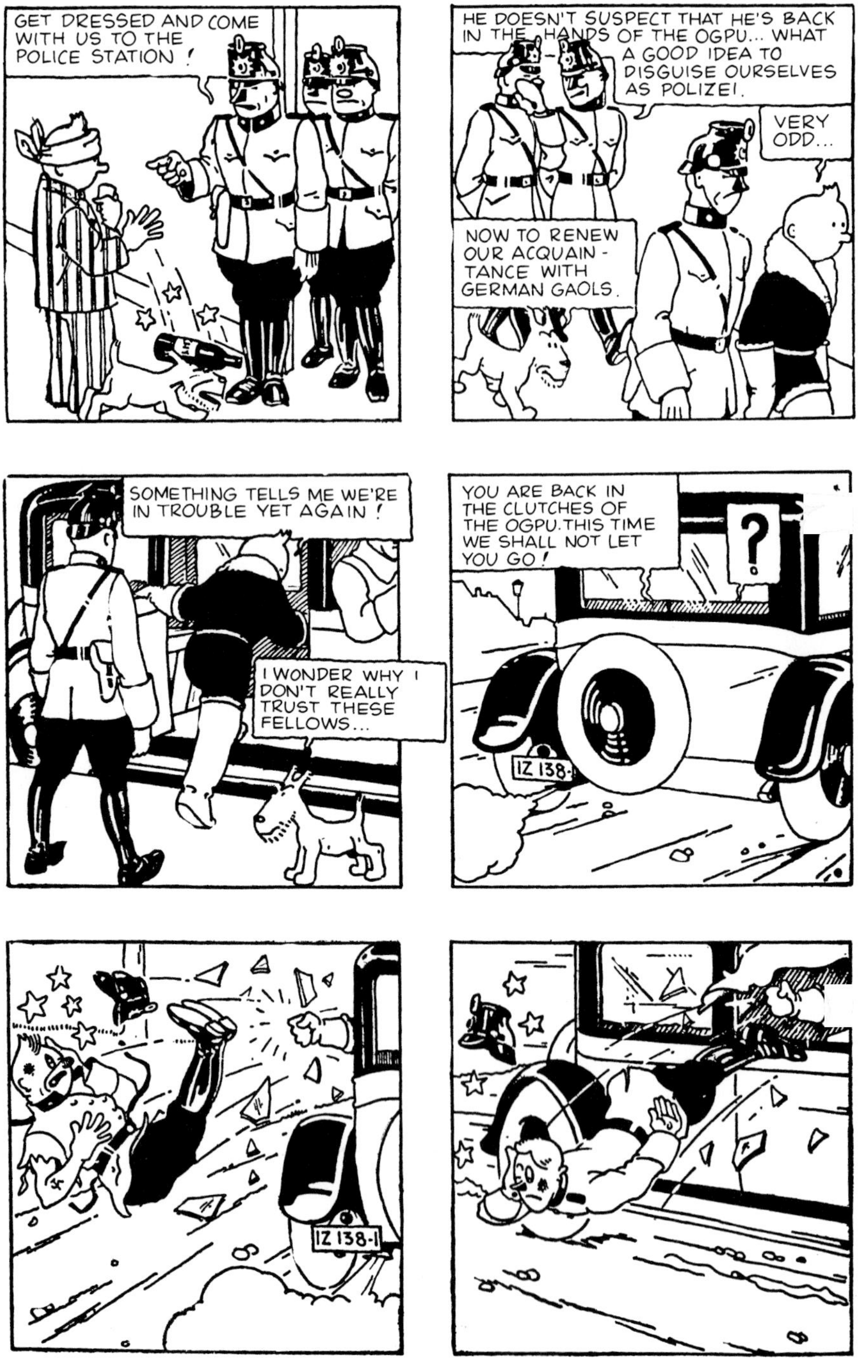

GET DRESSED AND COME WITH US TO THE POLICE STATION!
HE DOESN'T SUSPECT THAT HE'S BACK IN THE HANDS OF THE OGPU... WHAT A GOOD IDEA TO DISGUISE OURSELVES AS POLIZEI.
VERY ODD...
NOW TO RENEW OUR ACQUAINTANCE WITH GERMAN GAOLS.
SOMETHING TELLS ME WE'RE IN TROUBLE YET AGAIN!
I WONDER WHY I DON'T REALLY TRUST THESE FELLOWS...
YOU ARE BACK IN THE CLUTCHES OF THE OGPU. THIS TIME WE SHALL NOT LET YOU GO!
?
IZ 138-1
IZ 138-1

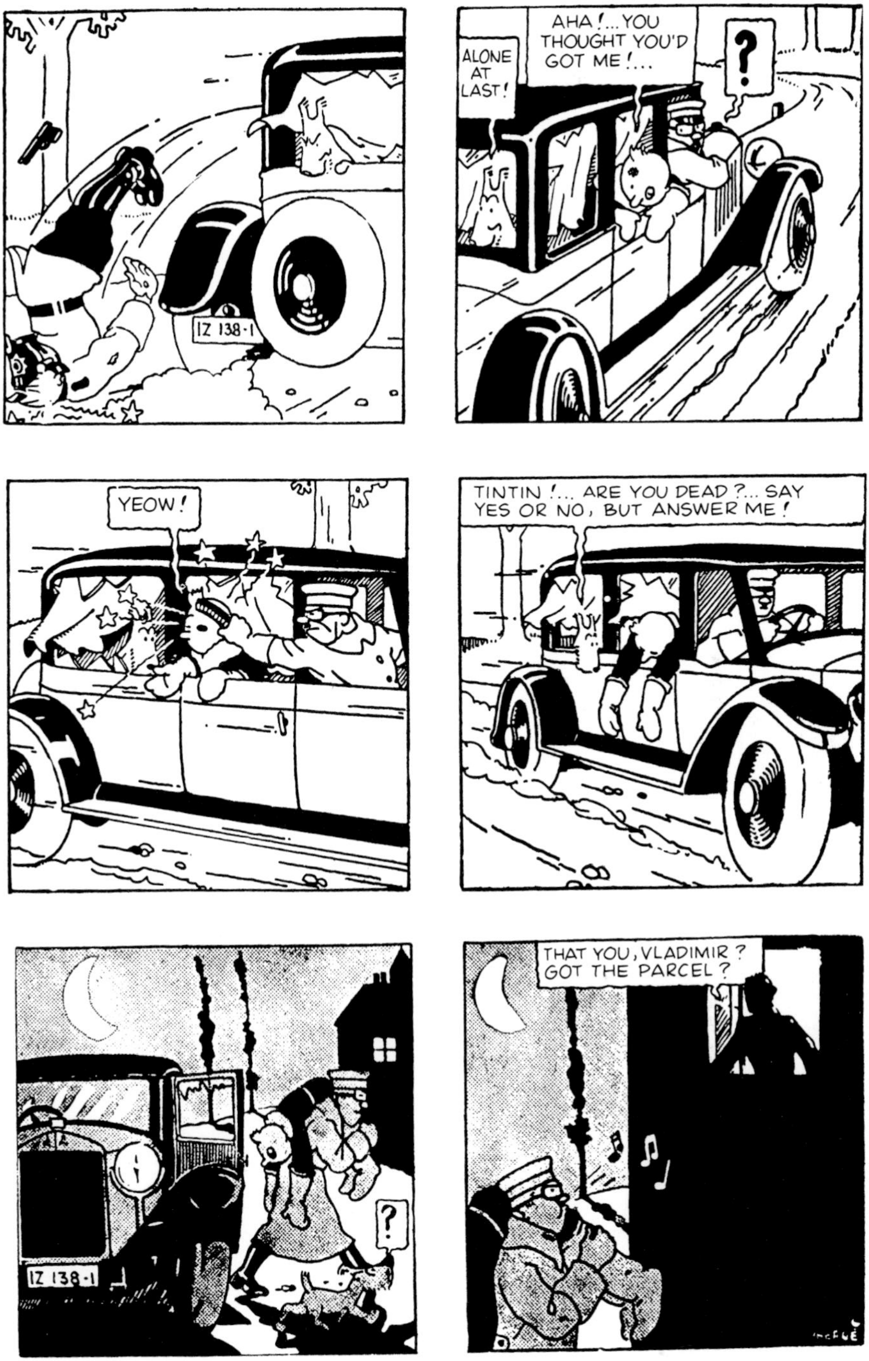
IZ 138-1
ALONE AT LAST!
AHA!... YOU THOUGHT YOU'D GOT ME!...
?
YEOW!
TINTIN!... ARE YOU DEAD?... SAY YES OR NO, BUT ANSWER ME!
IZ 138-1
?
THAT YOU, VLADIMIR? GOT THE PARCEL?
HERGÉ

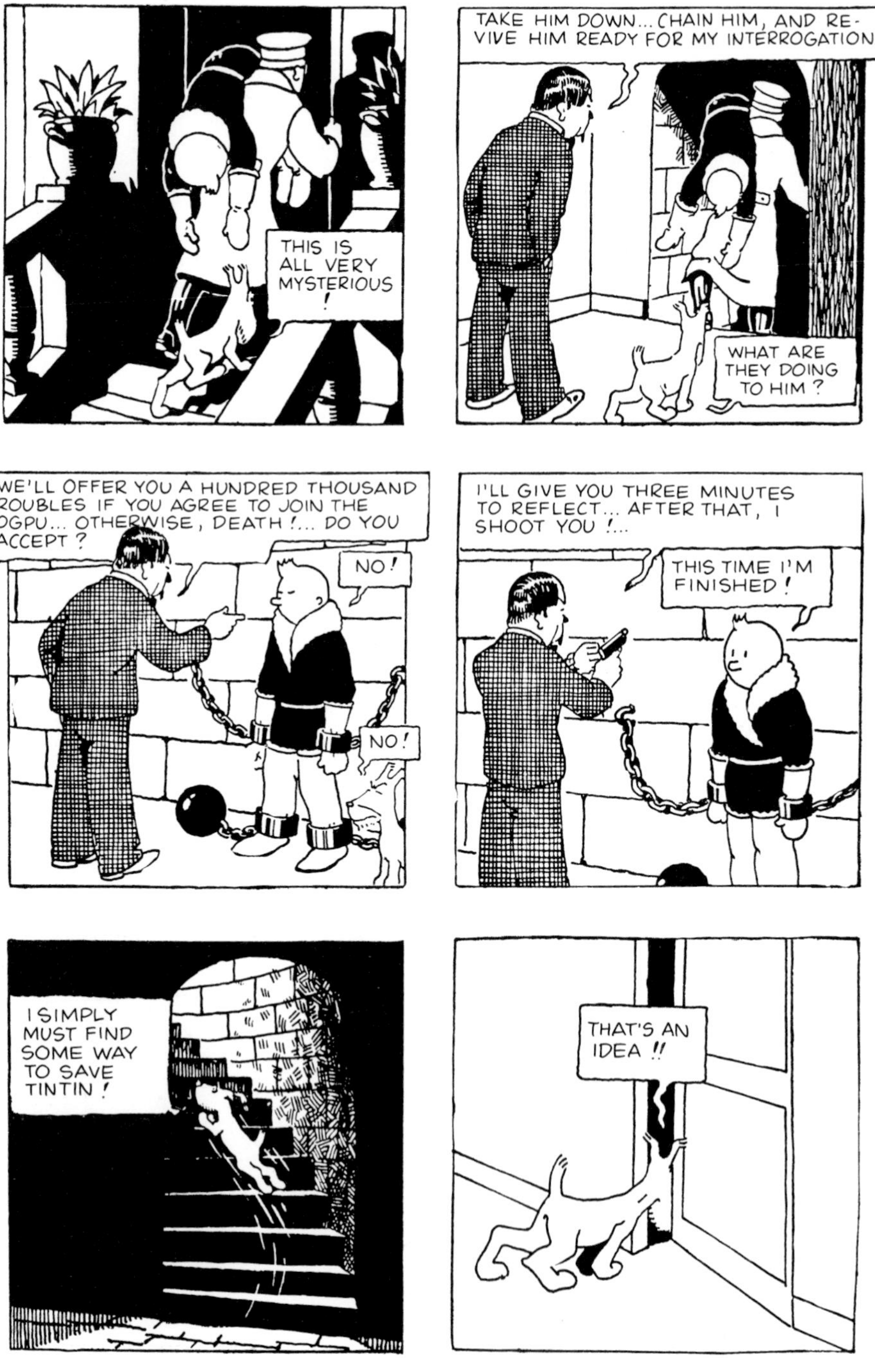
THIS IS ALL VERY MYSTERIOUS !
TAKE HIM DOWN... CHAIN HIM, AND RE-VIVE HIM READY FOR MY INTERROGATION.
WHAT ARE THEY DOING TO HIM ?
WE'LL OFFER YOU A HUNDRED THOUSAND ROUBLES IF YOU AGREE TO JOIN THE OGPU... OTHERWISE, DEATH !... DO YOU ACCEPT ?
NO !
NO !
I'LL GIVE YOU THREE MINUTES TO REFLECT... AFTER THAT, I SHOOT YOU !...
THIS TIME I'M FINISHED !
I SIMPLY MUST FIND SOME WAY TO SAVE TINTIN !
THAT'S AN IDEA !!

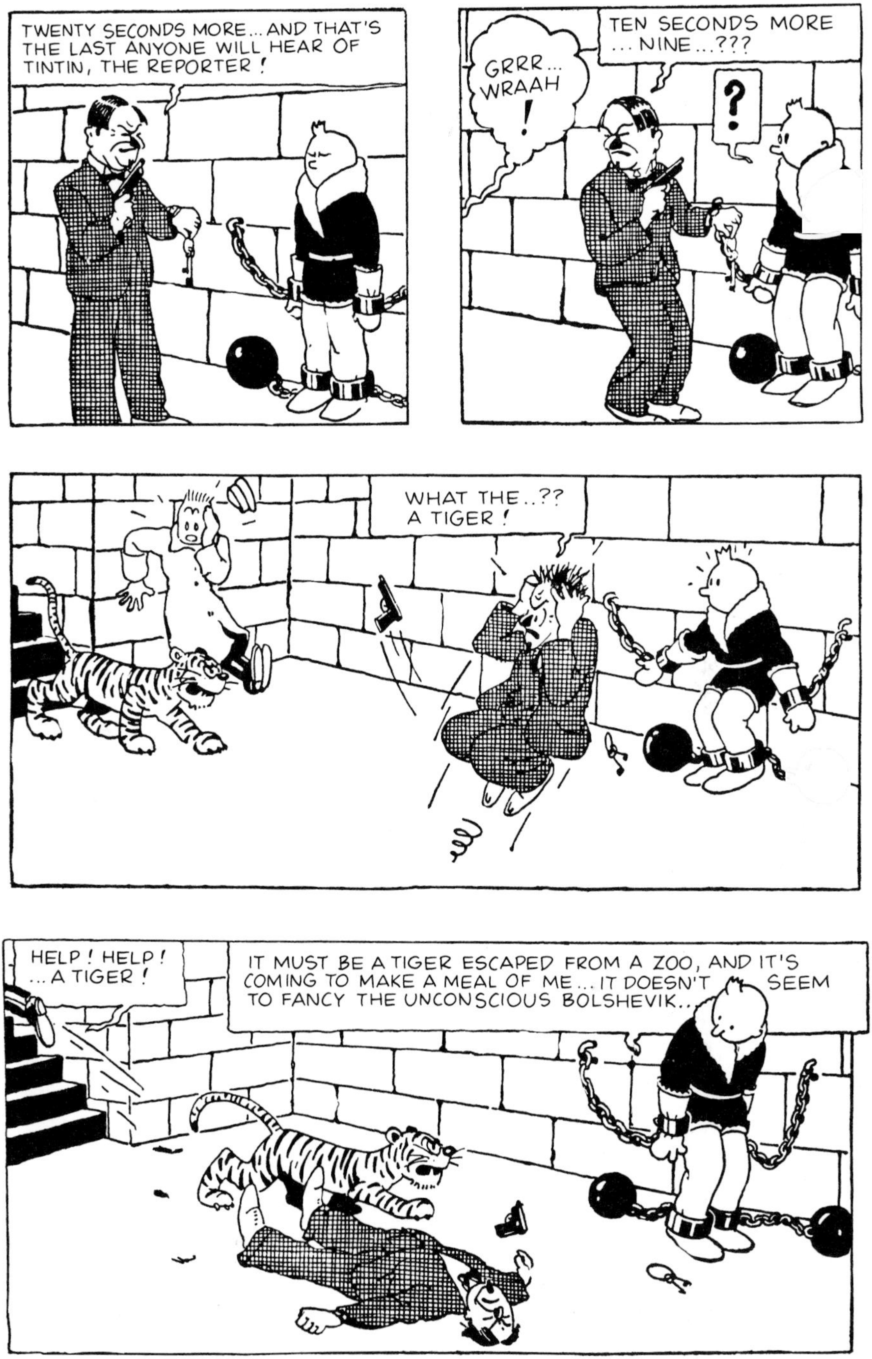
TWENTY SECONDS MORE... AND THAT'S THE LAST ANYONE WILL HEAR OF TINTIN, THE REPORTER !
GRRR... WRAAH !
TEN SECONDS MORE ... NINE...???
?
WHAT THE..?? A TIGER !
HELP ! HELP ! ...A TIGER !
IT MUST BE A TIGER ESCAPED FROM A ZOO, AND IT'S COMING TO MAKE A MEAL OF ME... IT DOESN'T SEEM TO FANCY THE UNCONSCIOUS BOLSHEVIK...

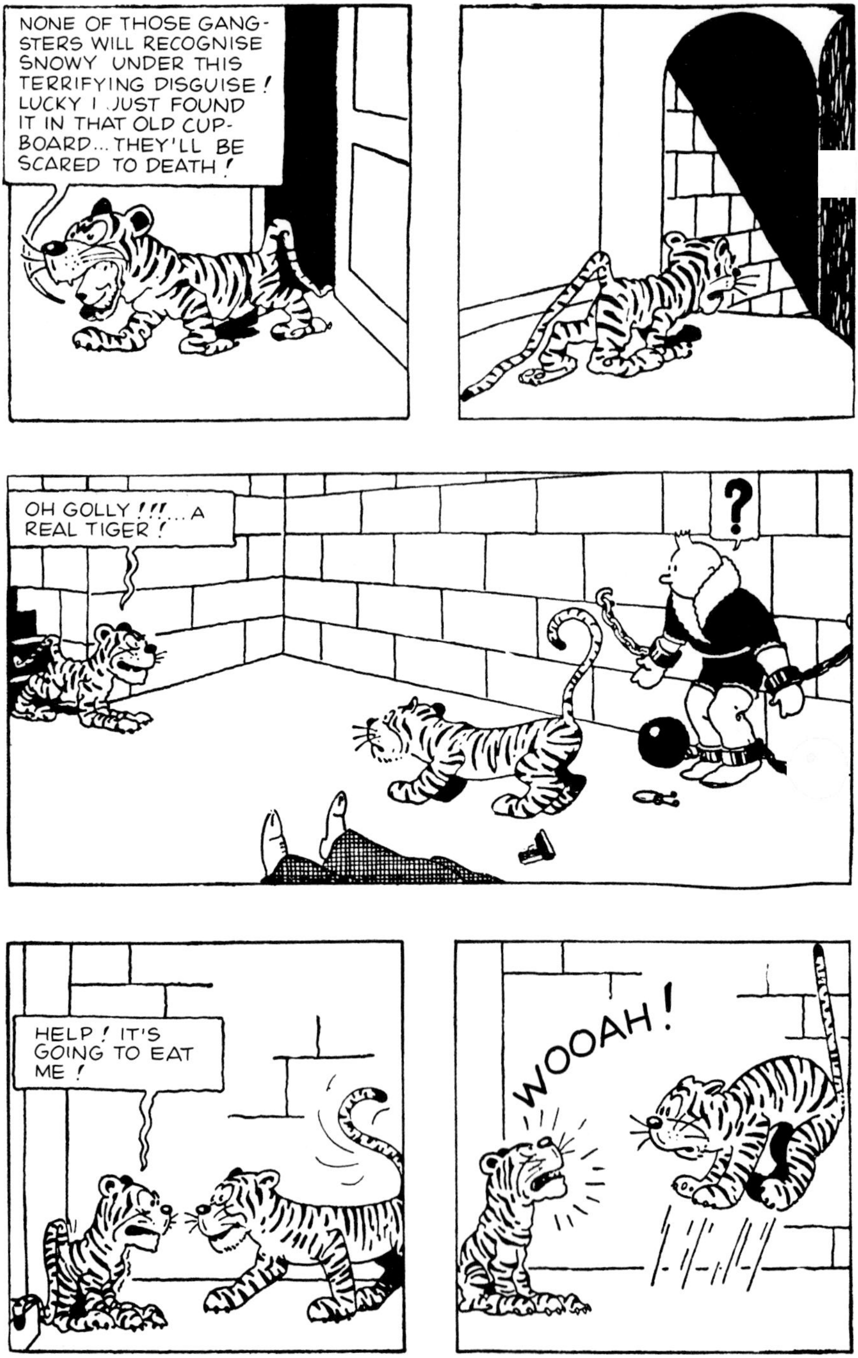
NONE OF THOSE GANGSTERS WILL RECOGNISE SNOWY UNDER THIS TERRIFYING DISGUISE! LUCKY I JUST FOUND IT IN THAT OLD CUPBOARD... THEY'LL BE SCARED TO DEATH!
OH GOLLY!!!... A REAL TIGER!
?
HELP! IT'S GOING TO EAT ME!
WOOAH!

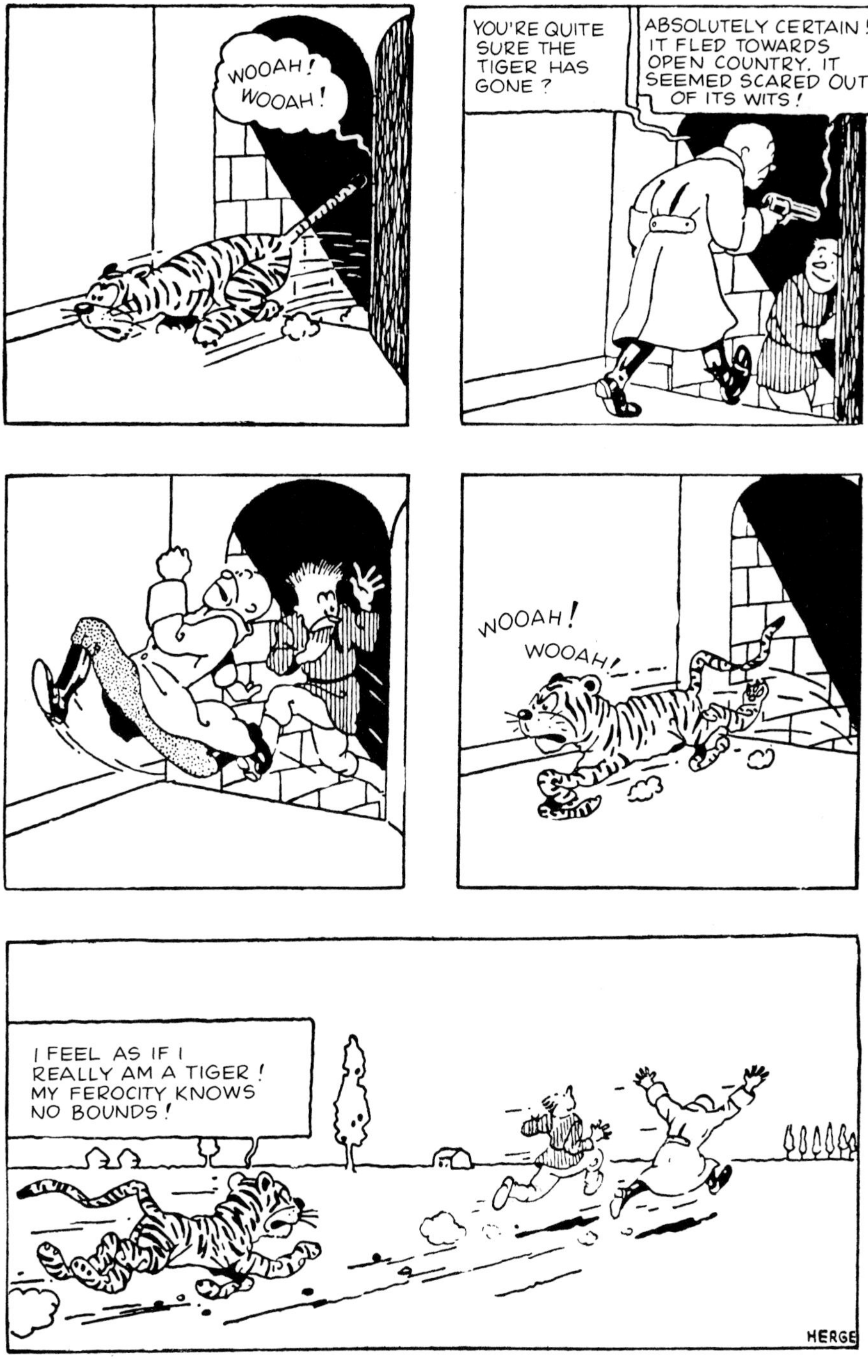
WOOAH! WOOAH!
YOU'RE QUITE SURE THE TIGER HAS GONE?
ABSOLUTELY CERTAIN! IT FLED TOWARDS OPEN COUNTRY. IT SEEMED SCARED OUT OF ITS WITS!
WOOAH!
WOOAH!
I FEEL AS IF I REALLY AM A TIGER! MY FEROCITY KNOWS NO BOUNDS!
HERGE

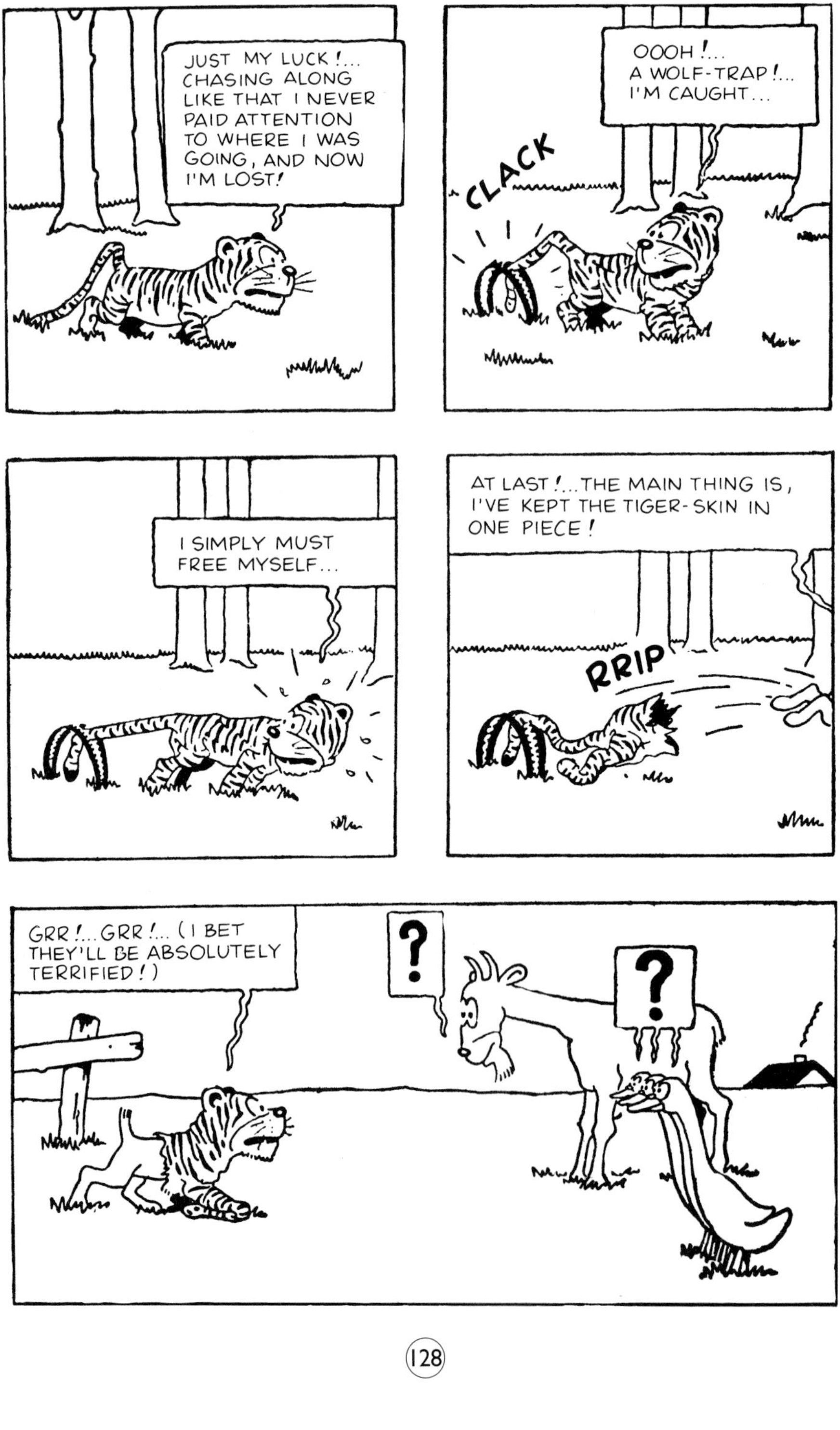
JUST MY LUCK!... CHASING ALONG LIKE THAT I NEVER PAID ATTENTION TO WHERE I WAS GOING, AND NOW I'M LOST!
OOOH!... A WOLF-TRAP!... I'M CAUGHT...
CLACK
I SIMPLY MUST FREE MYSELF...
AT LAST!...THE MAIN THING IS, I'VE KEPT THE TIGER-SKIN IN ONE PIECE!
RRIP
GRR!...GRR!... (I BET THEY'LL BE ABSOLUTELY TERRIFIED!)
?
?

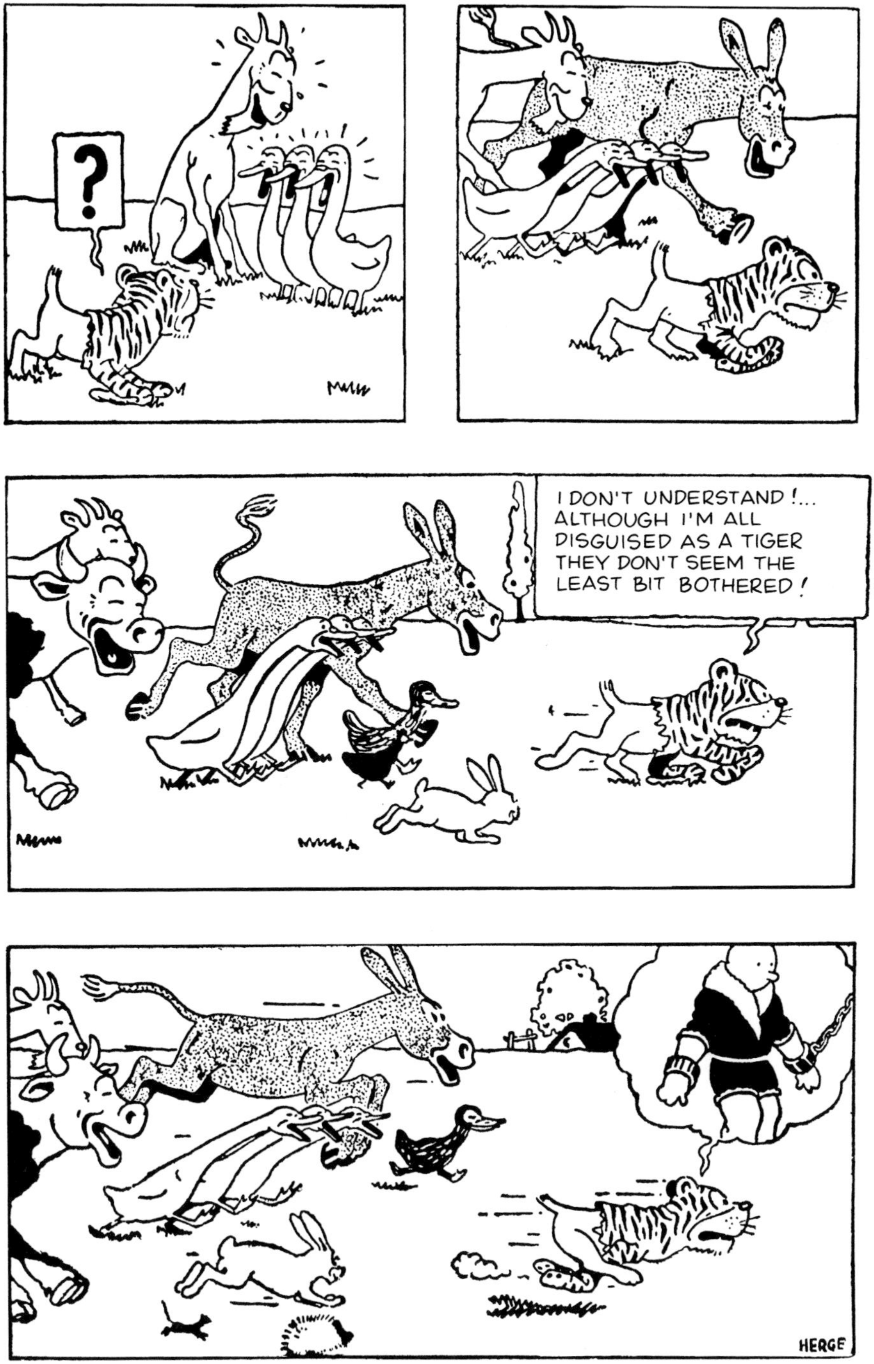
?
I DON'T UNDERSTAND !... ALTHOUGH I'M ALL DISGUISED AS A TIGER THEY DON'T SEEM THE LEAST BIT BOTHERED !
HERGE

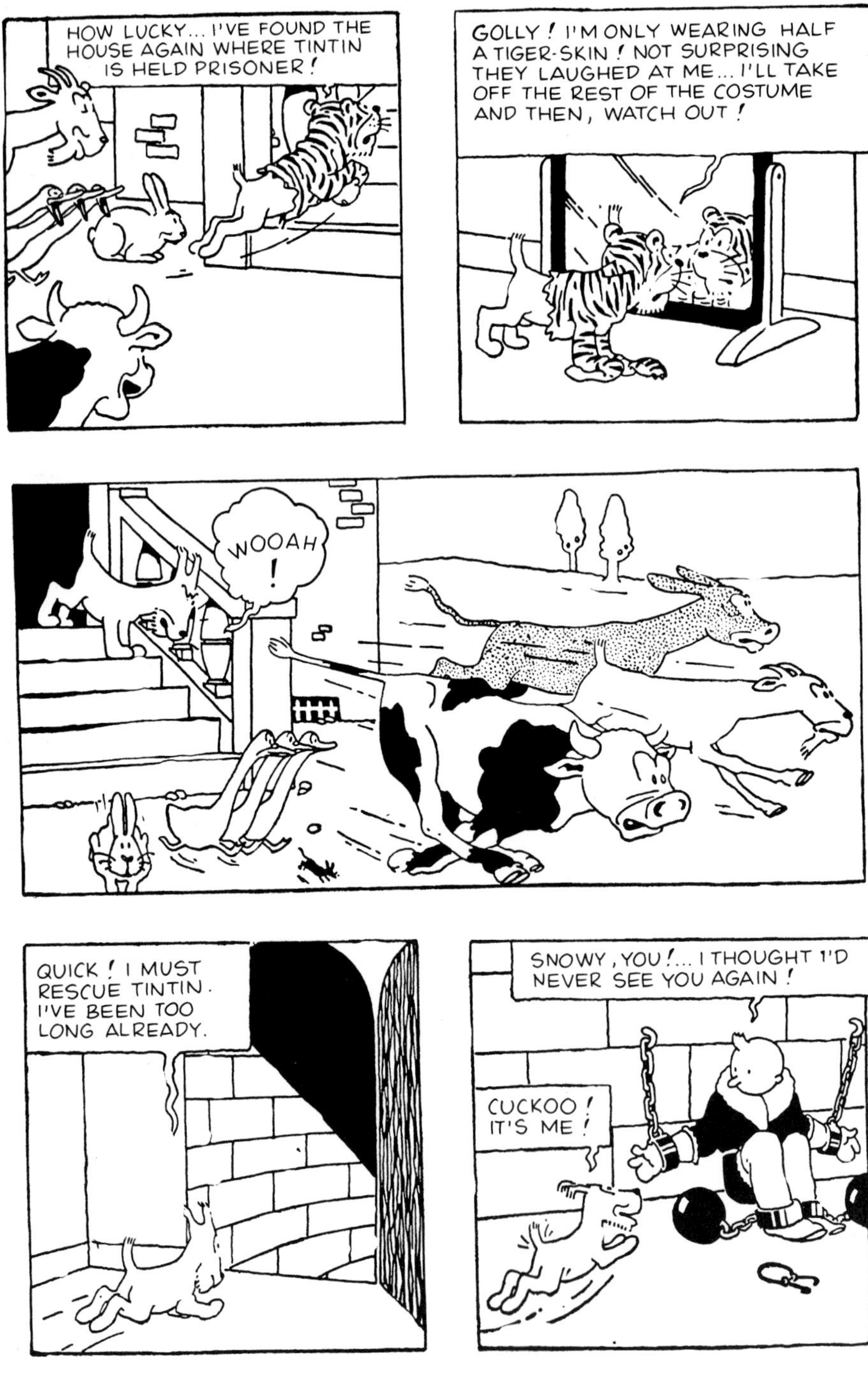
HOW LUCKY... I'VE FOUND THE HOUSE AGAIN WHERE TINTIN IS HELD PRISONER!
GOLLY! I'M ONLY WEARING HALF A TIGER-SKIN! NOT SURPRISING THEY LAUGHED AT ME... I'LL TAKE OFF THE REST OF THE COSTUME AND THEN, WATCH OUT!
WOOAH!
QUICK! I MUST RESCUE TINTIN. I'VE BEEN TOO LONG ALREADY.
SNOWY, YOU!... I THOUGHT I'D NEVER SEE YOU AGAIN!
CUCKOO! IT'S ME!

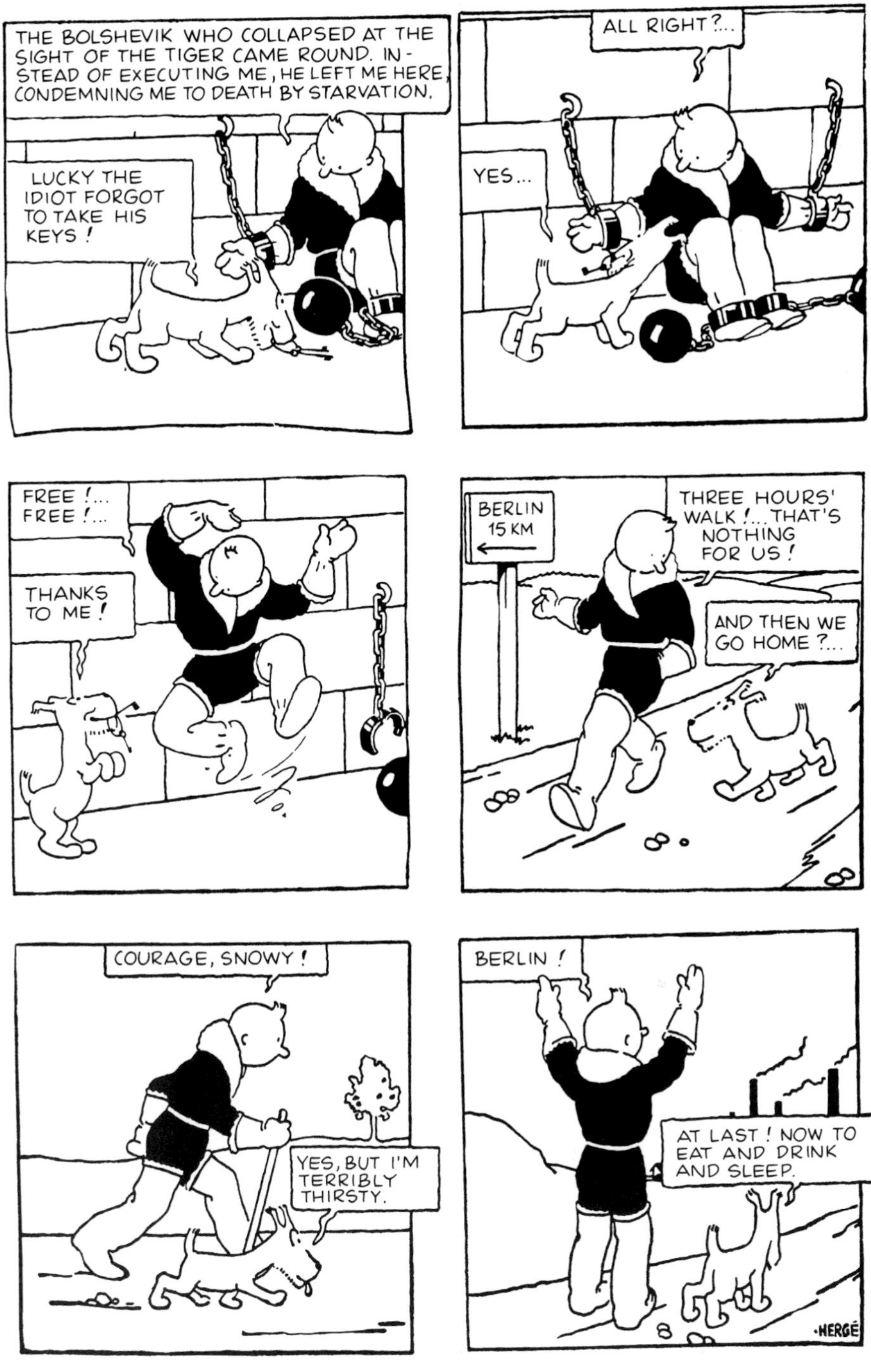
THE BOLSHEVIK WHO COLLAPSED AT THE SIGHT OF THE TIGER CAME ROUND. IN-STEAD OF EXECUTING ME, HE LEFT ME HERE, CONDEMNING ME TO DEATH BY STARVATION.
LUCKY THE IDIOT FORGOT TO TAKE HIS KEYS !
ALL RIGHT ?...
YES...
FREE !... FREE !...
THANKS TO ME !
BERLIN 15 KM
THREE HOURS' WALK !... THAT'S NOTHING FOR US !
AND THEN WE GO HOME ?...
COURAGE, SNOWY !
YES, BUT I'M TERRIBLY THIRSTY.
BERLIN !
AT LAST ! NOW TO EAT AND DRINK AND SLEEP.
HERGÉ

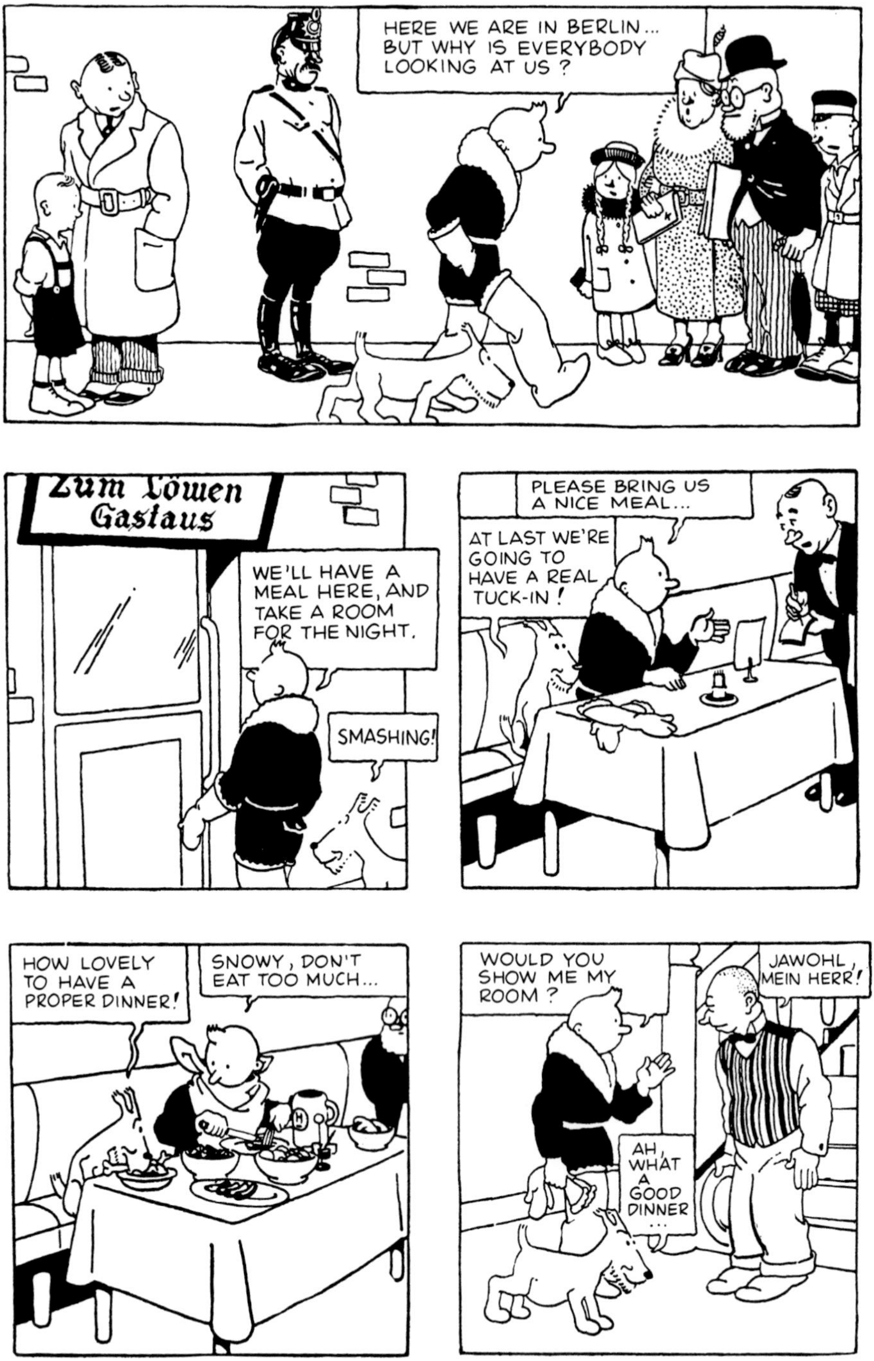
HERE WE ARE IN BERLIN... BUT WHY IS EVERYBODY LOOKING AT US ?
Zum Löwen Gastaus
WE'LL HAVE A MEAL HERE, AND TAKE A ROOM FOR THE NIGHT.
SMASHING!
PLEASE BRING US A NICE MEAL...
AT LAST WE'RE GOING TO HAVE A REAL TUCK-IN !
HOW LOVELY TO HAVE A PROPER DINNER!
SNOWY, DON'T EAT TOO MUCH...
WOULD YOU SHOW ME MY ROOM ?
JAWOHL, MEIN HERR!
AH, WHAT A GOOD DINNER ...

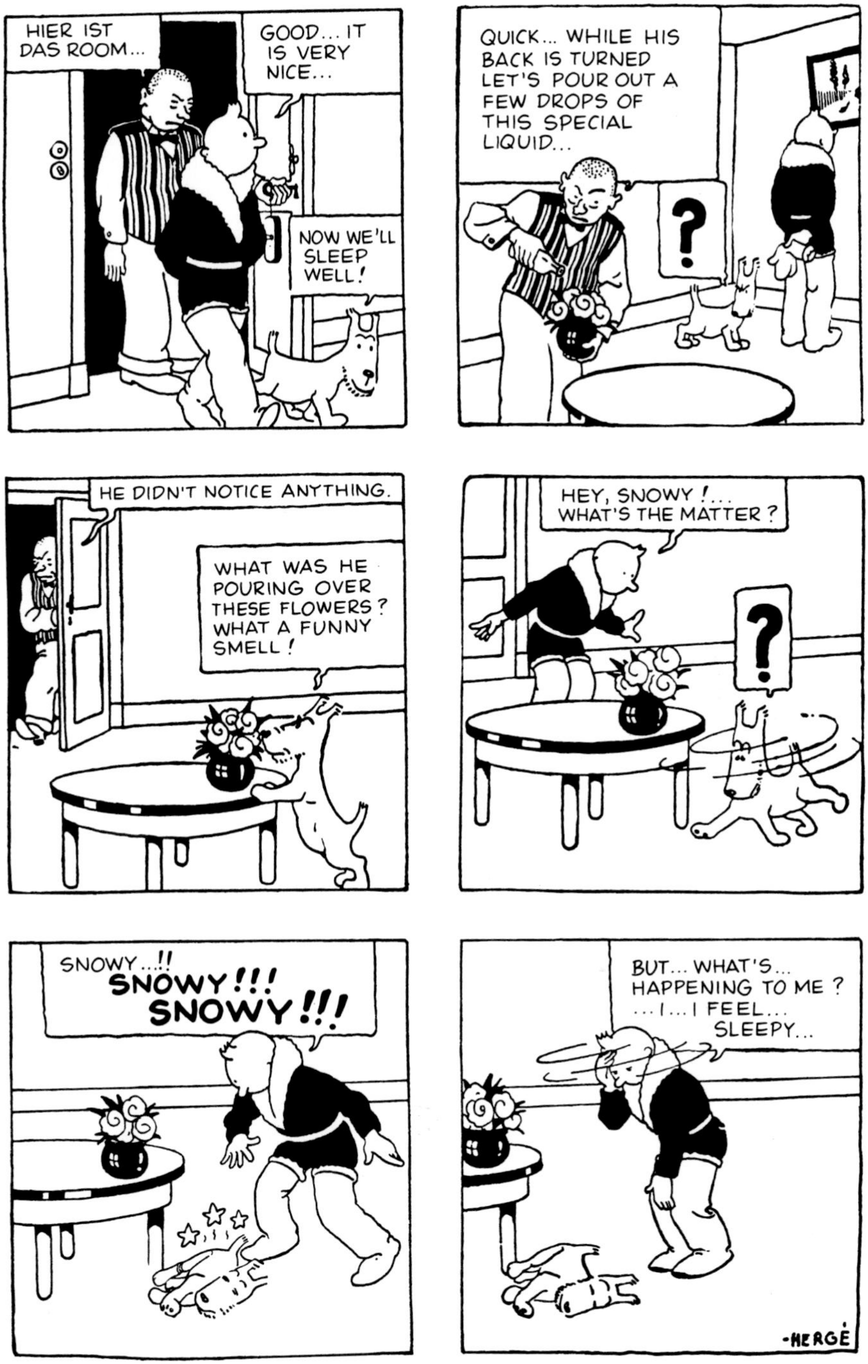
HIER IST DAS ROOM...
GOOD... IT IS VERY NICE...
NOW WE'LL SLEEP WELL!
QUICK... WHILE HIS BACK IS TURNED LET'S POUR OUT A FEW DROPS OF THIS SPECIAL LIQUID...
HE DIDN'T NOTICE ANYTHING.
WHAT WAS HE POURING OVER THESE FLOWERS? WHAT A FUNNY SMELL!
HEY, SNOWY!... WHAT'S THE MATTER?
SNOWY...!! SNOWY!!! SNOWY!!!
BUT... WHAT'S... HAPPENING TO ME? ...I... I FEEL... SLEEPY...
HERGÉ

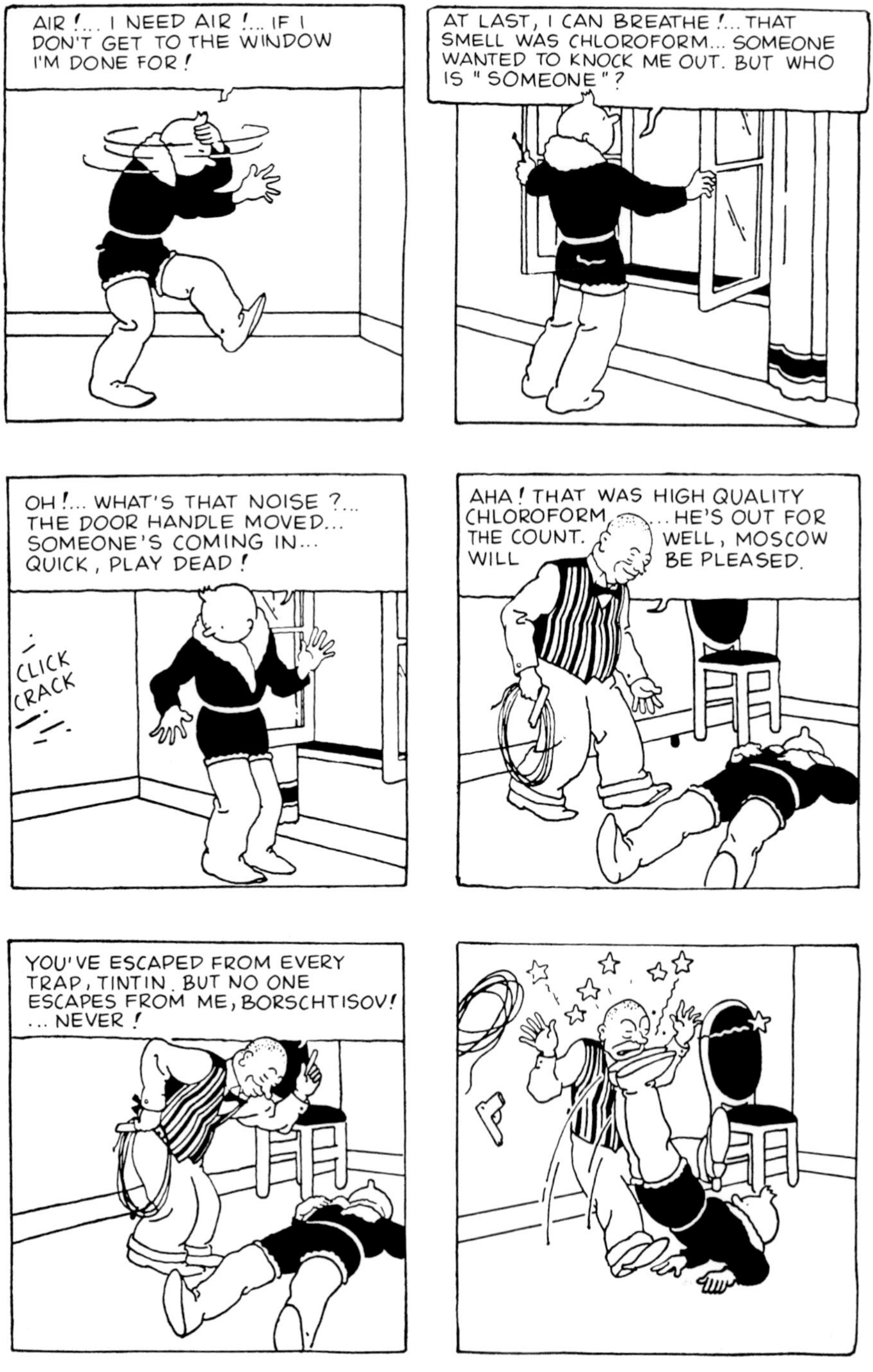
AIR !... I NEED AIR !... IF I DON'T GET TO THE WINDOW I'M DONE FOR !
AT LAST, I CAN BREATHE !... THAT SMELL WAS CHLOROFORM... SOMEONE WANTED TO KNOCK ME OUT. BUT WHO IS "SOMEONE"?
OH !... WHAT'S THAT NOISE ?... THE DOOR HANDLE MOVED... SOMEONE'S COMING IN... QUICK, PLAY DEAD !
CLICK CRACK
AHA ! THAT WAS HIGH QUALITY CHLOROFORM ... HE'S OUT FOR THE COUNT. WELL, MOSCOW WILL BE PLEASED.
YOU'VE ESCAPED FROM EVERY TRAP, TINTIN. BUT NO ONE ESCAPES FROM ME, BORSCHTISOV! ... NEVER !

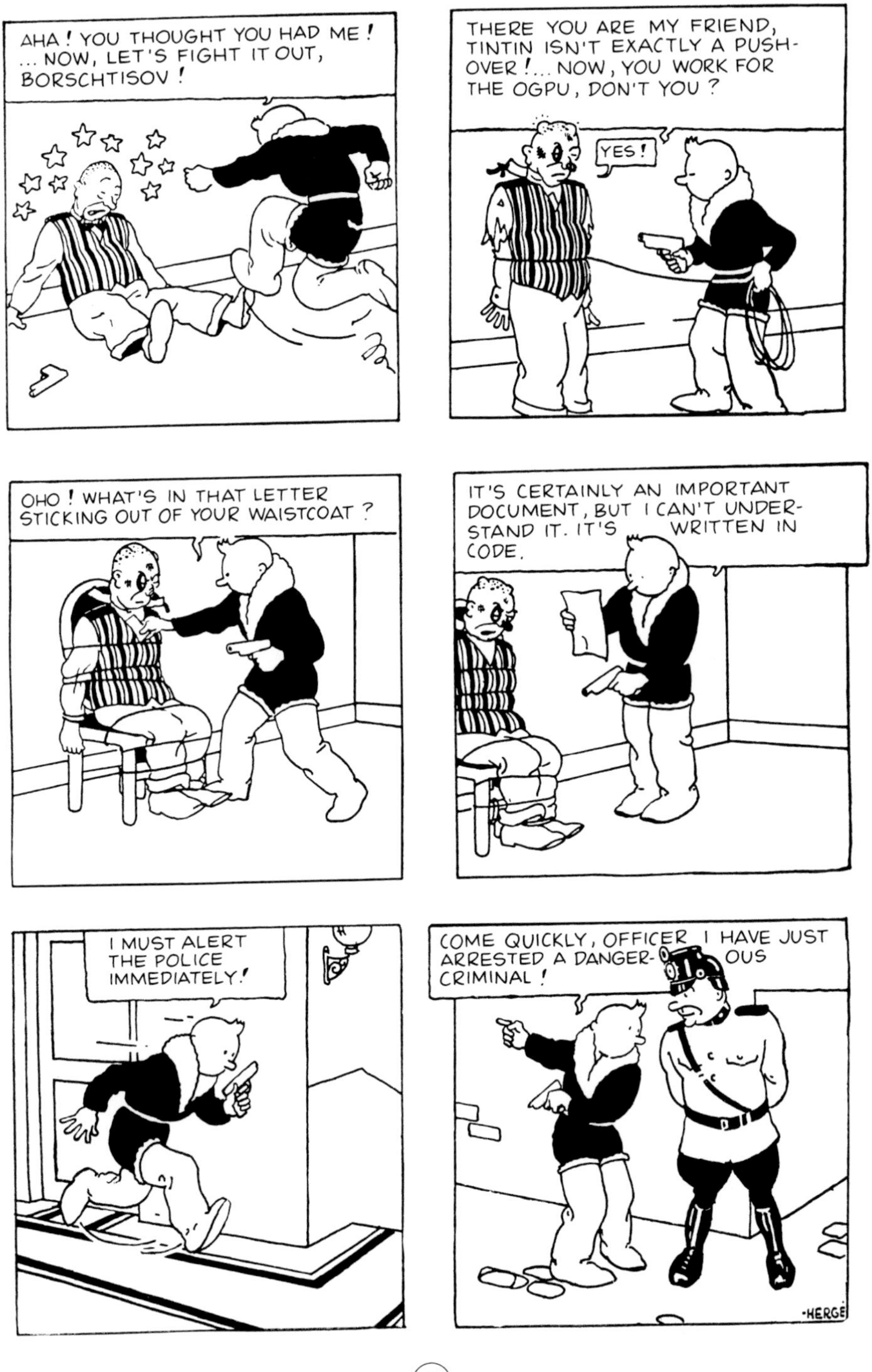
AHA ! YOU THOUGHT YOU HAD ME ! ... NOW, LET'S FIGHT IT OUT, BORSCHTISOV !
THERE YOU ARE MY FRIEND, TINTIN ISN'T EXACTLY A PUSH-OVER !... NOW, YOU WORK FOR THE OGPU, DON'T YOU ?
YES !
OHO ! WHAT'S IN THAT LETTER STICKING OUT OF YOUR WAISTCOAT ?
IT'S CERTAINLY AN IMPORTANT DOCUMENT, BUT I CAN'T UNDER-STAND IT. IT'S WRITTEN IN CODE.
I MUST ALERT THE POLICE IMMEDIATELY !
COME QUICKLY, OFFICER I HAVE JUST ARRESTED A DANGER-OUS CRIMINAL !
HERGÉ

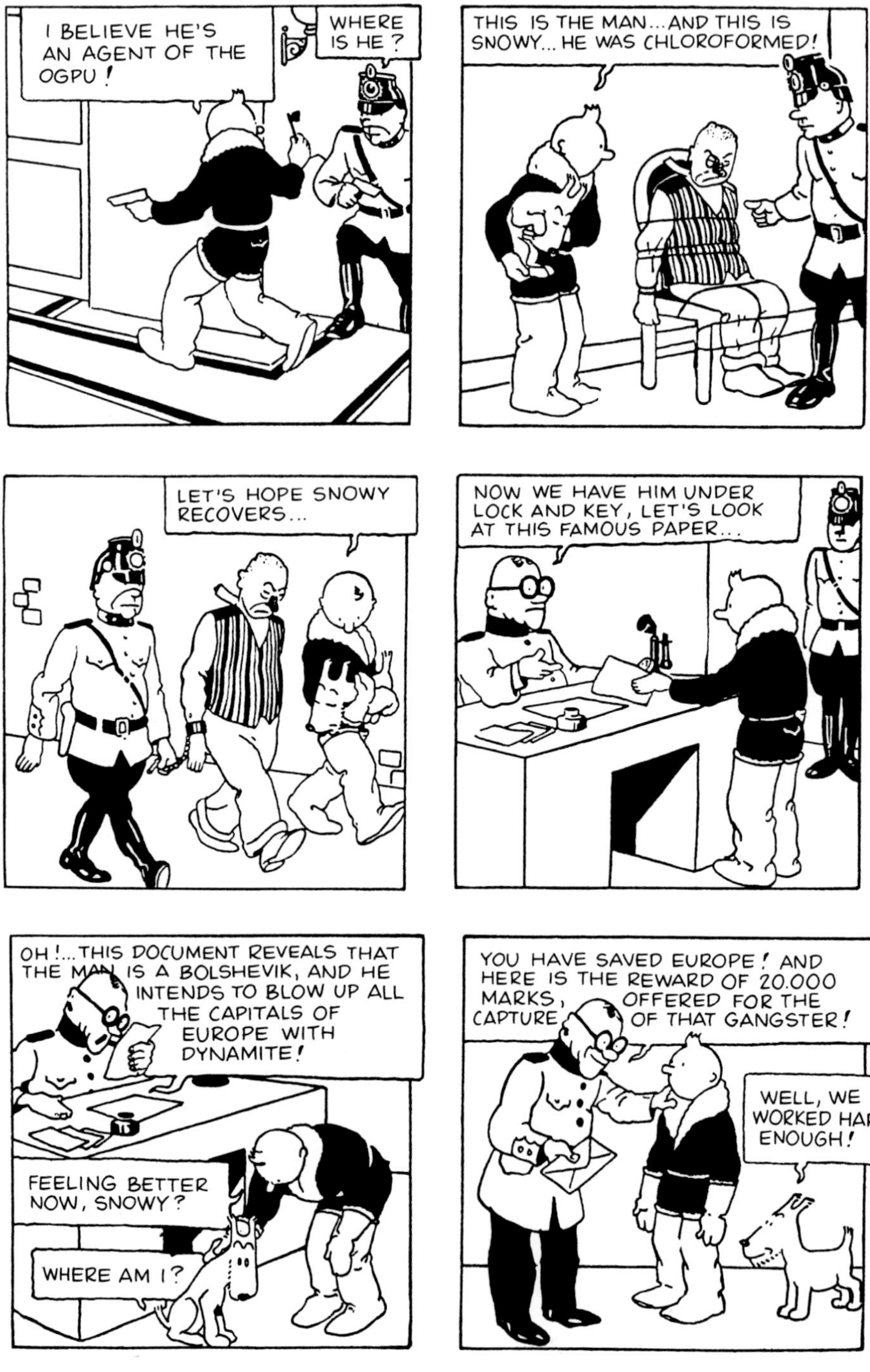
I BELIEVE HE'S AN AGENT OF THE OGPU!
WHERE IS HE?
THIS IS THE MAN... AND THIS IS SNOWY... HE WAS CHLOROFORMED!
LET'S HOPE SNOWY RECOVERS...
NOW WE HAVE HIM UNDER LOCK AND KEY, LET'S LOOK AT THIS FAMOUS PAPER...
OH!... THIS DOCUMENT REVEALS THAT THE MAN IS A BOLSHEVIK, AND HE INTENDS TO BLOW UP ALL THE CAPITALS OF EUROPE WITH DYNAMITE!
FEELING BETTER NOW, SNOWY?
WHERE AM I?
YOU HAVE SAVED EUROPE! AND HERE IS THE REWARD OF 20.000 MARKS, OFFERED FOR THE CAPTURE OF THAT GANGSTER!
WELL, WE WORKED HARD ENOUGH!

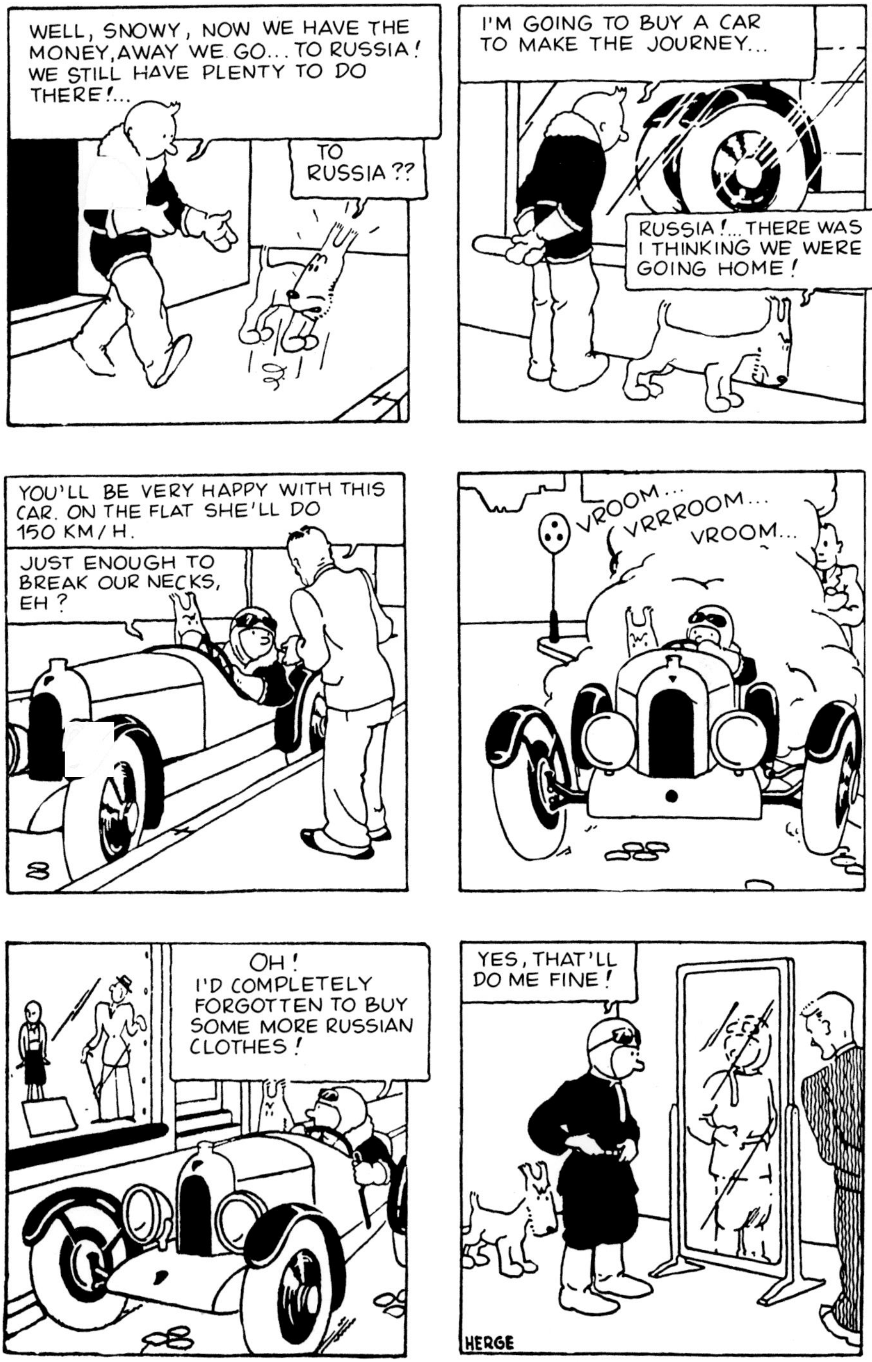
WELL, SNOWY, NOW WE HAVE THE MONEY, AWAY WE GO... TO RUSSIA! WE STILL HAVE PLENTY TO DO THERE!...
TO RUSSIA??
I'M GOING TO BUY A CAR TO MAKE THE JOURNEY...
RUSSIA!... THERE WAS I THINKING WE WERE GOING HOME!
YOU'LL BE VERY HAPPY WITH THIS CAR. ON THE FLAT SHE'LL DO 150 KM/H.
JUST ENOUGH TO BREAK OUR NECKS, EH?
VROOM...
VRRROOM...
VROOM...
OH! I'D COMPLETELY FORGOTTEN TO BUY SOME MORE RUSSIAN CLOTHES!
YES, THAT'LL DO ME FINE!
HERGE

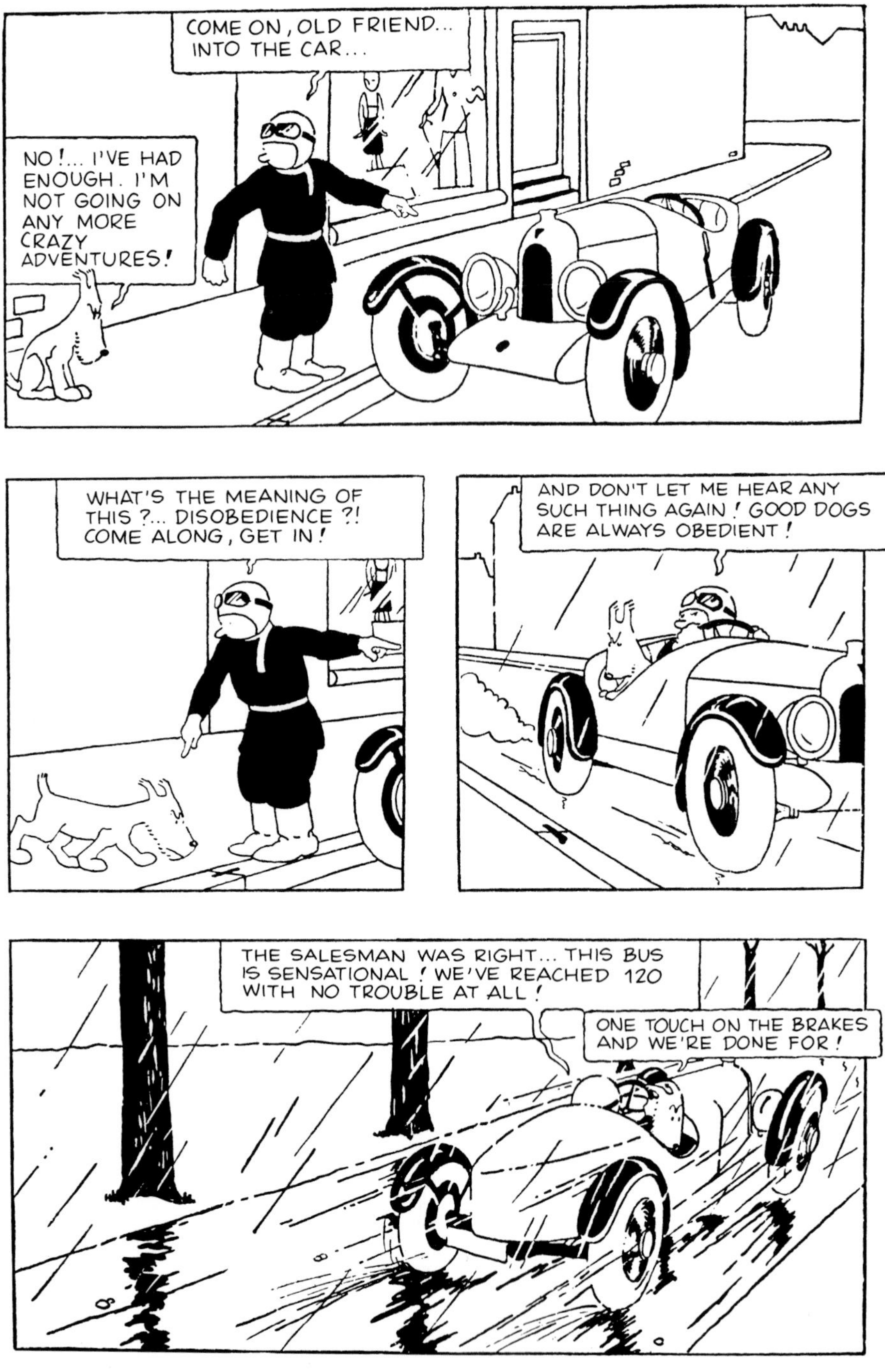
COME ON, OLD FRIEND... INTO THE CAR...
NO!... I'VE HAD ENOUGH. I'M NOT GOING ON ANY MORE CRAZY ADVENTURES!
WHAT'S THE MEANING OF THIS?... DISOBEDIENCE?! COME ALONG, GET IN!
AND DON'T LET ME HEAR ANY SUCH THING AGAIN! GOOD DOGS ARE ALWAYS OBEDIENT!
THE SALESMAN WAS RIGHT... THIS BUS IS SENSATIONAL! WE'VE REACHED 120 WITH NO TROUBLE AT ALL!
ONE TOUCH ON THE BRAKES AND WE'RE DONE FOR!

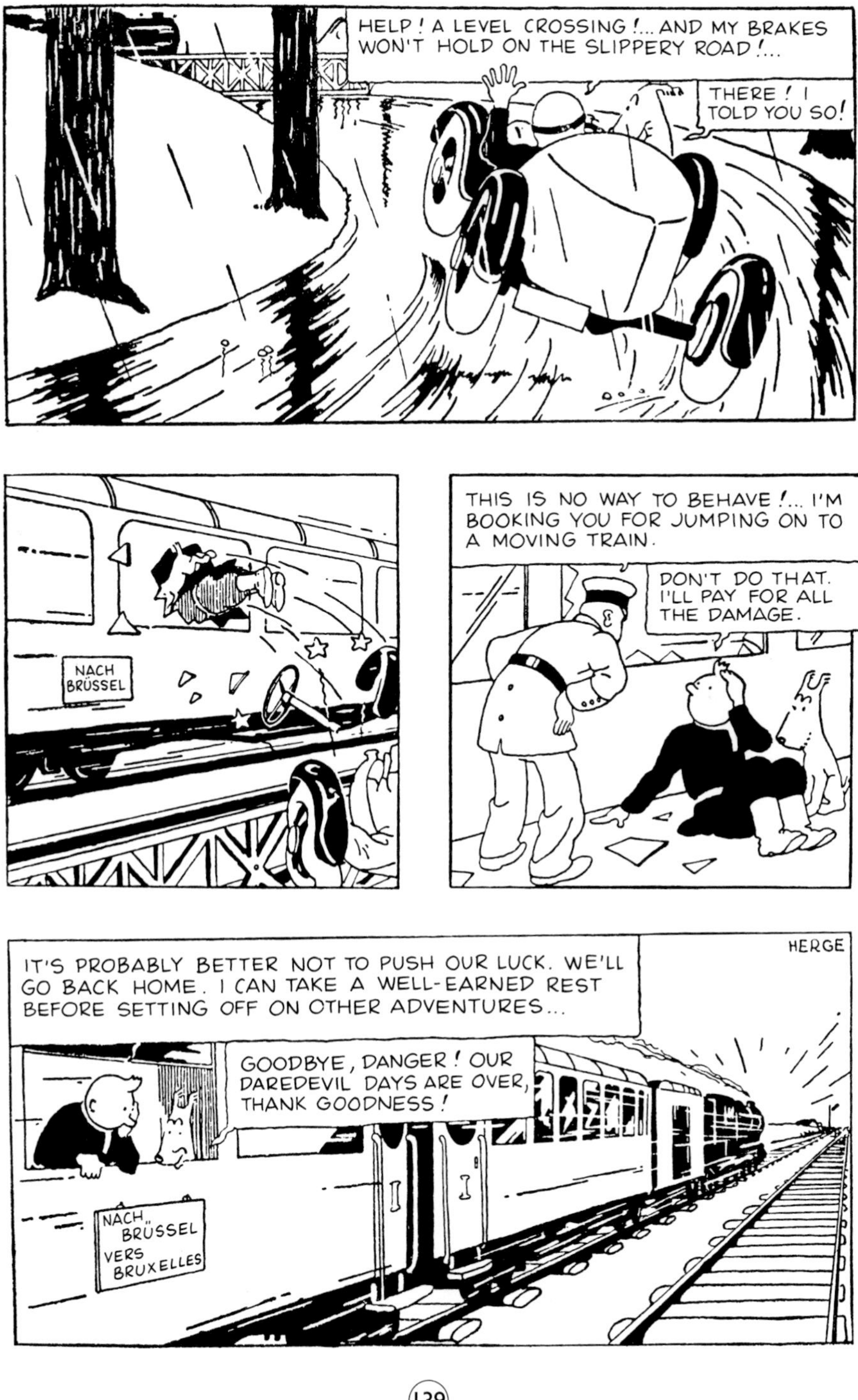
HELP! A LEVEL CROSSING!... AND MY BRAKES WON'T HOLD ON THE SLIPPERY ROAD!...
THERE! I TOLD YOU SO!
NACH BRÜSSEL
THIS IS NO WAY TO BEHAVE!... I'M BOOKING YOU FOR JUMPING ON TO A MOVING TRAIN.
DON'T DO THAT. I'LL PAY FOR ALL THE DAMAGE.
HERGE
IT'S PROBABLY BETTER NOT TO PUSH OUR LUCK. WE'LL GO BACK HOME. I CAN TAKE A WELL-EARNED REST BEFORE SETTING OFF ON OTHER ADVENTURES...
GOODBYE, DANGER! OUR DAREDEVIL DAYS ARE OVER, THANK GOODNESS!
NACH BRÜSSEL VERS BRUXELLES

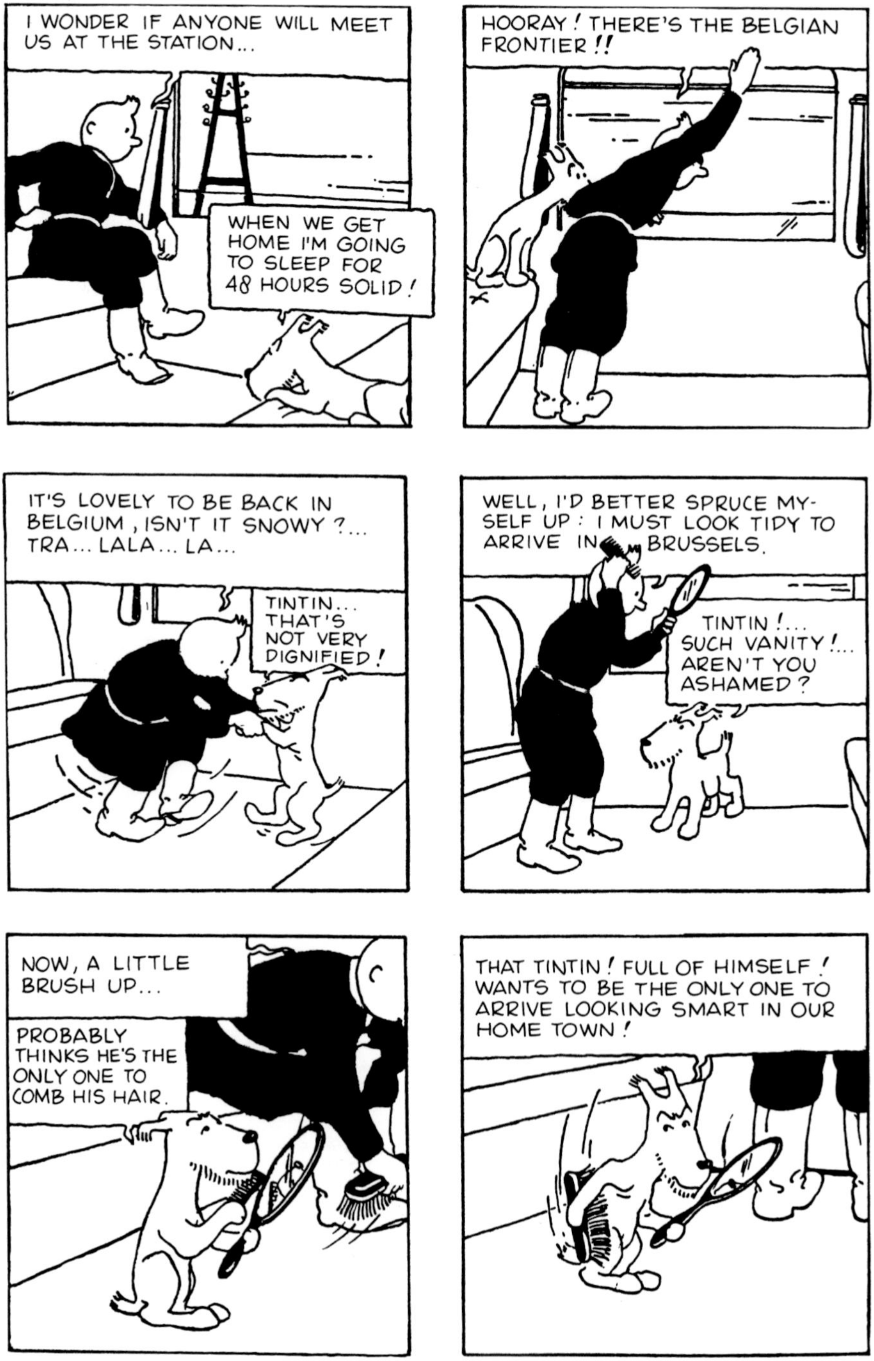
I WONDER IF ANYONE WILL MEET US AT THE STATION...
WHEN WE GET HOME I'M GOING TO SLEEP FOR 48 HOURS SOLID!
HOORAY! THERE'S THE BELGIAN FRONTIER!!
IT'S LOVELY TO BE BACK IN BELGIUM, ISN'T IT SNOWY?... TRA... LALA... LA...
TINTIN... THAT'S NOT VERY DIGNIFIED!
WELL, I'D BETTER SPRUCE MYSELF UP: I MUST LOOK TIDY TO ARRIVE IN BRUSSELS.
TINTIN!... SUCH VANITY!... AREN'T YOU ASHAMED?
NOW, A LITTLE BRUSH UP...
PROBABLY THINKS HE'S THE ONLY ONE TO COMB HIS HAIR.
THAT TINTIN! FULL OF HIMSELF! WANTS TO BE THE ONLY ONE TO ARRIVE LOOKING SMART IN OUR HOME TOWN!

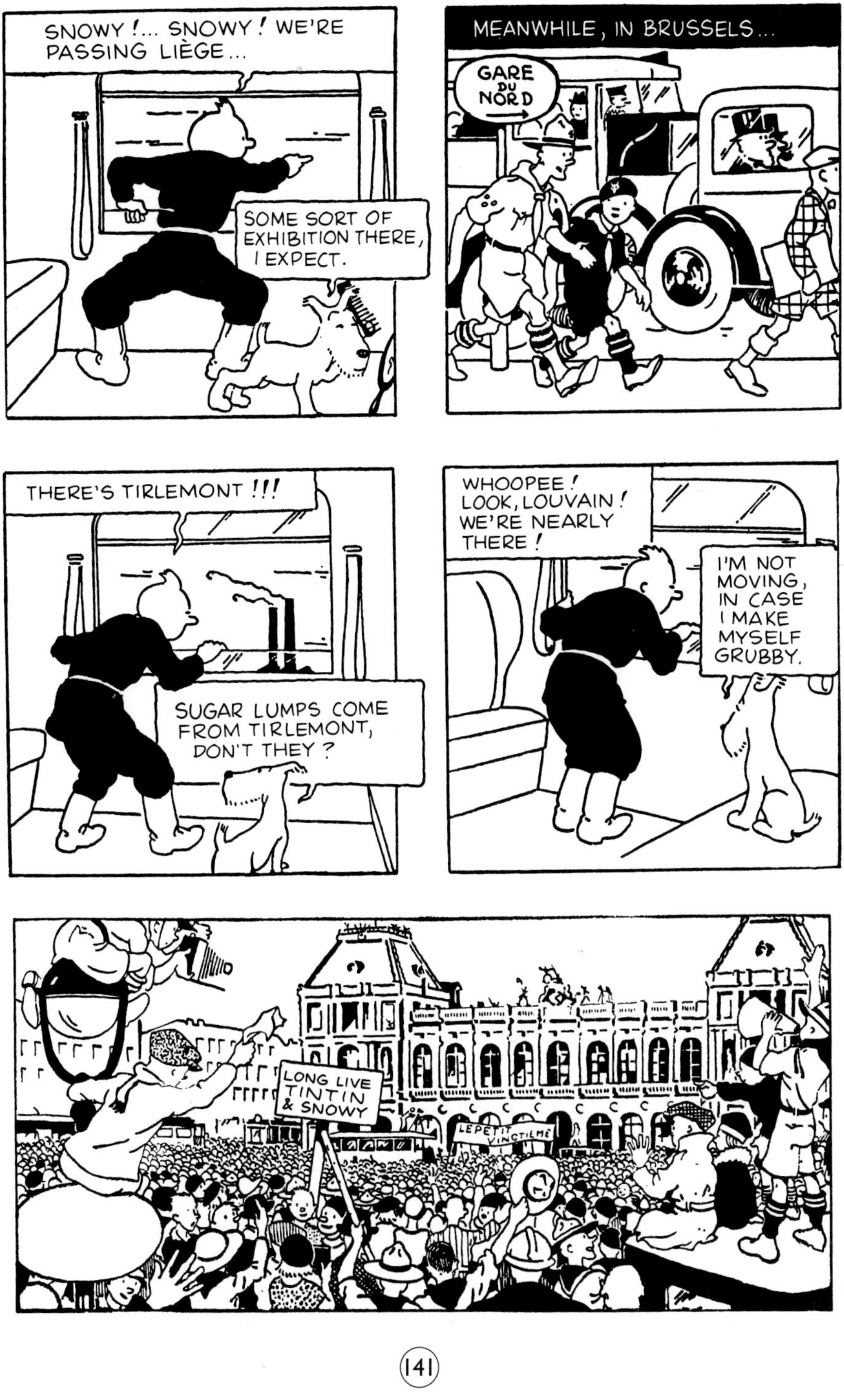
SNOWY !... SNOWY ! WE'RE PASSING LIÈGE ...
SOME SORT OF EXHIBITION THERE, I EXPECT.
MEANWHILE, IN BRUSSELS ...
GARE DU NORD
THERE'S TIRLEMONT !!!
SUGAR LUMPS COME FROM TIRLEMONT, DON'T THEY ?
WHOOPEE ! LOOK, LOUVAIN ! WE'RE NEARLY THERE !
I'M NOT MOVING, IN CASE I MAKE MYSELF GRUBBY.
LONG LIVE TINTIN & SNOWY
LE PETIT VINGTIÈME

HERGÉ
★
THE ADVENTURES OF
TINTIN
★
TINTIN
IN
AMERICA

EGMONT

TINTIN IN AMERICA

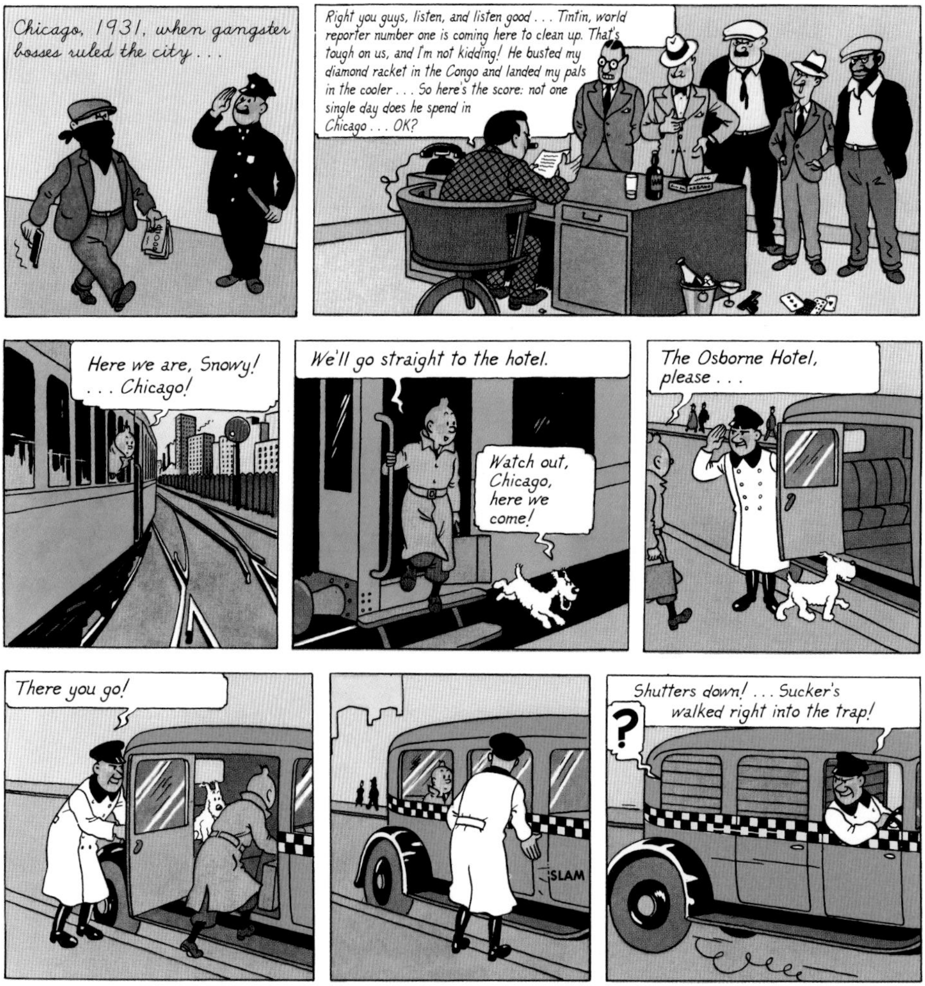
Chicago, 1931, when gangster bosses ruled the city . . .
Right you guys, listen, and listen good . . . Tintin, world reporter number one is coming here to clean up. That's tough on us, and I'm not kidding! He busted my diamond racket in the Congo and landed my pals in the cooler . . . So here's the score: not one single day does he spend in Chicago . . . OK?
Here we are, Snowy! . . . Chicago!
We'll go straight to the hotel.
Watch out, Chicago, here we come!
The Osborne Hotel, please . . .
There you go!
SLAM
?
Shutters down! . . . Sucker's walked right into the trap!

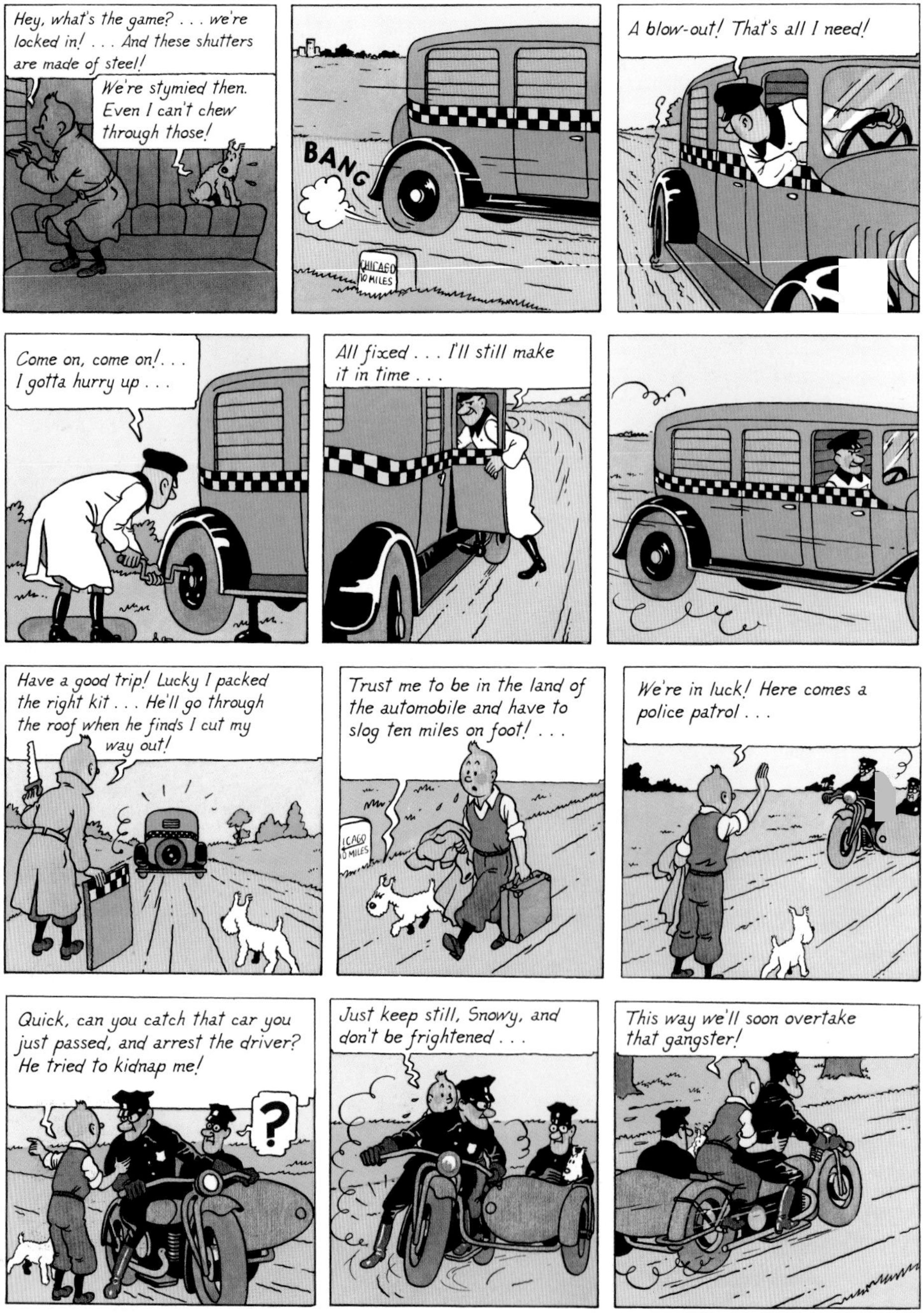

Hey, what's the game? . . . we're locked in! . . . And these shutters are made of steel!
We're stymied then. Even I can't chew through those!
BANG
CHICAGO 10 MILES
A blow-out! That's all I need!
Come on, come on! . . . I gotta hurry up . . .
All fixed . . . I'll still make it in time . . .
Have a good trip! Lucky I packed the right kit . . . He'll go through the roof when he finds I cut my way out!
Trust me to be in the land of the automobile and have to slog ten miles on foot! . . .
We're in luck! Here comes a police patrol . . .
Quick, can you catch that car you just passed, and arrest the driver? He tried to kidnap me!
?
Just keep still, Snowy, and don't be frightened . . .
This way we'll soon overtake that gangster!

That the car you mean?

Yes, it's him all right!

STOP!

Hands up, buddy!

You kidnapped me! Come on . . . Why?

They promised me five hundred bucks . . . They told me, if I got you into the taxi . . . dropped the steel shutters . . . and delivered you to the place they fixed . . .

What place?

The rendezvous . . . where I was to drive you? . . . OK, just to show I'm not really a crook, I'll spill the beans . . .

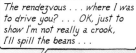

?

Look! A boomerang!

Thanks.

He's grabbed our bike!

'Bye, suckers!

Quick, all into the car!
After him!

Here, take my gun . . .

Thanks . . .

We're approaching the city . . .
Don't lose sight of him . . .

If Butch isn't on the lookout
with his car, I'm a dead duck!

OK, let her go!

Saved!

A cab driven by the cops . . .
hit side on by another car . . .

Say, what
a mess!

Some
crash!

DING
DING
DING

Gee! The poor kid . . .
He looks so
young . . .

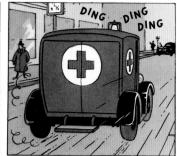

DING
DING
DING

148

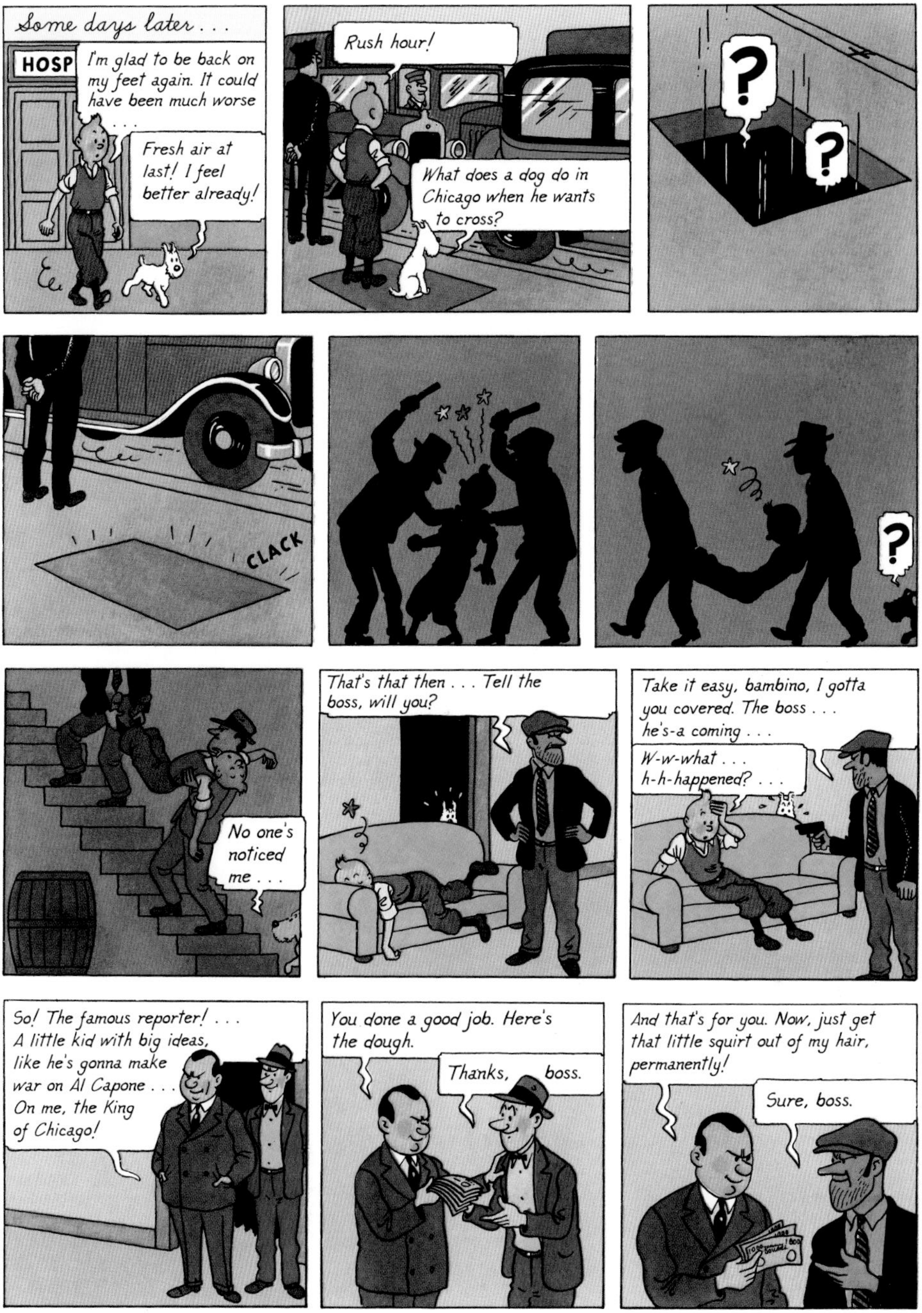
Some days later . . .
HOSP
I'm glad to be back on my feet again. It could have been much worse . . .
Fresh air at last! I feel better already!
Rush hour!
What does a dog do in Chicago when he wants to cross?
CLACK
No one's noticed me . . .
That's that then . . . Tell the boss, will you?
Take it easy, bambino, I gotta you covered. The boss . . . he's-a coming . . .
W-w-what . . . h-h-happened? . . .
So! The famous reporter! . . . A little kid with big ideas, like he's gonna make war on Al Capone . . . On me, the King of Chicago!
You done a good job. Here's the dough.
Thanks, boss.
And that's for you. Now, just get that little squirt out of my hair, permanently!
Sure, boss.

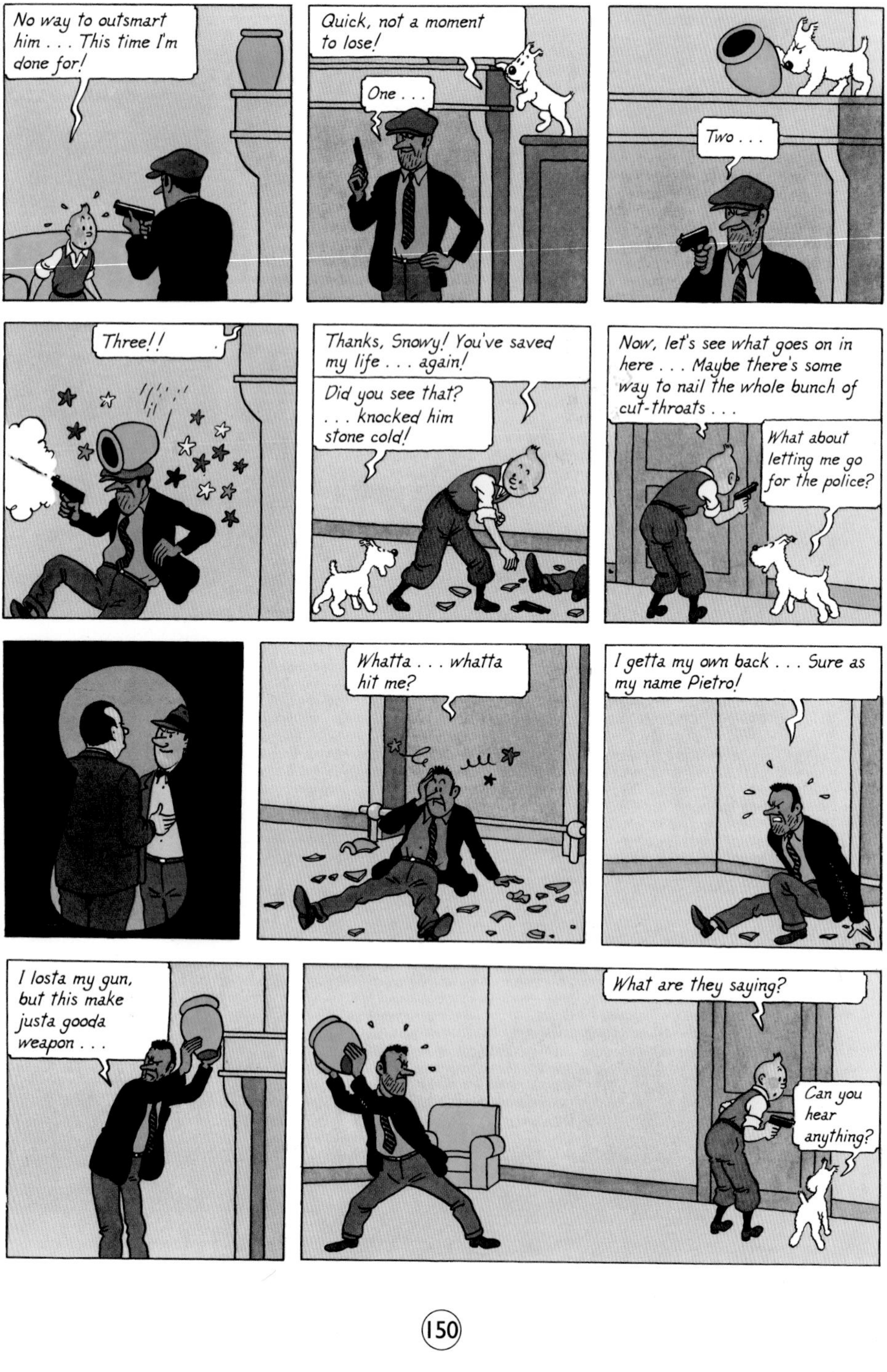

No way to outsmart him . . . This time I'm done for!
Quick, not a moment to lose!
One . . .
Two . . .
Three!!
Thanks, Snowy! You've saved my life . . . again!
Did you see that? . . . knocked him stone cold!
Now, let's see what goes on in here . . . Maybe there's some way to nail the whole bunch of cut-throats . . .
What about letting me go for the police?
Whatta . . . whatta hit me?
I getta my own back . . . Sure as my name Pietro!
I losta my gun, but this make justa gooda weapon . . .
What are they saying?
Can you hear anything?

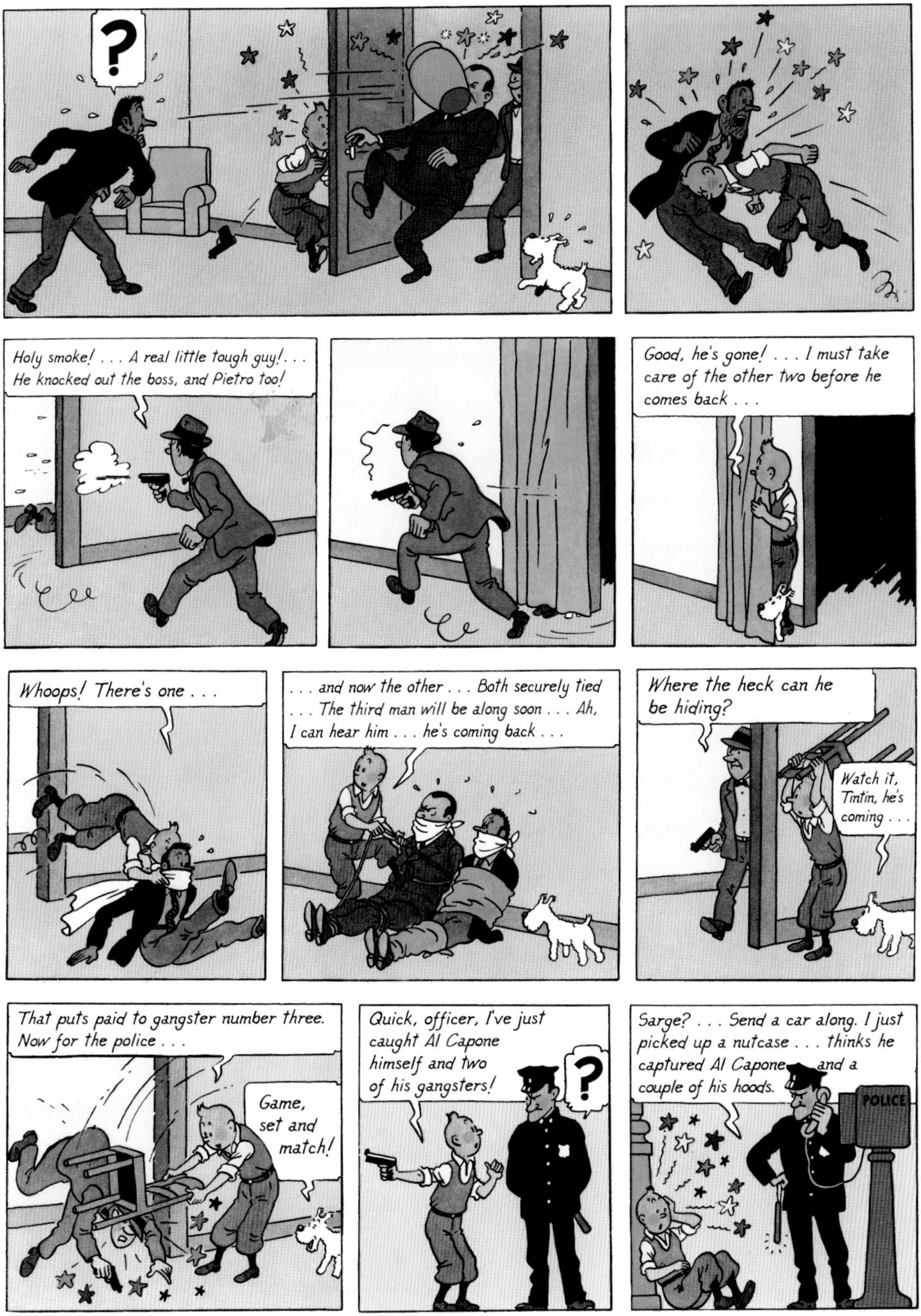
?
Holy smoke! . . . A real little tough guy! . . . He knocked out the boss, and Pietro too!
Good, he's gone! . . . I must take care of the other two before he comes back . . .
Whoops! There's one . . .
. . . and now the other . . . Both securely tied . . . The third man will be along soon . . . Ah, I can hear him . . . he's coming back . . .
Where the heck can he be hiding?
Watch it, Tintin, he's coming . . .
That puts paid to gangster number three. Now for the police . . .
Game, set and match!
Quick, officer, I've just caught Al Capone himself and two of his gangsters!
?
Sarge? . . . Send a car along. I just picked up a nutcase . . . thinks he captured Al Capone and a couple of his hoods.
POLICE

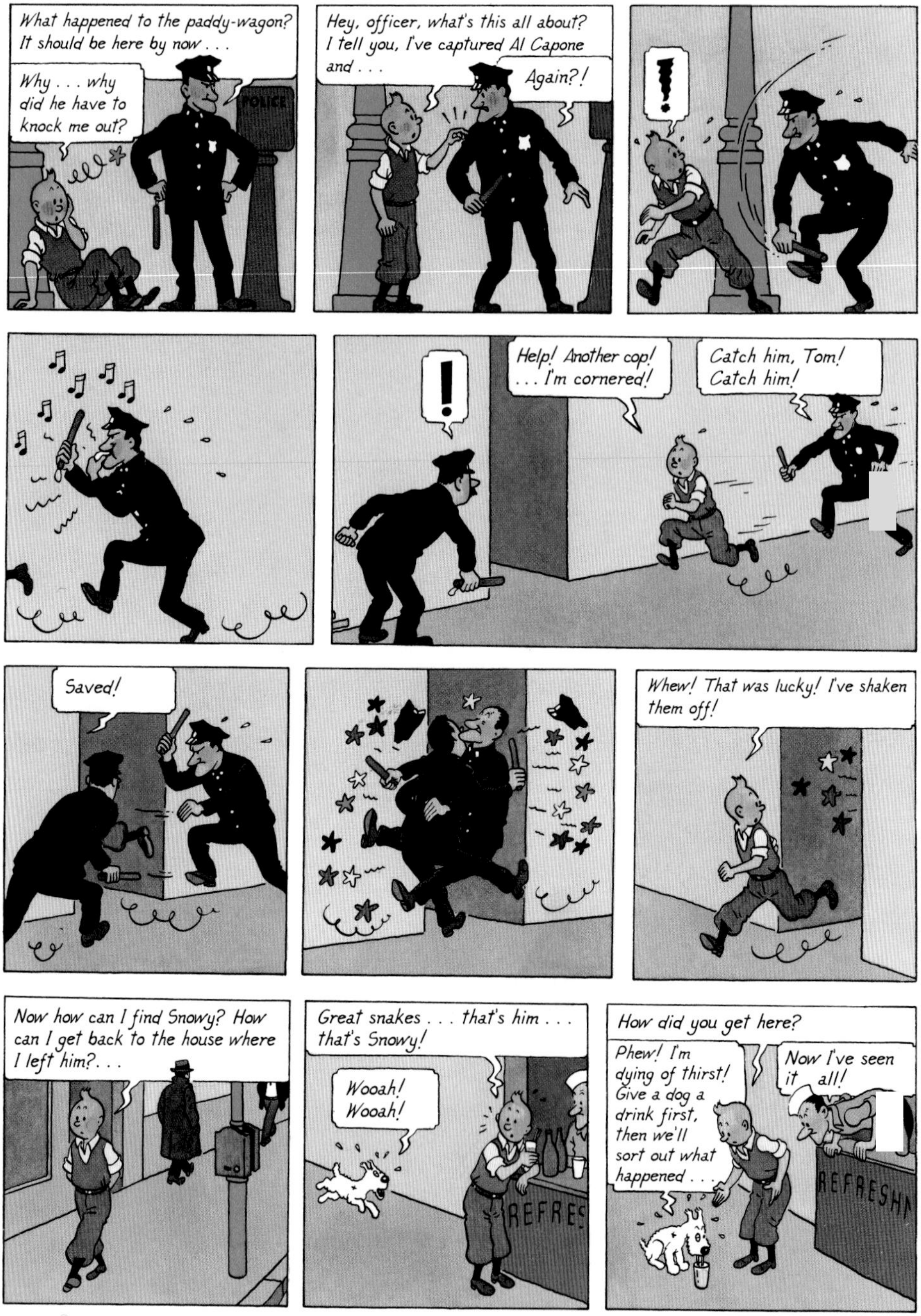
What happened to the paddy-wagon? It should be here by now . . .
Why . . . why did he have to knock me out?
POLICE
Hey, officer, what's this all about? I tell you, I've captured Al Capone and . . .
Again?!
!
!
Help! Another cop! . . . I'm cornered!
Catch him, Tom! Catch him!
Saved!
Whew! That was lucky! I've shaken them off!
Now how can I find Snowy? How can I get back to the house where I left him?. . .
Great snakes . . . that's him . . . that's Snowy!
Wooah! Wooah!
REFRES
How did you get here?
Phew! I'm dying of thirst! Give a dog a drink first, then we'll sort out what happened . . .
Now I've seen it all!
REFRESH

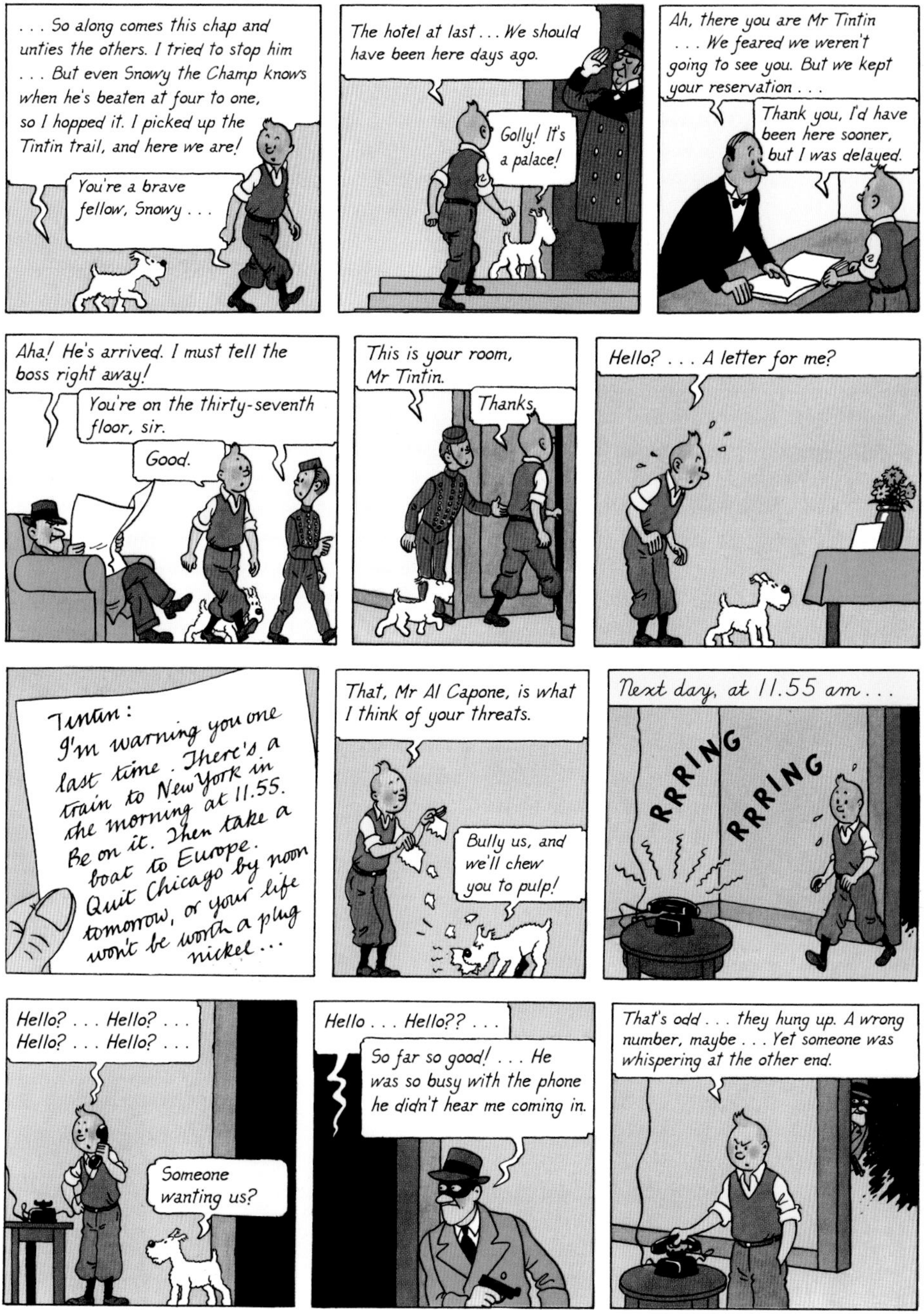
. . . So along comes this chap and unties the others. I tried to stop him . . . But even Snowy the Champ knows when he's beaten at four to one, so I hopped it. I picked up the Tintin trail, and here we are!
You're a brave fellow, Snowy . . .
The hotel at last . . . We should have been here days ago.
Golly! It's a palace!
Ah, there you are Mr Tintin . . . We feared we weren't going to see you. But we kept your reservation . . .
Thank you, I'd have been here sooner, but I was delayed.
Aha! He's arrived. I must tell the boss right away!
You're on the thirty-seventh floor, sir.
Good.
This is your room, Mr Tintin.
Thanks.
Hello? . . . A letter for me?
Tintin:
I'm warning you one last time. There's a train to New York in the morning at 11.55. Be on it. Then take a boat to Europe. Quit Chicago by noon tomorrow, or your life won't be worth a plug nickel . . .
That, Mr Al Capone, is what I think of your threats.
Bully us, and we'll chew you to pulp!
Next day, at 11.55 am . . .
RRRING
RRRING
Hello? . . . Hello? . . . Hello? . . . Hello? . . .
Someone wanting us?
Hello . . . Hello?? . . .
So far so good! . . . He was so busy with the phone he didn't hear me coming in.
That's odd . . . they hung up. A wrong number, maybe . . . Yet someone was whispering at the other end.

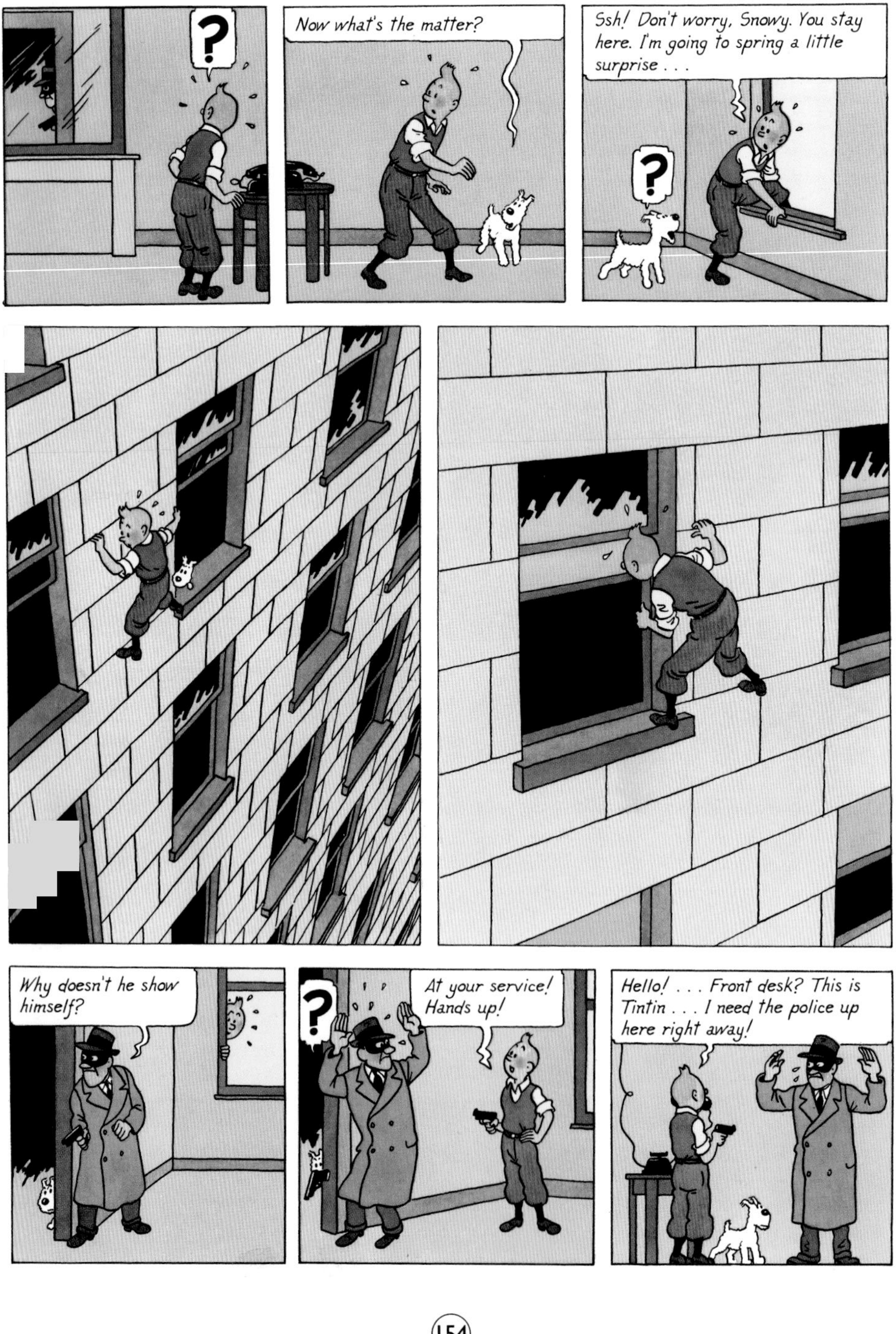
?
Now what's the matter?
Ssh! Don't worry, Snowy. You stay here. I'm going to spring a little surprise . . .
?
Why doesn't he show himself?
?
At your service! Hands up!
Hello! . . . Front desk? This is Tintin . . . I need the police up here right away!

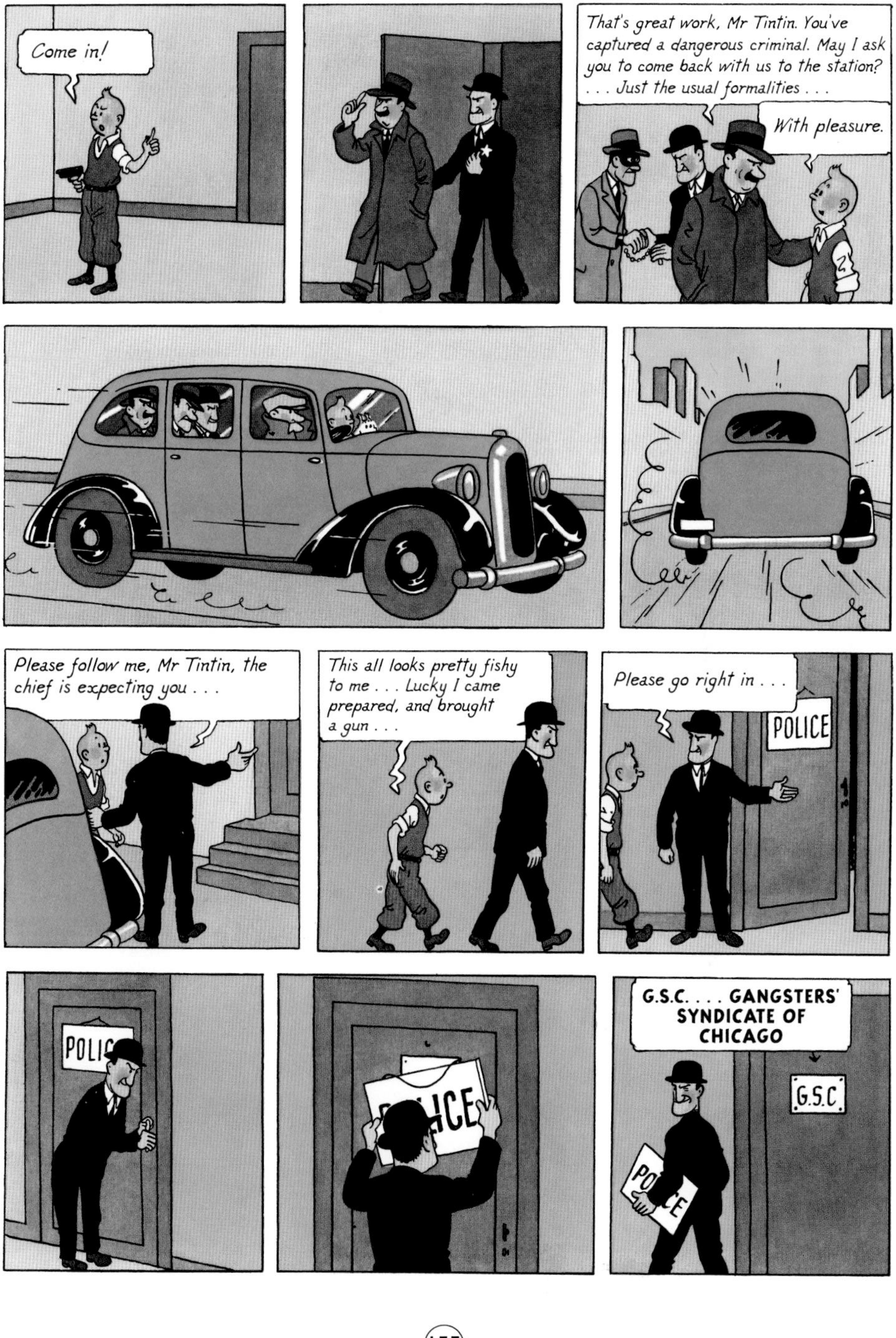
Come in!
That's great work, Mr Tintin. You've captured a dangerous criminal. May I ask you to come back with us to the station? . . . Just the usual formalities . . .
With pleasure.
Please follow me, Mr Tintin, the chief is expecting you . . .
This all looks pretty fishy to me . . . Lucky I came prepared, and brought a gun . . .
Please go right in . . .
POLICE
POLICE
G.S.C. . . . GANGSTERS' SYNDICATE OF CHICAGO
G.S.C
POLICE

My dear Mr Tintin, this is a pleasure! I'm glad to meet you. Do please sit down . . . Have a cigar? . . . No? . . . Then I'll come straight to the point . . .

I'm Bobby Smiles, boss of the rival gangs fighting Al Capone and his mob. I'm hiring you at $2000 a month to help me bring him down. If you rub Capone out yourself, there's a bonus of twenty grand . . . Agreed? . . . Here's your contract. Sign there.

Get your hands up, you crook! . . . And I'll take care of that paper . . . Just remember, I came to Chicago to clean the place up, not to become a gangster's stooge!

So I'll make a start by arresting you!

Oh? . . . Is that so?

Marvellous little gadget, just under my foot!

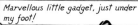

I've been tricked . . . and now I'm trapped . . . Ugh! Smoke! . . . What a peculiar smell . . . It's like . . .

Help! It's gas! . . . They mean to kill me . . . Quick, my handkerchief!

Useless! . . . I'm done for! . . . I'm choking . . . My lungs . . . they're burning . . .

There he is, Nick! . . . O.X2Z gas sure does knock 'em out!

To the waterfront, fast. Lake Michigan for him!

No one here. All clear, Nick, bring him along!

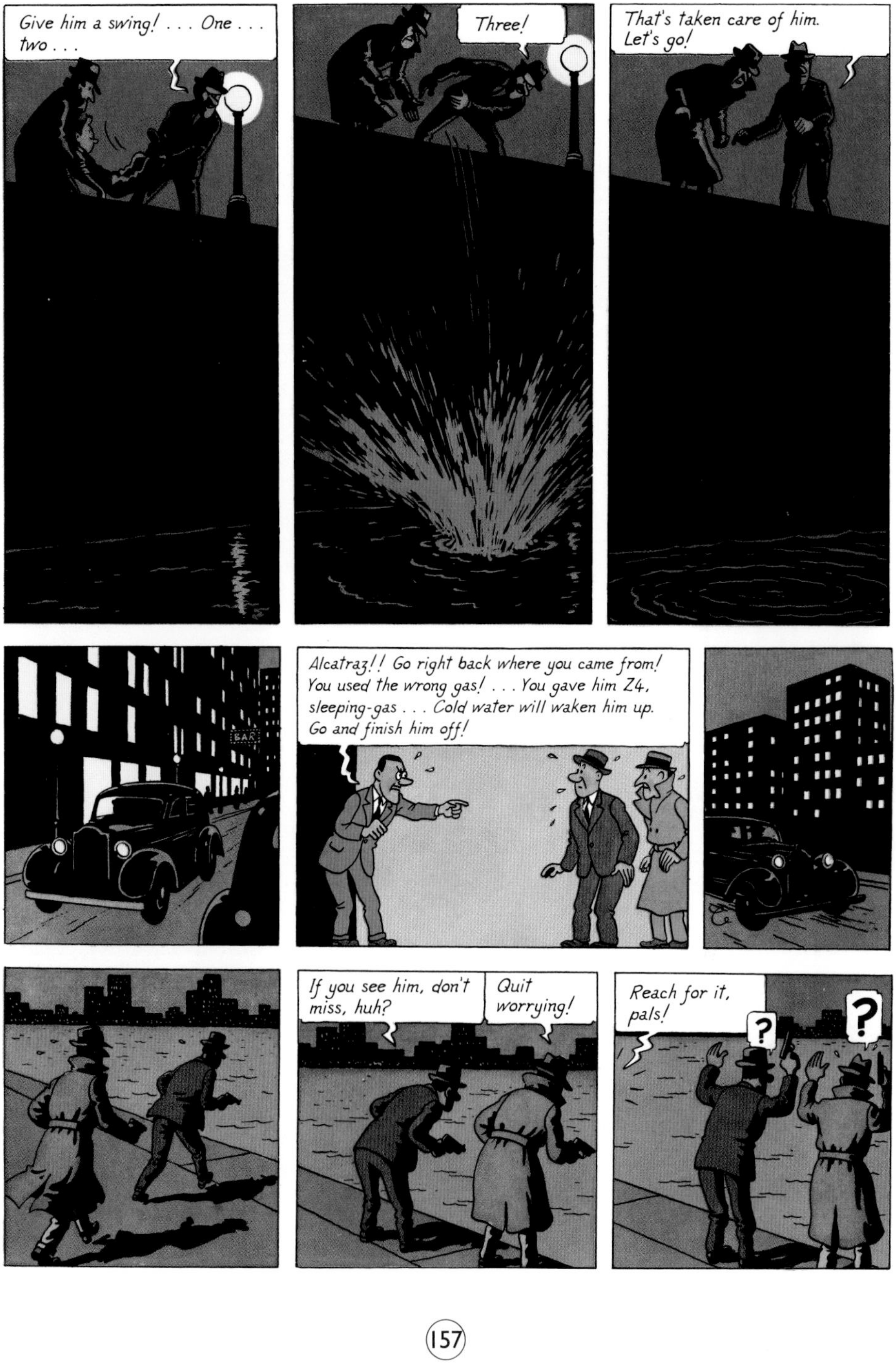
Give him a swing! . . . One . . . two . . .
Three!
That's taken care of him. Let's go!
BAR
Alcatraz!! Go right back where you came from! You used the wrong gas! . . . You gave him Z4, sleeping-gas . . . Cold water will waken him up. Go and finish him off!
If you see him, don't miss, huh?
Quit worrying!
Reach for it, pals!
?
?

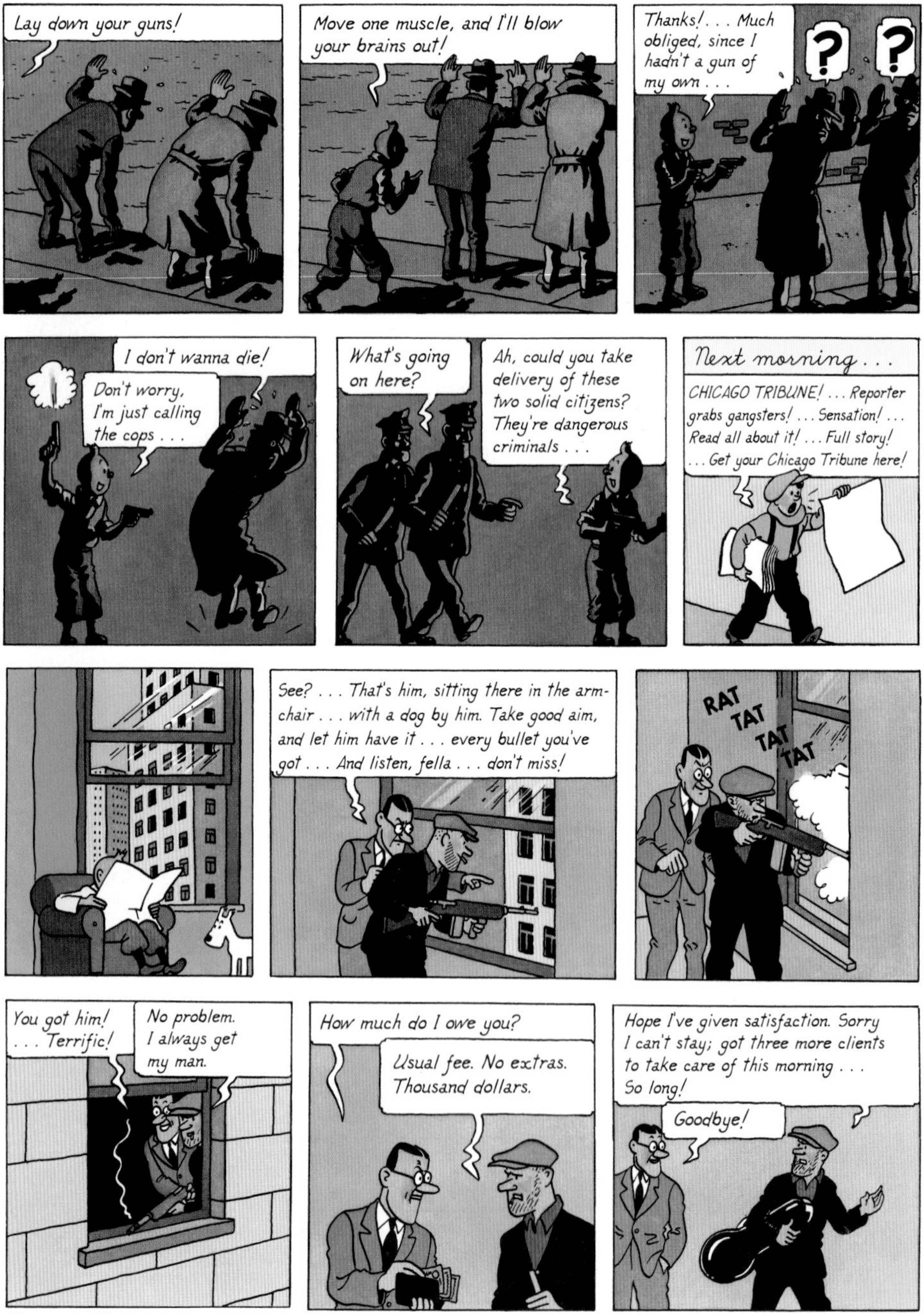
Lay down your guns!
Move one muscle, and I'll blow your brains out!
Thanks! . . . Much obliged, since I hadn't a gun of my own . . .
?
?
I don't wanna die!
Don't worry, I'm just calling the cops . . .
What's going on here?
Ah, could you take delivery of these two solid citizens? They're dangerous criminals . . .
Next morning . . .
CHICAGO TRIBUNE! . . . Reporter grabs gangsters! . . . Sensation! . . . Read all about it! . . . Full story! . . . Get your Chicago Tribune here!
See? . . . That's him, sitting there in the arm-chair . . . with a dog by him. Take good aim, and let him have it . . . every bullet you've got . . . And listen, fella . . . don't miss!
RAT TAT TAT TAT
You got him! . . . Terrific!
No problem. I always get my man.
How much do I owe you?
Usual fee. No extras. Thousand dollars.
Hope I've given satisfaction. Sorry I can't stay; got three more clients to take care of this morning . . . So long!
Goodbye!

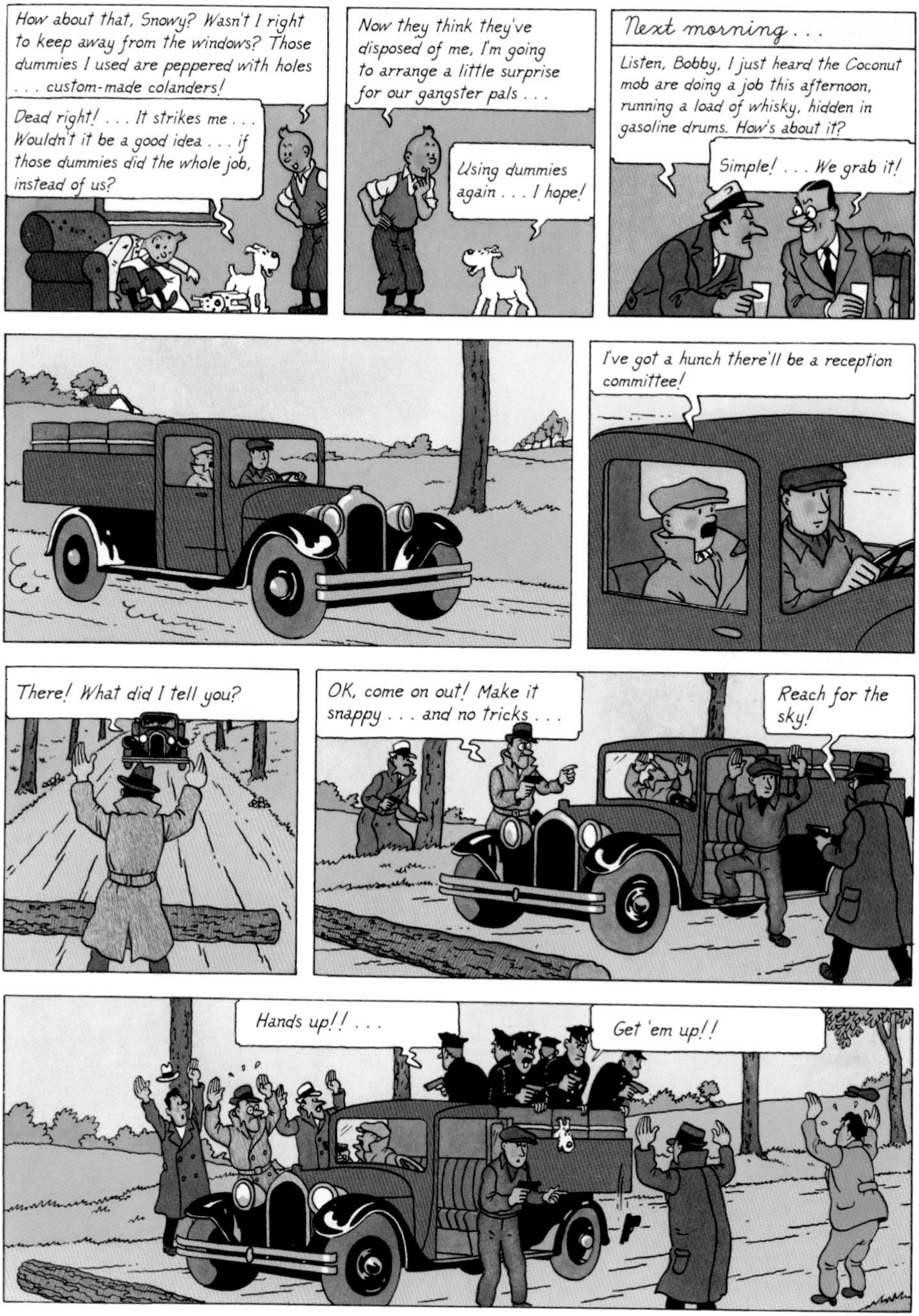
How about that, Snowy? Wasn't I right to keep away from the windows? Those dummies I used are peppered with holes . . . custom-made colanders!
Dead right! . . . It strikes me . . . Wouldn't it be a good idea . . . if those dummies did the whole job, instead of us?
Now they think they've disposed of me, I'm going to arrange a little surprise for our gangster pals . . .
Using dummies again . . . I hope!
Next morning . . .
Listen, Bobby, I just heard the Coconut mob are doing a job this afternoon, running a load of whisky, hidden in gasoline drums. How's about it?
Simple! . . . We grab it!
I've got a hunch there'll be a reception committee!
There! What did I tell you?
OK, come on out! Make it snappy . . . and no tricks . . .
Reach for the sky!
Hands up!! . . .
Get 'em up!!

You did a fine job, Mr Tintin . . . a fine job! Thanks to you, we've landed a really big fish, I . . .

Hey! What's that?

BANG
BANG
BANG

See ya, fellas!

Suffering catfish! Getting away under my very nose! And Bobby Smiles, too, the big boss!

Don't worry, I'll bring Bobby Smiles to justice!

A few days later . . .

These two telegrams are about Bobby Smiles. They say he's been seen in Redskin City, a small place near the Indian Reservations. Come on Snowy; it's Redskin City for us!

But . . . but . . . You don't really mean us to go into Indian country, do you Tintin?

Two whole days on the train! . . . Oh well, we're here at last, and that's what matters!

REDSKIN
CITY

Just look, Snowy . . . A real Red Indian.

I have a feeling we look a bit out of place here, Snowy . . .

$5

$10

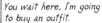
You wait here, I'm going to buy an outfit.

Redskin dogs! OK, so I'm a paleface . . . Haven't you redskins ever seen one before?

It's the very latest fashion . . . cartridge belt slung to the right . . . Last winter's models, all to the left . . .

Good. Just what I want!

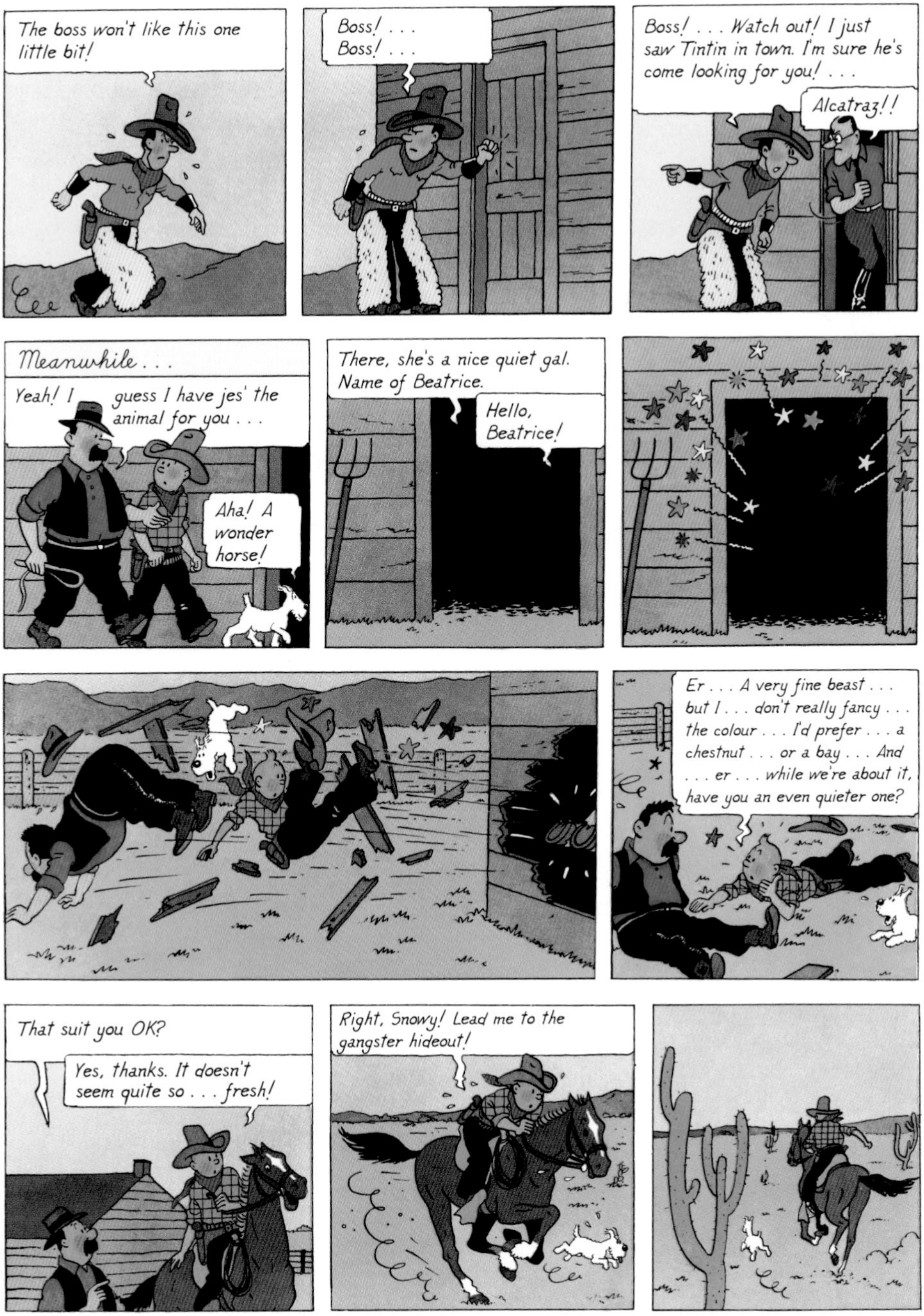

The boss won't like this one little bit!
Boss! . . . Boss! . . .
Boss! . . . Watch out! I just saw Tintin in town. I'm sure he's come looking for you! . . .
Alcatraz!!
Meanwhile . . .
Yeah! I guess I have jes' the animal for you . . .
Aha! A wonder horse!
There, she's a nice quiet gal. Name of Beatrice.
Hello, Beatrice!
Er . . . A very fine beast . . . but I . . . don't really fancy . . . the colour . . . I'd prefer . . . a chestnut . . . or a bay . . . And . . . er . . . while we're about it, have you an even quieter one?
That suit you OK?
Yes, thanks. It doesn't seem quite so . . . fresh!
Right, Snowy! Lead me to the gangster hideout!

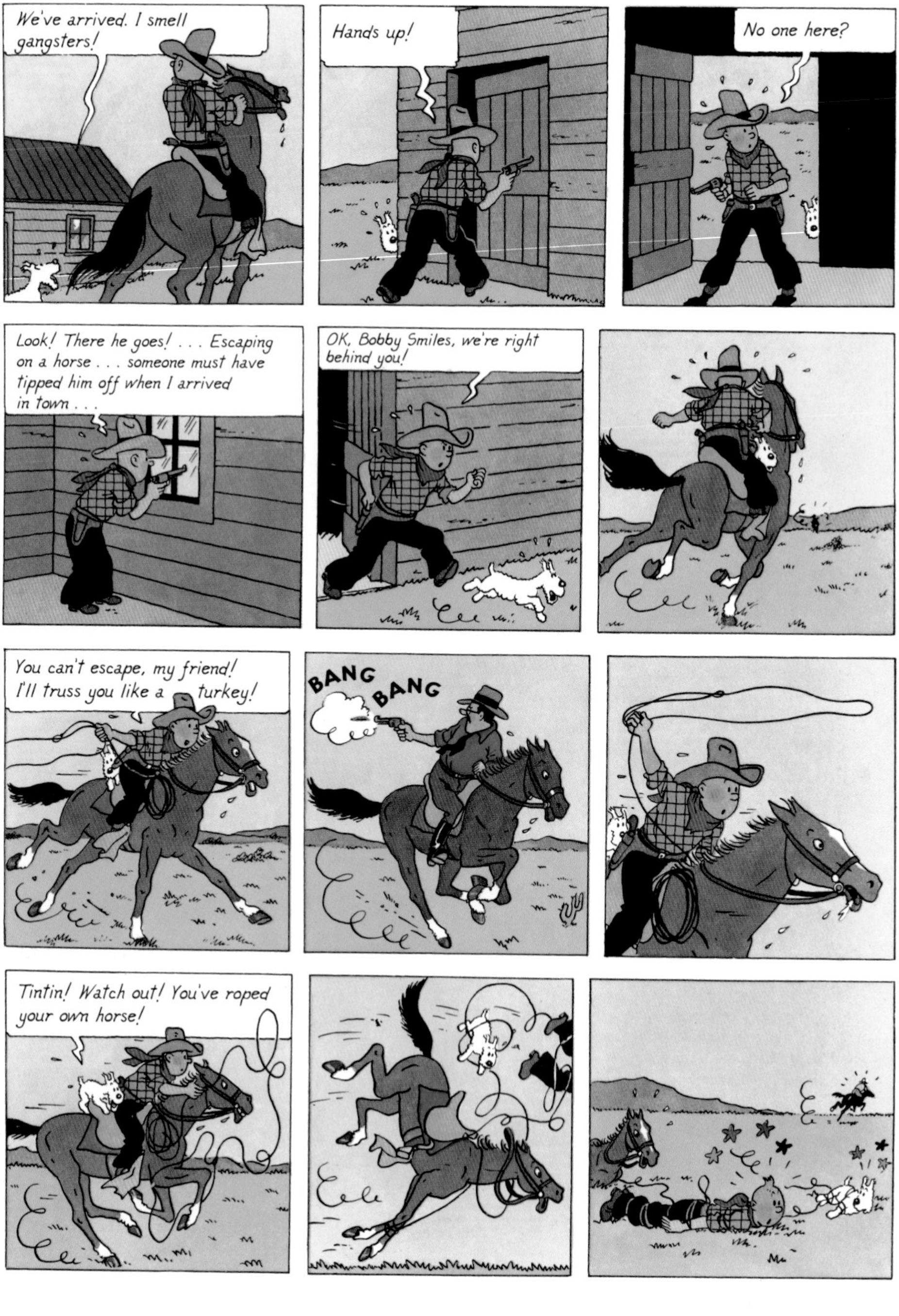
We've arrived. I smell gangsters!
Hands up!
No one here?
Look! There he goes! . . . Escaping on a horse . . . someone must have tipped him off when I arrived in town . . .
OK, Bobby Smiles, we're right behind you!
You can't escape, my friend! I'll truss you like a turkey!
BANG
BANG
Tintin! Watch out! You've roped your own horse!

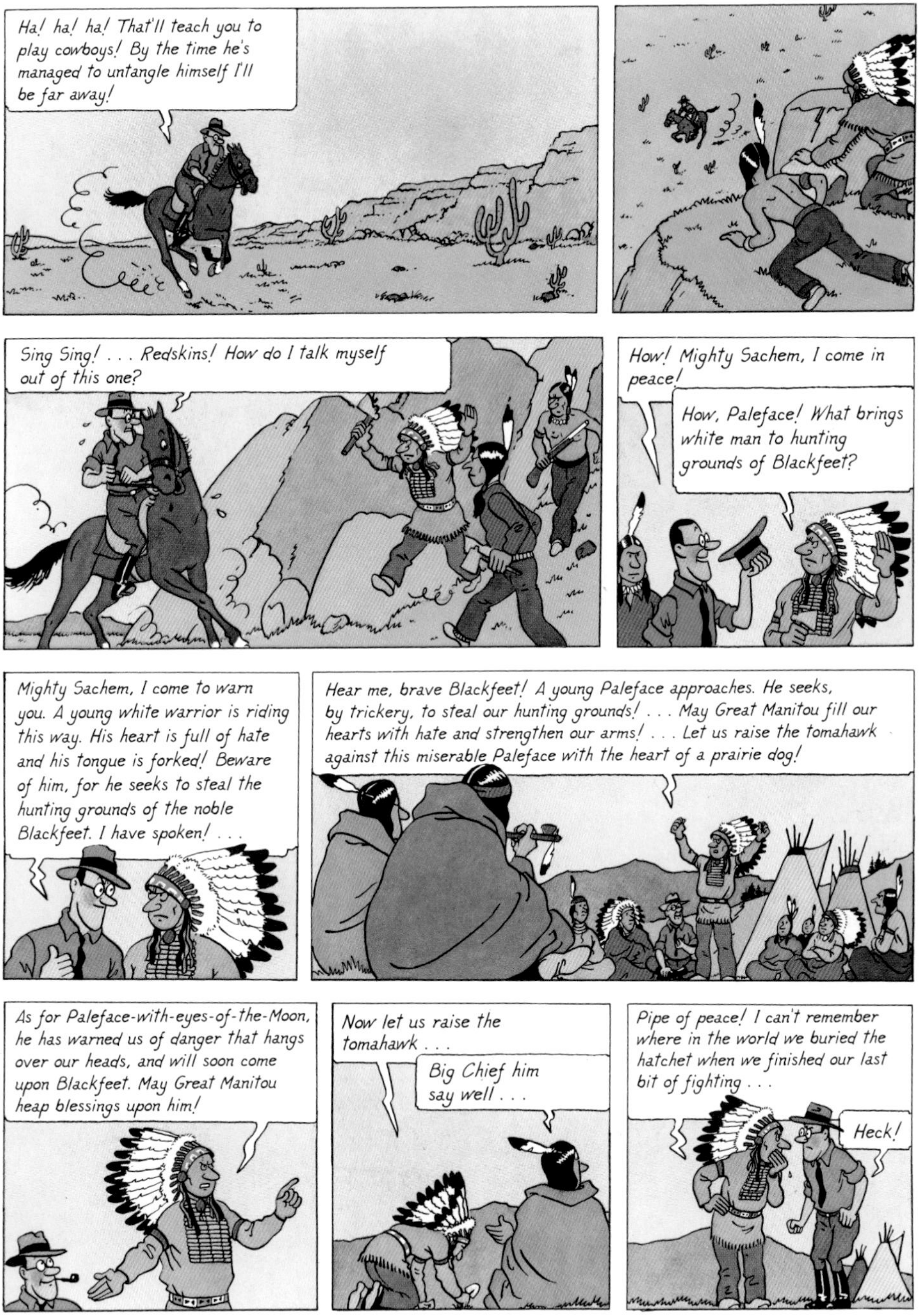

Ha! ha! ha! That'll teach you to play cowboys! By the time he's managed to untangle himself I'll be far away!
Sing Sing! . . . Redskins! How do I talk myself out of this one?
How! Mighty Sachem, I come in peace!
How, Paleface! What brings white man to hunting grounds of Blackfeet?
Mighty Sachem, I come to warn you. A young white warrior is riding this way. His heart is full of hate and his tongue is forked! Beware of him, for he seeks to steal the hunting grounds of the noble Blackfeet. I have spoken! . . .
Hear me, brave Blackfeet! A young Paleface approaches. He seeks, by trickery, to steal our hunting grounds! . . . May Great Manitou fill our hearts with hate and strengthen our arms! . . . Let us raise the tomahawk against this miserable Paleface with the heart of a prairie dog!
As for Paleface-with-eyes-of-the-Moon, he has warned us of danger that hangs over our heads, and will soon come upon Blackfeet. May Great Manitou heap blessings upon him!
Now let us raise the tomahawk . . .
Big Chief him say well . . .
Pipe of peace! I can't remember where in the world we buried the hatchet when we finished our last bit of fighting . . .
Heck!

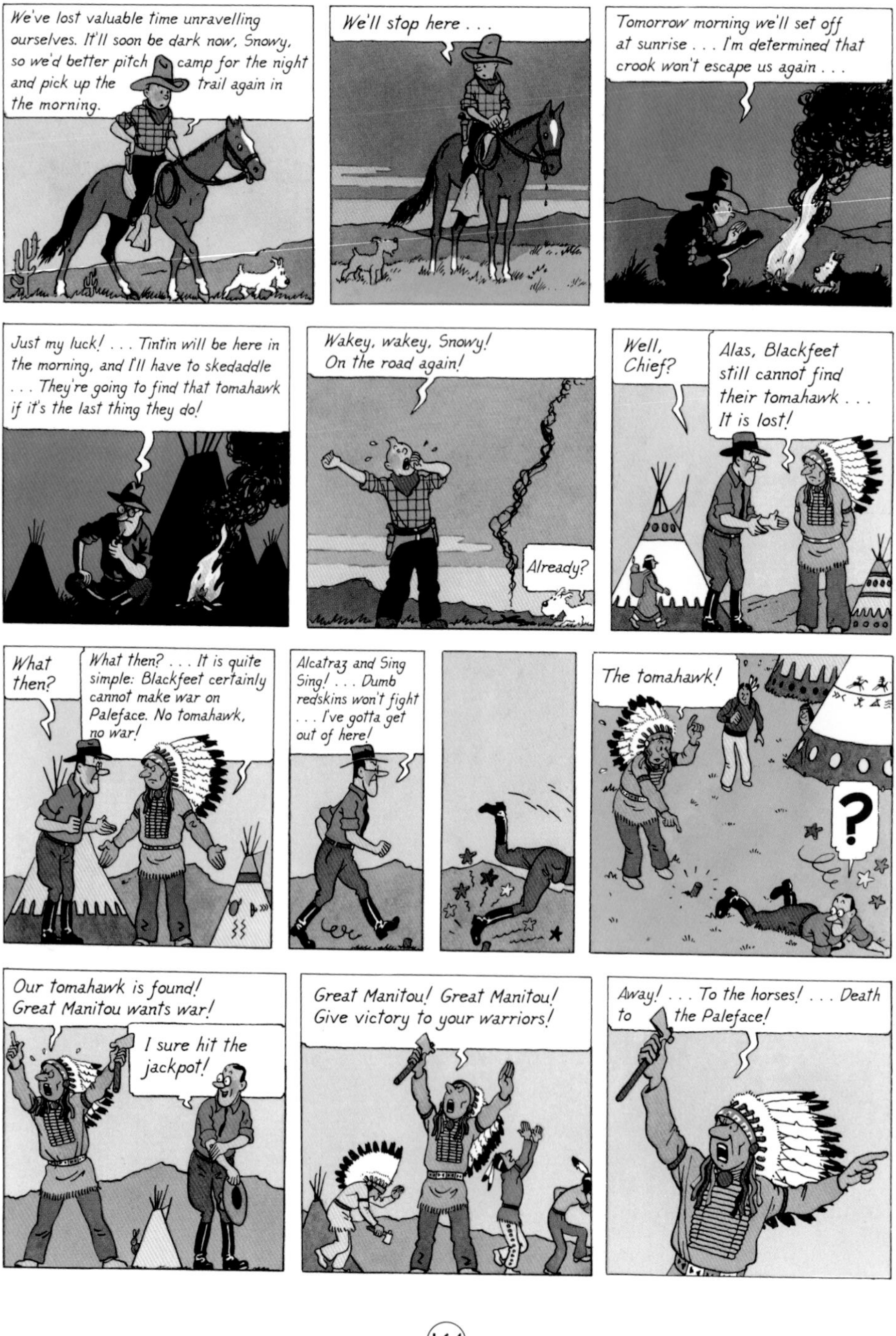

We've lost valuable time unravelling ourselves. It'll soon be dark now, Snowy, so we'd better pitch camp for the night and pick up the trail again in the morning.
We'll stop here . . .
Tomorrow morning we'll set off at sunrise . . . I'm determined that crook won't escape us again . . .
Just my luck! . . . Tintin will be here in the morning, and I'll have to skedaddle . . . They're going to find that tomahawk if it's the last thing they do!
Wakey, wakey, Snowy! On the road again!
Already?
Well, Chief?
Alas, Blackfeet still cannot find their tomahawk . . . It is lost!
What then?
What then? . . . It is quite simple: Blackfeet certainly cannot make war on Paleface. No tomahawk, no war!
Alcatraz and Sing Sing! . . . Dumb redskins won't fight . . . I've gotta get out of here!
The tomahawk!
?
Our tomahawk is found! Great Manitou wants war!
I sure hit the jackpot!
Great Manitou! Great Manitou! Give victory to your warriors!
Away! . . . To the horses! . . . Death to the Paleface!

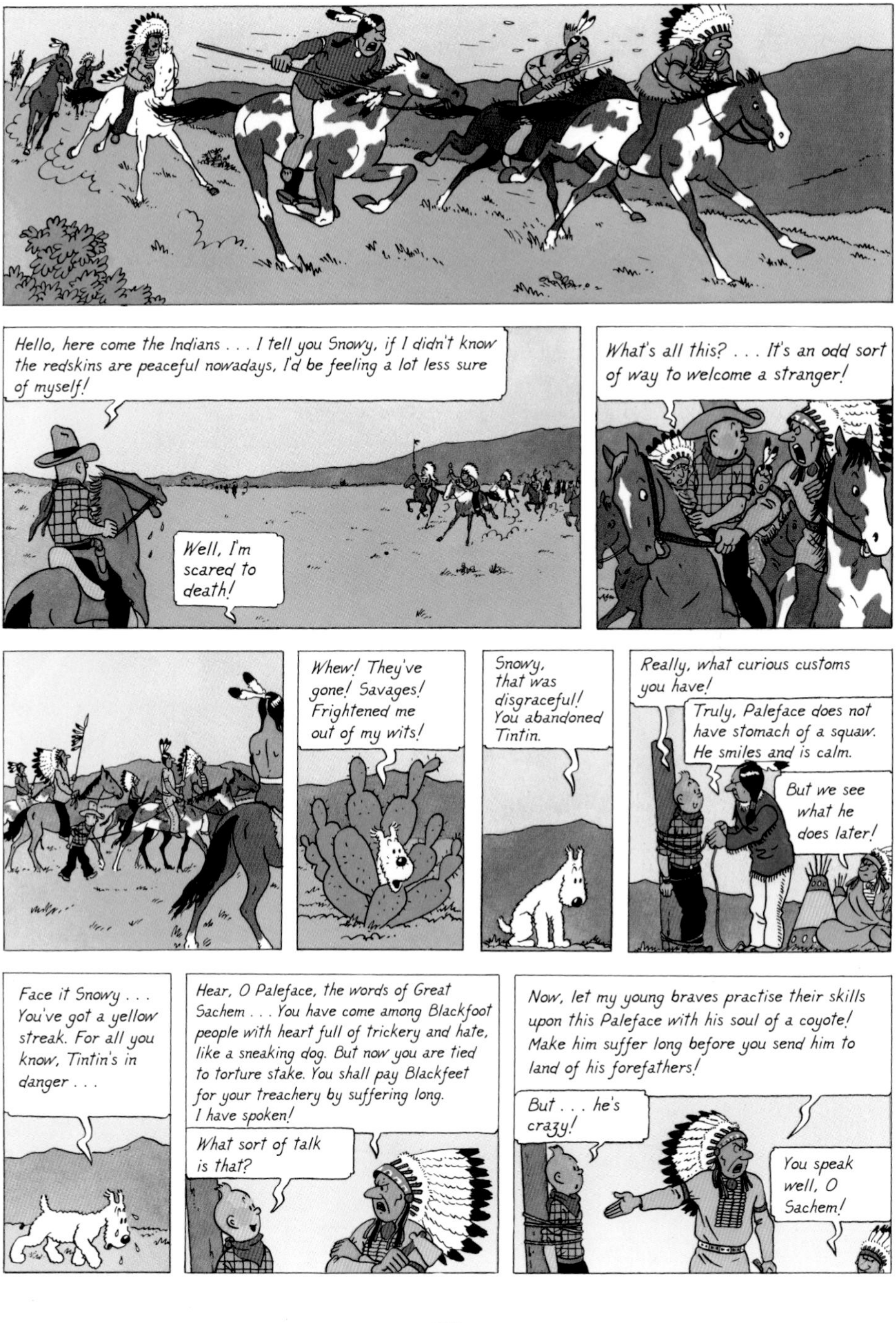
Hello, here come the Indians . . . I tell you Snowy, if I didn't know the redskins are peaceful nowadays, I'd be feeling a lot less sure of myself!
Well, I'm scared to death!
What's all this? . . . It's an odd sort of way to welcome a stranger!
Whew! They've gone! Savages! Frightened me out of my wits!
Snowy, that was disgraceful! You abandoned Tintin.
Really, what curious customs you have!
Truly, Paleface does not have stomach of a squaw. He smiles and is calm.
But we see what he does later!
Face it Snowy . . . You've got a yellow streak. For all you know, Tintin's in danger . . .
Hear, O Paleface, the words of Great Sachem . . . You have come among Blackfoot people with heart full of trickery and hate, like a sneaking dog. But now you are tied to torture stake. You shall pay Blackfeet for your treachery by suffering long. I have spoken!
What sort of talk is that?
Now, let my young braves practise their skills upon this Paleface with his soul of a coyote! Make him suffer long before you send him to land of his forefathers!
But . . . he's crazy!
You speak well, O Sachem!

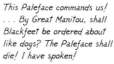

Sachem, this little joke's gone far enough! Untie these ropes and let me go!

This Paleface commands us! ... By Great Manitou, shall Blackfeet be ordered about like dogs? The Paleface shall die! I have spoken!

Resin! ... That's an idea!

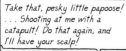

PLOP

Oho! A catapult!

It worked!

Take that, pesky little papoose! ... Shooting at me with a catapult! Do that again, and I'll have your scalp!

What a nerve! Behaving like that to Big Chief Keen-eyed-Mole, the Great Sachem himself! ... Nasty brat!

Keep out of my sight for three moons, or else ...

They shouldn't let papoose play with catapult ...

PLOP

By Great Wacondah! ... You too! You dare show disrespect to Big Chief Keen-eyed-Mole!

Me? ...

Yes! ... You!

Sachem! You strike my brother! ... Browsing-Bison, he is innocent ... He do no wrong!

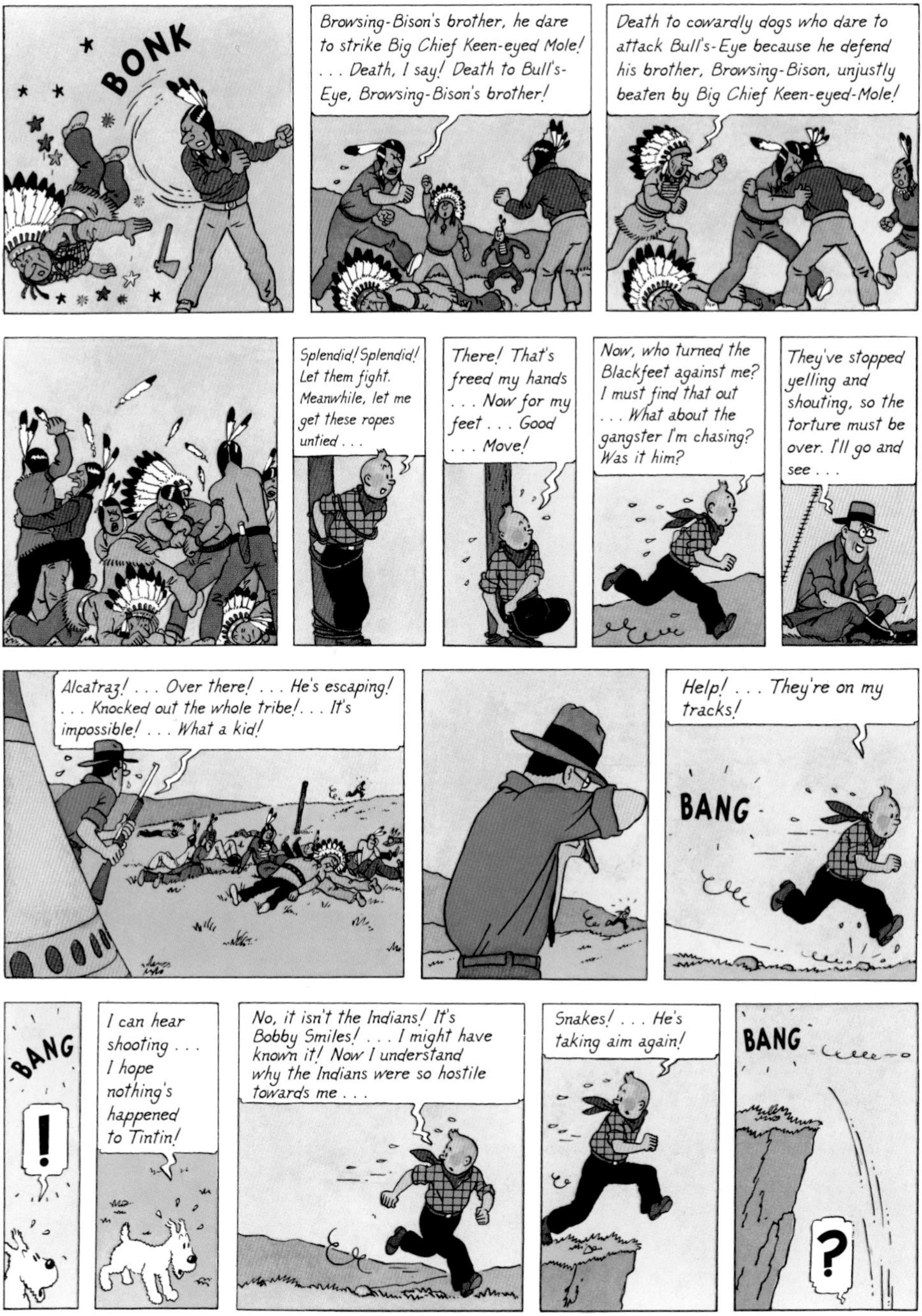
BONK
Browsing-Bison's brother, he dare to strike Big Chief Keen-eyed Mole! . . . Death, I say! Death to Bull's-Eye, Browsing-Bison's brother!
Death to cowardly dogs who dare to attack Bull's-Eye because he defend his brother, Browsing-Bison, unjustly beaten by Big Chief Keen-eyed-Mole!
Splendid! Splendid! Let them fight. Meanwhile, let me get these ropes untied . . .
There! That's freed my hands . . . Now for my feet . . . Good . . . Move!
Now, who turned the Blackfeet against me? I must find that out . . . What about the gangster I'm chasing? Was it him?
They've stopped yelling and shouting, so the torture must be over. I'll go and see . . .
Alcatraz! . . . Over there! . . . He's escaping! . . . Knocked out the whole tribe! . . . It's impossible! . . . What a kid!
Help! . . . They're on my tracks!
BANG
BANG
!
I can hear shooting . . . I hope nothing's happened to Tintin!
No, it isn't the Indians! It's Bobby Smiles! . . . I might have known it! Now I understand why the Indians were so hostile towards me . . .
Snakes! . . . He's taking aim again!
BANG
?

Alcatraz! ... What a drop! ... The canyon goes down hundreds of feet ... I can scarcely see the bottom ...

Quick! Quick! I must save Tintin!

That'll teach you, smartalec! Meddling little busybody ... I've got you out of my hair for good.

What's he looking at? ... Surely it can't be ... Tintin's fallen over that precipice ... ?

And now, back to Chicago.

Wooah! ... Wooah! ... Wooah!

It's that dratted dog of Tintin's! ... OK, he can follow his owner!

BANG

Wooaah! ...

Hello, Snowy! We both seem to have come by the same route!

I fell into space, like you. It was fantastic: there was this bush, and I fell right into it. It bent and dropped me on this ledge. So here I am, safe and sound, instead of smashed to bits in the canyon.

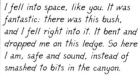

Golly, what a stroke of luck!

Still, we're only safe for the time being ... I can't see any possible way of escape from here ...

What are you sniffing at there, Snowy? . . . Have you found something? . . .

Good gracious! . . . Amazing! . . . It looks like some sort of cave . . . Why don't we see if it leads anywhere?

Here goes!

Where are we?
Careful, Snowy! . . . Don't take any chances!

It's heading upwards more and more . . .

Where are we going to come out?

Look! A huge gallery, decorated with Indian paintings . . .

The Blackfeet probably hid in this cave when they were being hunted by their enemies . . .

This is the other exit . . .

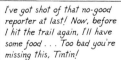
Still going upwards! . . . Where can this tunnel be leading?

Ah, now it's starting to go down . . .

. . . then it's taking us up again, steeply . . .

I've got shot of that no-good reporter at last! Now, before I hit the trail again, I'll have some food . . . Too bad you're missing this, Tintin!

Hey, what goes on around here? Must be an earthquake! The ground's shaking under me . . .

?

Whew! What a weight!

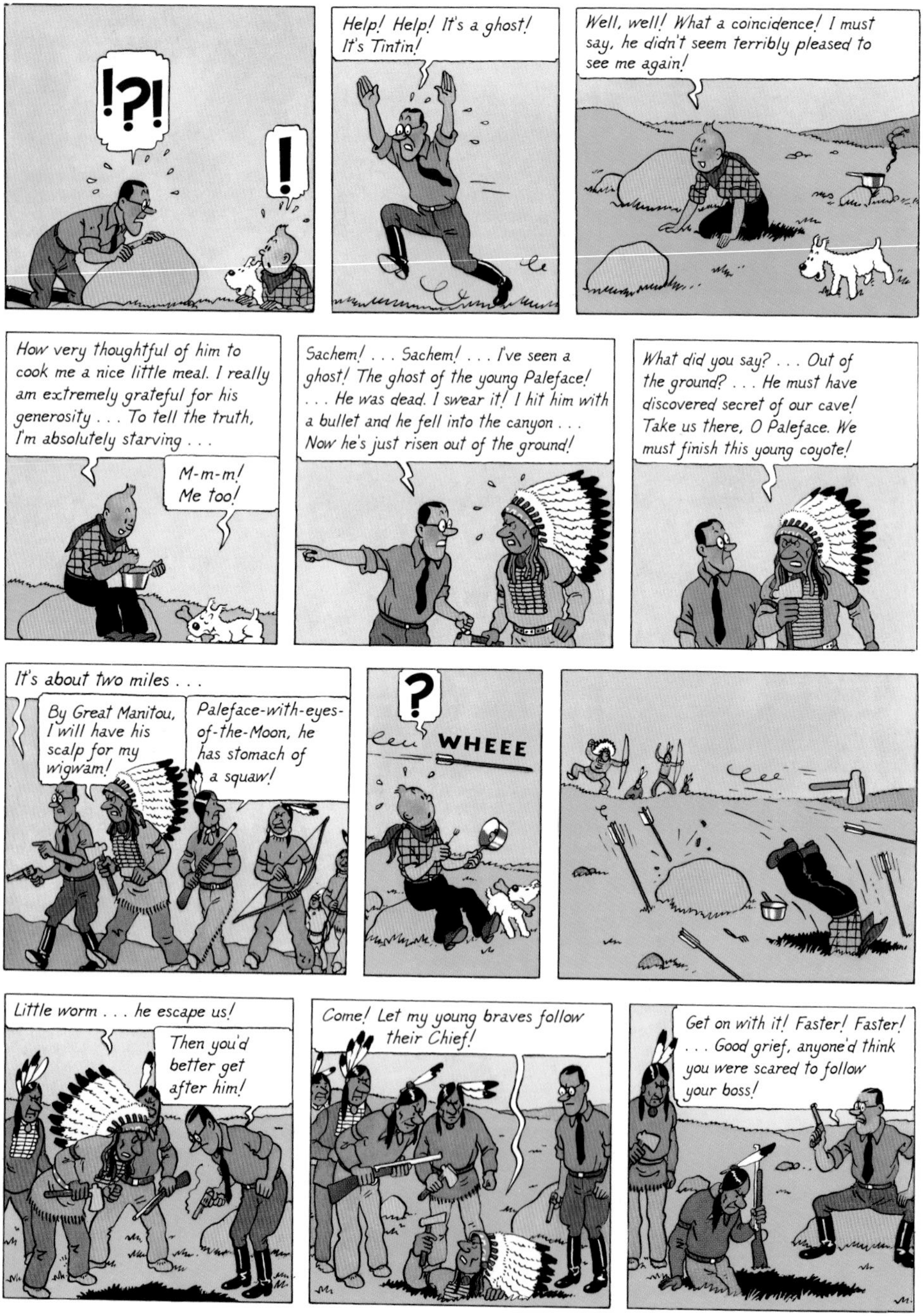
!?!
!
Help! Help! It's a ghost! It's Tintin!
Well, well! What a coincidence! I must say, he didn't seem terribly pleased to see me again!
How very thoughtful of him to cook me a nice little meal. I really am extremely grateful for his generosity . . . To tell the truth, I'm absolutely starving . . .
M-m-m! Me too!
Sachem! . . . Sachem! . . . I've seen a ghost! The ghost of the young Paleface! . . . He was dead. I swear it! I hit him with a bullet and he fell into the canyon . . . Now he's just risen out of the ground!
What did you say? . . . Out of the ground? . . . He must have discovered secret of our cave! Take us there, O Paleface. We must finish this young coyote!
It's about two miles . . .
By Great Manitou, I will have his scalp for my wigwam!
Paleface-with-eyes-of-the-Moon, he has stomach of a squaw!
?
WHEEE
Little worm . . . he escape us!
Then you'd better get after him!
Come! Let my young braves follow their Chief!
Get on with it! Faster! Faster! . . . Good grief, anyone'd think you were scared to follow your boss!

Over ten minutes since they went down. I wonder what's happening . . .

At last! There you are! . . . Well?

Great Wacondah has sent victory to his braves! Little Paleface is vanquished.

Our great Sachem did the deed. He brings his victim . . .

Fine! Fine! . . .

Yet again Big Chief Keen-eyed-Mole, he is worthy of his name. After heap big battle in darkness, with help of Great Wacondah, I, Sachem of Blackfeet, conquer the Paleface. Let my young warriors drag him from hole!

See! . . . Pestilential prairie-dog! He trouble us no more.

By Great Manitou! It is not the young Paleface!

Wriggling rattlesnakes! I made mistake! It is Lame Duck!

I have idea . . . Let us leave Little Paleface there, to starve to death in his burrow!

Do what you like, but get rid of him! This has gone on too long!

This end, heap big rock . . . other end, sheer drop! What can Paleface do? No way out but death . . .

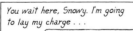

Don't be afraid, Snowy. We aren't going to moulder away down here. They think we're trapped, but we're getting out. Look I've emptied my cartridges and collected the powder. There! Now we'll blast their rocks to blazes!

You think it'll work?

You wait here, Snowy. I'm going to lay my charge . . .

Take care you don't blow us up as well!

Done it! . . . Now . . . there'll be a tremendous explosion . . . and that rock will pop like a champagne cork . . . Any minute now, we'll be free!

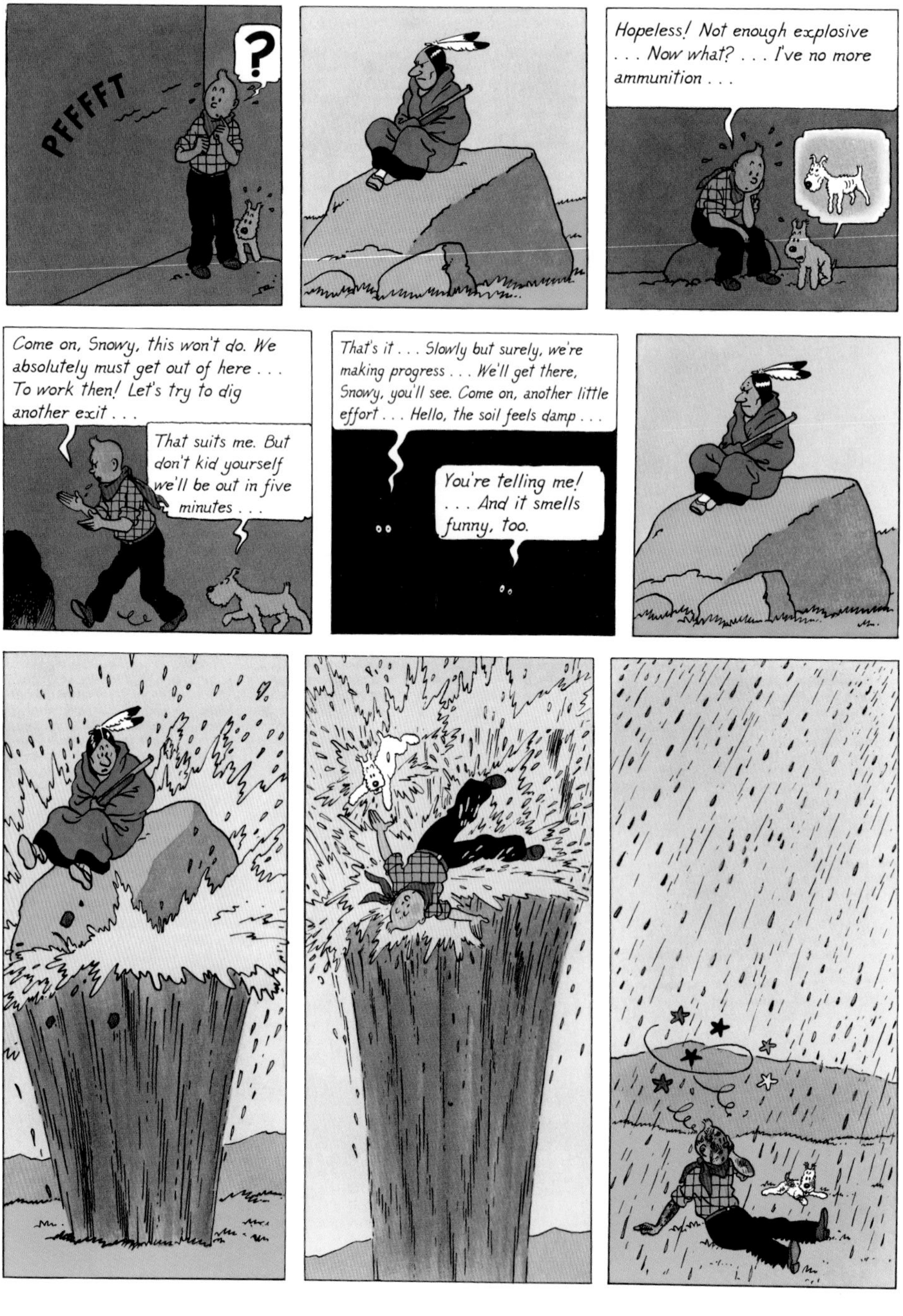
PFFFFT
?
Hopeless! Not enough explosive . . . Now what? . . . I've no more ammunition . . .
Come on, Snowy, this won't do. We absolutely must get out of here . . . To work then! Let's try to dig another exit . . .
That suits me. But don't kid yourself we'll be out in five minutes . . .
That's it . . . Slowly but surely, we're making progress . . . We'll get there, Snowy, you'll see. Come on, another little effort . . . Hello, the soil feels damp . . .
You're telling me! . . . And it smells funny, too.

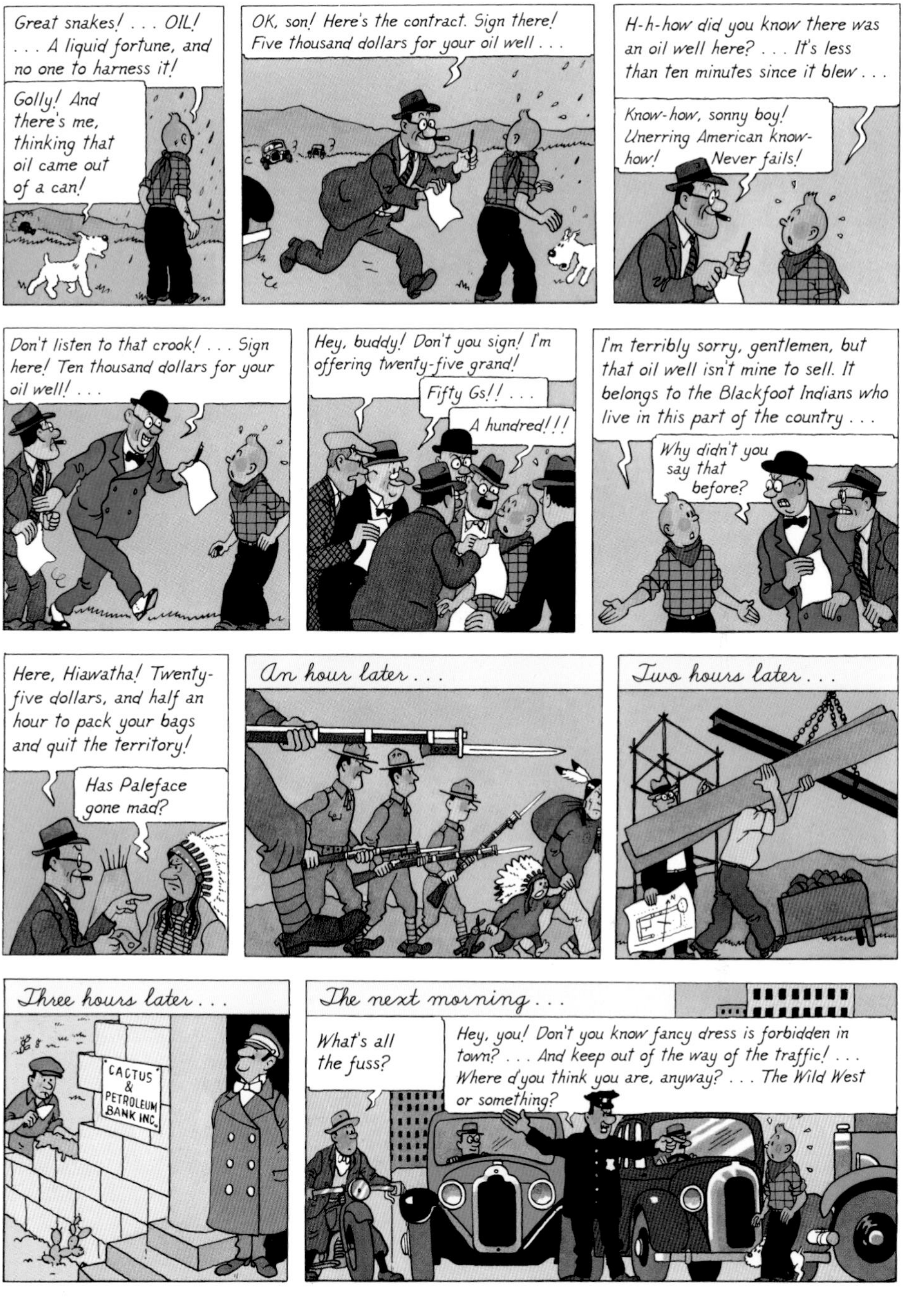

Great snakes! . . . OIL! . . . A liquid fortune, and no one to harness it!
Golly! And there's me, thinking that oil came out of a can!
OK, son! Here's the contract. Sign there! Five thousand dollars for your oil well . . .
H-h-how did you know there was an oil well here? . . . It's less than ten minutes since it blew . . .
Know-how, sonny boy! Unerring American know-how! Never fails!
Don't listen to that crook! . . . Sign here! Ten thousand dollars for your oil well! . . .
Hey, buddy! Don't you sign! I'm offering twenty-five grand!
Fifty Gs!! . . .
A hundred!!!
I'm terribly sorry, gentlemen, but that oil well isn't mine to sell. It belongs to the Blackfoot Indians who live in this part of the country . . .
Why didn't you say that before?
Here, Hiawatha! Twenty-five dollars, and half an hour to pack your bags and quit the territory!
Has Paleface gone mad?
An hour later . . .
Two hours later . . .
Three hours later . . .
CACTUS & PETROLEUM BANK INC.
The next morning . . .
What's all the fuss?
Hey, you! Don't you know fancy dress is forbidden in town? . . . And keep out of the way of the traffic! . . . Where d'you think you are, anyway? . . . The Wild West or something?

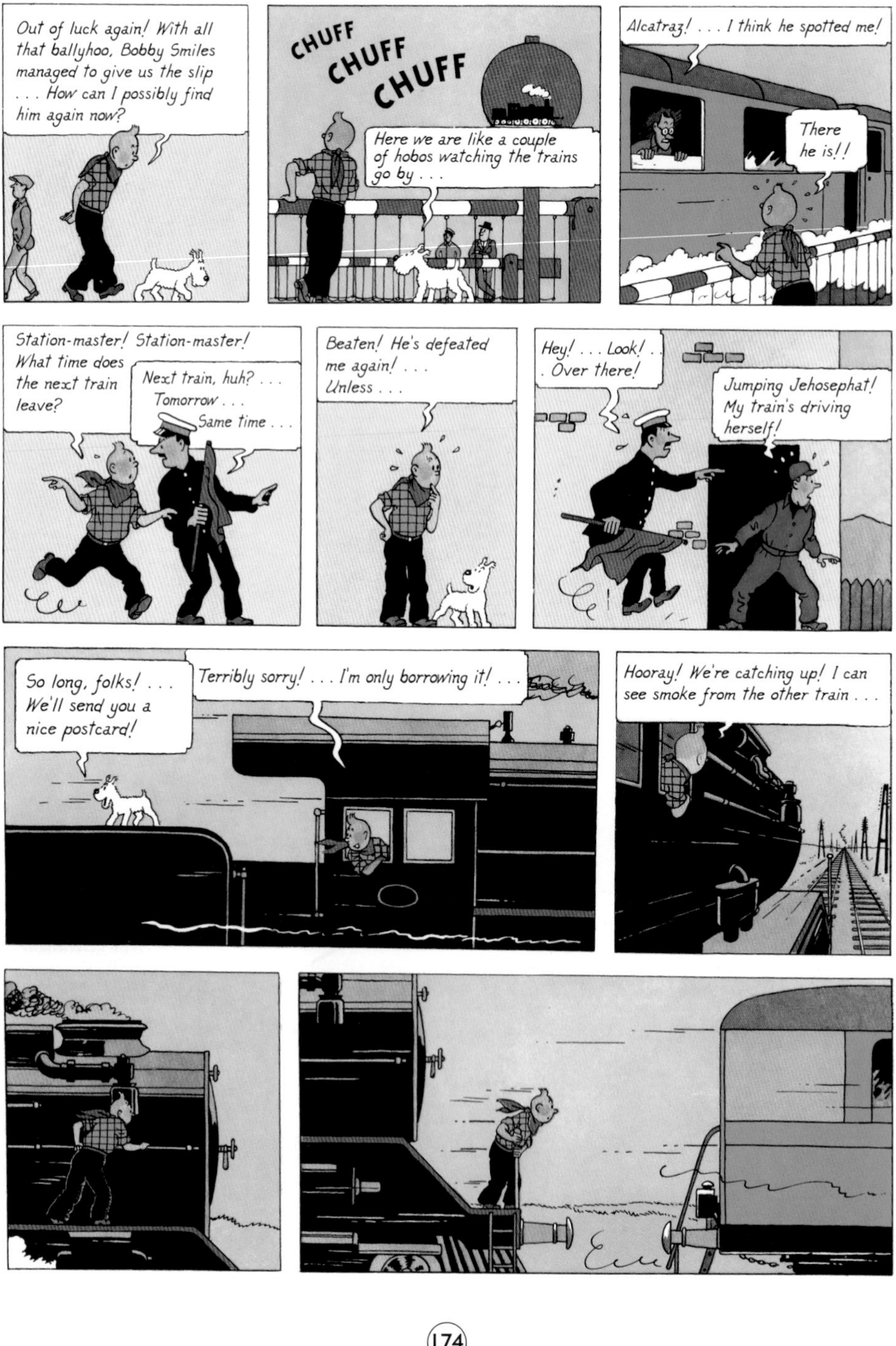
Out of luck again! With all that ballyhoo, Bobby Smiles managed to give us the slip . . . How can I possibly find him again now?
CHUFF CHUFF CHUFF
Here we are like a couple of hobos watching the trains go by . . .
Alcatraz! . . . I think he spotted me!
There he is!!
Station-master! Station-master! What time does the next train leave?
Next train, huh? . . . Tomorrow . . . Same time . . .
Beaten! He's defeated me again! . . . Unless . . .
Hey! . . . Look! . . . Over there!
Jumping Jehosephat! My train's driving herself!
So long, folks! . . . We'll send you a nice postcard!
Terribly sorry! . . . I'm only borrowing it! . . .
Hooray! We're catching up! I can see smoke from the other train . . .

Hello? . . . Block one-five-two? . . . There's a loco running crazy on the track . . . Yes . . . She mustn't overtake the Flyer . . . Switch her on to number seven . . .

Right you are, boss! Count on me!

Phew! Just in time! Here comes the Flyer . . . with the runaway train on her tail . . .

Drat! We've been switched to another track . . .

Quick, stop the engine, and back up. We'll soon be on the right track . . .

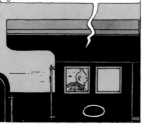

That's torn it! The brake lever's jammed. Now I understand. This engine was in for repairs!

BLOCK 16

Only one way to clear this here track, Jem, and that's dynamite. We got plenty of time. Next train won't be coming through till tomorrow morning . . .

Sure was lucky we found this old boulder on the track, Slim. Just imagine if the Flyer was to hit it in the morning! . . . Brother, what a wreck! Fair makes my blood freeze!

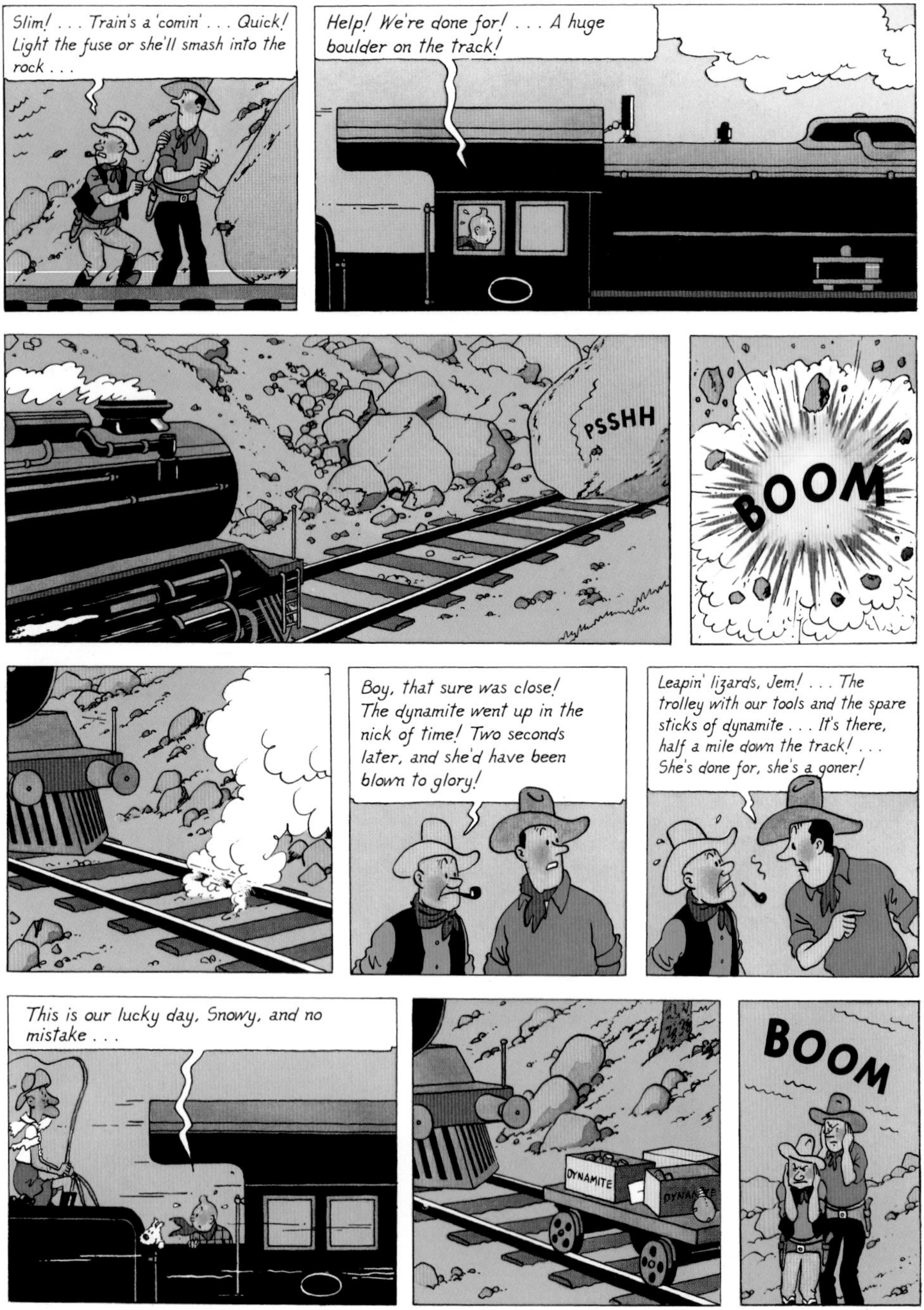

Slim! . . . Train's a 'comin' . . . Quick! Light the fuse or she'll smash into the rock . . .
Help! We're done for! . . . A huge boulder on the track!
PSSHH
BOOM
Boy, that sure was close! The dynamite went up in the nick of time! Two seconds later, and she'd have been blown to glory!
Leapin' lizards, Jem! . . . The trolley with our tools and the spare sticks of dynamite . . . It's there, half a mile down the track! . . . She's done for, she's a goner!
This is our lucky day, Snowy, and no mistake . . .
DYNAMITE
BOOM

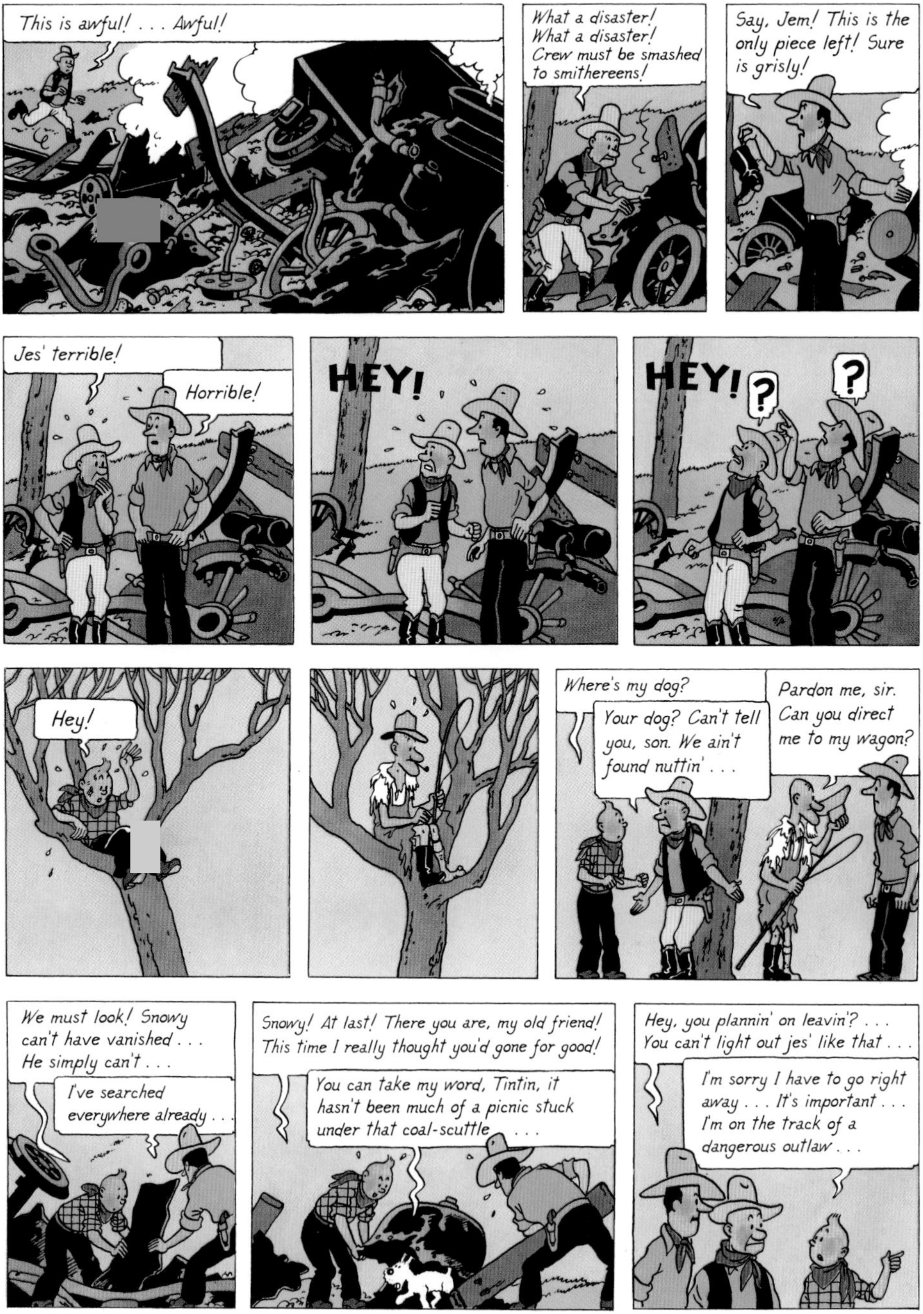

This is awful! . . . Awful!
What a disaster! What a disaster! Crew must be smashed to smithereens!
Say, Jem! This is the only piece left! Sure is grisly!
Jes' terrible!
Horrible!
HEY!
HEY!
?
?
Hey!
Where's my dog?
Your dog? Can't tell you, son. We ain't found nuttin' . . .
Pardon me, sir. Can you direct me to my wagon?
We must look! Snowy can't have vanished . . . He simply can't . . .
I've searched everywhere already . . .
Snowy! At last! There you are, my old friend! This time I really thought you'd gone for good!
You can take my word, Tintin, it hasn't been much of a picnic stuck under that coal-scuttle . . .
Hey, you plannin' on leavin'? . . . You can't light out jes' like that . . .
I'm sorry I have to go right away . . . It's important . . . I'm on the track of a dangerous outlaw . . .

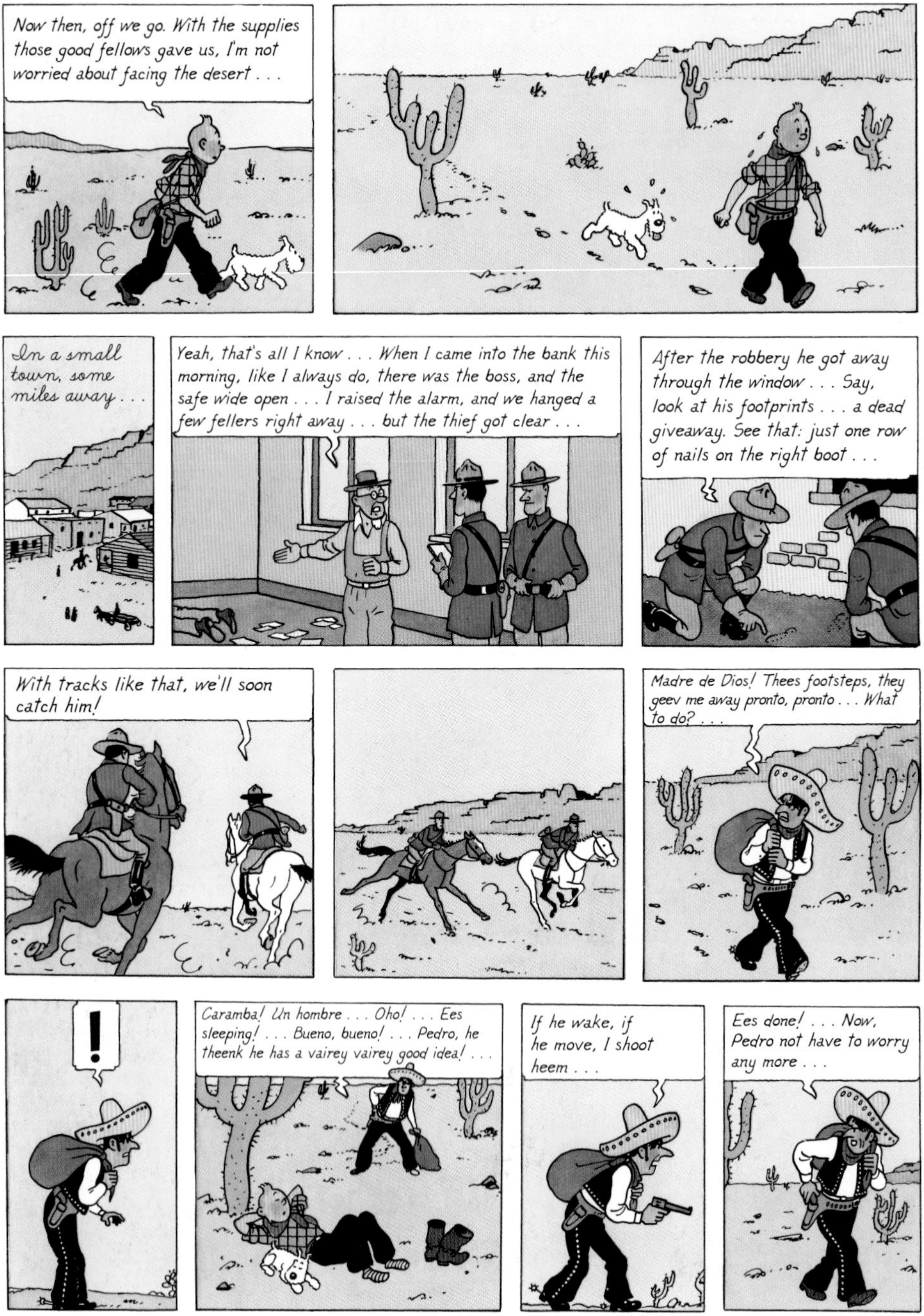

Now then, off we go. With the supplies those good fellows gave us, I'm not worried about facing the desert . . .
In a small town, some miles away . . .
Yeah, that's all I know . . . When I came into the bank this morning, like I always do, there was the boss, and the safe wide open . . . I raised the alarm, and we hanged a few fellers right away . . . but the thief got clear . . .
After the robbery he got away through the window . . . Say, look at his footprints . . . a dead giveaway. See that: just one row of nails on the right boot . . .
With tracks like that, we'll soon catch him!
Madre de Dios! Thees footsteps, they geev me away pronto, pronto . . . What to do? . . .
!
Caramba! Un hombre . . . Oho! . . . Ees sleeping! . . . Bueno, bueno! . . . Pedro, he theenk he has a vairey vairey good idea! . . .
If he wake, if he move, I shoot heem . . .
Ees done! . . . Now, Pedro not have to worry any more . . .

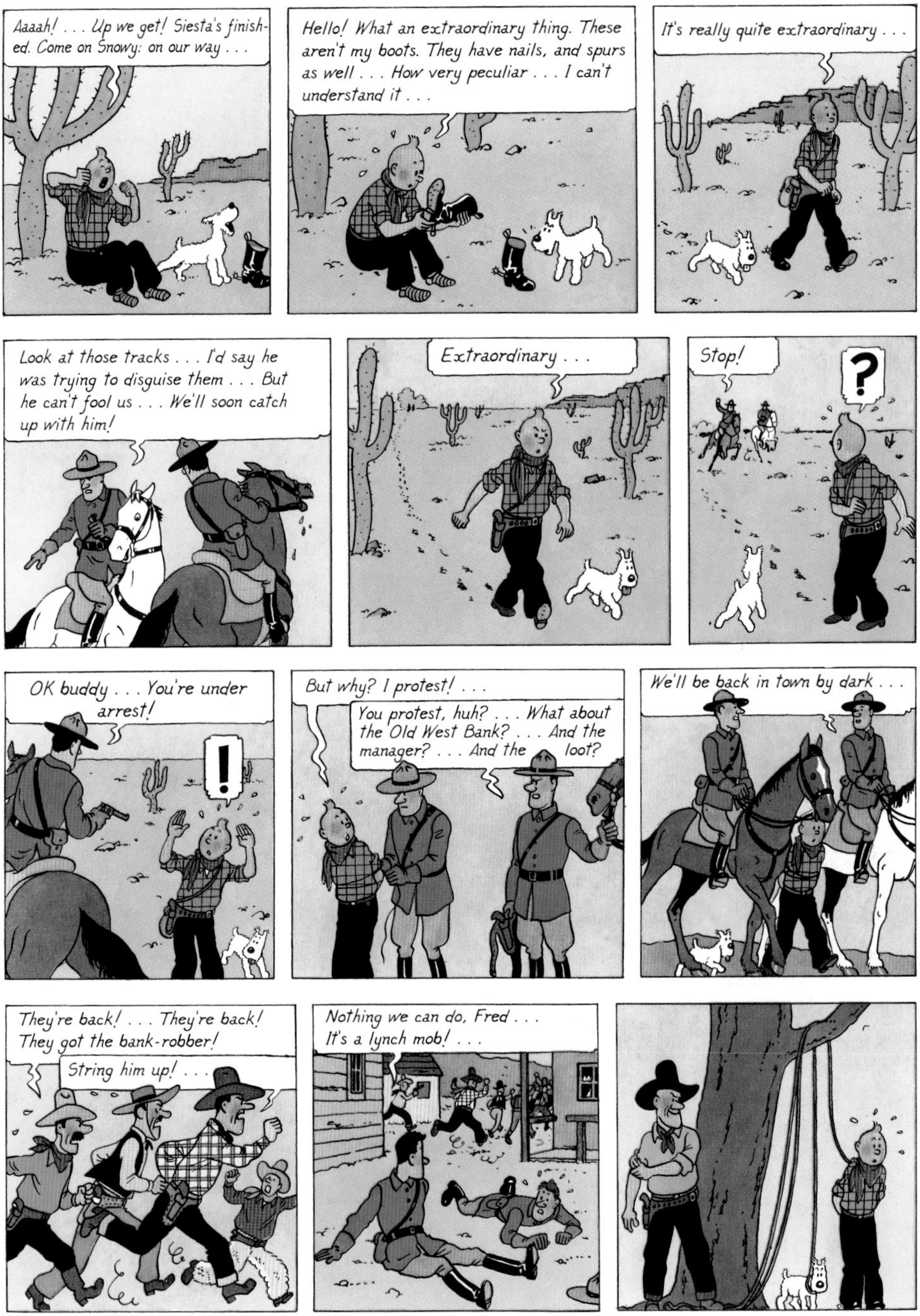
Aaaah! . . . Up we get! Siesta's finish-ed. Come on Snowy: on our way . . .
Hello! What an extraordinary thing. These aren't my boots. They have nails, and spurs as well . . . How very peculiar . . . I can't understand it . . .
It's really quite extraordinary . . .
Look at those tracks . . . I'd say he was trying to disguise them . . . But he can't fool us . . . We'll soon catch up with him!
Extraordinary . . .
Stop!
?
OK buddy . . . You're under arrest!
!
But why? I protest! . . .
You protest, huh? . . . What about the Old West Bank? . . . And the manager? . . . And the loot?
We'll be back in town by dark . . .
They're back! . . . They're back! They got the bank-robber!
String him up! . . .
Nothing we can do, Fred . . . It's a lynch mob! . . .

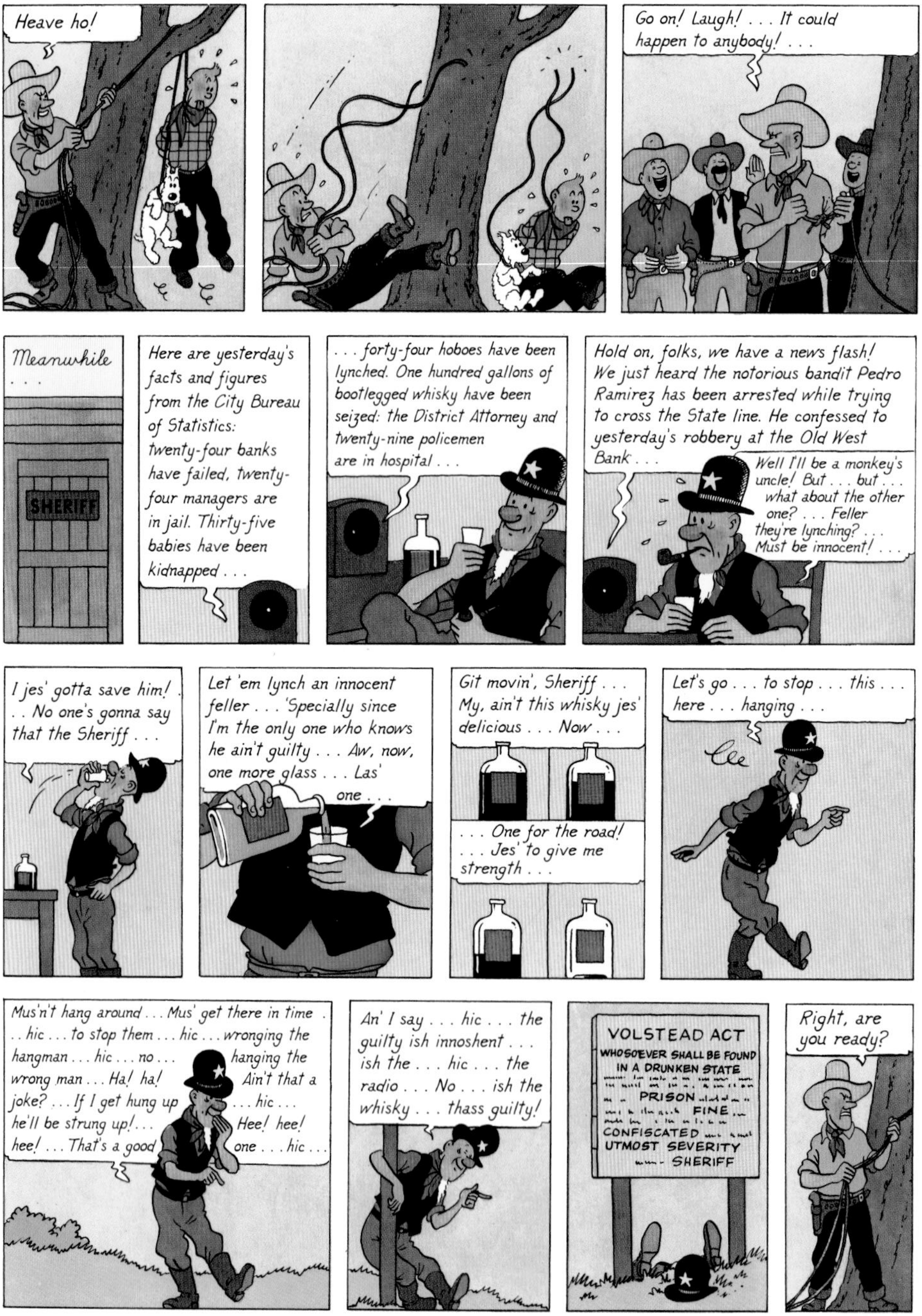

Heave ho!
Go on! Laugh! . . . It could happen to anybody! . . .
Meanwhile . . .
SHERIFF
Here are yesterday's facts and figures from the City Bureau of Statistics: twenty-four banks have failed, twenty-four managers are in jail. Thirty-five babies have been kidnapped . . .
. . . forty-four hoboes have been lynched. One hundred gallons of bootlegged whisky have been seized: the District Attorney and twenty-nine policemen are in hospital . . .
Hold on, folks, we have a news flash! We just heard the notorious bandit Pedro Ramirez has been arrested while trying to cross the State line. He confessed to yesterday's robbery at the Old West Bank . . .
Well I'll be a monkey's uncle! But . . . but . . . what about the other one? . . . Feller they're lynching? . . . Must be innocent! . . .
I jes' gotta save him! . . . No one's gonna say that the Sheriff . . .
Let 'em lynch an innocent feller . . . 'Specially since I'm the only one who knows he ain't guilty . . . Aw, now, one more glass . . . Las' one . . .
Git movin', Sheriff . . . My, ain't this whisky jes' delicious . . . Now . . .
. . . One for the road! . . . Jes' to give me strength . . .
Let's go . . . to stop . . . this . . . here . . . hanging . . .
Mus'n't hang around . . . Mus' get there in time . . hic . . . to stop them . . . hic . . . wronging the hangman . . . hic . . . no . . . hanging the wrong man . . . Ha! ha! Ain't that a joke? . . . If I get hung up . . . hic . . . he'll be strung up! . . . Hee! hee! hee! . . . That's a good one . . . hic . . .
An' I say . . . hic . . . the guilty ish innoshent . . . ish the . . . hic . . . the radio . . . No . . . ish the whisky . . . thass guilty!
VOLSTEAD ACT
WHOSOEVER SHALL BE FOUND IN A DRUNKEN STATE
PRISON
FINE
CONFISCATED
UTMOST SEVERITY
SHERIFF
Right, are you ready?

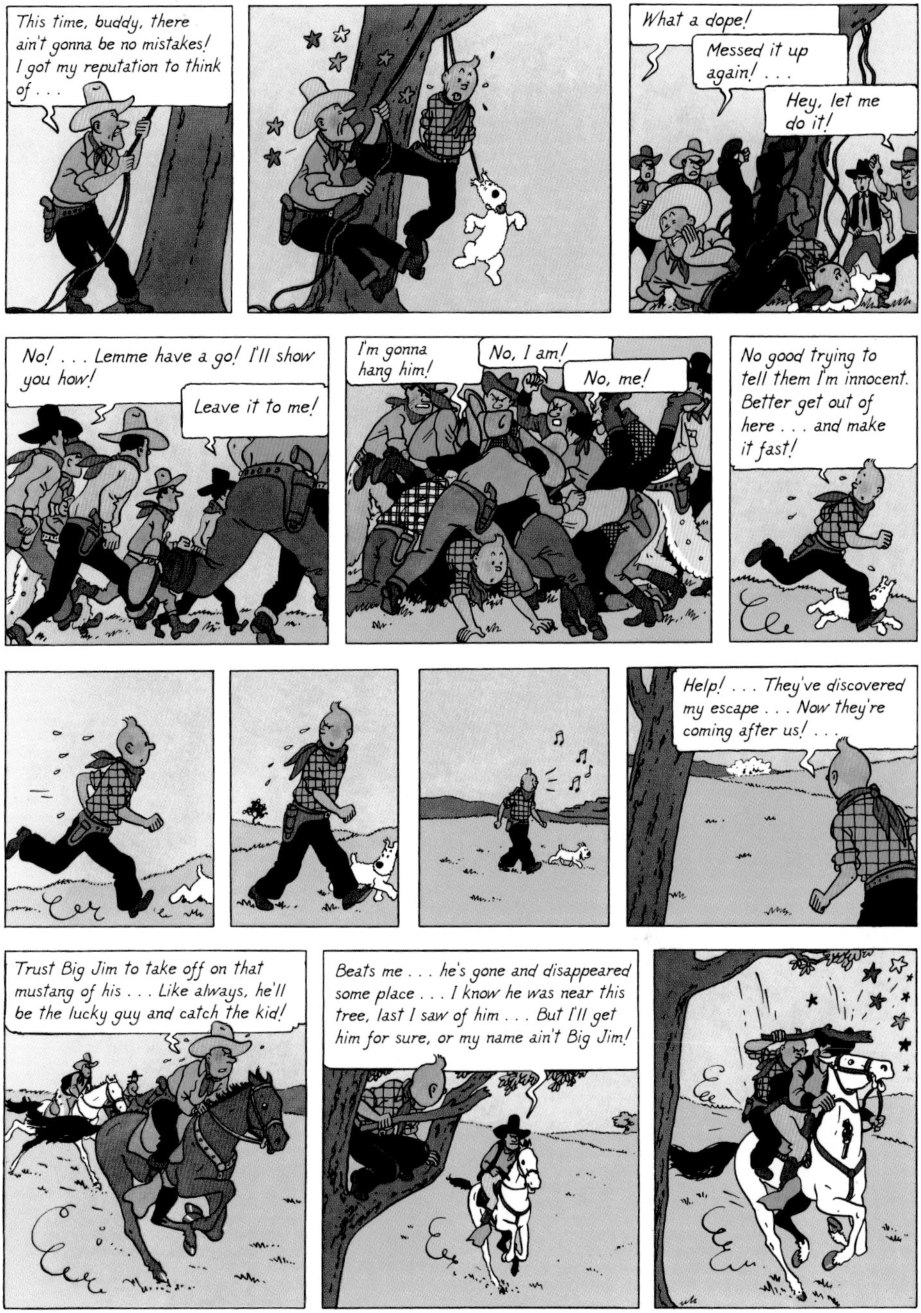
This time, buddy, there ain't gonna be no mistakes! I got my reputation to think of . . .
What a dope!
Messed it up again! . . .
Hey, let me do it!
No! . . . Lemme have a go! I'll show you how!
Leave it to me!
I'm gonna hang him!
No, I am!
No, me!
No good trying to tell them I'm innocent. Better get out of here . . . and make it fast!
Help! . . . They've discovered my escape . . . Now they're coming after us! . . .
Trust Big Jim to take off on that mustang of his . . . Like always, he'll be the lucky guy and catch the kid!
Beats me . . . he's gone and disappeared some place . . . I know he was near this tree, last I saw of him . . . But I'll get him for sure, or my name ain't Big Jim!

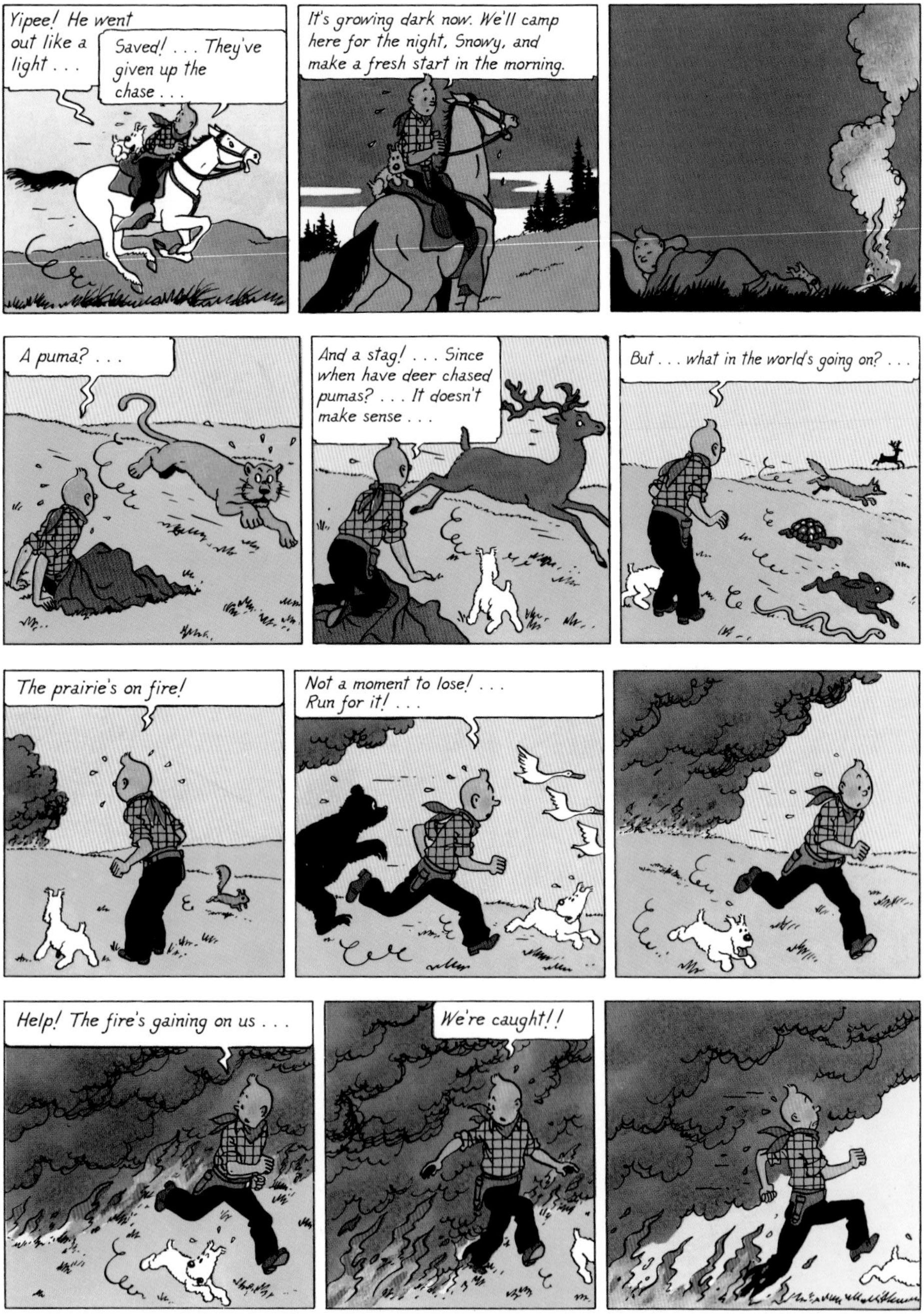

Yipee! He went out like a light . . .
Saved! . . . They've given up the chase . . .
It's growing dark now. We'll camp here for the night, Snowy, and make a fresh start in the morning.
A puma? . . .
And a stag! . . . Since when have deer chased pumas? . . . It doesn't make sense . . .
But . . . what in the world's going on? . . .
The prairie's on fire!
Not a moment to lose! . . . Run for it! . . .
Help! The fire's gaining on us . . .
We're caught!!

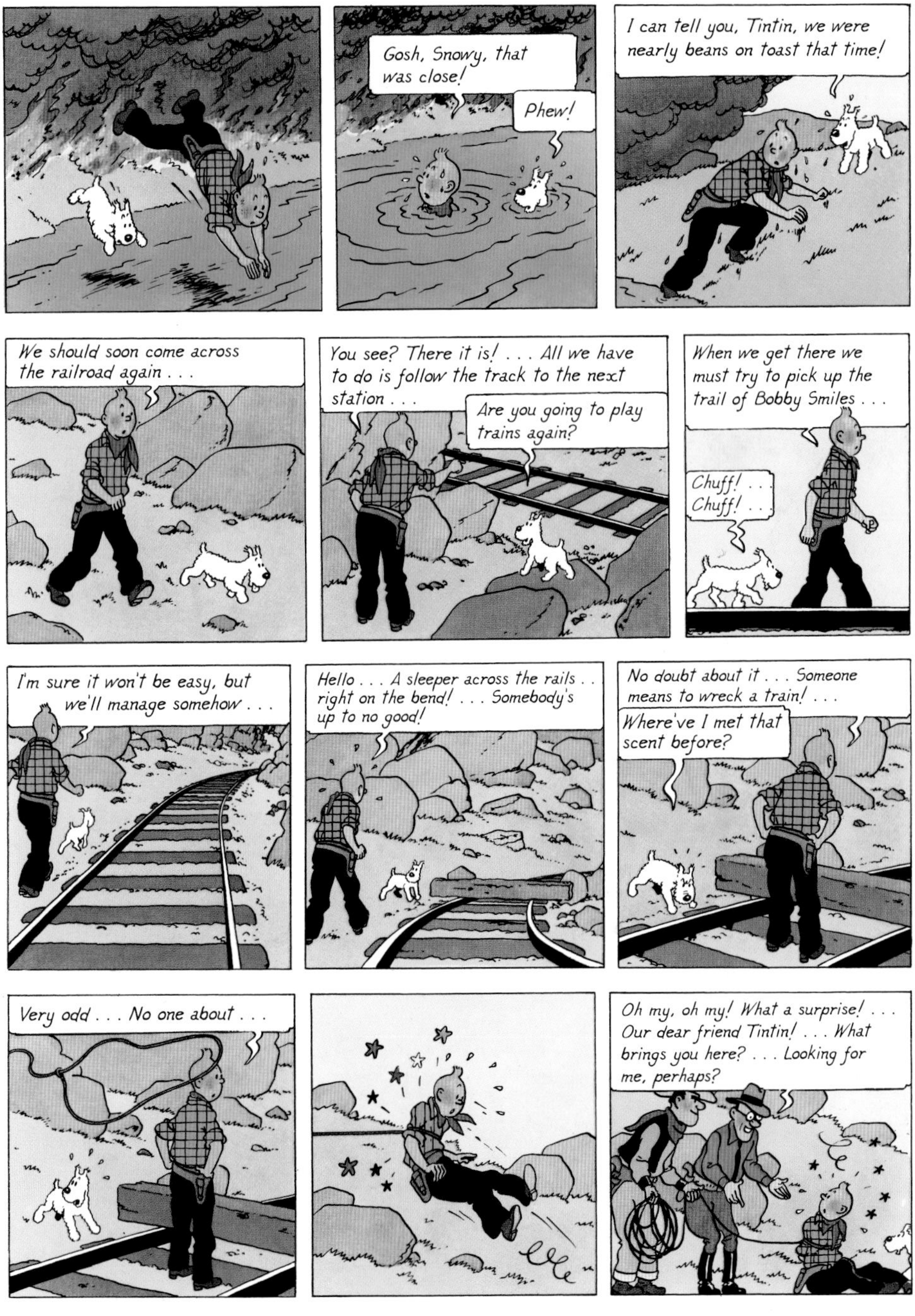
Gosh, Snowy, that was close!
Phew!
I can tell you, Tintin, we were nearly beans on toast that time!
We should soon come across the railroad again . . .
You see? There it is! . . . All we have to do is follow the track to the next station . . .
Are you going to play trains again?
When we get there we must try to pick up the trail of Bobby Smiles . . .
Chuff! . . . Chuff! . . .
I'm sure it won't be easy, but we'll manage somehow . . .
Hello . . . A sleeper across the rails . . right on the bend! . . . Somebody's up to no good!
No doubt about it . . . Someone means to wreck a train! . . .
Where've I met that scent before?
Very odd . . . No one about . . .
Oh my, oh my! What a surprise! . . . Our dear friend Tintin! . . . What brings you here? . . . Looking for me, perhaps?

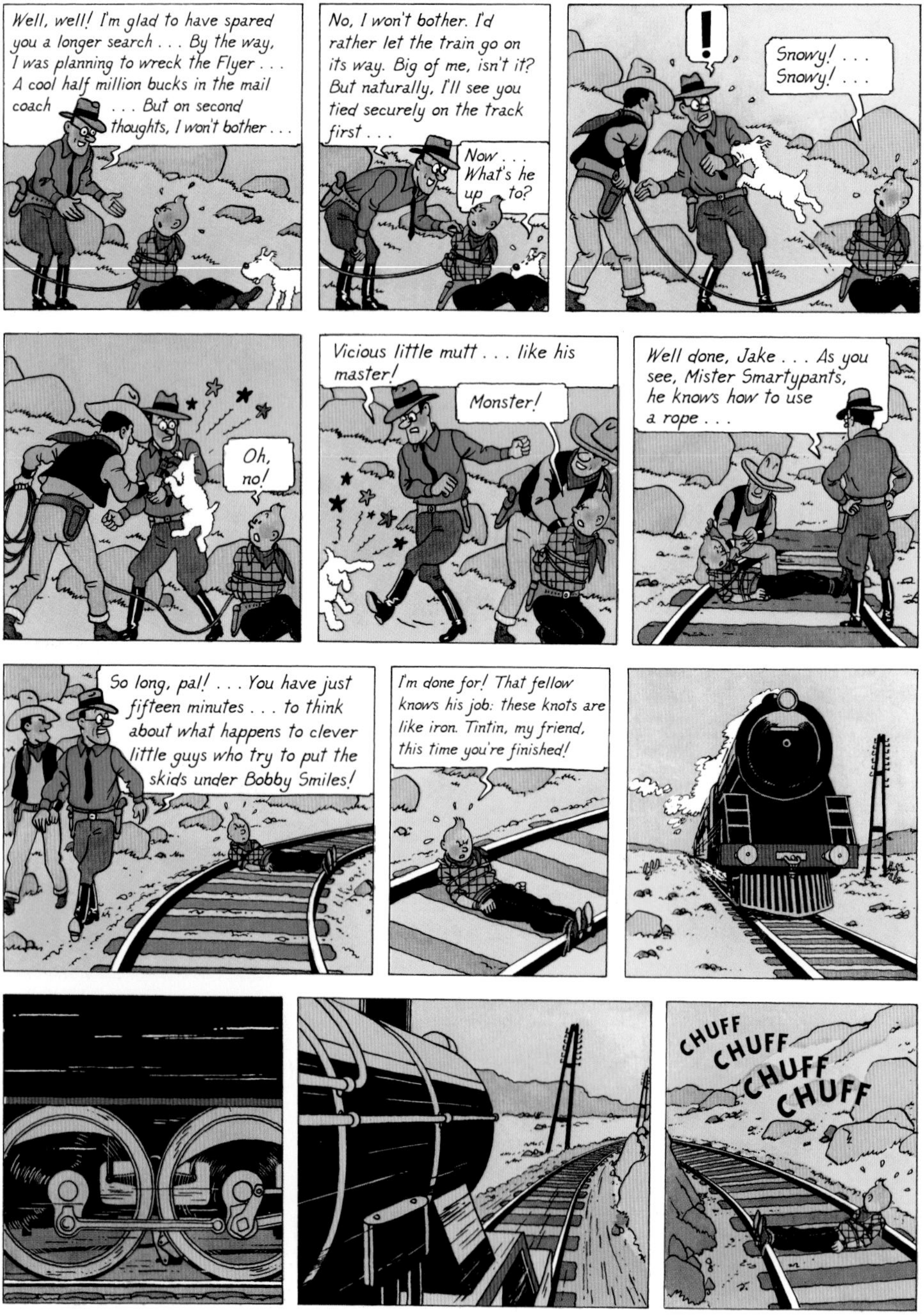

Well, well! I'm glad to have spared you a longer search . . . By the way, I was planning to wreck the Flyer . . . A cool half million bucks in the mail coach . . . But on second thoughts, I won't bother . . .
No, I won't bother. I'd rather let the train go on its way. Big of me, isn't it? But naturally, I'll see you tied securely on the track first . . .
Now . . . What's he up to?
!
Snowy! . . . Snowy! . . .
Oh, no!
Vicious little mutt . . . like his master!
Monster!
Well done, Jake . . . As you see, Mister Smartypants, he knows how to use a rope . . .
So long, pal! . . . You have just fifteen minutes . . . to think about what happens to clever little guys who try to put the skids under Bobby Smiles!
I'm done for! That fellow knows his job: these knots are like iron. Tintin, my friend, this time you're finished!
CHUFF
CHUFF
CHUFF
CHUFF

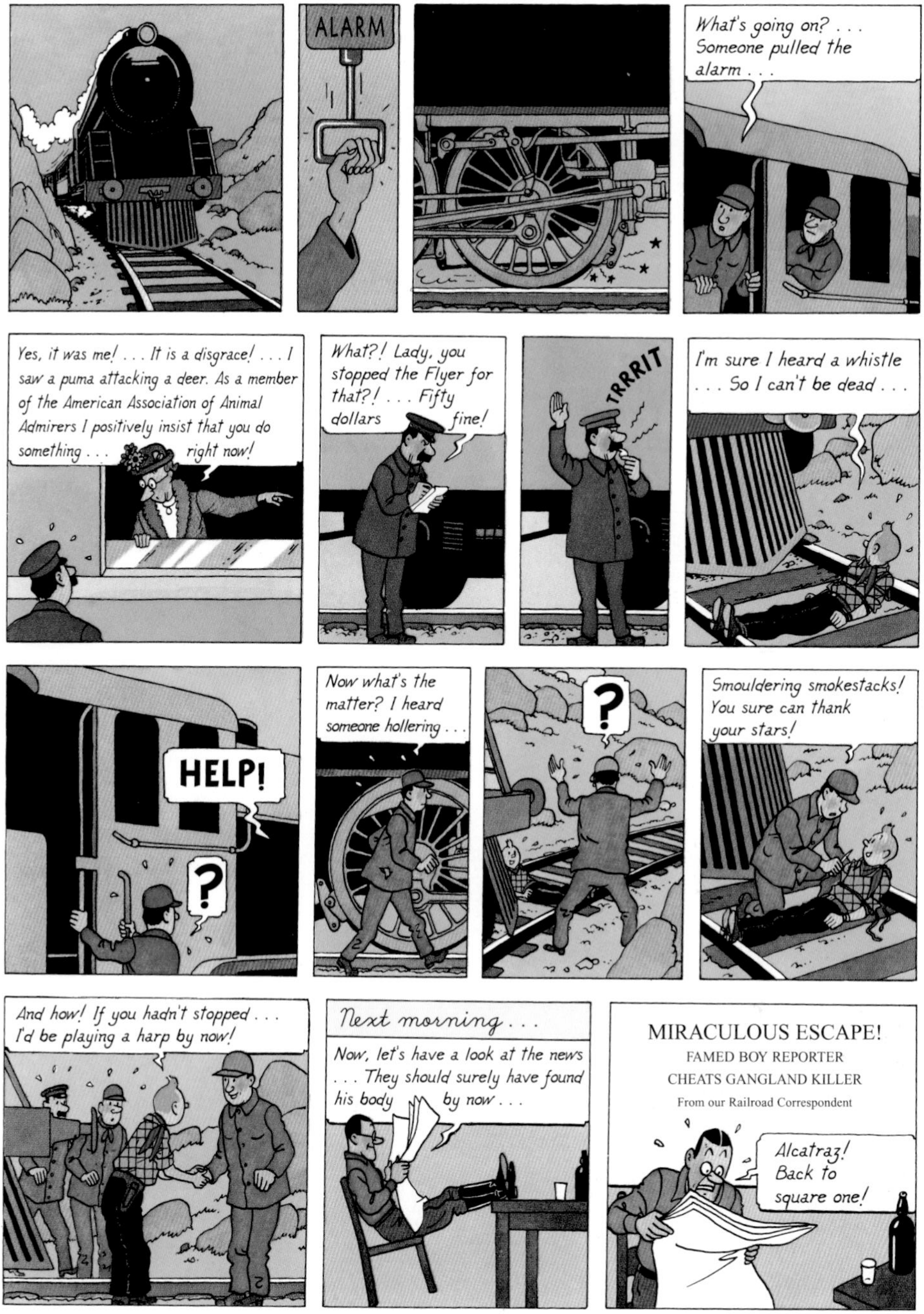
ALARM
What's going on? . . . Someone pulled the alarm . . .
Yes, it was me! . . . It is a disgrace! . . . I saw a puma attacking a deer. As a member of the American Association of Animal Admirers I positively insist that you do something . . . right now!
What?! Lady, you stopped the Flyer for that?! . . . Fifty dollars fine!
TRRRIT
I'm sure I heard a whistle . . . So I can't be dead . . .
HELP!
?
Now what's the matter? I heard someone hollering . . .
?
Smouldering smokestacks! You sure can thank your stars!
And how! If you hadn't stopped . . . I'd be playing a harp by now!
Next morning . . .
Now, let's have a look at the news . . . They should surely have found his body by now . . .
MIRACULOUS ESCAPE!
FAMED BOY REPORTER
CHEATS GANGLAND KILLER
From our Railroad Correspondent
Alcatraz! Back to square one!

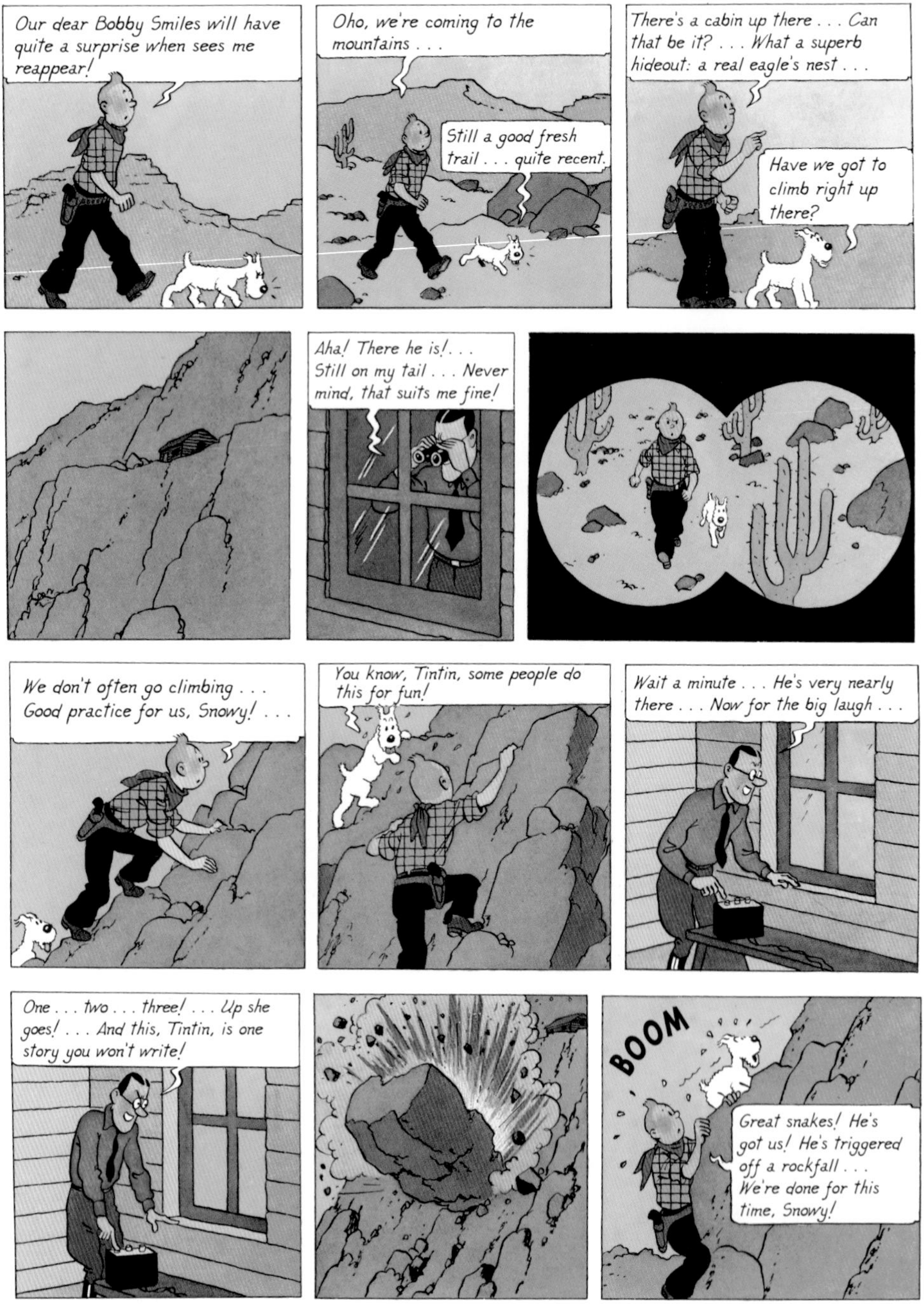
Our dear Bobby Smiles will have quite a surprise when sees me reappear!
Oho, we're coming to the mountains . . .
Still a good fresh trail . . . quite recent.
There's a cabin up there . . . Can that be it? . . . What a superb hideout: a real eagle's nest . . .
Have we got to climb right up there?
Aha! There he is! . . . Still on my tail . . . Never mind, that suits me fine!
We don't often go climbing . . . Good practice for us, Snowy! . . .
You know, Tintin, some people do this for fun!
Wait a minute . . . He's very nearly there . . . Now for the big laugh . . .
One . . . two . . . three! . . . Up she goes! . . . And this, Tintin, is one story you won't write!
BOOM
Great snakes! He's got us! He's triggered off a rockfall . . . We're done for this time, Snowy!

I had to blow up half the mountain, but, boy, it did the trick!

Tintin, my dear departed friend, here's to you!

And to you, too!

Back from the dead!

Back from the dead, indeed! If I hadn't been protected by an overhanging rock . . .

. . . I'd be dead as a doornail!

Well, better late than never!

BANG

Nice shooting, eh, Mr Smiles?

Believe me, it's far better to give in. As you see, I always get there in the end.

Don't try any funny business!

Three days later, in Chicago . . .

Hello? . . . Yeah? . . . Chief of Police? . . . That's me! . . . Tintin? Nope! Not a squeak! . . . Been gone a long while now . . . Trouble? . . . Sure is! . . . Nope . . . Ain't heard a word . . .

Come in!

RAT TAT TAT

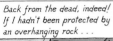

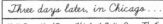

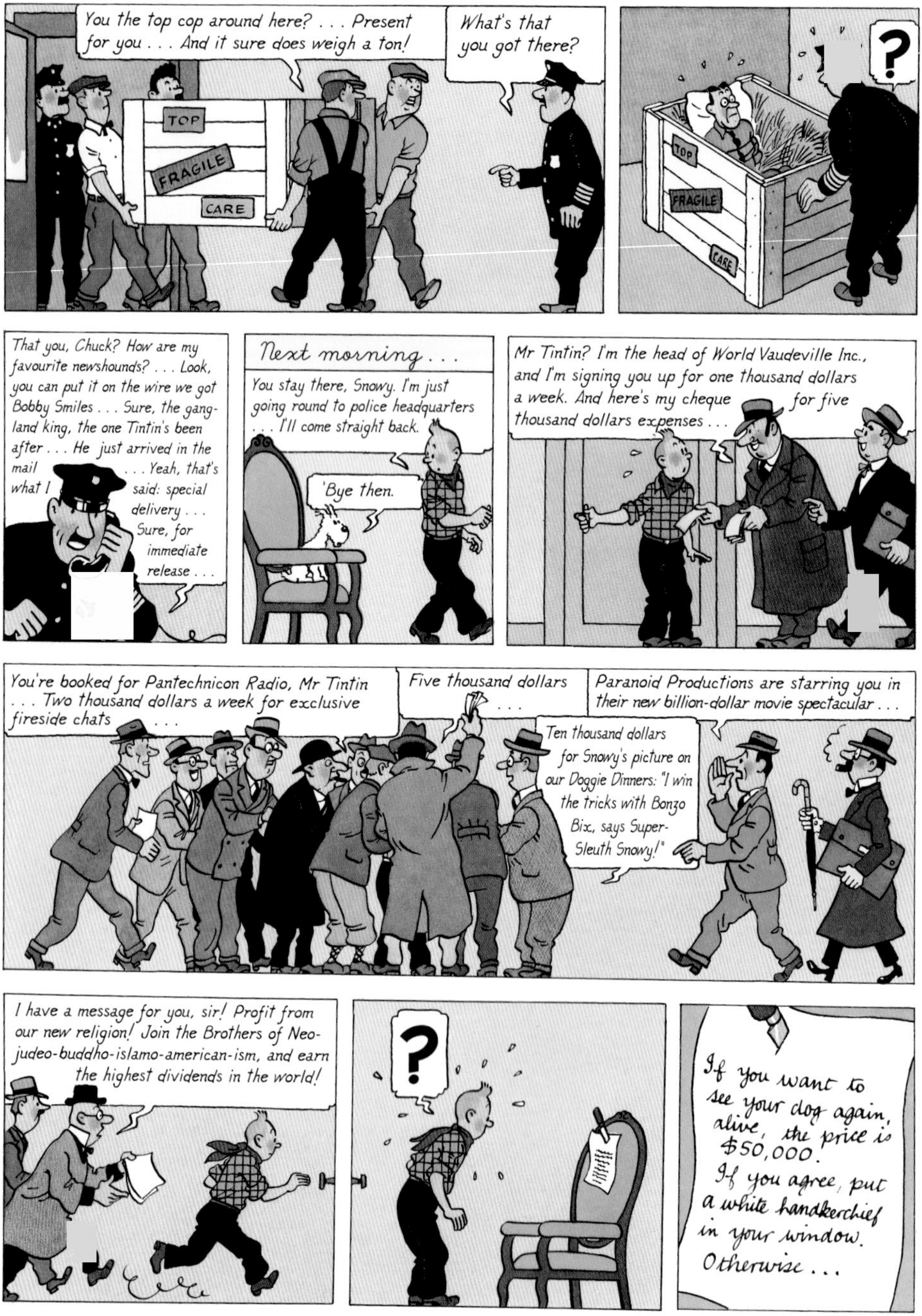
You the top cop around here? . . . Present for you . . . And it sure does weigh a ton!
What's that you got there?
?
That you, Chuck? How are my favourite newshounds? . . . Look, you can put it on the wire we got Bobby Smiles . . . Sure, the gangland king, the one Tintin's been after . . . He just arrived in the mail . . . Yeah, that's what I said: special delivery . . . Sure, for immediate release . . .
Next morning . . .
You stay there, Snowy. I'm just going round to police headquarters . . . I'll come straight back.
'Bye then.
Mr Tintin? I'm the head of World Vaudeville Inc., and I'm signing you up for one thousand dollars a week. And here's my cheque for five thousand dollars expenses . . .
You're booked for Pantechnicon Radio, Mr Tintin . . . Two thousand dollars a week for exclusive fireside chats . . .
Five thousand dollars . . .
Paranoid Productions are starring you in their new billion-dollar movie spectacular . . .
Ten thousand dollars for Snowy's picture on our Doggie Dinners: "I win the tricks with Bonzo Bix, says Super-Sleuth Snowy!"
I have a message for you, sir! Profit from our new religion! Join the Brothers of Neo-judeo-buddho-islamo-american-ism, and earn the highest dividends in the world!
?
If you want to see your dog again, alive, the price is $50,000.
If you agree, put a white handkerchief in your window.
Otherwise . . .

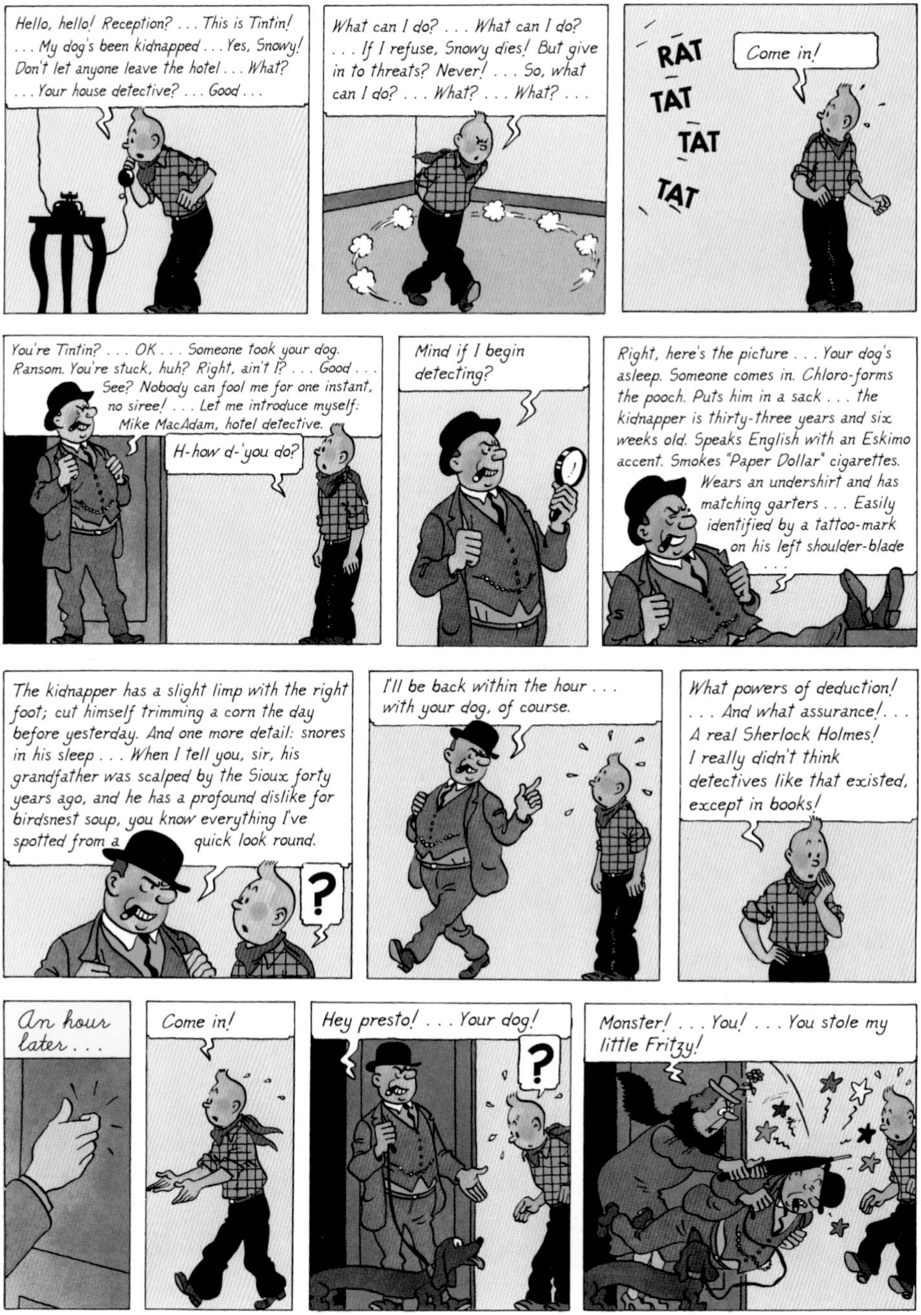

Hello, hello! Reception? . . . This is Tintin! . . . My dog's been kidnapped . . . Yes, Snowy! Don't let anyone leave the hotel . . . What? . . . Your house detective? . . . Good . . .
What can I do? . . . What can I do? . . . If I refuse, Snowy dies! But give in to threats? Never! . . . So, what can I do? . . . What? . . . What? . . .
RAT TAT TAT TAT
Come in!
You're Tintin? . . . OK . . . Someone took your dog. Ransom. You're stuck, huh? Right, ain't I? . . . Good . . . See? Nobody can fool me for one instant, no siree! . . . Let me introduce myself: Mike MacAdam, hotel detective.
H-how d-'you do?
Mind if I begin detecting?
Right, here's the picture . . . Your dog's asleep. Someone comes in. Chloro-forms the pooch. Puts him in a sack . . . the kidnapper is thirty-three years and six weeks old. Speaks English with an Eskimo accent. Smokes "Paper Dollar" cigarettes. Wears an undershirt and has matching garters . . . Easily identified by a tattoo-mark on his left shoulder-blade . . .
The kidnapper has a slight limp with the right foot; cut himself trimming a corn the day before yesterday. And one more detail: snores in his sleep . . . When I tell you, sir, his grandfather was scalped by the Sioux forty years ago, and he has a profound dislike for birdsnest soup, you know everything I've spotted from a quick look round.
?
I'll be back within the hour . . . with your dog, of course.
What powers of deduction! . . . And what assurance! . . . A real Sherlock Holmes! I really didn't think detectives like that existed, except in books!
An hour later . . .
Come in!
Hey presto! . . . Your dog!
?
Monster! . . . You! . . . You stole my little Fritzy!

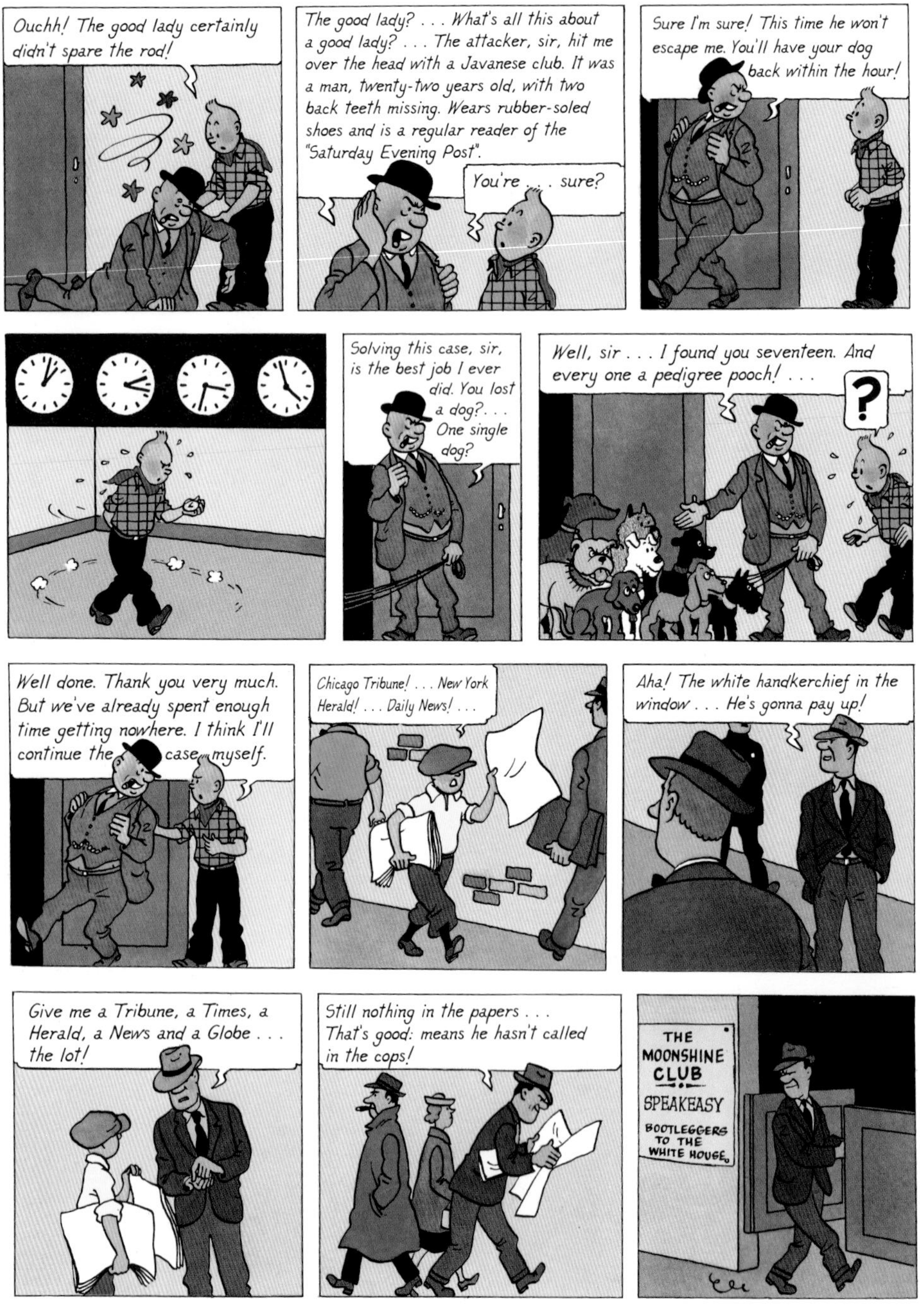
Ouchh! The good lady certainly didn't spare the rod!
The good lady? . . . What's all this about a good lady? . . . The attacker, sir, hit me over the head with a Javanese club. It was a man, twenty-two years old, with two back teeth missing. Wears rubber-soled shoes and is a regular reader of the "Saturday Evening Post".
You're . . . sure?
Sure I'm sure! This time he won't escape me. You'll have your dog back within the hour!
Solving this case, sir, is the best job I ever did. You lost a dog?. . . One single dog?
Well, sir . . . I found you seventeen. And every one a pedigree pooch! . . .
?
Well done. Thank you very much. But we've already spent enough time getting nowhere. I think I'll continue the case myself.
Chicago Tribune! . . . New York Herald! . . . Daily News! . . .
Aha! The white handkerchief in the window . . . He's gonna pay up!
Give me a Tribune, a Times, a Herald, a News and a Globe . . . the lot!
Still nothing in the papers . . . That's good: means he hasn't called in the cops!
THE MOONSHINE CLUB
SPEAKEASY
BOOTLEGGERS TO THE WHITE HOUSE

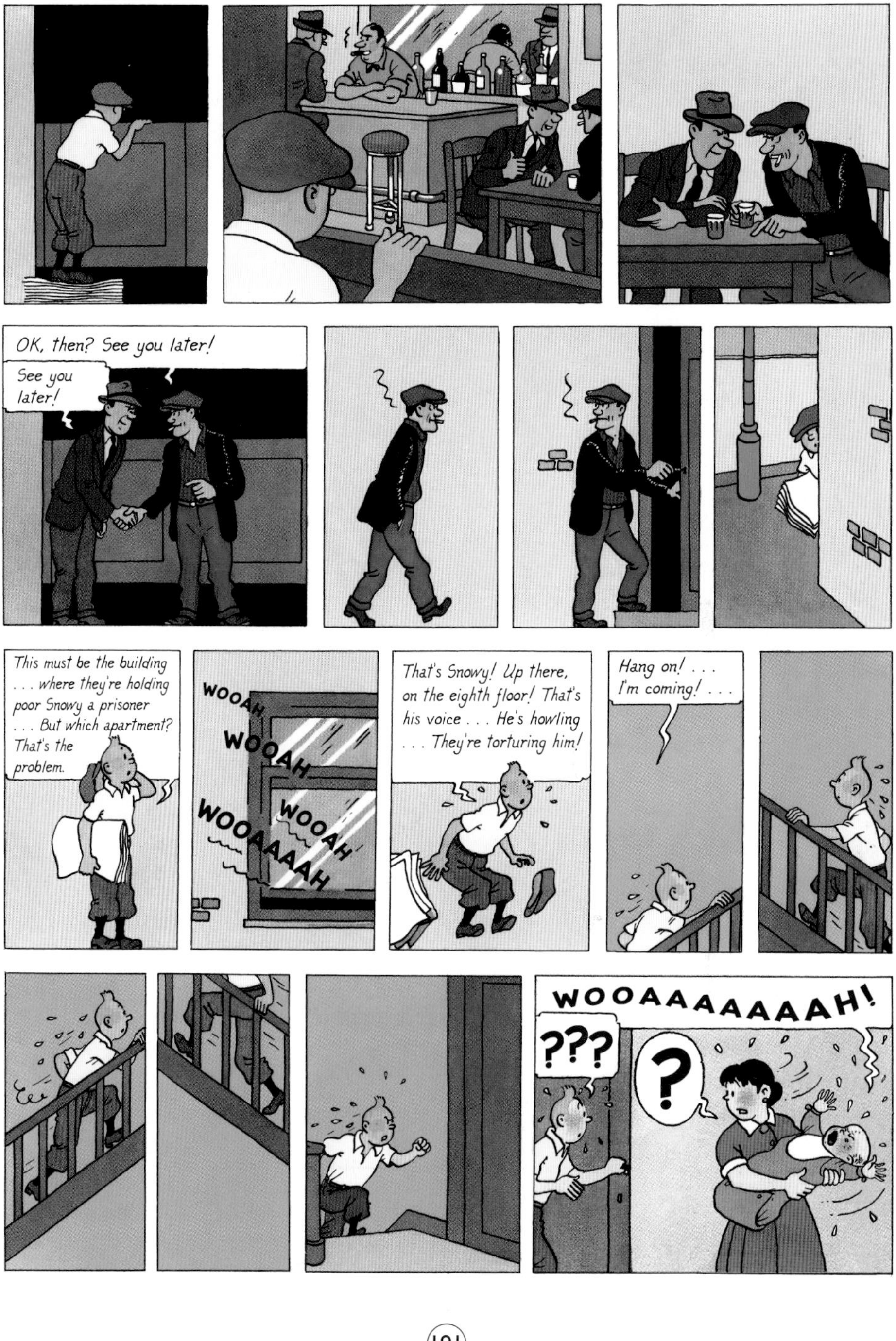
OK, then? See you later!
See you later!
This must be the building . . . where they're holding poor Snowy a prisoner . . . But which apartment? That's the problem.
WOOAH
WOOAH
WOOAH
WOOAAAAAH
That's Snowy! Up there, on the eighth floor! That's his voice . . . He's howling . . . They're torturing him!
Hang on! . . . I'm coming! . . .
WOOAAAAAAAAH!
???
?

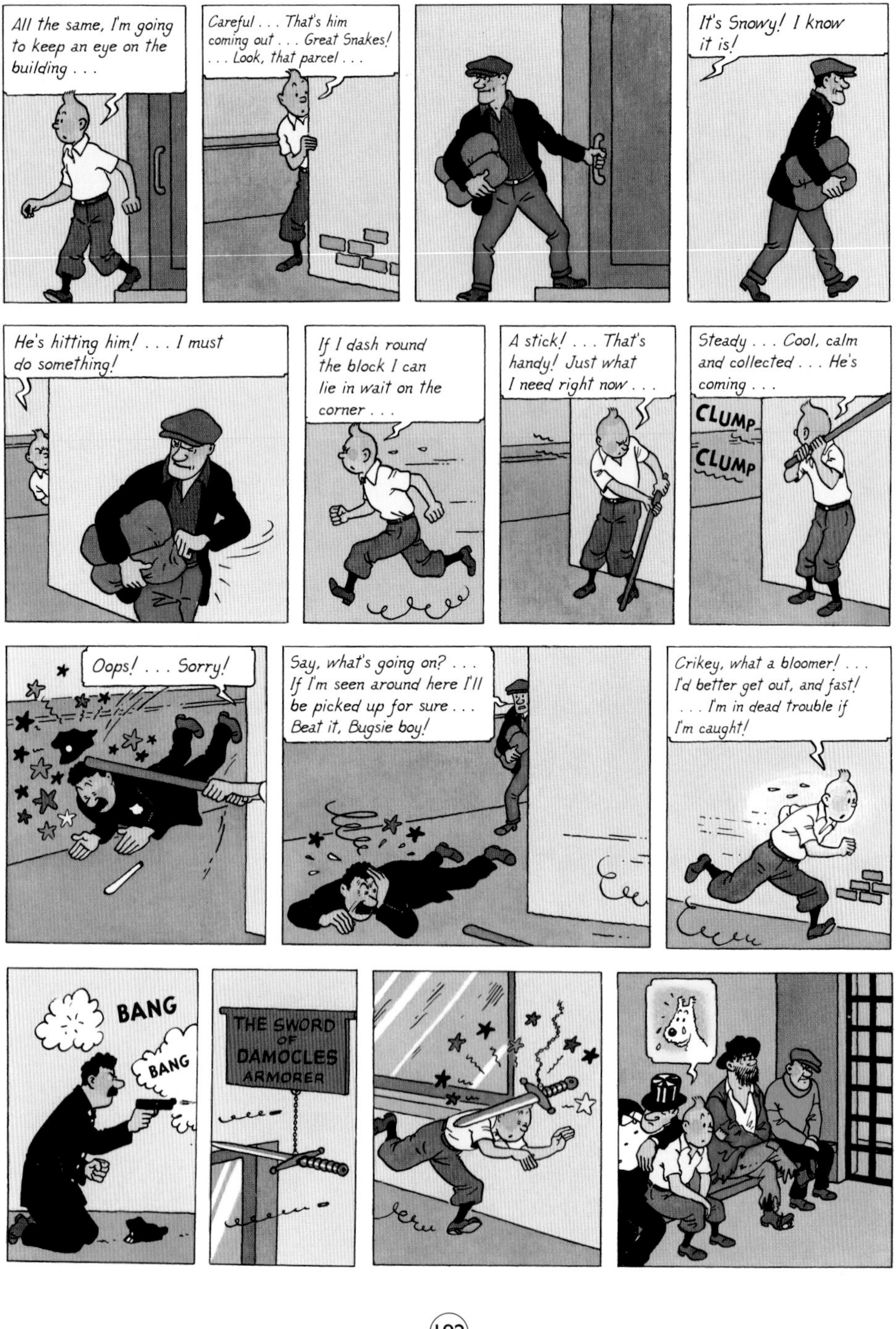

All the same, I'm going to keep an eye on the building . . .
Careful . . . That's him coming out . . . Great Snakes! . . . Look, that parcel . . .
It's Snowy! I know it is!
He's hitting him! . . . I must do something!
If I dash round the block I can lie in wait on the corner . . .
A stick! . . . That's handy! Just what I need right now . . .
Steady . . . Cool, calm and collected . . . He's coming . . .
CLUMP
CLUMP
Oops! . . . Sorry!
Say, what's going on? . . . If I'm seen around here I'll be picked up for sure . . . Beat it, Bugsie boy!
Crikey, what a bloomer! . . . I'd better get out, and fast! . . . I'm in dead trouble if I'm caught!
BANG
BANG
THE SWORD OF DAMOCLES ARMORER

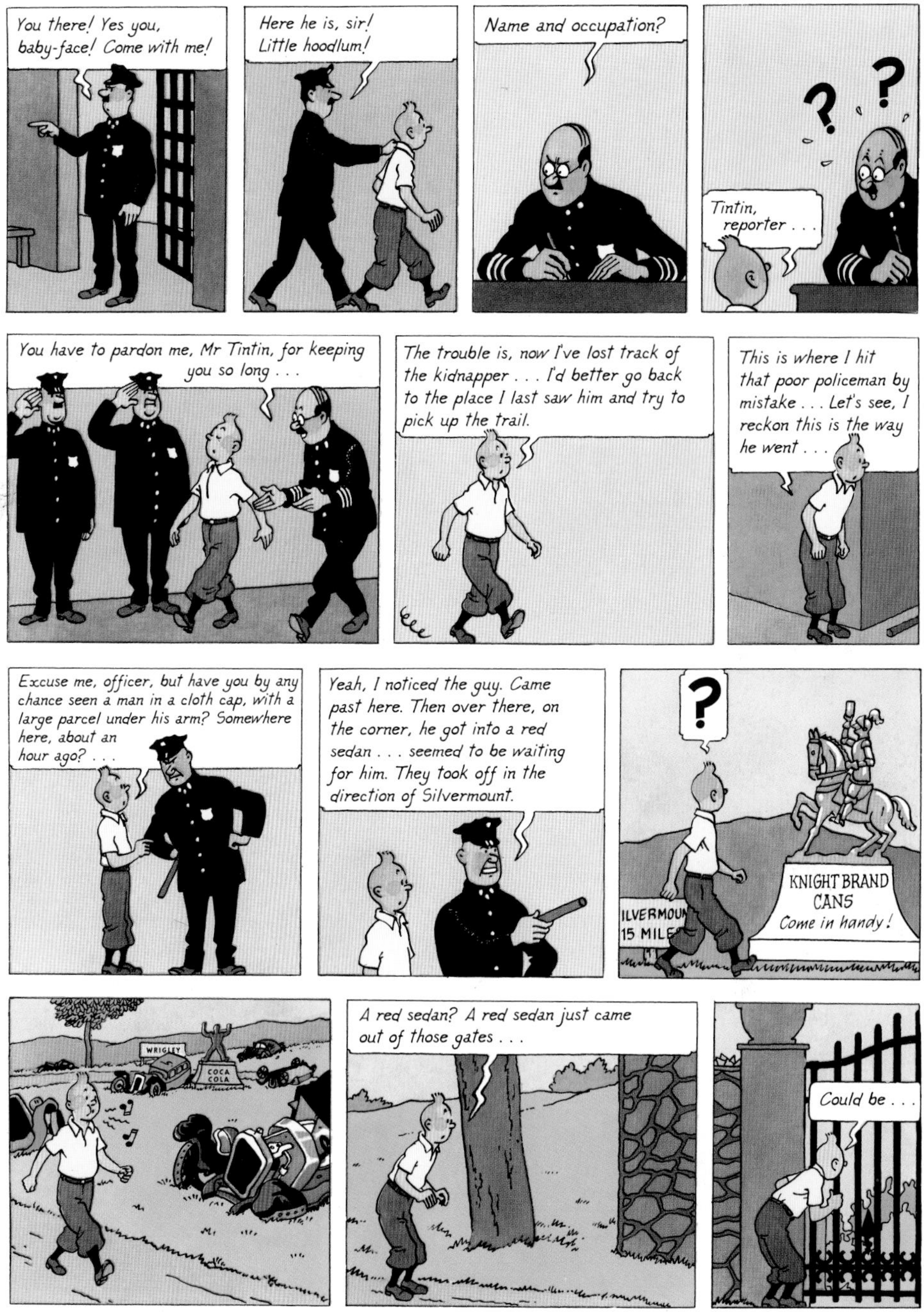
You there! Yes you, baby-face! Come with me!
Here he is, sir! Little hoodlum!
Name and occupation?
Tintin, reporter . . .
You have to pardon me, Mr Tintin, for keeping you so long . . .
The trouble is, now I've lost track of the kidnapper . . . I'd better go back to the place I last saw him and try to pick up the trail.
This is where I hit that poor policeman by mistake . . . Let's see, I reckon this is the way he went . . .
Excuse me, officer, but have you by any chance seen a man in a cloth cap, with a large parcel under his arm? Somewhere here, about an hour ago? . . .
Yeah, I noticed the guy. Came past here. Then over there, on the corner, he got into a red sedan . . . seemed to be waiting for him. They took off in the direction of Silvermount.
?
KNIGHT BRAND CANS Come in handy!
ILVERMOUN
15 MILE
WRIGLEY
COCA COLA
A red sedan? A red sedan just came out of those gates . . .
Could be . . .

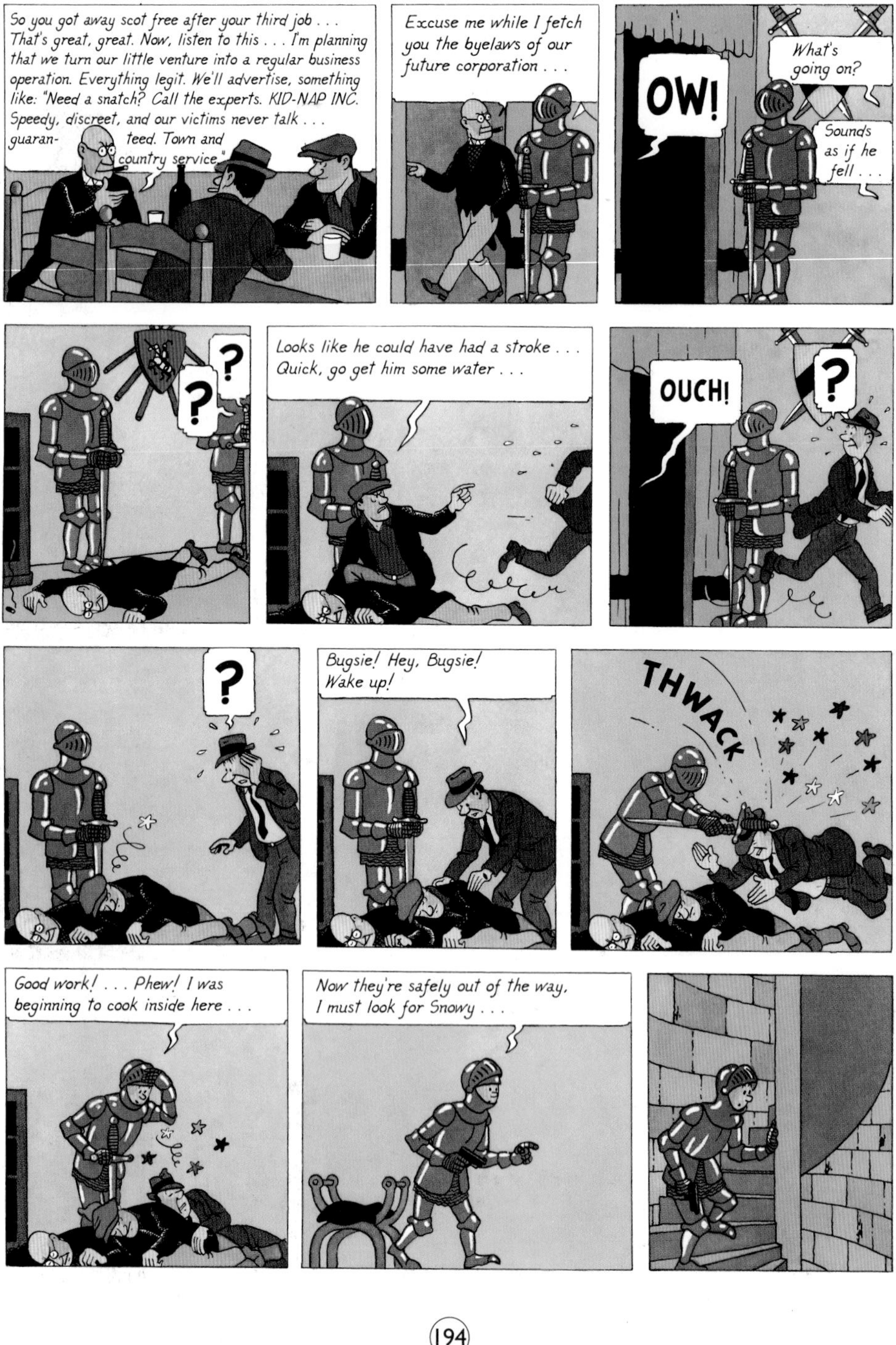
So you got away scot free after your third job . . . That's great, great. Now, listen to this . . . I'm planning that we turn our little venture into a regular business operation. Everything legit. We'll advertise, something like: "Need a snatch? Call the experts. KID-NAP INC. Speedy, discreet, and our victims never talk . . . guaranteed. Town and country service."
Excuse me while I fetch you the byelaws of our future corporation . . .
OW!
What's going on?
Sounds as if he fell . . .
?
?
Looks like he could have had a stroke . . . Quick, go get him some water . . .
OUCH!
?
?
Bugsie! Hey, Bugsie! Wake up!
THWACK
Good work! . . . Phew! I was beginning to cook inside here . . .
Now they're safely out of the way, I must look for Snowy . . .

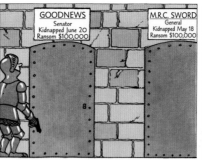

GOODNEWS
Senator
Kidnapped June 20
Ransom $100,000

M.R.C. SWORD
General
Kidnapped May 18
Ransom $100,000

SNOWY
Dog
Kidnapped June 25
Ransom $50,000

!

Snowy! . . .
Snowy! . . .

ped June 25
om $50,000

Wooah!
Wooah!

It's me, Snowy. Hang on just a little longer. I'm going to find the keys to your cell.

What happened? . . . Ooh, have I got a headache! . . . Yet I only had one glass of whisky . . . I wonder . . .

Hey! . . . Just you keep quiet for a bit!

Here I am, Snowy! You see, Tintin hasn't let you down!

Snowy! My dear old Snowy!

I never thought . . . I'd ever see you again . . .

KIDNAP INC.
RULES FOR GUESTS

Ssh! A whistle! . . . One of the gangsters upstairs must have raised the alarm . . . We'd better watch out . . .

That's a snappy outfit Tintin . . .

He's around here somewhere. I give you ten minutes . . . Bring him to me . . . bound and gagged. Now, get going . . . Scram!

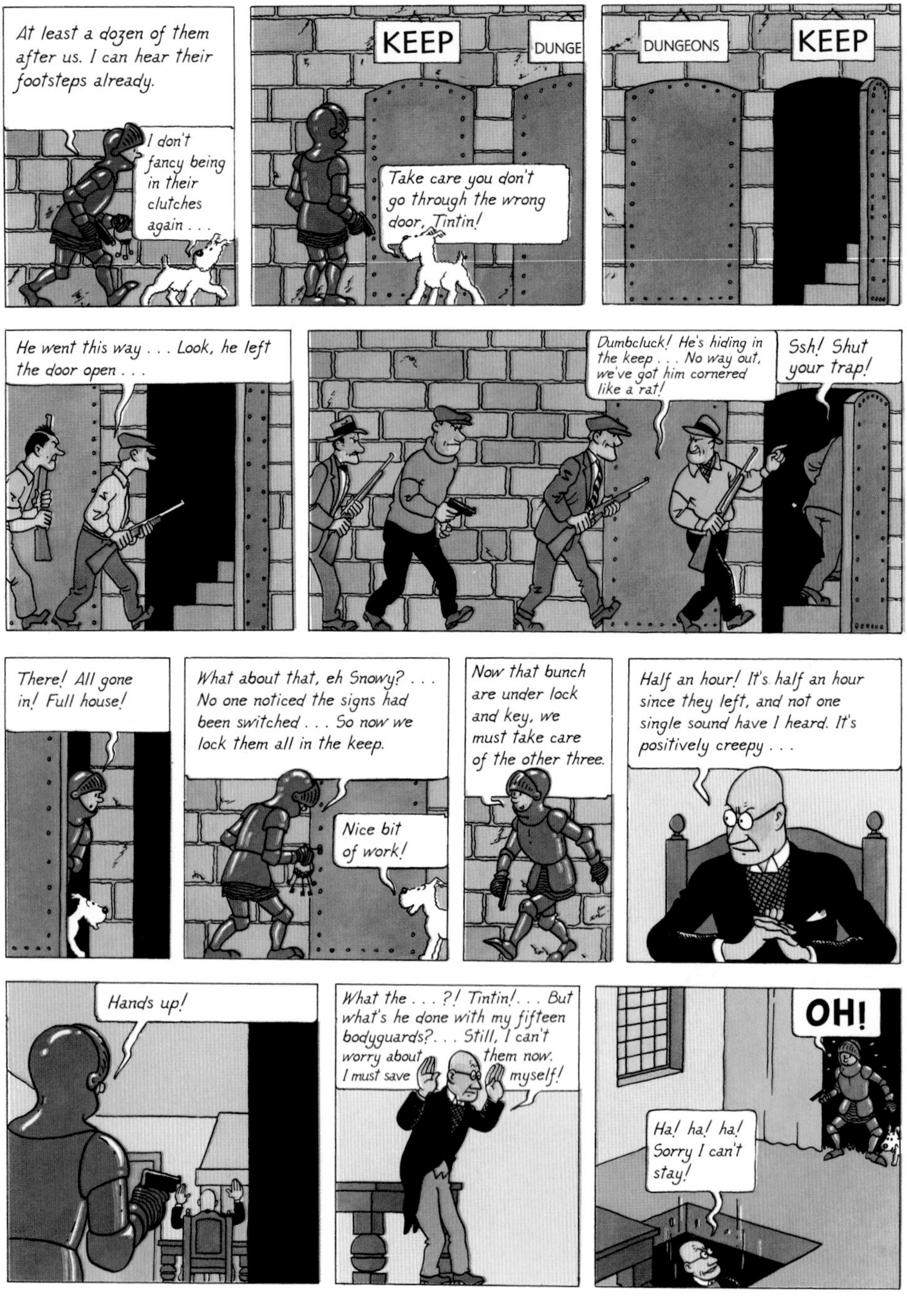
At least a dozen of them after us. I can hear their footsteps already.
I don't fancy being in their clutches again . . .
KEEP
DUNGE
Take care you don't go through the wrong door, Tintin!
DUNGEONS
KEEP
He went this way . . . Look, he left the door open . . .
Dumbcluck! He's hiding in the keep . . . No way out, we've got him cornered like a rat!
Ssh! Shut your trap!
There! All gone in! Full house!
What about that, eh Snowy? . . . No one noticed the signs had been switched . . . So now we lock them all in the keep.
Nice bit of work!
Now that bunch are under lock and key, we must take care of the other three.
Half an hour! It's half an hour since they left, and not one single sound have I heard. It's positively creepy . . .
Hands up!
What the . . . ?! Tintin! . . . But what's he done with my fifteen bodyguards? . . . Still, I can't worry about them now. I must save myself!
OH!
Ha! ha! ha! Sorry I can't stay!

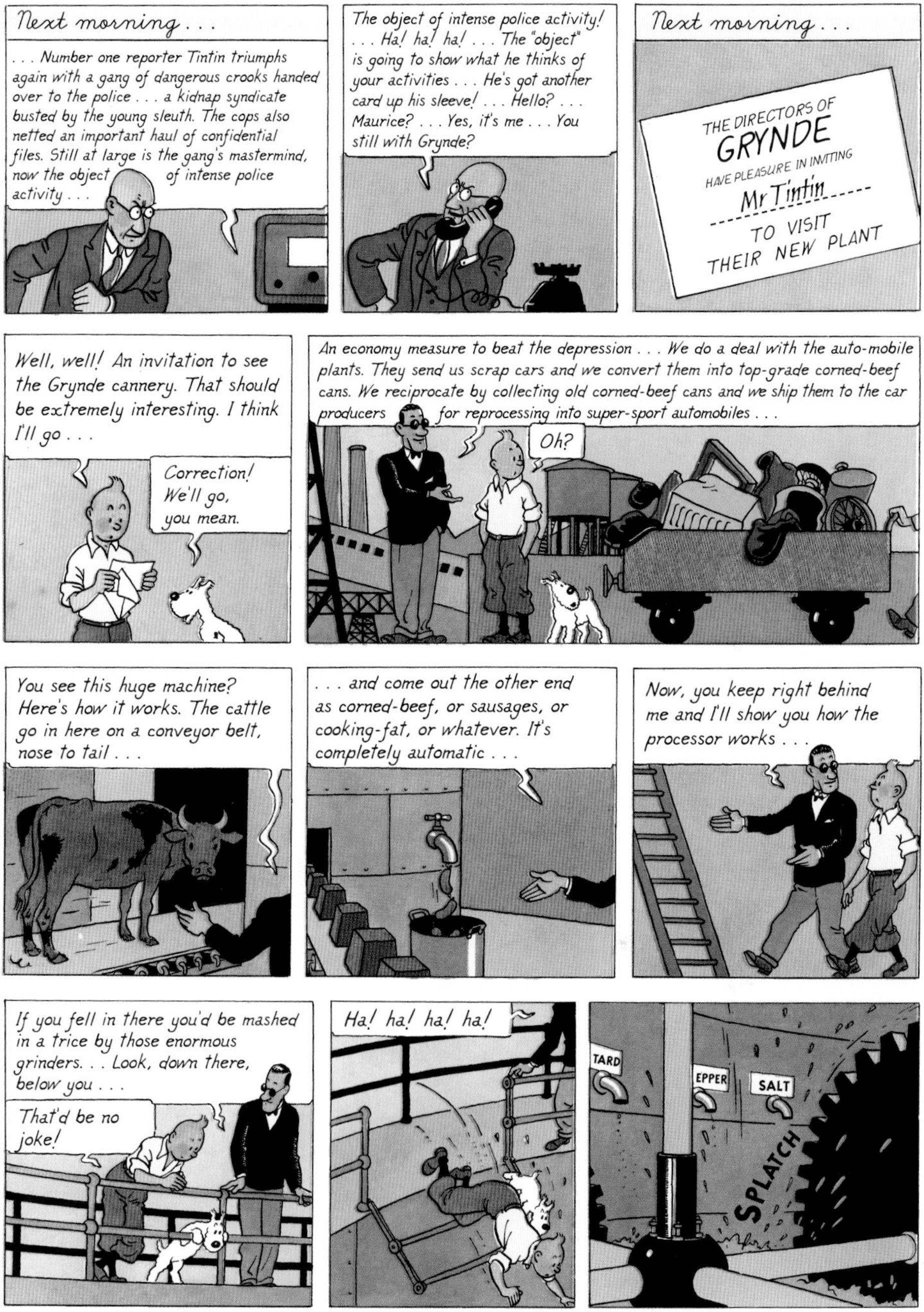
Next morning . . .
. . . Number one reporter Tintin triumphs again with a gang of dangerous crooks handed over to the police . . . a kidnap syndicate busted by the young sleuth. The cops also netted an important haul of confidential files. Still at large is the gang's mastermind, now the object of intense police activity . . .
The object of intense police activity! . . . Ha! ha! ha! . . . The "object" is going to show what he thinks of your activities . . . He's got another card up his sleeve! . . . Hello? . . . Maurice? . . . Yes, it's me . . . You still with Grynde?
Next morning . . .
THE DIRECTORS OF GRYNDE HAVE PLEASURE IN INVITING Mr Tintin TO VISIT THEIR NEW PLANT
Well, well! An invitation to see the Grynde cannery. That should be extremely interesting. I think I'll go . . .
Correction! We'll go, you mean.
An economy measure to beat the depression . . . We do a deal with the auto-mobile plants. They send us scrap cars and we convert them into top-grade corned-beef cans. We reciprocate by collecting old corned-beef cans and we ship them to the car producers for reprocessing into super-sport automobiles . . .
Oh?
You see this huge machine? Here's how it works. The cattle go in here on a conveyor belt, nose to tail . . .
. . . and come out the other end as corned-beef, or sausages, or cooking-fat, or whatever. It's completely automatic . . .
Now, you keep right behind me and I'll show you how the processor works . . .
If you fell in there you'd be mashed in a trice by those enormous grinders. . . Look, down there, below you . . .
That'd be no joke!
Ha! ha! ha! ha!
TARD
EPPER
SALT
SPLATCH

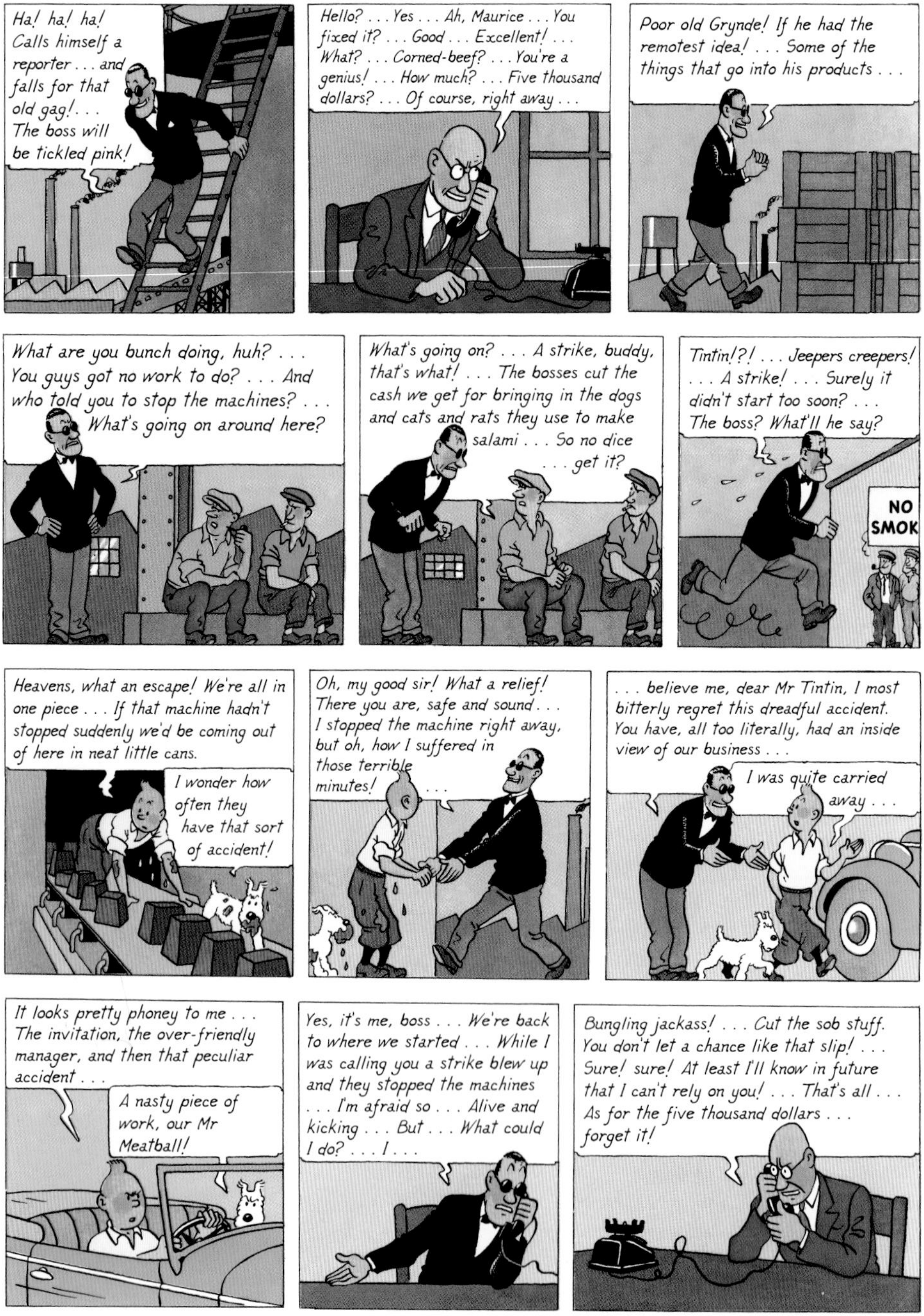
Ha! ha! ha! Calls himself a reporter . . . and falls for that old gag! . . . The boss will be tickled pink!
Hello? . . . Yes . . . Ah, Maurice . . . You fixed it? . . . Good . . . Excellent! . . . What? . . . Corned-beef? . . . You're a genius! . . . How much? . . . Five thousand dollars? . . . Of course, right away . . .
Poor old Grynde! If he had the remotest idea! . . . Some of the things that go into his products . . .
What are you bunch doing, huh? . . . You guys got no work to do? . . . And who told you to stop the machines? . . . What's going on around here?
What's going on? . . . A strike, buddy, that's what! . . . The bosses cut the cash we get for bringing in the dogs and cats and rats they use to make salami . . . So no dice . . . get it?
Tintin!?! . . . Jeepers creepers! . . . A strike! . . . Surely it didn't start too soon? . . . The boss? What'll he say?
NO SMOK
Heavens, what an escape! We're all in one piece . . . If that machine hadn't stopped suddenly we'd be coming out of here in neat little cans.
I wonder how often they have that sort of accident!
Oh, my good sir! What a relief! There you are, safe and sound . . . I stopped the machine right away, but oh, how I suffered in those terrible minutes! . . .
. . . believe me, dear Mr Tintin, I most bitterly regret this dreadful accident. You have, all too literally, had an inside view of our business . . .
I was quite carried away . . .
It looks pretty phoney to me . . . The invitation, the over-friendly manager, and then that peculiar accident . . .
A nasty piece of work, our Mr Meatball!
Yes, it's me, boss . . . We're back to where we started . . . While I was calling you a strike blew up and they stopped the machines . . . I'm afraid so . . . Alive and kicking . . . But . . . What could I do? . . . I . . .
Bungling jackass! . . . Cut the sob stuff. You don't let a chance like that slip! . . . Sure! sure! At least I'll know in future that I can't rely on you! . . . That's all . . . As for the five thousand dollars . . . forget it!

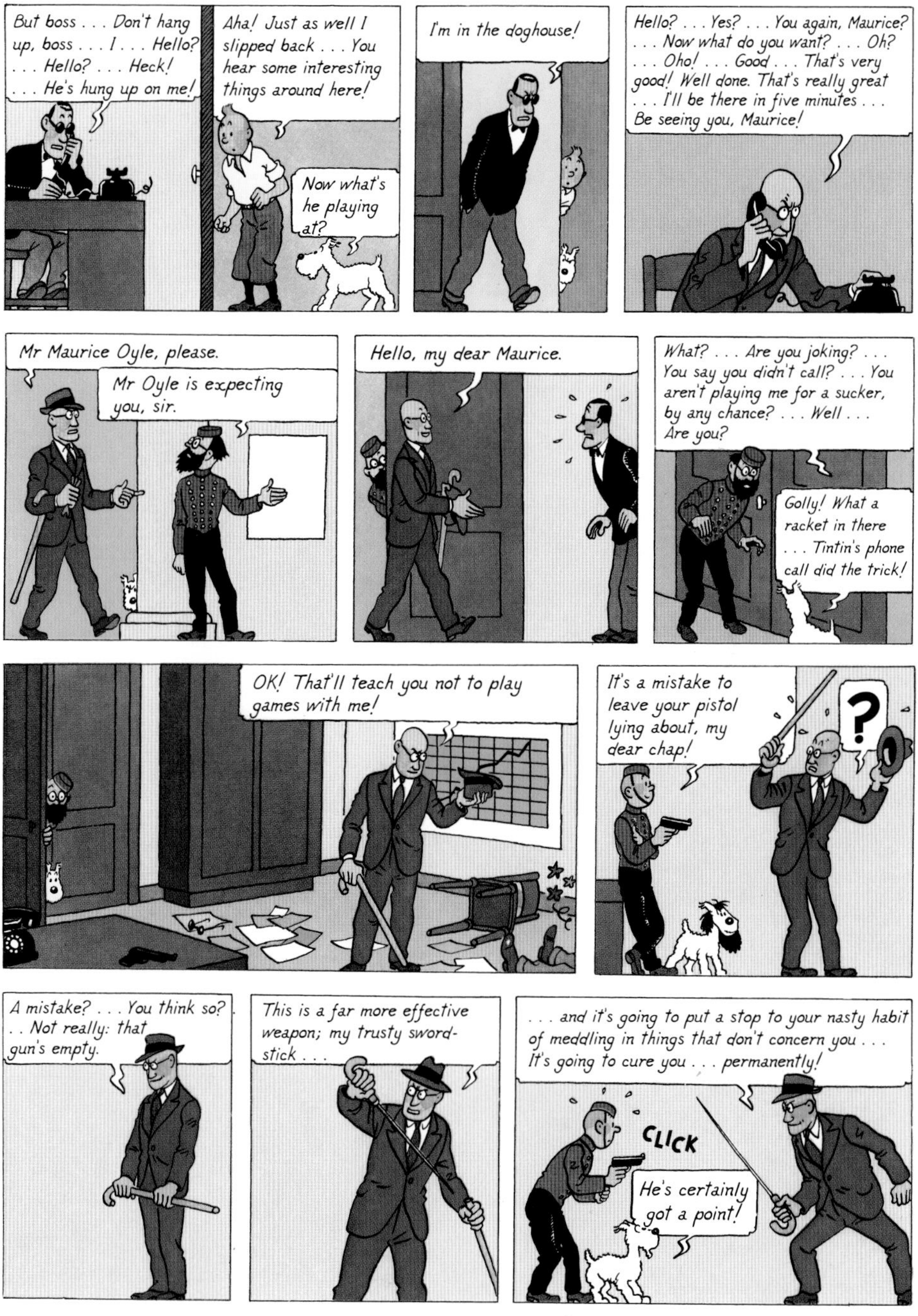
But boss . . . Don't hang up, boss . . . I . . . Hello? . . . Hello? . . . Heck! . . . He's hung up on me!
Aha! Just as well I slipped back . . . You hear some interesting things around here!
Now what's he playing at?
I'm in the doghouse!
Hello? . . . Yes? . . . You again, Maurice? . . . Now what do you want? . . . Oh? . . . Oho! . . . Good . . . That's very good! Well done. That's really great . . . I'll be there in five minutes . . . Be seeing you, Maurice!
Mr Maurice Oyle, please.
Mr Oyle is expecting you, sir.
Hello, my dear Maurice.
What? . . . Are you joking? . . . You say you didn't call? . . . You aren't playing me for a sucker, by any chance? . . . Well . . . Are you?
Golly! What a racket in there . . . Tintin's phone call did the trick!
OK! That'll teach you not to play games with me!
It's a mistake to leave your pistol lying about, my dear chap!
?
A mistake? . . . You think so? . . Not really: that gun's empty.
This is a far more effective weapon; my trusty sword-stick . . .
. . . and it's going to put a stop to your nasty habit of meddling in things that don't concern you . . . It's going to cure you . . . permanently!
CLICK
He's certainly got a point!

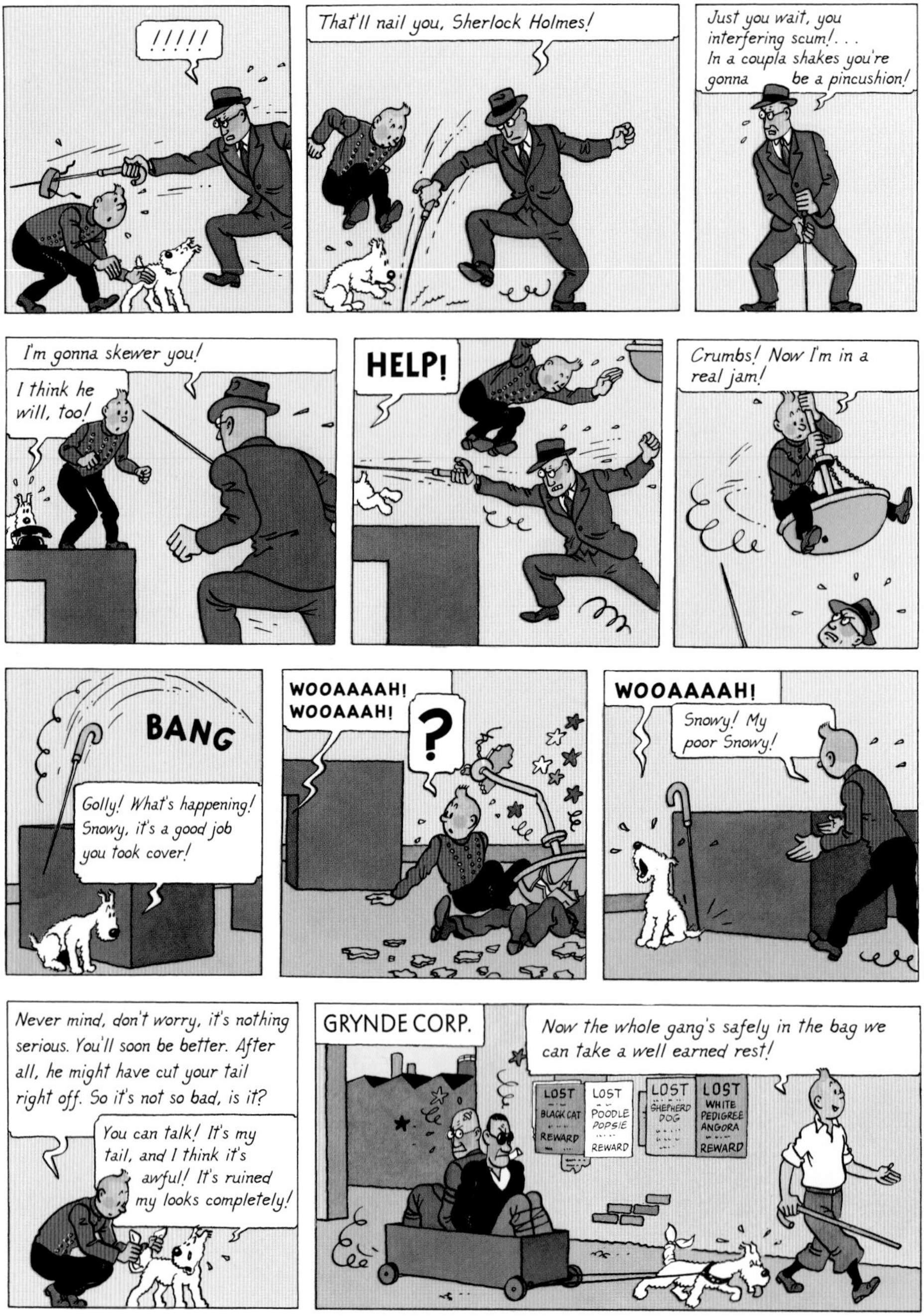
!!!!!
That'll nail you, Sherlock Holmes!
Just you wait, you interfering scum!... In a coupla shakes you're gonna be a pincushion!
I'm gonna skewer you!
I think he will, too!
HELP!
Crumbs! Now I'm in a real jam!
BANG
Golly! What's happening! Snowy, it's a good job you took cover!
WOOAAAAH! WOOAAAH!
?
WOOAAAAH!
Snowy! My poor Snowy!
Never mind, don't worry, it's nothing serious. You'll soon be better. After all, he might have cut your tail right off. So it's not so bad, is it?
You can talk! It's my tail, and I think it's awful! It's ruined my looks completely!
GRYNDE CORP.
Now the whole gang's safely in the bag we can take a well earned rest!
LOST BLACK CAT REWARD
LOST POODLE POPSIE REWARD
LOST SHEPHERD DOG
LOST WHITE PEDIGREE ANGORA REWARD

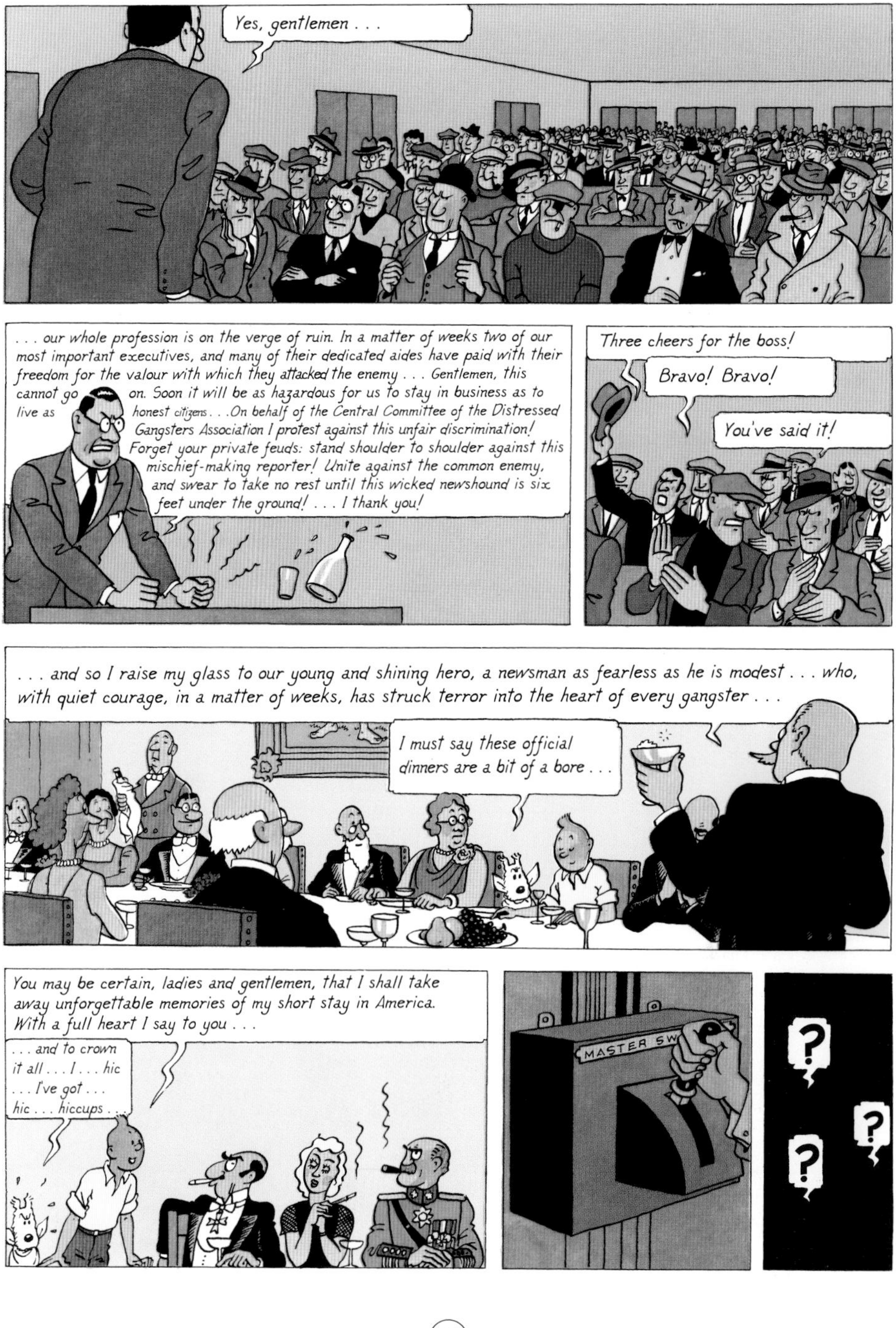
Yes, gentlemen . . .
. . . our whole profession is on the verge of ruin. In a matter of weeks two of our most important executives, and many of their dedicated aides have paid with their freedom for the valour with which they attacked the enemy . . . Gentlemen, this cannot go on. Soon it will be as hazardous for us to stay in business as to live as honest citizens . . . On behalf of the Central Committee of the Distressed Gangsters Association I protest against this unfair discrimination! Forget your private feuds: stand shoulder to shoulder against this mischief-making reporter! Unite against the common enemy, and swear to take no rest until this wicked newshound is six feet under the ground! . . . I thank you!
Three cheers for the boss!
Bravo! Bravo!
You've said it!
. . . and so I raise my glass to our young and shining hero, a newsman as fearless as he is modest . . . who, with quiet courage, in a matter of weeks, has struck terror into the heart of every gangster . . .
I must say these official dinners are a bit of a bore . . .
You may be certain, ladies and gentlemen, that I shall take away unforgettable memories of my short stay in America. With a full heart I say to you . . .
. . . and to crown it all . . . I . . . hic . . . I've got . . . hic . . . hiccups . . .
MASTER SW

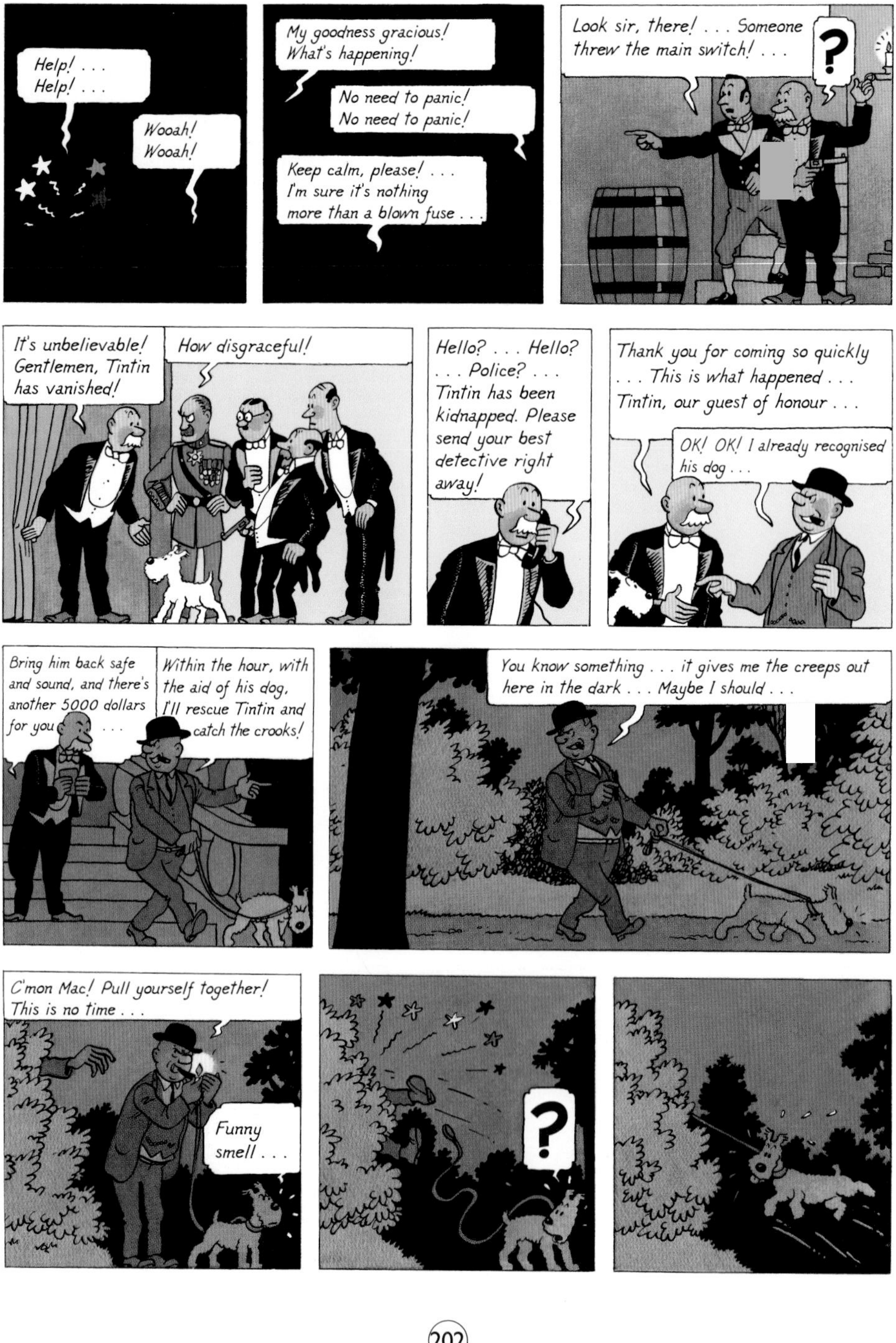
Help! . . .
Help! . . .
Wooah!
Wooah!
My goodness gracious! What's happening!
No need to panic! No need to panic!
Keep calm, please! . . . I'm sure it's nothing more than a blown fuse . . .
Look sir, there! . . . Someone threw the main switch! . . .
?
It's unbelievable! Gentlemen, Tintin has vanished!
How disgraceful!
Hello? . . . Hello? . . . Police? . . . Tintin has been kidnapped. Please send your best detective right away!
Thank you for coming so quickly . . . This is what happened . . . Tintin, our guest of honour . . .
OK! OK! I already recognised his dog . . .
Bring him back safe and sound, and there's another 5000 dollars for you . . .
Within the hour, with the aid of his dog, I'll rescue Tintin and catch the crooks!
You know something . . . it gives me the creeps out here in the dark . . . Maybe I should . . .
C'mon Mac! Pull yourself together! This is no time . . .
Funny smell . . .
?

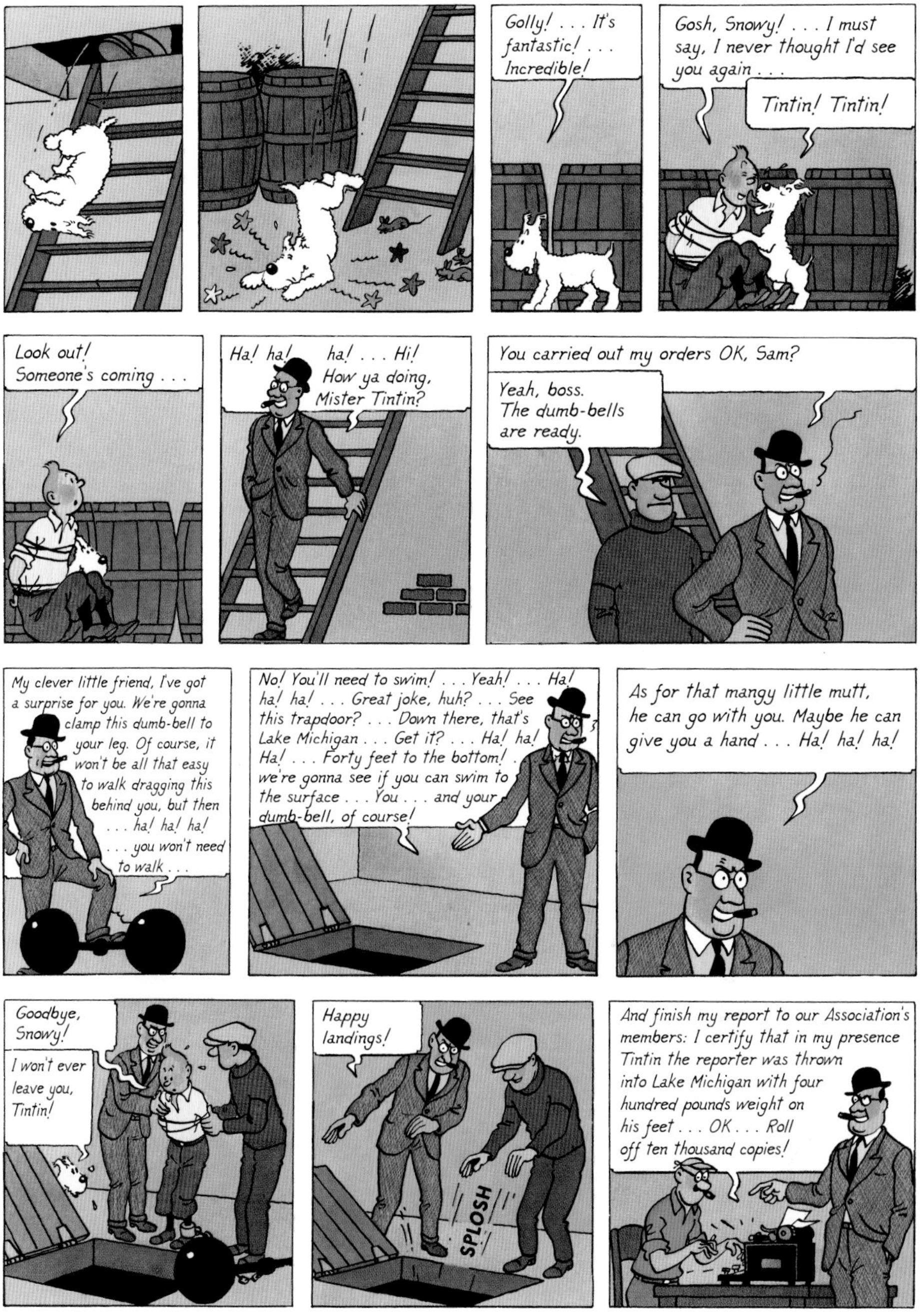
Golly! . . . It's fantastic! . . . Incredible!
Gosh, Snowy! . . . I must say, I never thought I'd see you again . . .
Tintin! Tintin!
Look out! Someone's coming . . .
Ha! ha! ha! . . . Hi! How ya doing, Mister Tintin?
You carried out my orders OK, Sam?
Yeah, boss. The dumb-bells are ready.
My clever little friend, I've got a surprise for you. We're gonna clamp this dumb-bell to your leg. Of course, it won't be all that easy to walk dragging this behind you, but then . . . ha! ha! ha! . . . you won't need to walk . . .
No! You'll need to swim! . . . Yeah! . . . Ha! ha! ha! . . . Great joke, huh? . . . See this trapdoor? . . . Down there, that's Lake Michigan . . . Get it? . . . Ha! ha! Ha! . . . Forty feet to the bottom! . . we're gonna see if you can swim to the surface . . . You . . . and your dumb-bell, of course!
As for that mangy little mutt, he can go with you. Maybe he can give you a hand . . . Ha! ha! ha!
Goodbye, Snowy!
I won't ever leave you, Tintin!
Happy landings!
SPLOSH
And finish my report to our Association's members: I certify that in my presence Tintin the reporter was thrown into Lake Michigan with four hundred pounds weight on his feet . . . OK . . . Roll off ten thousand copies!

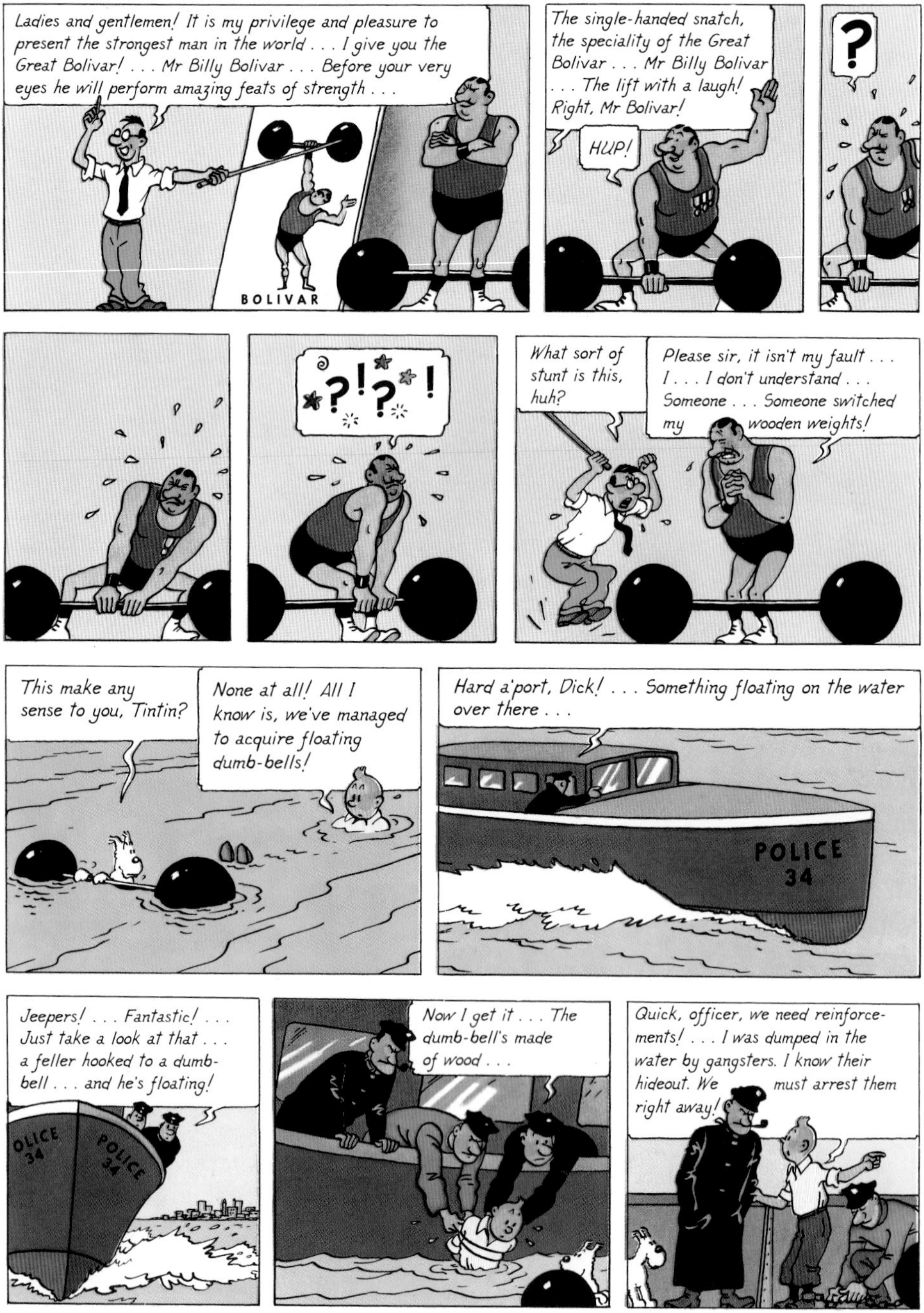
Ladies and gentlemen! It is my privilege and pleasure to present the strongest man in the world . . . I give you the Great Bolivar! . . . Mr Billy Bolivar . . . Before your very eyes he will perform amazing feats of strength . . .
BOLIVAR
The single-handed snatch, the speciality of the Great Bolivar . . . Mr Billy Bolivar . . . The lift with a laugh! Right, Mr Bolivar!
HUP!
?
?!?!
What sort of stunt is this, huh?
Please sir, it isn't my fault . . . I . . . I don't understand . . . Someone . . . Someone switched my wooden weights!
This make any sense to you, Tintin?
None at all! All I know is, we've managed to acquire floating dumb-bells!
Hard a'port, Dick! . . . Something floating on the water over there . . .
POLICE 34
Jeepers! . . . Fantastic! . . . Just take a look at that . . . a feller hooked to a dumb-bell . . . and he's floating!
POLICE 34
Now I get it . . . The dumb-bell's made of wood . . .
Quick, officer, we need reinforcements! . . . I was dumped in the water by gangsters. I know their hideout. We must arrest them right away!

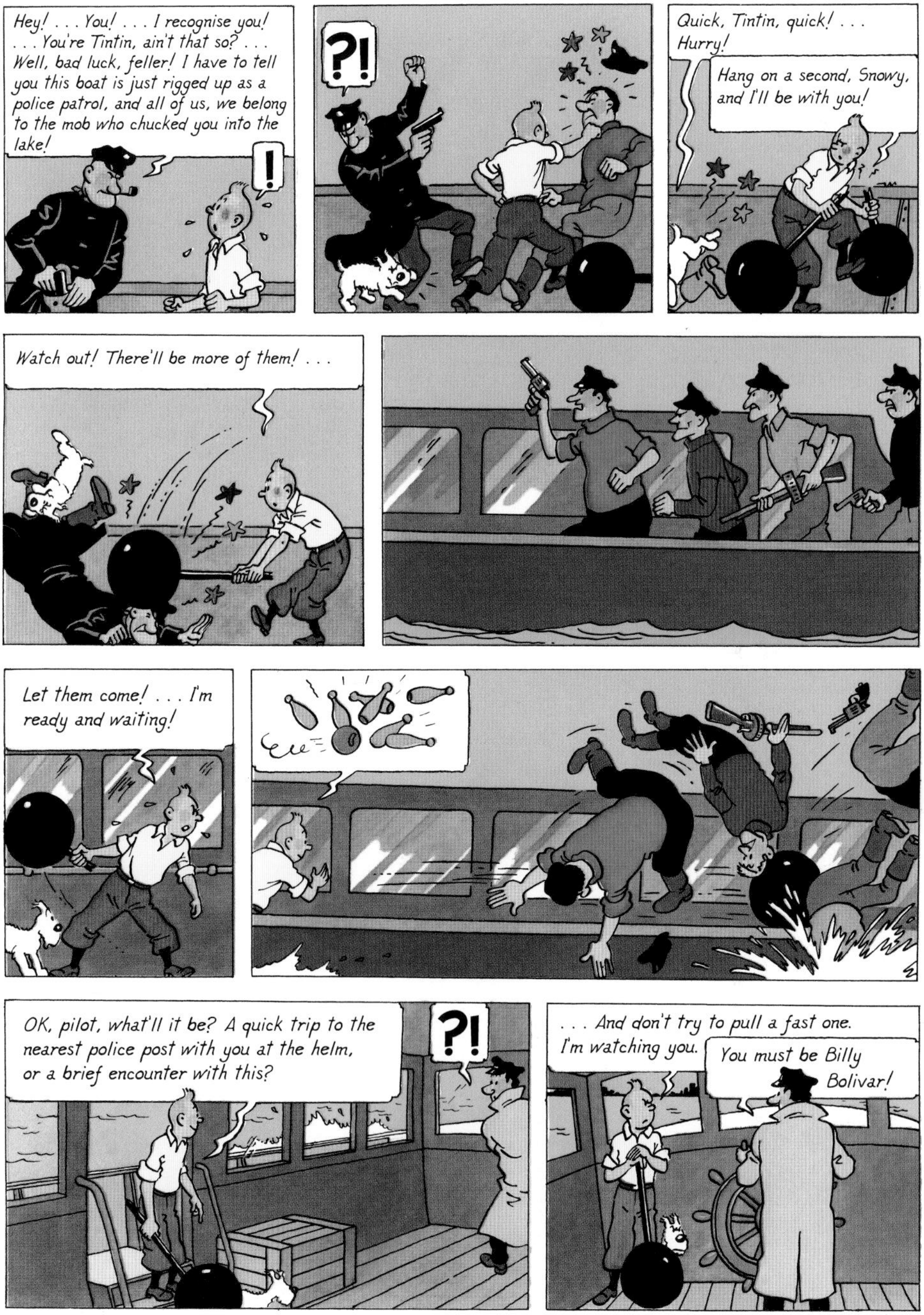

Hey! . . . You! . . . I recognise you! . . . You're Tintin, ain't that so? . . . Well, bad luck, feller! I have to tell you this boat is just rigged up as a police patrol, and all of us, we belong to the mob who chucked you into the lake!
!
?!
Quick, Tintin, quick! . . . Hurry!
Hang on a second, Snowy, and I'll be with you!
Watch out! There'll be more of them! . . .
Let them come! . . . I'm ready and waiting!
OK, pilot, what'll it be? A quick trip to the nearest police post with you at the helm, or a brief encounter with this?
?!
. . . And don't try to pull a fast one. I'm watching you.
You must be Billy Bolivar!

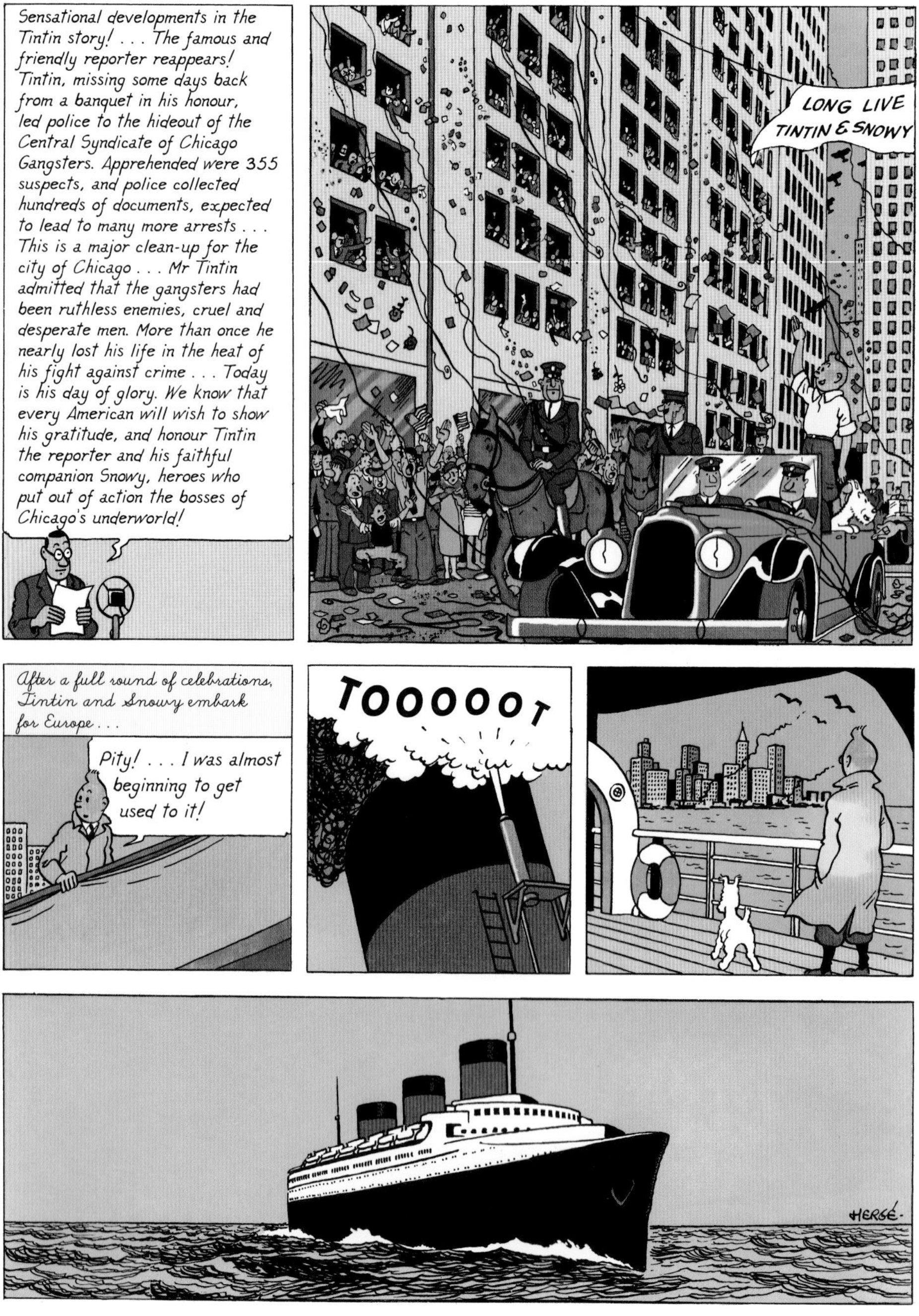
Sensational developments in the Tintin story! . . . The famous and friendly reporter reappears! Tintin, missing some days back from a banquet in his honour, led police to the hideout of the Central Syndicate of Chicago Gangsters. Apprehended were 355 suspects, and police collected hundreds of documents, expected to lead to many more arrests . . . This is a major clean-up for the city of Chicago . . . Mr Tintin admitted that the gangsters had been ruthless enemies, cruel and desperate men. More than once he nearly lost his life in the heat of his fight against crime . . . Today is his day of glory. We know that every American will wish to show his gratitude, and honour Tintin the reporter and his faithful companion Snowy, heroes who put out of action the bosses of Chicago's underworld!
LONG LIVE TINTIN & SNOWY
After a full round of celebrations, Tintin and Snowy embark for Europe . . .
Pity! . . . I was almost beginning to get used to it!
TOOOOOT
HERGÉ